STARS
ACROSS
THE
OCEAN

STARS ACROSS THE OCEAN

KIMBERLEY FREEMAN

hachette
AUSTRALIA

Published in Australia and New Zealand in 2017
by Hachette Australia
(an imprint of Hachette Australia Pty Limited)
Level 17, 207 Kent Street, Sydney NSW 2000
www.hachette.com.au

10 9 8 7 6 5 4 3 2 1

National Library of Australia
Cataloguing-in-Publication data:

Freeman, Kimberley, 1970– author.
Stars across the ocean / Kimberley Freeman.

978 0 7336 3354 6 (paperback)

Birthparents – Identification – Fiction.
Birthmothers – Fiction.
Women – Fiction.

Cover design by Christabella Designs
Cover photograph © Mark Owen/Trevillion Images
Author photograph courtesy of Craig Peihopa
Text design by Bookhouse, Sydney
Typeset in 12.6/16.8pt Adobe Garamond Pro by Bookhouse, Sydney
Printed and bound in Australia by McPherson's Printing Group

MIX
Paper from
responsible sources
FSC® C001695

The paper this book is printed on is certified against the
Forest Stewardship Council® Standards. McPherson's Printing
Group holds FSC® chain of custody certification SA-COC-005379.
FSC® promotes environmentally responsible, socially beneficial
and economically viable management of the world's forests.

For my mother

The Present

'M um?'

'She gets confused. Don't be upset if she—'

'Mum?' I say it more firmly, more like I might have as a teenager, benign exasperation. I am looking right at my mother's face; she is looking right back at me, but it's as though a veil has come down between us. On one side, the nurse and me and the pale green walls of the clinic. On the other, my mother. Lost at sea.

'Victoria?' she says at last, the veil dropping.

I smile. 'It's me. Here I am.' She's the only person who calls me by my full name. To everyone else I'm Tori, a contemporary no-fuss name. She named me for a queen. I'm not a queen.

'I wandered into traffic,' she says, by way of an explanation for the abrasions on her pale, softly lined face.

'I heard.'

'Could have been worse, I suppose. I didn't break anything.' She sniffs. 'You didn't come all the way from Australia for this, surely?'

The nurse pats my mother's thigh through the blankets. 'I'll leave you girls to it, shall I, Mrs Camber?'

'*Professor* Camber.' My mother and I both correct the nurse at once, in identical voices of weary outrage.

'Well, look whose memory is improving,' the nurse says as she leaves, and it isn't kindly. I thought nurses were kind, but the way this one has spoken about my mother is anything but; 'The old dear.' 'Madam.' 'The silly duck.' Mum is only seventy, and there's nothing silly or duck-like about her.

Alone now, I return my gaze to Mum's face. She looks frightened. The fear jumps into me, making my stomach go cold. Why is she frightened? Should I be frightened? I fake a smile over it. 'So,' I say.

She smiles too. Somehow my smile reassures her. 'You didn't come all the way from Australia for this, surely,' she says again, and I don't know if she's repeating it for effect, or because she's forgotten she already said it.

'The accident? Not really. It's . . . the other . . .'

Her eyes slide sideways. My mother was a great beauty in her youth, and great beauty does not leave a face ever, really. Yes, her hair is the colour of steel, her cheeks are hollow, and the skin around her lips is crisscrossed by lines; but her eyes are still huge and blue, almost violet, the lashes still long and dark.

A weak beam of sunlight spears through the window, and I hear muffled seagulls riding on the currents above the Bristol channel. Mum works in Bristol, but has always lived here in Portishead. Her house is a five-minute walk from the clinic. She must have walked past it a thousand-thousand times on her afternoon strolls, never suspecting she would end up in here: the 'home for ladies who have gone doo-lally' as she'd often called it.

Will she work in Bristol for much longer, though? Her reluctant retirement has been the thorn under the skin of all her emails to me over the past eighteen months.

'It's not as bad as they think,' she says at last. 'I forget some things, remember others . . .'

'When your doctor phoned she said it's not the first time you've wandered.'

'I took a wrong turn on the way home from work one day. They changed the bus route and it confused me. Don't listen to Doctor Chaudry, she's young and thinks she knows everything.'

I don't push it further. Four times, the doctor has said. Four times over two years Mum has been found, bewildered and lost. 'We can assume there have been other times, when she's managed to get herself home and not told me,' Dr Chaudry has said. Tests, a diagnosis have all been carried out without my knowledge. The outcome was no surprise. Locksley College's fearsome Emeritus Professor of History, Margaret Camber: doo-lally.

Definitely doo-lally.

And while that's a terrible diagnosis for any woman to receive, it seems doubly so for a woman who has been so fiercely clever her whole life.

Triply so, because she's my mum.

I sit and hold her hand in the softly lit room, not able to believe that it's actually happening. That my mother is not invincible. That sickness and mortality will prey on her, just as they prey on all of us. My head grinds with jetlag. I can't grasp whole thoughts, just the edges of them. I am sad and I want my mum to comfort me but, bafflingly, it seems it's my job to comfort her.

'How long are you staying?' she asks after a while.

'As long as you need me to.'

'Geoff will be annoyed if I keep you here too long.'

'Geoff will be fine.'

The quiet descends again. Then, 'How long are you staying?'

'As long as . . . I'm not sure. I haven't booked a return flight.'

'I need you to go to the office for me.'

'Your office? At Locksley?'

She nods, and I notice her body is filling with energy. She grows stiff. 'They'll throw it all out and I'm not done sorting it yet.'

'Your papers and books? You want me to pack them up?'

'There's things in there . . . they've heaped them all in the middle of the room. Scoundrels.'

'Of course, Mum. Of course. Where would I find the key?'

'With my other keys. My handbag is in that drawer.'

She indicates a bureau on the other side of the bed. I slide open the deep bottom drawer and pull out her handbag, then find a handful of keys.

'I'll go straight up there when the nurse kicks me out,' I tell her.

Her body relaxes again. 'I thought I saw him, you know. Emile.'

'Who's Emile?'

'I realise now that's not possible. I got mixed up. But I saw him and I walked towards him and didn't check for cars.'

'Who's Emile?' I ask again.

She shakes her head sadly. 'I just wanted to ask him how it ended.' She trails into mutters. The veil is down again. I'm not even sure she knows I'm here.

I stroke her hand and say nothing. The nurse comes in, cheerily announcing afternoon tea time. I don't know whether it's the jetlag or seeing my mother like this, but it doesn't feel like afternoon tea time. It feels like midnight.

●

Locksley College is on a long tree-lined street just over the Clifton Suspension Bridge. It has always delighted my mother that she crosses an icon of Victorian architecture every day on her way to work, given that she is a nineteenth-century historian. To be precise, Mum's field is the nineteenth-century English private sphere. She even hosted a short television series once, on BBC2, called

Victorian Women's Lives. That was back in the 1990s, when I was still young enough to be embarrassed by the way my male peers at work talked about how attractive my mother was: Mum was fifty, I was nineteen, and it seemed the whole world had decided that I should stand in her shadow.

I crawl the kerb looking for a place to park the rental car. I am really too tired to drive, but I survived the two-hour journey along the M4 from Heathrow, so to stay home when Mum is so desperate for me to look in on her office seems cruelly cautious. I find a spot and pay the meter, and then cross the road to Beech House (constructed 1901, so *just* Victorian) and head up to the third floor via stone stairs worn into smooth grooves, to Mum's office.

I feel . . . not guilty; perhaps furtive is the word I'm looking for. I glance around before slotting the key into the lock. All is quiet. It's after six. Everyone has either gone home to enjoy the long English evening, or they are on summer sabbatical. I close the door behind me and I'm engulfed with the smells I associate with my mother: old books and rose oil. I take a moment, a few breaths, then survey the task.

My stomach tightens with anger. Mum is right: some 'scoundrel' has pulled all of her papers out of drawers and off shelves, and thrown them haphazardly into boxes in the middle of the room, all piled on top of each other, none sealed. It's a terrible mess. The books are stacked on the desk and on the floor all around, the bowed bookshelves bare except for dust.

'Oh, Mum. I'm sorry,' I say under my breath as I pull out a sheaf of papers – old pages from a recipe book dated 1881 – and fan myself with them. The room is stuffy and hot. The task looks insurmountable.

I make a vow to come back in the morning, early. After a good night's sleep. And then I'll find the Dean and perhaps I'll punch him right between the eyes for harassing my mother to retire before she is ready and for letting some clown make such a mess of these precious documents.

I sit heavily at Mum's desk. Through the window, I see leaves and branches moving in an evening breeze, slightly distorted by the thick glass. Between two stacks of books is a tiny square of paper, frail and crisp under my fingers as I pick it up. The writing is in faded ink, long sloping letters. Underlined, at the top of the page:

To my child, whom I could not keep.

It is only one page long, and a quick glance tells me it ends mid-sentence, and so I know that this page has become separated from its siblings. I imagine the rough men who moved Mum's things finding it as they left, perhaps under one of their dirty shoes, and carelessly flinging it onto the desk.

To my child. Whom I could not keep.

I'm crying now. I'm tired. Mum's sick, and I haven't told her I lost another one. Another baby. Eleven weeks, this time. I had been so close, dangerously close to announcing the happy news. And here I am about to turn forty, and there has been no child in my life. Never will be, probably.

All my children, whom I could not keep.

I blink away tears, frustrated by my own self-pity, and read the first page.

•

To my child, whom I could not keep.

First, above all, never doubt that I loved you. I love you still.

You were created with love, born with love, and taken from me, all for love. I have tried to find you now for months, but my family – especially my sister, who I thought would be kinder to me – steadfastly refuse to tell me where you are, save to say that you are well cared for. By now, you have bestowed your first smiles upon your new mama, perhaps even your first words. You have learned to love the rhythms and timbre of her voice, the feel of her arms around you, the little bed you sleep in. It cuts me sharp as a blade; but I cannot bring myself to imagine taking you from where you are safe and happy. If I did find you, if I did hold you against me as I long to do, I would be doing so in a world of uncertainty and penury. Father has made it clear to me the penalty I would pay for our family's lost reputation. Love will not keep us from the poor house.

But I have not forgotten you and never will, my girl. Though you may never read it, I am compelled to write down the events that—

•

That's it. I wonder how long Mum has been in possession of this letter, if the rest of it must be around here somewhere. People all over the world are always sending Mum such documents, found in the back of old books and in great-grandmothers' musty trunks after funerals. She has been trying to convince Locksley to set up a proper archive for all this material, but in the new Dean's eyes, if the documents aren't about wars and politics – men's business – the funding is thin.

I leave the page where I found it. My head is heavy and I won't be able to stay awake much longer.

I scrawl a 'DO NOT TOUCH' sign, lock the door behind me, and return to Mum's house.

•

The forgotten but familiar smell of my mother's house greets me as I let myself in. I switch on the light in the entrance and put down my suitcase. I'll take it upstairs later; for now, I am in search of food and somewhere to lie down.

As the light goes on in the kitchen, I blink in confusion. At first, I think Mum has hung pale yellow bunting everywhere, but I see that instead she has covered the cupboards with sticky reminder notes. Some are perfectly clear: *Hairdresser Tuesday 3 p.m.* Others are less so: *Other book* or *Last round marks* or *Ask Beth* or *1875*. But there are so many, and my eyes travel over them, telling my brain what it doesn't want to hear. Mum knows she is losing her memory; these are her attempts to preserve it.

From cupboard to cupboard I go, on a sticky-note tour of my mother's mind. I can't make any coherent sense of it, but I suppose that is what memory looks like: flashes diverging and coalescing. On one note, midway up the cupboard where the teacups are kept, is simply a name all in capital letters: *EMILE VENSON*.

It takes my jetlagged brain a few moments to catch up. Mum said that name today. Emile. *I thought I saw him, you know.*

She'd said something about finding out how things had ended. My mother has been single a very long time. My father, who is dead now, left when I was only two. Many men have been interested in Mum, but she shows no interest in return. I don't know why. Is Emile a lover? Has he left her? How did I not know? Also, how did I not know my mother was writing her memories on sticky notes? How did I allow the distance between here and Australia to become a distance between her heart and mine?

I press my hips against the counter top and lean forward on my elbows. The kitchen is perfectly quiet and I can hear my own blood thrumming past my ears. Then the refrigerator motor surges to life, making me jump.

Food. Bed.

Then I can close my eyes and think about Mum, and the ocean that has grown between us.

CHAPTER 1
Agnes

1874

Agnes had counted the steps between the lower and upper floors of Perdita Hall hundreds of times. Seventeen. Wide at the bottom, narrower after the turn in the staircase, leading up to a wooden landing whose boards creaked under her feet as she made her way down the faded – but perfectly respectable – hall runner that led to Captain Forest's office. If she turned the other way, to the right, she would come to the door of Mrs Watford, the senior mistress. That was a well-worn path for Agnes, hauled in again and again for misdemeanours. The thought of never having to see Mrs Watford again was a satisfying one, and the feeling was no doubt returned. The senior mistress's last words to her had been, 'At least when you leave we won't have to open the gate; I expect you'll simply climb over it like you usually do.'

Agnes approached Captain Forest's closed door, and she hesitated a moment, glancing out the window at the end of the hall. She could see out over the chapel, the gardens, the workrooms and the dormitories that had been her home for nineteen years. The only

1

home she had ever known. She wondered if she'd miss it, but that hardly seemed possible: she was aching for life to begin.

Agnes knocked quickly and quietly.

'Come,' he called, and Agnes opened the door.

She had met Captain Forest only once that she could remember. History recorded that Captain Forest met every child when they were first admitted to Perdita Hall, but as Agnes had been a baby then, she had no recollection. The other time was around her tenth birthday. She remembered him as kind, but distracted. At ten, each child in the foundling hospital was given their first trial apprenticeship, either here or with one of the trades or families in the village, and Captain Forest would treat them to tea in his office and a pep talk about what being a Perdita boy or girl meant. He had given her a slice of sponge cake and it had melted on her tongue, buttery and sweet.

Agnes briefly wondered if there would be cake today, but decided not. She was nineteen now, no longer a child. Today, everything changed.

Captain Forest sat at an immense oak desk. On the wall behind him was an ornate barometer. Paintings hung everywhere: translucent turquoise waters and ships ploughing through foam. A brass sextant sat before him, holding down papers.

Agnes went to stand in front of the desk, hands folded across her ribs on her grey cotton dress.

The warm spring light through his window illuminated the silver in his moustache and muttonchop sideburns. 'Miss Agnes Resolute, I take it?'

'Good morning, Captain Forest.'

He smiled and indicated the chair beside her. 'Do sit down.'

Agnes did as she was told, running her fingertips over the fine carvings on the chair's arms.

Captain Forest hooked a pair of spectacles over his ears and leafed through the documents in front of him. 'You have been here all your life, Agnes. Just a babe when we took you in.'

'Aye, sir.'

'I see you completed your apprentice work in the laundry here at Perdita.'

'Sewing and mending, sir. I took to it.' Agnes was an accomplished seamstress mostly because she enjoyed the quiet in the mending room above the laundry, which gave her imagination time and space to roam.

'Excelled at reading and writing, not so suited to infirmary or kitchen work, an adequate parlour-maid to the Bennett family in upper Hatby . . .' He leafed through the pages, her history recorded flat and neat. 'Oh, dear. You have been cautioned for behaviour many times, Miss Resolute. That *is* disappointing.'

Agnes didn't know if this comment called for a response, but an unspoken one jumped into her head. *Can you blame a caged bird for beating its wings against the bars?*

Finally, he looked up. 'Agnes, on the occasion of your nineteenth birthday, I take great delight in releasing you from your obligation to Perdita Hall.'

Her face could not contain her smile. 'Thank you, sir.'

'You will be released with all your papers, references, and of course a small sum of money to take you into the city to look for work.' One of Captain Forest's edicts was that Perdita boys and girls needed to travel ten miles to York to make a new life: coach fare and a month's board. 'My brother runs a laundry near Petergate; he could offer you—'

'I doubt that I'll stay long in York,' she declared, though she didn't know why. Perhaps it was simply the prospect of Captain Forest taking control of her opportunities again.

His hairy eyebrows shot up. 'No? You have broader horizons?'

Agnes glanced around at his paintings of ships, and wondered how he could ask that. 'Aye, sir. I do.' The truth was she didn't know what she was going to do. She had written away to a ladies' home that would take her for a few weeks and help her find a position, but she hoped to work a month or so and save a little and then head somewhere with a view of the sea. She had never seen the sea.

'I admire your courage, but listen to me: find good honest work and don't live beyond your means or aspire above your station. That is the key to happiness. None of this . . . misbehaviour, and you'll be happy.'

Agnes was well used to holding her tongue while receiving such lectures. 'Thank you, sir. I intend to be happy.'

He shuffled the papers back into the folder and tied the ribbons around it with a flourish. He stood, and with ceremony, handed it to her. Her history, finished with. Her future, waiting just outside the high iron gates of Perdita Hall.

'Fare well, Miss Resolute. You are named after a fine square-rigger that was nimble and steadfast. May you emulate her and uphold the good name of this fine institution.'

'Thank you, Captain Forest,' she said, with a shake of his curiously soft hand. 'Fare well.'

She left and sat on the stairs, untying the ribbons on the folder. Her skirt pooled around her, and she could feel the cool of the stone through the layers of material. Agnes was keen to see what Mrs Robbins in the laundry had said about her in her letter of recommendation. They had never got on, and she needed good recommendations to get work as a seamstress. The first document she came to, however, was the list of information about her admission to Perdita Hall, and she paused to read it.

It was set out in a table. *Name: Agnes (suggest Resolute).* Every Perdita child was surnamed after a famous ship. HMS *Resolute* was a Royal Navy gun-brig that had been broken up before her birth.

Father: Unknown.
Mother: Unknown.

Agnes skimmed past those. The facts were no surprise, but they still had the power to cause her pain, dull and dim though it now was.

Surrendered in person?: No. Left in portico early morning.

More lines, more details. Her weight and length, her lack of distinguishing marks, her head listed as *well shaped* and her ears as *rather small*. Agnes self-consciously touched her ears. She'd never thought them too small before now.

Her eyes ran all the way to the bottom of the document, and there she saw it.

Token: button with unicorn.

A tiny jolt of recognition, like a moth against glass. Most children were left with some token from their destitute mother: a ribbon or a lock of hair or even a piece of string found on the street. Agnes had always assumed she had no token, given that she was not surrendered in person, not ever intended to be identified or collected. But she had been left with a button. A unicorn button.

The memory is upon her in an instant, brightly lit around the edges. The voices of children and hoofbeats. She is very small, maybe five or six, and she is in the village with her classmates and a teacher. Across the road she sees a tall, fair woman, with a straight spine, who argues with a ruddy-faced man. The man tries to be quiet and calm, but the woman denounces him imperiously.

'Do not seek to control me!' she cries, and flounces across the road towards the children.

Agnes has been so closely watching the argument that she has lagged behind, and now in her hurry to catch up with her classmates she trips and falls, hands flying out in front of her, elbow landing in a muddy puddle.

Then the tall, fair woman is there, helping her up.

5

'You've made your dress all dirty,' she says, with a small smile, brushing off a damp leaf. Agnes is bewitched by the woman's high colour and bright eyes. She looks as though she has won something. Her miserable opponent skulks away on the other side of the road.

Then Miss Candlewick grabs her arm roughly, thanking the fair woman and hustling Agnes back towards the group. 'Come along,' she says. 'Naughty, wilful child.'

'Who was that beautiful lady?' Agnes asks.

'Genevieve. Lord Breckby's daughter,' Miss Candlewick says with a frown. 'Do you think her beautiful?'

'Aye. Beautiful and fierce.'

'What nonsense,' Miss Candlewick replies, then in a quieter voice, 'Though you would think that; cut of the same cloth you are.'

•

'Sitting on the stairs like an urchin, Miss Resolute?'

Agnes quickly gathered the folder together and tied it again, taking care to ensure her hands did not shake. 'No, ma'am. I dropped the papers and had to gather them.' She looked up into the eyes of Mrs Archer, the home-management mistress. Agnes and home management had never got on particularly well, and Mrs Archer had always thought this to be a moral failure on Agnes's part.

In truth, Agnes and moral failure were almost synonymous at Perdita Hall.

'You're still a Perdita girl for another few days, Agnes,' Mrs Archer said in her sharp, southern accent. 'Mind how you present yourself.'

Agnes watched her go. She might have laughed. That would be her last lecture from Mrs Archer. Agnes stood and smoothed her skirts, and headed for her dormitory. Back in her childhood memory, she'd thought Miss Candlewick's 'cut of the same cloth' an offhand comment, comparing naughty Agnes to wild Genevieve. But now, she suspected something quite different.

•

Motherless. Was there a sadder word in the English language? Agnes had often considered that question while sitting on this narrow bed, in this crowded dormitory, over the past nineteen years.

Afternoon sun struggled through the high beech trees that crowded against the windows. She didn't open the folder again. She didn't want others to hang about and ask her questions. When she was ready, in her own time, she would share some of the details within with Gracie Badger, her dearest friend of childhood. But for now, as other girls chatted and folded their clothes and read to each other from books, she thought again about being motherless, about believing herself a girl from nowhere and nobody, and how a button with a unicorn on it might mean she had provenance.

One could endure a great deal as a foundling. Becoming inured to suffering was Perdita Hall's great gift. The children were taught from the outset that while nobody had wanted them, it did not mean they were valueless in society. When Agnes misbehaved, which had been often, it was assumed she did so because she felt adrift or abandoned in the world. 'Look at the next bed and know you are not alone in feeling so,' Mrs Watford had told her again and again. After she climbed a beech tree and plopped over the wall to hunt for mushrooms in the woods. After she was discovered to have drawn lurid pictures in her notebook rather than copy out spelling words. After she had got into a screaming row with that mealy-mouthed Charlotte Pelican, who insisted that because God created Eve second, woman should always be second to man.

Agnes had to admit, though, that the staff were mostly kind, and even those who were unkind only served to toughen the overly hesitant, or humble the overly proud. Perdita Hall presumed itself a good place for a foundling to grow up, and perhaps that was the truth. But the highly controlled environment had pressed against Agnes from all sides. Nineteen years of rising at six, praying at six and ten, pissing at six and fifteen, mustering at six and forty-five for lessons or work; following the bugle to breakfast, lunch, dinner . . . nineteen years lived between the heavily inked lines of the Perdita schedule.

And of course no matter how kind the institution, everyone here longed for a mother. Most of the children imagined mothers as warm and soft and loving. Agnes, though, imagined mothers were mirrors, showing daughters who they might be, what they might become beyond the schedule, beyond the gates.

Maybe mothers owned riding coats with unicorn buttons, just like the one Agnes had seen on that coat . . .

But no, she couldn't conclude that. Not yet. She had to see the token with her own eyes to be certain. The tokens were all in Captain Forest's office. Everyone knew that. He kept some in a glass-fronted cabinet and showed them to visitors: Agnes had glimpsed them on her tenth-birthday visit, when she had sponge cake. She had ever after thought it such a strange collection of things to be on display, let alone to be proud of: knotted strings and pins and scraps of stained lace. The thing that seemed to unify the collection was that the items were so pathetic.

But thirty years of operation and nearly seven hundred children later, many other tokens had been handed in with abandoned children. Once they were described in the paperwork, according to Captain Forest's cleaner, an ex-Perdita girl herself, they were sorted into a chest of drawers. That meant Agnes needed to get into Captain Forest's office when nobody was there.

•

Agnes was a well-practised liar when she needed to be, though even she baulked a little at lying in order to miss church. Still, nothing seemed so pressing to her at this moment than to *know*. She prayed to God to forgive her as Nurse Maggie, fetched by her nearest dorm-mate Alexandra Orion, sat lightly on the edge of her bed and pressed a warm palm against Agnes's forehead. The dorm was chilly and quiet, girls slowly climbing out of bed in the early morning light. Church bells sounded in the distance, from the village of Hatby. Perdita's chapel had no bell beyond an old ship's bell hung in the vestibule.

'No fever,' Nurse Maggie observed, in her thick Scottish accent.

'A stomach ache.'

'How bad?'

Agnes winced. 'Awful.'

Agnes knew Nurse Maggie would take no chances. Six years ago a bout of typhoid fever went through Perdita Hall, killing four children. Captain Forest had been inconsolable.

'Rash?'

Agnes shook her head, but Nurse Maggie bunched up her nightdress nonetheless, to check her legs and trunk. She pressed her hand under the waistband of Agnes's bloomers into her tummy, a little cruelly, Agnes thought.

'You'll have to go to the infirmary until the physician can get here,' Nurse Maggie said. 'We'll have a time of it calling one in on a Sunday morning.'

'I don't mind waiting.'

Nurse Maggie narrowed her eyes. She was not easily fooled and Agnes's reputation preceded her, so she wilted a little further into her rumpled bed.

'Right, then,' Nurse Maggie said. 'Up you get. I'll take you over.'

Agnes smoothed down her yellowed nightdress, a hand-me-down whose ribbons were all frayed, and gingerly climbed out. Her slippers were under her bed, and she slid her feet into them and reached for her threadbare dressing gown. Nurse Maggie, who was an imposing woman of nearly six feet, waited with a grim face, then took Agnes's elbow and steered her along the dormitory between all the beds, down the stairs and out across the quadrangle. Agnes's breath fogged in the early morning air. She could hear some of the junior boys playing games on the grass on the other side of the wall that divided the boys from the girls, before the ship bell rang. Birdsong filled the clear morning air, but the sun hadn't risen above the dark stone buildings. Agnes's soles grew damp with dew. She hadn't been given new slippers at the start of winter, on account of her approaching departure from Perdita Hall. Nurse Maggie marched along ahead of her, but Agnes knew better than to try to keep up. If she was able to keep up, she was well enough for church: Nurse Maggie's pace was a test, for certain.

The infirmary was at the back of the main building of Perdita Hall, the same building that housed Captain Forest's office. Nurse Maggie waited for Agnes at the large double doors, then closed them behind her. Around behind the staircase and down to the half-lit basement level, and then through the lime-washed corridor to the infirmary, with its low dark ceiling. A yeasty, cold smell welcomed them.

One other child was there, a lad of about twelve with a wet cough.

Nurse Maggie showed Agnes to a bed at the opposite end of the ward and cautioned her to stay still, that they would send for the physician the moment Sunday morning service ended.

'I'm off to chapel now,' she said, striding over to the boy and tucking his blankets in firmly. 'I'll be back within the hour.'

Agnes nodded, then lay very still, listening. Ten minutes passed. Twenty. The boy's wet cough went on and on, but in a gap where he drew breath, she heard it dimly: the ship's bell on the chapel. The service was starting.

And everyone, except the sick boy and Agnes, was there.

She flipped back her scratchy blanket.

The boy stared at her with red-rimmed eyes. 'What are you doing?'

'Hush now. If you tell, there'll be trouble.'

He descended into another coughing fit, and guilt speared Agnes's heart. He was just a boy, a sick one at that, and she was torn between hoping Nurse Maggie would return soon to tend him, and hoping Nurse Maggie would stay away long enough that Agnes may find what she needed to find. That she was thinking such thoughts on a Sunday, instead of praying in chapel, struck her with doubly guilty force. 'Sorry, God,' she muttered, and hurried away from the infirmary.

Agnes stopped to listen at the top of the stairs. The tick-tock of the immense grandfather clock in the foyer, but no other sounds. She slipped out then rounded the bottom of the staircase up to the offices. One step at a time, her whole body tensed against discovery. Once she was in the dim corridor, she allowed herself to breathe. There were plenty of places to hide up here, should somebody return from chapel early.

Agnes approached Captain Forest's office for the second time in a week. This time, her heart was thudding. If she was found sneaking about where she oughtn't be, in her dressing gown and slippers, they might take away her references or refuse to give her the travelling money. She opened the door and slipped in, then closed it behind her gently. She was in. Excitement bubbled warmly inside her. The room smelled of lemon wax and the macassar oil Captain Forest wore in his hair. She glanced around at the cabinets and chests of drawers, all polished to gleaming. She opened the closest one, beside his desk, and found only papers. Next, she tried the drawers under the window. The top drawer squeaked so loudly on opening that Agnes was certain someone would hear. She straightened her back, heart speeding. What excuse could she make if she was found rifling through things that weren't hers, in a place she wasn't allowed, after lying about being sick to get out of church? How was she to describe to another the strange, mad impulse that had caused her to act this way? After all, if she found

11

the unicorn button, perhaps it was utterly unlike the one in her mind's eye . . .

But a minute passed, and nobody came. She returned her attention to the drawer. Wooden dividers had been built into it and each square contained tokens. There were so many squares. How would she find the unicorn button? She began sifting through the tokens with her fingers, then noticed that each square in the drawer had a card slid into the back, and each card had a year written on it. 1874. 1873. 1872 . . . She ran her eyes over the cards, then realised she needed to go to the next drawer down.

1859, 1858 . . . and there it was, 1855. The year she had arrived. A dozen or so tokens rattled in the square. She saw it almost immediately.

She withdrew the unicorn button with trembling fingers.

It was *exactly* as she remembered it.

•

Agnes had been ten, and it was the third day of her first week in the laundry. Mrs Watford had declared that ten hours a day in a steaming workroom would finally cure Agnes of her wickedness, but within a day Mrs Robbins had seen the quality of her needlework and shifted her to the sewing room. Yes, she still learned how to scrub and rinse and mangle and shake and hang, but for the most part her work was pleasant and dry.

That's when the basket had come in. Delivered by a tall, bent man who said he was a servant from Breckby Manor, the immense estate on the hilltop above Hatby owned by Lord Caspian Breckby.

'I have secondhand clothes from his Lordship's daughter,' he said, sliding the basket onto the long bench where the folding usually took place. 'Miss Genevieve says that all of these are to be given to charity. Perhaps some of the young lasses here can make use of them.'

Agnes had been instructed to secure all the buttons and hooks, darn any holes and tighten any loose seams. She remembered Genevieve from their encounter, and was thrilled for a chance to work with her clothes, even though they were off-casts. First to hand was a riding jacket. Agnes had never ridden a horse but had formed an opinion of them as a potent symbol of freedom. She and Gracie made up stories while sharing a bed at night, in which a herd of wild horses broke down the gates of Perdita Hall, and only the two girls could tame them. The fantasy always ended with them escaping onto the moors riding bareback, at one with the night and the clouds shredding across the moon. But on the riding jacket was something even more enchanting than horses: round crimson buttons, with a gold unicorn rearing on its hind legs. A horse with a stabbing device! As she secured each button with thread, Agnes was overcome by wild imaginings, in which she, dressed only in her nightdress and this tiny-waisted riding coat, forged a bloody path out of Perdita Hall for good.

One unicorn button had been missing from the cuff, and Mrs Robbins had instructed Agnes to sew on a button that didn't match. After that, she never saw the riding coat again. None of the clothes went to Perdita girls: they would have caused jealousies and fights. Mrs Robbins sold them on and the money went to Captain Forest, as did all the money they earned, to pay for their keep. But Agnes had never forgotten the buttons – the perfect match for this button that she held now, which may have unlocked the secret of her provenance. For what other conclusion could she draw? Surely she must be the illegitimate daughter of the noble and striking, yet famously wild Genevieve Breckby.

•

'Are you certain this is the right thing to do?'

Agnes glanced at Gracie. It was early evening on Monday, and they had asked permission for a walk outside the gates, to go

13

to Hatby to consult the coach times for Agnes's departure in two days. As if Agnes hadn't memorised every coach departure from the village over her lifetime. Their real objective was to take the path up through the sycamore woods and out through the churchyard to Breckby Manor.

'I am more than certain,' Agnes said, leading Gracie around a muddy patch on the path. Her friend was blind in one eye and always tripping over things. The woods were dark and cool, quiet but for the sound of birds hopping on and off branches and small creatures moving in the undergrowth. 'Miss Candlewick has been dead for two years, so I can't ask her. I will have to ask at the source. Would you not do the very same thing, Gracie?'

'I don't know,' Gracie said uncertainly, tucking an errant ginger curl back under her bonnet.

Gracie said and did everything uncertainly. Her heart was so kind and so full of good will that she was able to see everyone's perspective, even if they were awful. It meant she rarely had any conviction about her own thoughts and feelings, could not decide whom to love and whom to hate.

Agnes grasped her hand. 'What am I to do but to go and see her, look at her face and tell her I am her child?'

Gracie fixed her with her good eye. The other wandered to the left. 'She wouldn't admit you were her child. She rid herself of you, remember?'

Agnes blocked the squeeze of pain this statement made her feel, and they resumed walking. 'She left me with the button, and then she sent the riding coat to Perdita's. Surely she was trying to tell me who she was. Perhaps she never wanted to give me up. Perhaps she had no choice.'

'I saw her once, in the village,' Gracie said. 'She seemed the kind of woman who makes her own choices.'

Gracie was right. 'I saw her once too,' Agnes said, and the words came out more wistfully than she would have liked.

'She was pretty. I mean . . . she was striking.'

Gracie was right: Genevieve Breckby had such an imposing demeanour, such a well-formed frame, that she almost resembled a Roman statue come to life. Even though Genevieve had only spoken to her that one time, Agnes had seen her in the village two more times in her childhood. Genevieve had made a deep impression on Agnes, not the least reason being the rumours that she was headstrong, sharp-tongued, and slipped constantly from her father's and her husband's attempts to control her. It was these stories that so inflamed Agnes's imagination. She didn't want a mother for cuddles and kisses: she had long ago made her peace with that privation. Nobody could grow up in Perdita Hall without being a little crooked in the heart, and love was not something she expected or understood. Not even the idea that she may be related to nobility, and thus not destined for hard work and penury, had the power to move her as much as the notion that this drive to be free, which had ever beaten in her blood like the workings of a thundering engine, might be an inherited trait. That there might be another woman in the world whose heart knew her heart, whose passions recognised hers.

That she might not be so alone.

In truth, Agnes did not even know whether Genevieve still lived at Breckby Manor. There had been talk of a scandalous end to a marriage, and Agnes hadn't seen her for many years. But she could hardly leave Hatby without at least trying to find out the truth. She released Gracie's hand to open the church gate and they made their way across the churchyard, under the low-dipping branches.

At the other side, Gracie stopped. 'From here you should go alone,' she said, settling on the stone border of a garden bed, her grey skirts bunched around her.

15

Agnes crouched in front of her, taking her hands. 'Thank you, my dear friend. I won't leave you here long.'

'Take the time that you need,' Gracie said. 'I will be happy sitting here with the breeze and the branches.' She smiled. 'Imagine, Agnes, if in two years' time when I am due to leave, I find the very same thing written on my papers. *Button with unicorn.* We could be sisters.'

Agnes didn't point out that they could never be sisters, they were manufactured from entirely different material for any biological link to exist; but Gracie was like a sister in a different way. She had loved and listened to Agnes even as everyone else mocked her or corrected her; and Agnes adored Gracie and protected her.

Agnes rose, smoothed down her skirts, and marched with purpose out of the churchyard and up the path to Breckby Manor.

Its imposing front gates were closed, and Agnes hoped she wouldn't have to climb into the grounds – that wouldn't be the ideal way to approach her long-lost family. But she put her hand through and lifted the latch, and it was not locked. She pushed the gate and it creaked loudly. A moment later, two gigantic, sleek dogs came thundering towards her. She stood very still, tensed to slip back out the gate, but they came with tails wagging and tongues lolling. She bent to pat their heads. One of them went over on its back and she rubbed its belly roughly.

As she lavished pats on the dogs, she lifted her head and looked around her. The foregrounds of Breckby Manor were encircled by a wide carriageway that passed in front of the house and branched off towards stables. The circular garden was full of bright flowers and carefully managed trees. Agnes crossed the garden, accompanied by the dogs. She spied some little mournful crosses by the pond, underneath a slender willow. They were marked for dead pets: Persimmon, Xerxes, Fluff, Calico. The packed earth of the carriageway crunched under her feet, and then she was climbing the four wide stone stairs to the portico and, finally, ringing the brass bell by the door. The dogs, well trained, did not advance up the stairs.

She waited. A cloud moved over the sun.

Then the door opened, and an elderly smiling-faced butler appeared. 'How may I help you, Miss?'

'I would like to see Genevieve.' She realised she ought to use the more formal 'Miss Breckby' but her mother's name was fixed in her head now.

His smile was immediately transformed to a frown. 'And who are you?'

'My name is Agnes Resolute. I am from Perdita Hall. And it's important I speak to Genevieve.'

He shifted so he could pull the door closed behind him, but she still had a glimpse of a cavernous entry hall, with a servant dusting a row of imposing portraits. 'The younger Miss Breckby no longer lives here, Miss.'

Agnes's heart fell. She had known this was a possibility, but nonetheless the confirmation took the wind from her sails. 'Where does she live, then? Because I need to find her.'

'I am not likely to tell a foundling where the Breckby family might or might not be. Their movements are no business of yours. Now, good day.'

He moved to slip back into the house, but she grasped his sleeve. 'Please,' she said. 'I must find her.'

'Good *day*, Miss. If you don't leave immediately I shall ensure a report is sent back to Captain Forest about this . . . harassment.' He shook off her hand and she stood back and let him go.

Hell fire.

Agnes turned and made her way back down the stairs, across the garden, and out the gate. Powerful feelings traversed her body, causing her hands to shake. But she would not cry. Tears were for the weak. She had endured a lifetime of disappointments; this one would not break her.

Gracie leapt to her feet as Agnes strode back into the churchyard.

'I can tell by your face it didn't go well,' Gracie said.

'Aye, flower. It certainly did not.'

'But you aren't to worry. I've been sitting here thinking. You remember Cole Briar, don't you?'

Agnes blinked back at Gracie. Why was she talking about Cole Briar? The day he had graduated from Perdita Hall was one of the best days of her life. She couldn't count the number of times he'd sought her out in the gardens behind the church and tried to kiss her or grope her. Every time she had complained to Mrs Watford she'd been told that if she had been in her dormitory and not running wild in the garden, she would have nothing to worry about. 'Aye, I remember his bad manners. What of him?'

'He used to work for the Breckbys. Maybe he knows summat.'

'I'd just as like kiss an eel as ask for his help.' But even as she said this, Agnes was already changing her mind. Cole had never left Hatby. He worked for the local bootmaker, and if he knew something, he would be easily persuaded by Agnes to tell it.

'Agnes?' Gracie said, after she had been silent for a few long moments.

'Aye, then.' Agnes linked her arm through Gracie's. 'Come with me. I'm not doing it alone.'

•

Hatby's high street was a grim, straight road of grey stone buildings. Apart from a horse and cart outside the post office, and an elderly couple gazing in the window of the milliner, Agnes and Gracie were the only ones on the street. Shadows grew long in front of them as they made their way down to Tucker's Bootmaker. The shop was narrow, wedged between the candlemaker and an empty shop that had once been a tea room. Agnes pushed open the door, with Gracie close behind her. The shop smelled of leather and dust. Behind the counter, in a corner, sat Cole Briar. Tools and strips of leather hung on the walls all around him. He had his head bent over a boot, crimping the leather with a hand tool.

'Cole,' Agnes said.

He glanced up. He had a long nose and greasy skin, and lank dark hair that fell in two hanks over either side of his brow. When he saw Agnes, a slow smile grew on his face.

'Well now, see thee here. If it isn't Agnes Resolute.'

'And Gracie Badger,' Gracie said.

Cole ignored her, put down his boot and moved towards them. 'Why are you in the village, looking for Cole Briar, eh? Is it my lucky day?'

Agnes fought with her irritation, applied a sweet smile. 'Aye, Cole. That it might be.'

'Do tell.' He was a good six inches taller than her, and he stood so close she could smell his musty clothes.

'You worked for the Breckbys, didn't you?'

'Aye. My last three years at Perdita I was sent out as their footman. The inside of that house is so big a man could get lost in it.'

'Did you ever hear them mention Genevieve? Where she had gone?'

He looked at her a moment, his eyes sharp and bright. She knew he was thinking over what to say next. 'Why do you want to know?'

'Can you not just answer the question?'

'No I can't. I need to know what's in it for me.'

Gracie squeezed closer to Agnes.

'Do you actually know anything or are you just pretending?' Agnes asked defiantly. 'Because I'm warning you, Cole Briar, I'll give you a threp in the stones if you don't tell the truth.'

He shifted his weight from one foot to the other, still not speaking. Then said, 'I know something. I used to collect their mail.'

Agnes's heart lifted. 'You did?'

'Aye. So, now I ask again: what's in it for me?'

'You can have a kiss.'

He leaned in but she took a step back, nearly knocking Gracie over. 'Not yet. When you tell me something.'

'Aye, here's the deal. One small kiss to get me to speak, one long kiss when I've told you her address.' He emphasised the last word with raised eyebrows.

Her address? It was worth kissing an eel. She put her face up and he leaned down and pressed his lips hard against hers. She allowed the pressure to rest there for two seconds, then stood back. 'Aye, then. What do you know?'

'Genevieve went to live in London with her sister, Marianna. That's what the housekeeper told me. I picked up Marianna's letters every Thursday at the post office. Belgrave Place, London. Now, about that long kiss. I'll give you the house number when we're done.'

Agnes glanced at Gracie, who appeared puzzled and fascinated at the same time.

'Go on, then,' Gracie said. 'You promised.'

Agnes took a step forward, allowed Cole to place his hands around her waist. Then he bent and kissed her forcefully, prising open her lips with his tongue and probing her mouth roughly. She screwed her eyes tightly shut and thought about something else. London. Her mother. The unicorn button. His hands slid down and over her hips, and he was reaching around for her bottom when she broke off the kiss and leapt back.

'Give over. I never gave permission for *that*.'

He laughed. 'Can't blame me for trying, Agnes Resolute. You've always been the top of my list.' He gave Gracie a wink and Gracie smiled at him guilelessly.

'Right. House number?'

He gave her the full address and asked for another kiss, which she refused angrily. Finally, she was free of the smell of the shop and out on the chilly street.

'London,' Gracie breathed. 'What a shame she's so far away.'

Agnes stopped and turned to Gracie. 'The distance doesn't matter. I'll have to go,' she said.

Gracie's eyebrows shot up. 'What nonsense, Agnes. You'll not be able to afford it. You can't . . . you won't . . .'

'I'll use some of the money for my first month's board.' Agnes glanced back towards the bootmaker to make sure Cole hadn't followed her. 'Gracie, Genevieve Breckby might very well be my mother.'

'Can owt I say stop you?' Gracie asked.

'You know you can't stop me,' Agnes answered.

'Aye,' Gracie said with a smile. 'Nobody ever has once you've got an idea in your head.'

●

It was a blustery afternoon when Agnes finally stood at the coach stop outside the Hatby post office, ready to begin her new life. Gracie stood with her, clutching her hand, as Agnes's trunk was loaded onto the carriage. It looked pathetically small alongside the large, elaborate trunks of the other travellers. A woman not much older than Agnes was bossing one of the footmen in an arch voice. She wore a plum-coloured silk dress with an enormous bow on the bustle. Agnes glanced down at her own dress. Every Perdita girl was tasked with making her own leaving dress in the months before her departure. That morning, Agnes had finally pulled on the dress – sewn of the regulation pale grey broadcloth but enlivened with lace collar and cuffs Gracie had made for her – then fastened all the hooks and buttons, and gathered the tape that kept the modest bustle sitting sweetly. She had thought she looked very fine indeed, but she knew that next to this woman she did not look fine. The most she could say was she looked neat.

Agnes watched as the coach driver spoke to the passengers one by one and admitted them to the coach. She was the last in line. He held out his hand for the slip of paper that had her fare on it.

'York?' he said in a gruff voice.

'The railway station. I'm going to London.'

He lifted an overgrown eyebrow. 'London, eh? I can sell you the train fare here, much cheaper. It's a long way to London. They'll charge you fifteen shillings if you buy your fare at the station.'

Fifteen shillings! She had been given twenty, enough for the coach to York and then a month's board. 'How much is it if I buy a ticket from you?'

'I'll give it to you for twelve. And I'll throw in your coach fare for two and six; that's half the price.'

Agnes did calculations in her head, her blood cooling rapidly. She had heard the train was cheaper than coach, but of course it was two hundred miles or so between York and London. She was a fool to think she could afford it.

She looked at Gracie, who shook her head sadly, her bad eye roaming to the left. 'You won't have enough money to get back if things go wrong. Perhaps London will have to wait.'

Wait? She had been waiting her whole life for something. Maybe this was the something.

'I'll take it,' she said to the coach driver. When she found her mother, she would not need money.

'Agnes—'

'It will be fine, Gracie. You will see.' She untied the drawstring on the purse hanging from her wrist and withdrew the money, counting it out carefully into the coach driver's rough palm. She slid her train ticket into her purse then she yanked it closed. It hung limp and light, weighted down by only a few coins and the folded piece of paper that identified who she was and explained why she had no certificate of birth.

'Hop on board,' the driver said, returning to his seat at the front of the coach.

Gracie was shoving something into Agnes's hands. 'Here,' she said.

'What is this?' It was soft and small, wrapped in old newspaper.

'A gift. And . . . you might need it more than ever. Don't be afraid to sell it if you have to.'

'You oughtn't have got me a gift.' Agnes drew Gracie into an embrace. 'I love you, dear friend.'

'Write to me,' she said. 'The moment you arrive.'

'I will.' Then Agnes was stepping up and into the coach, where the women sat. The men had arranged themselves on the outside seats. She squeezed in between the woman in the plum dress and another, elderly lady who seemed affronted by having to give Agnes space on the seat. She turned her elbows out territorially, and Agnes tried to imagine what Genevieve would do if the elderly woman was so rude to her. She pulled her spine straight and held her space, and tilted her chin up for good measure. Some of Genevieve's features were vague in Agnes's memory, but she could easily remember the noble set of her chin.

The horses set off and the coach began to bounce along the road. She gazed out the window, watching beech trees and oaks slide past, then a glimpse of the front gate of Perdita Hall, behind branches and houses. She leaned back and closed her eyes. Her pulse seemed thick in her throat.

The decision was made now.

She opened her eyes and turned to the package, unpicking the string and pulling the newspaper away. The elderly woman sniffed disdainfully. Agnes pulled out Gracie's gift, a lace shawl.

Gracie was the best lacemaker in Perdita Hall. As clumsy as she was walking about, her one good eye was sharp-focused on close work and her hands as steady as rods. Ordinarily, what she made had to be sold. How had she managed to hold this back? Agnes smiled, thinking of Gracie, who was so afraid of getting in trouble, hiding this shawl from the eyes of the lacemakers' mistress, fearing discovery, wrapping it and bringing it outside the gates. Her heart lurched, thinking about Gracie left alone at Perdita Hall without Agnes to protect her and read to her.

Agnes swore to herself she wouldn't sell it. No matter how bad things became.

She pulled it around her shoulders, elbows bumping the other passengers. The plum-dressed woman drew her mouth down in a little moue of disapproval, but Agnes didn't mind. She was willing to wager that plum-dress woman owned nothing so precious as Gracie's gift, because it was made with love.

The coach rattled along, away from her old life and towards the new.

CHAPTER 2

It was four in the afternoon when Agnes finally alighted at a coaching inn a hundred yards from the railway station. She waited while the footman took her trunk down, and he showed her with an extended hand which direction she should take.

The railway station was a huge limestone-and-brick building on Tanner Row. She made her way around the noisy platform, under the iron train shed. A hissing black engine sat at the platform, smelling of coal and grease, its long line of wooden carriages hitched behind. People milled about, hauling baggage, saying farewells; children laughing and carousing, adults cautioning them, staff weaving between them on missions of their own. Everything around her was coated in a fine film of soot. A porter hurried past and she called out, 'Excuse me, is this the train to London?'

He shook his head. 'Edinburgh. Go ask at the ticket office.'

'But I have a ticket already.'

He had disappeared into the crowd and didn't hear her, but he had gestured to the ticket office and so she walked down the platform and waited in a queue until an older gentleman with snow-white muttonchops and a flat black cap asked if he could help her. She fished her ticket out of her purse and showed him. 'When is the next train to London?'

'Twenty minutes. But this ticket is for the one o'clock service.' He handed it back.

'One o'clock? Then I've missed it?' Her heart fell sharply.

He shook his head. 'One o'clock in the morning, Miss. We will be boarding in eight hours.'

So, that was why the ticket had been so cheap. Her stomach tightened with anger. The gentleman was already turning his attention to the woman behind her, who was far better dressed, so Agnes slunk out of the way and wandered back up the platform with her little trunk, found a seat and sat and watched a while. The bells on the Minster rang out evensong and then died on the breeze. The flow of people on and off trains mesmerised her. As each train departed, in clouds of hissing steam, it left behind an empty quiet. But then, minutes later, people would start to arrive and gather again; the pace returned, the trumpet would sound, a train would steam into the platform. And so on.

Not one of them took her to London. She glanced at the clock above the platform. It was nearly seven o'clock and her stomach was rumbling. Movement at the corner of her eye caught her attention. The ticket master approached, a small china cup in each hand. Curious, she watched him. He offered one of the cups to her.

'Coffee?' he asked.

Agnes would have preferred roast beef, but at least it was something in her stomach. She took the cup and said, 'Thank you.'

'So, you're going to wait until the train comes?'

'I have nowhere else to go or be.'

'I am locking up the office and going home in ten minutes. The night guard won't return until midnight, so you'll be alone on the platform.'

Agnes shivered.

'Keep your eye out for urchins,' he said.

'I will.' She lifted the cup to her lips, took one sip, then bumped her elbow on the back of the seat and spilled the coffee down the front of her dress. 'Hell fire,' she said, then clapped a hand over her mouth. 'I'm so sorry, sir. I oughtn't repay your generosity with coarse language.'

The ticket master chuckled and took her cup. 'Would you like me to pour you another?'

'No, thank you.' The coffee was too strong and swirled in her empty stomach.

'I will leave the lamps lit for you,' he said, and moved away. Shortly afterwards, she heard a door being locked and the sound of receding footsteps.

Agnes sat and waited. The evening grew quiet. An hour passed. Another. Her body sagged. She lay down on her side on the bench, tucking her purse under her head like a pillow. It was a Perdita habit to sleep on one's valuables, when things were always being nicked. The hard wood pushed back at her hips, and it was impossible to get comfortable. She waited. A cold wind crept down the railway tracks, swirling up grit.

She was just starting to nod off when she heard footsteps. Alert suddenly, she sat up. At the far end of the platform stood a gentleman, silhouetted against the gas lamps. Agnes wondered if he might be the night guard, but he wasn't in a uniform. He began to pace the platform, ten yards, twenty, but turning back before he came near her. She could see he had a small carpet bag, and presumed he was waiting for the same train as her. He wore a

27

top hat, a well-made great coat, and brown leather gloves. On his next circuit of the platform, he caught her eye and smiled at her.

Agnes couldn't help but smile in return. He had such a handsome face, such kindness in his eyes. He came no nearer to her, and Agnes relaxed. With a gentleman on the platform, she wouldn't have to worry about urchins as the ticket master had warned her.

She began to nod again, and as the gentleman was now at the opposite end of the platform, seemingly determined not to crowd her, she lay down her head again and closed her eyes. Time stuttered. She fell into a dream. She was back at Perdita Hall. She could hear Gracie on the other side of the wall that enclosed the grounds and she knew she needed to get to her. She started to climb but found the wall grew higher and higher, until it became an impossible teetering thing. She clung to it with her fingers, but they were cold and a wind was blowing and then she was falling . . .

Agnes's eyes opened. She was alone on the platform again. How long had she slept? She sat up, wondering what had happened to the well-dressed gentleman. As she put her feet on the ground, she realised the familiar shape of her trunk was not behind her knees. She leapt up, checked under the bench.

It had gone.

'No,' she said, and scooped up her purse to run to the other end of the platform, looking for her trunk, looking for the gentleman, anyone. 'No!' she called and her voice was whipped away on the wind. Agnes returned to the bench and sat heavily.

Had the gentleman taken her trunk? But why? What use would two dresses and some plain cotton underwear be to him? He wouldn't get a shilling for the lot if he tried to sell it. But it was all she owned. Her clothes, her slippers, her nightgown, not to mention her letters of reference and embroidery samples, without which finding a good position would prove very difficult. All she had left was a little money, a coffee-stained dress, and the shawl Gracie had made for her.

Doubt sang to her. Perhaps she oughtn't board the train at all. Perhaps she should return on the morning coach to Perdita Hall and ask for guidance. It had worked out terribly so far. Why did she think London would work out any better? She had heard stories of the poor houses, and she knew she didn't want to end up in one.

But then she scolded herself. She had a shawl to cover the coffee stain. She had enough money to get by for a little while. She had skills as a seamstress that would find her work. But most of all, she had a ticket to London on the one o'clock train.

And London was where her mother lived.

•

The single advantage of a one o'clock train was that the third-class carriage held few passengers, so she was able to lay herself out on the hard wooden seat and close her eyes. Sleep was impossible, though, due to the noisy rattling and juddering, and the thick choking stench of coal. Hours later, when the sun had risen thinly and the train pulled into King's Cross Station, her eyes were gritty from tiredness and coal dust. She alighted with only the clothes on her back and the purse in her hands, and made her way along the vast arched concourse, trying not to look lost and unsure – even though she had never seen such a crowd, never heard such a tumult, and had no idea what she was to do next.

'Excuse me? Miss?'

Agnes ignored the voice, but the gentle tap on her arm caught her attention. She turned to see a plump, white-haired woman in a blue-and-grey dress and matching hat. She had kind eyes and deep lines in her powdery white skin, but Agnes was in no mood for chat.

'What is it?' she said, a snap of warning in her voice.

The woman's smile faded on her lips. 'You forgot your luggage. I saw you get off the train. You must have left it on board.'

Guilt speared Agnes's heart; she had repaid this woman's attempt at kindness with heat. 'I am so sorry. I have had a bad time of it,' she said.

'Oh, dear,' the woman said, placing her own travelling bag on the ground between them and taking Agnes's hand. This small gesture of human comfort, on top of Agnes's weariness and uncertainty, made her chest burn. But she didn't cry. She couldn't remember the last time she'd cried; perhaps as a child.

'My trunk was stolen,' Agnes said. 'In York, before I boarded the train.'

'Have you friends here in London? Relatives? Someone who can help you?'

'I have seven shillings and a few pennies and the dress you see. That is all.'

The woman shook her head, clicking her tongue. 'No, no, dear. London isn't a place to be for a girl with so little.'

'Can you tell me where to go? I have to survive, at least for a week or so.'

'You might find a cheap room somewhere in the East End.' The woman bent to her bag and pulled out of it a map almost worn through on its folds. She opened it and folded it backwards, and Agnes noticed her fingers were jammed with gold rings, sapphires and rubies. 'This is us here, and this . . .' She jabbed a chubby finger. 'This is the direction you should head in. It's a few miles. Here, you can keep this map. High time I bought a new one.'

'Thank you,' Agnes said. She knew she should say, *You are too generous and I can't possibly accept a gift from a stranger*, but she desperately needed the map and didn't want to be taken at her word.

The woman took her by the shoulders. 'Don't have anything else stolen,' she said. 'What you have left is of high value, but only once.'

Agnes dropped her eyes. 'I have no intention of having my honour stolen, madam. I thank you for the warning, though.'

'London is quite the worst place to live if you are poor. If things get desperate, you must leave. Go back home.'

Agnes nodded; didn't tell her she had no home. The woman picked up her bag and hurried off. Agnes peered at the map, got her bearings, and began to walk.

Agnes had spent many years behind the gates of Perdita Hall, with only visits to Hatby to give her knowledge of the outside world. Of course she had read about London in books, but nothing could have prepared her for the intense impressions of sight, sound and smell when stepping into the London morning. The endless stream of people, faces blurring past until she could hardly distinguish them one from another. The way the light didn't fall soft and flowing but was brutally interrupted in cold blocks of shadow by the buildings. The shops: Lord, so many shops, all of them shouting at her in large letters. An old beggar here. A shrill-voiced woman selling limp turnips from a wheelbarrow there. A minstrel band with a hurdy-gurdy and monkeys, the music rising and falling on the wind. The din of rattling carriages hurtling past each other. As she walked, it all seemed to shift and tilt around her. Over everything, the smell of horse dung, coal and a faint unyielding odour of sewage. The number of people on the main roads, heads down with determination as they moved about between coal-smirched shops and offices, had intensified. The clop of hooves and rattle of carriages was incessant. She slipped into a side alley, feeling the quiet on all of her senses. She stopped a moment, took a few deep breaths.

'You can do this, Agnes,' she said softly. 'You'll not be frightened of a busy street, like a child.'

Once more she stepped out into the traffic. A mile passed. Two. The buildings began to change around her: these were not so grand. The parks were not so private. The coaches were not so shiny. A sign told her she was on Bethnal Green Road, and she thought that sounded a pretty name and wondered if she'd come far enough east now to find a cheap room. Agnes turned off the main road and followed her instincts down towards narrow lanes where she could hear children's voices.

Agnes stood at the head of one of the lanes and looked down. Crumbling brick buildings with windows broken and boarded. Children – so many children – barefoot and in ill-fitting and ragged clothing sitting on steps and in gutters while their mothers pegged faded laundry on long lines hung between windowsills. Broken furniture and muddy puddles. Skinny dogs winding between skinny legs.

Yes, she believed she would find something cheap here, and she was not too proud to take it. All she had to do was keep her purpose in sight: find a way to stay in London, then find her mother. Somehow.

Slowly, she made her way down the alley, picking around dog faeces embedded between cobbles. The smell made her recoil. A woman with sunken cheeks and a hungry gaze caught her eye and glared at her suspiciously.

'Who are you?' she said.

'I'm Agnes,' she replied. 'I need a place to live. Only short term.'

'Ask Minnie,' she said, stabbing her finger in the direction of a woman with wild red curls barely contained beneath a grey headscarf. She sat on the stairs of a dark grey tumbledown building of wood, weaving a basket and swatting away what appeared to be a dozen children. Agnes approached her warily.

'Minnie?'

'Who's asking?'

'I'm Agnes and I need a room, and—'

'I don't have a room. I have a bed. You can have it for sixpence a night, meals included.' Her worn hands worked their practised movements on the basket.

'Can I see it?'

She sighed, put her work aside, shouted at the oldest girl to mind the others and beckoned to Agnes. 'Come on, then.'

They entered a dark room that smelled of damp and mould. The kitchen was little more than a corner of a large living room, where two mattresses were butted against each other on the floor. Instead of shining things, there were broken things. Instead of light and air, there was gloom and stuffiness and the smell of urine. Minnie led her through to a tiny adjoining space with two beds in it, separated by a curtain that hung unevenly on a rail. The window was half-boarded over, so there was hardly any light. 'There,' she said, pointing at one of the beds. 'The other is mine and me husband's. But he's away out in the west country a few months, chasing some work in the mines.'

Agnes took a deep breath. All would be well. She would make it all well. One step at a time. 'I'll take it,' she said.

'Four nights' rent in advance?'

Agnes opened her purse and retrieved two shillings. They were snatched from her fingers. 'Aye, then,' said Minnie. 'Himself will be pleased.' She patted her tummy. 'Another on the way.'

'How many will that make?'

'Six, but we have me sister's two wee twins with us too. Poor Lizzie died in the having of them. Weren't anything we could do but take them in.' Minnie's eyes narrowed. 'You don't mind the sound of children, I hope.'

'I'm very used to it,' Agnes said, and it was true. She'd lived at Perdita Hall without privacy, surrounded by children: this could hardly be significantly different. 'What time is lunch?'

'Half after twelve. If you're not here, you miss out.'

'I have some business elsewhere in town. I'll be back by then.'

'Ooh, business, have we?' Minnie said in a mocking tone. 'You must be verrrry important.' She pocketed Agnes's money and said again, 'If you're not here, you miss out.'

Agnes nodded and forced a smile. Perhaps, before half past twelve, she would have met her mother and be welcomed into her home. Then she wouldn't care a jot if she missed out on Minnie's lunch.

·

With the worn map the woman at the railway station had given her, Agnes plotted her route to her mother's house. Genevieve lived on Belgrave Place, which looked to be a walk of at least two miles. She arranged Gracie's lace shawl so it covered the coffee stain and tidied her long, golden hair. Then Agnes stepped out of the grim grey dwelling and made her way out of the eastern streets towards the better-heeled end of town. She was tired from walking, but fascinated by all she saw. On her route, she passed galleries and churches and theatres, and saw ladies in the most divine frocks and some gentlemen dressed just as handsomely. She saw high, fast carriages drawn by gleaming horses. She heard cathedral bells and smelled smoke and flowers. At length, she passed a large green square enclosed by privets, where bronze statues sat among the chestnuts and plane trees. Here she stopped, consulted her map one last time, caught her breath, then took the turn into Belgrave Place.

A few moments later, she was standing in front of the address that Cole Briar had given her in what seemed another lifetime but was only a handful of days ago. Genevieve's house. It was a tall, narrow townhouse, painted white, with a small columned portico and dormer windows nestled among the dark brown roof tiles. It spoke of wealth, but not grandeur. Agnes took two deep breaths, then walked up three stone steps to ring the bell.

A long time passed. Long enough for her to think nobody was home, when a clunk near the post slot in the door caught her attention. A white hand had pulled the brass stopper up, and a voice emerged.

'Are you here about the position?' it said. A woman's voice. She sounded uncertain.

'No, I'm—'

The stopper slapped back into place, the woman, her voice now muffled, said, 'Good day.' Then footsteps retreated.

Agnes rang the doorbell again and waited. This time, nothing but a long silence. One more time she rang, but the woman didn't return, nor did a butler or maid come.

Are you here about the position?

Agnes turned and descended the three stairs back to the street. It was too soon to do so now, but she would ring that bell again tomorrow. And tomorrow, she would give the right answer.

CHAPTER 3

Agnes missed lunch after all. She thought she knew her way back but didn't and got lost and had to retrace her steps. By the time she made it back to Bethnal Green she was starving, exhausted, and her feet were swollen and sore. At least she missed the rain, which started shortly after she walked up the stairs and into Minnie's home. Minnie offered her a grunt in greeting from the floor where she sat with a pile of mending as little children crawled on and off her, crying.

'Can I help you with owt?' Agnes said, sitting beside her. The floor was hard and cold. Rain battered the windows.

'Can you make it stop raining?' Minnie grumbled.

'I can sew. Or I can entertain the wee ones.'

'Be my guest,' she said, shrugging off a little boy of about four.

'Come on,' Agnes said, grasping his hand and the hand of the smaller girl in Minnie's lap. 'I'll tell you all a story.'

Agnes lined them up in front of her, and two older girls and a boy joined them too. A few children were missing but Minnie didn't seem concerned. As the rain deepened overhead, and a mournful dripping noise came from somewhere near the kitchen, Agnes told them all a story about two girls who escaped from an orphanage on a unicorn. The smallest child crawled into her lap. Agnes could feel through her skirt that she was hot with fever, and her face was tired and grey. Agnes stroked her hair gently. The four-year-old boy was clearly hungry. She could hear his stomach yowling and when she slid an arm around him to comfort him during a scary part of the story, she could feel his ribs through his back. His legs were twisted with rickets. They passed the afternoon like this, and even Minnie smiled and chuckled through Agnes's story, which grew wilder and more elaborate the longer she went.

'Right, now,' Agnes said, when her throat was sore and the tiredness of the day caught up with her. 'I need a rest. Away with you.'

'You heard the lady; get off her,' Minnie said, far more harshly. Then to Agnes she said, 'Supper is half after five. You must be hungry.'

'Famished.'

'I'll call you when it's ready.'

Agnes took to her bedroom, if that's what it could be called. She lay down and looked up at the dirty, peeling ceiling. She could still smell the children on her clothes, and wondered if they'd ever had a bath. At Perdita Hall everyone had to be neat and tidy. Captain Forest had been fixated on making them ready for good honest work, on keeping them out of the poor house. *Pride in your appearance is pride in yourself.* For once, she felt lucky to have been a foundling at Perdita. These children at Minnie's had a mother, but they had far less than Agnes had had in every other way.

Minnie's supper was bread and dripping, which was often served at the foundling hospital. The differences were acute. The bread was not freshly baked by the boys in the village, but hard and flowered with mould. The dripping was not golden and savoury, but tasted stale and greasy. The meal was served at the kitchen table with the children, all seven of them standing around it while Agnes and Minnie sat on the only two chairs. By this time, Agnes's stomach was rumbling with hunger, and as the piece of bread landed in front of her, she glanced around to see that each of the children only had half a slice each. They ate as though they might never see another meal. Agnes, despite her hunger pains, could not bring the bread to her mouth.

Minnie had already eaten and was shepherding the children out, when Agnes caught the little thin boy, the one with rickets, and handed him her bread. 'Go on, you have it,' she said. 'I'm not hungry.'

The boy's eyes went round. Minnie gave Agnes an irritated look. 'I'll not reduce your rent for that,' she said, but the bread was already gone and the boy had limped off.

'I don't expect you to,' Agnes said. 'The poor lad is starving.'

'He does well enough,' Minnie grumped. 'Don't be telling me how to be a mother, when you've no children of your own and know nothing.'

Agnes didn't answer. She returned, instead, to her bedroom and lay down, still dressed in her coffee-stained grey leaving dress. Hunger fought to keep her awake, but weariness claimed her. She slept deep and dreamless until morning.

•

Agnes woke the next day to the sound of children on the other side of the curtain, whining for Minnie to wake up and feed them. She heard Minnie groan as she woke, and Agnes felt a strong wave of pity for her. It was one thing to be poor and hard on luck, but another altogether to be those things with children to provide for.

Agnes rose and went to the kitchen for a bowl of the thinnest porridge she had ever eaten. It ran off her spoon so rapidly that she was forced to lift the bowl to her lips and drink it. The boy with rickets watched her with ravenous eyes, so she left half for him and returned to her room to tidy herself. She pulled on her gloves, smoothed the shawl over her shoulders, and set out with purpose back to Belgrave Place.

The rain had stopped but the sky was still the colour of slate, and there were many puddles along her way. Once out of Bethnal Green, she stopped at a shop window and examined her reflection, making sure she had no dirt on her face. The coffee stain was hidden, but she had to be careful not to move too much lest the shawl slip aside and reveal it. She told herself that today could be the day: perhaps Genevieve would meet her and invite her in, and Agnes would remind her of their encounter all those years ago, and Genevieve would remember it too. Perhaps she would say, 'I knew when I looked at that little girl that she was somebody who mattered in my world.' These thoughts buoyed her on the long walk, even as her shoes grew damp from the wet ground and her head grew light from hunger.

Finally, she was back at Belgrave Place. As she stepped under the portico, light rain began to spit down. Heart thundering, she clanged the bell, then waited for the little voice at the post slot.

But this time, the door opened and a man stood there. He was in his early twenties, clean-shaven but for tidy sideburns, with thick, dark auburn hair, and warm brown eyes. He looked as though he had just arrived home, for his cravat was untied but still hung about his collar. He wore a soft white shirt and a dark grey waistcoat with a golden pocket watch chain visible. A scent of something woody or perhaps cinnamon or perhaps both enveloped her, and she reacted to it with a leap of excitement to her heart that she hadn't experienced before.

'May I help you?' he asked.

'Aye, I've come about the position,' she said, boldly.

The corner of his lip turned up in a smile. 'You're from the north. That's a Yorkshire accent if ever I heard one. What's your name, Miss?'

'Agnes Forest, sir.' She didn't want to give away who she was, and a surname like Resolute drew far too many questions.

'Come in, Miss Forest. I'll have a quick word to you in the drawing room and I'll explain to you about Marianna.'

Marianna. Genevieve's sister. Agnes wondered if it was she who had answered the door yesterday, or if it was Genevieve herself. Had she already spoken to her own mother? The thought thrilled her so much she barely noticed the rich interior of the house. The ornate plasterwork, the gleaming brass lamps, the floral damask wallpaper, the dozens of framed paintings and miniatures, the ornaments and clocks and urns and carved side tables. It could not have been more different from Minnie's place. The young man led Agnes into a light-filled room and asked her to sit on a long chaise, while he sat opposite on an upholstered chair.

'Miss Forest,' he said, 'my name is Julius Halligan, and I am Marianna's nephew.'

Agnes's mind whirled. If Marianna's sister was Genevieve, did this mean she was looking at her own brother? Was that the reason she had had such a strong reaction to the first sight of him? 'It is very good to meet you, sir,' she managed.

'From the advertisement in the newspaper, you will have gathered that the position requires you to keep Marianna company – and you must call her Marianna; she despises being called Madam.' His eyes went to the doorway, as though making sure the lady in question wasn't listening to him.

So, the position was as a lady's companion. Now Agnes felt on firmer footing, and knew what kind of truths she might have to bend.

'You read well, I take it?' he asked her. 'Her eyes are mostly fine but reading gives her a headache.'

'Oh yes, sir. And I know when to talk and when to listen. I would make a fine companion for . . . Marianna.' Her eyes roamed the room briefly, then came back to his face. She'd hoped for a portrait of Genevieve somewhere, but the paintings were all landscapes.

He forced a smile. 'It's a little trickier than you might imagine. This is the first time I have advertised for such a role. I suppose I have been her companion until recently, but now I have finished my studies and am off to the hospital at odd hours, she gets lonely and . . . I worry about her.'

'I am sure I could keep her spirits up.'

'Sometimes, though, she wakes in the middle of the night. I should say . . . most nights. She doesn't sleep easily and she looks for company then, too.'

Agnes drew up short of saying, *I would do anything to get inside this house.* 'I am perfectly willing to wake and read to her or chat with her or walk with her.'

'Ah, that won't be necessary. She doesn't leave the house.'

Agnes thought about the little voice at the post slot, the way its owner had refused to open the door.

'You have references, I take it?' Julius asked.

'Sir, I can be nowt but honest with you. I arrived in London from York two days ago, and all I had was stolen from me. I had references, and they were good ones. My last job was as a lady's companion too. In York.' Agnes realised this wasn't precisely as honest as she'd promised him. 'But they went, along with my spare clothes.'

He eyed her, and she knew he didn't believe her. 'And before that? What other positions have you held?' He glanced at her hands, no doubt looking for signs of menial work. Her needlework had saved her once again: she had seen the permanently ruddy hands of girls who worked in the laundry.

'I was a governess for a year to a little girl named . . . Gracie,' she lied. 'As I said, reading and talking and listening . . . all the skills I need for this position, Mister Halligan.'

Julius did not look particularly convinced, but Agnes kept smiling, head high.

'Are there any other tasks, sir?' she asked. 'Any other . . . people in the house who might require my companionship?'

'No, it is just we two: Marianna and me. And the cook and maids hardly need company; they can come up with quite enough noisy nonsense between them.'

Just we two. So, where was Genevieve? Agnes felt herself wilt, the strain of the last few days, the awful suspicion that she'd come all this way for nothing weighing down upon her.

'Well, Miss Forest,' he continued. 'I do thank you for calling. If you can leave me an address where I might find you, should I wish to offer you the position?'

She told him the address at Bethnal Green and he almost recoiled when he heard it. She knew then she wouldn't get the position. He certainly hadn't given her any indication that he thought her suitable. What now? *What now?*

Through these urgent, panicked thoughts, she still managed to smile and say thank you and good day and accompany him to the door.

The rain fell steadily now. Julius eyed the sky and said, 'Oh, dear. Have you an umbrella?'

She shook her head. 'Stolen,' she said. 'Along with everything else.'

As she stepped out under the portico he said, 'Wait.' He reached for the stand in the entranceway and retrieved for her an old, worn umbrella with a wooden handle. 'Keep it,' he said. 'We have others.'

She considered him a moment, felt a sense of loss that she might never see him again, might never know this family that could be hers. Then she took the umbrella and raised it. 'Thank you for your kindness,' she said, and stepped out into the rain.

•

Agnes didn't immediately return to Bethnal Green. She was raw with panic now, having learned Genevieve was not where she'd hoped and having so little money. As she picked over wet cobbles, she cursed herself and cursed herself again. Why hadn't she listened to Gracie? Why hadn't she listened to that infernal Captain Forest, come to think of it? *Find good honest work and don't live beyond your means or aspire above your station.* She had failed on every count.

So today, she had to find a job. But she wouldn't let go of trying to find Genevieve. Not because she had ideas above her station. She had no ambition to be welcomed in the family, to enjoy their wealth and influence. She simply wanted to belong to somebody.

•

Agnes's feet were sore by the time she arrived at the third dressmaker, this time above a shop selling watches and clocks on Cheapside. The first two had dismissed her quickly, telling her there wasn't enough work for a new seamstress. But here, as she stood by the door and waited for the young woman who had let her in to fetch the dressmaker, she could see many projects in progress; at least five dressmaker dummies half-clothed, a dozen bolts of cloth stacked across a long counter, a table covered in poorly organised paperwork. The room was quiet and softly lit by the daylight at the window, and smelled faintly musty. Agnes could imagine herself working here.

From a back room, a harried-looking woman emerged, an embroidery ring in her hand and pins stored in her bodice in uneven lines. 'Mary says you're looking for work.'

'Aye, ma'am. I worked in sewing, mending and embroidery at Perdita Hall, a foundling hospital, for nine years.'

'You have samples? References?'

Agnes's hopes were already dashed. 'No, my trunk was stolen but I—'

'Come back when you have samples.'

43

'If I could just—'

'I'm very busy, dear. I'll look at your work when you have some to show me.'

'This dress,' Agnes said, remembering suddenly, spreading her arms.

The woman approached, peering, running her hands over seams. 'Not bad. I'll need to see some embroidery. Come back and see me next week.'

'But I—'

She turned and disappeared into the back room again. Mary, the younger girl, who had appeared at her shoulder, shrugged an apology.

So, she couldn't work without samples or references. Her references were irretrievable now. If she spent all her remaining money on material and thread for embroidery samples and still didn't get a job, then she wouldn't be able to pay Minnie her rent.

Tired and discouraged, she walked back to the house at Bethnal Green, longing to remove her shoes, which the rain puddles had soaked through, and lie still for a little while.

Minnie looked up from her basket weaving as Agnes entered the gloomy room. 'You have a letter.'

'A letter?' Her heart beat faster. Julius had sent a note already. Was that a good sign?

'I left it on your bed.'

She hurried away to her bedroom and snatched up the letter. Hands trembling, she picked off the seal.

Thank you for coming by today, but I regret to inform you . . .

That was all she read. She flung the letter away from her and buried her face in her mattress so she wouldn't cry.

•

Agnes was not foolish enough to return to Belgrave Place and cause a scene, declaring herself Genevieve's long-lost daughter. She had seen the way Julius looked at her, and knew that she had to think of a better way to find out where Genevieve had gone. If she turned up again with no reason, exposing herself as a liar and a sneak, he would not listen to a word out of her mouth before he had her on the street. She had to be canny, and in the meantime she needed ongoing work and so she went out the next morning to buy a shilling's worth of cloth and thread and a selection of embroidery needles. In the gloomy little bedroom in Bethnal Green she worked, starting with embroidering a rose over the coffee stain on her grey dress. The days seemed to go on forever and she was so hungry. She always gave at least some of her food to the little boy with rickets – Freddy was his name – and she daren't spend another penny on food from the street vendors back in the good part of town. So, she starved, working in low light until her hands ached, making samples she could show the seamstress. Sometimes, all the children assembled on the bed with her and she told them stories while she sewed. Days passed and it was time to pay Minnie another two shillings. Now she had two left. She worked faster, made mistakes, had to unpick and start again. It sometimes felt as though she were sewing her own destiny: panicked, careless, trying to make it work but having to turn back again and again and try to get it right. At night she dreamed about thread navigating through seas of cloth.

One afternoon, nearly a week after she had arrived in London, she was sewing on her bed when she heard the sound of voices raised in argument from the street.

'Don't you touch them!'

'I'll do as I please.'

'You can't come back here and start thrashing them!'

Agnes put aside her sewing and crept to the threshold of the bedroom, where she leaned out. The voices were directly outside the front door of the house, one of them clearly Minnie's, one an unknown man. A child cried, or perhaps it was two or even three children. Agnes felt the change in atmosphere as though foul weather had moved in; a storm brewed.

Then a shadow darkened the door to the house and Agnes ducked back into the bedroom and returned to her work. She had glimpsed him, though: a huge beefy man with a dirty face and a ragged beard. Minnie's husband, she presumed. In the living room, he was roaring at Minnie and the children for being dirty and untidy and for not having a meal ready for him. Agnes's pulse flicked fast at her throat. He sounded like a monster, and his bed was separated from hers only by a curtain. It had not been bad sleeping in such proximity to Minnie, but with this huge, hairy creature so close?

The argument went on, and Agnes heard her name mentioned.

'I've got a lass here paying us sixpence a night just to sleep in Lizzie's old bed and eat a bit of bread. See? I'm not as stupid and useless as you say.'

'Sixpence. You could have given her our bed and charged twice that.'

Lizzie was Minnie's dead sister. Agnes shivered at the thought of sleeping in a dead woman's bed.

'Then there wouldn't have been room for you. Now, you be nice to her or she'll leave and then we'll have nothing.'

On and on it went, and Agnes tried to hear music in her head instead as she dipped the needle into the cloth, again and again, sewing herself away from this awful situation and into her future.

•

That night, Agnes met Minnie's husband at supper. He resembled the picture of Father Bear that had been in the book of Goldilocks she had read as a child. He wore a grey shirt that might have once been white, and a filthy pair of trousers held up with rope. He sat glowering at her across the table, while Minnie and the children stood around, struck dumb by his presence. Whatever he had earned away in the mines, he had largely spent on whiskey by the smell of him. He ate two pieces of bread while the children had a quarter-slice each, and Agnes got only a half. She didn't speak. Her entire mind was focused on calculating when she could leave.

Minnie caught her after supper and said, 'Errol's not all bad.'

Agnes said nothing.

'Just . . . if you have anything of value, hide it. Or keep it on you.'

'I have nothing of value,' Agnes said.

'Even if you think it isn't of value,' Minnie said. 'He's been known to sell things for grog.'

'Aye, be right,' Agnes said. Her money and Gracie's shawl were in the bag under her mattress, and she could keep her cloth and thread there too.

Then she remembered, she also had Julius Halligan's umbrella under there: a spear of daylight shot through her clouded mind.

Agnes wasn't out of ideas yet.

•

She barely slept, listening to the snores and mumbles of Errol beyond the curtain. He had taken his pleasure with his wife without any care that Agnes could hear it all, but Agnes felt more relieved than shocked. At least she didn't have to fear him coming through the curtain to force himself on her. She was too nervous to eat breakfast, so she shared it all with Freddy, then slipped out before Minnie could ask her where she was off to.

The day had warmed, and she was flushed and uncomfortable by the time she finally arrived at Belgrave Place. She stood a little while in the shade of a nearby tree while she cooled down, checking the pins in her hair. She suspected that she might look dirty or dishevelled, that in fact only Gracie's shawl kept her from looking like a pauper. She said a little thank you to Gracie on the breeze, then walked up to the front door and rang the bell. Heart speeding.

The door was opened by a plain young woman in a navy day dress and white apron. 'May I help you?'

'May I come in?' Agnes held out the umbrella. 'I wanted to return this to Julius and Marianna. Are they home?'

The parlour-maid took a step back, allowing Agnes into the entryway, and looked at the umbrella with a frown. 'They are not expecting—'

'I know they're not expecting me, but—'

'Who is it, Daisy?' A woman in her middle years had appeared at the head of the passage that led into the house. She had fair hair streaked with white, piled high on her head. A plain, cream-coloured house gown skimmed rather too loosely over her frame, as though she had recently lost weight. Nonetheless, she was not a thin woman. Tall and well built, with square wrists and straight white fingers unadorned by jewels. This must be Marianna. Her aunt. Agnes noticed she hung back in the doorway, one hand gripped tightly at the threshold, almost disappearing behind it.

'Ma'am, I am Agnes Forest. Julius very kindly let me borrow this umbrella when I came to speak to him about the position as your companion.'

'You came about the position?'

'Aye, and although I didn't get it, I—'

'You're from the north?' Her eyes were clear and light, blue or grey, and they fixed directly on Agnes. 'I know that accent. You're from Yorkshire. My family are from there.'

And in those last lines, Agnes heard the faintest burr of Marianna's own northern accent, hidden beneath the clipped tones of a good education and a London life.

'I am that, ma'am, I'm from Hatby. And I need to speak with you.'

'Hatby! Why, that is where I spent my childhood.'

48

Footsteps sounded on the stairs, and a moment later Julius was there, fastening his cuffs and frowning. He stiffened when he saw Agnes. 'What are you doing here?'

'Julius, this lass is from Hatby,' Marianna said.

'I came to return the umbrella,' Agnes said.

'I didn't ask for it to be returned.'

Agnes glanced at Marianna, who was smiling at her. She told herself to ask quickly about Genevieve, but now Julius was here she knew he would have her thrown out. She opened her mouth to ask again for a moment alone with Marianna, but then Marianna spoke.

'As the other lass said no, Julius, why not this one?'

Hope lit up all through Agnes's blood. 'Then the position is still vacant? Or vacant again?'

Julius glanced from Marianna to Agnes and back. She could tell he was choosing his words carefully. 'Marianna, this girl has no references. I have two other girls in mind ahead of her.'

'My references were all stolen,' Agnes said quickly. 'A thief took my luggage at a coaching inn in York.'

'There,' Marianna said. 'It's hardly her fault.' She turned to Agnes. 'You can read? I would so love to hear more of that accent. It reminds me of happier days.'

The parlour-maid, Daisy, had fetched Julius's coat and gloves. 'Here you are, sir.'

He checked his pocket watch. 'I'll be late if I don't go now,' he muttered, as Daisy helped him into his coat. His eyes never left Agnes's face. She tried to read his expression. He was angry. Perhaps he felt thwarted too. She understood that. 'Fine, then,' he said. 'Fine. Marianna, if this is who you want, then fine.'

'Thank you, sir,' Agnes said, all on a big gush of breath, because never had she been more grateful. 'I won't let you down.'

Julius pulled on his gloves, then pointed his index finger at her. 'See that you don't.'

49

'Oh, Julius,' Marianna said dismissively. 'How badly wrong can it go? She's not going to steal our silverware, are you, my dear?'

'I promise you no, ma'am. I'm after good honest work. That's all.'

'Hear that, Julius? Good honest work.' Her fingers released from their grip on the threshold and she took one step forward. 'Go on, go to work. We'll sort everything out here.'

Julius left, but not before he gave Agnes a stern gaze of warning, but she simply smiled back at him sweetly. She had been gazed at sternly plenty of times in her life, and wasn't about to be intimidated now. Not now that she was in the last place Genevieve Breckby had lived. ·

CHAPTER 4

Though nothing ought to have persuaded her to return to Bethnal Green, Agnes had grown fond enough of the children, especially little Freddy, that she felt she should say goodbye. Errol was out when she arrived, and she solemnly gave Minnie her last two shillings and told her to look after the little ones.

'I can't accept such generosity,' Minnie said, but her hand had already closed over the coins.

'You have mouths to feed. I have a good job to go to now. I will be fine.'

Minnie nodded and said a gruff goodbye. Freddy found a piece of old ribbon to give her and Agnes left them behind, guilty but relieved.

This time, arriving at the house at Belgrave Place, Agnes was welcomed. Daisy called for Marianna, who collected her and led her up to her new room. She felt light, as though her limbs were filled with air.

'Now, you'll eat in the kitchen with the other servants,' Marianna said, climbing the very steep stairs to the third floor without any shortness of breath. 'But you must sleep up here, near us. I sleep very badly. I expect Julius explained.'

'Aye, ma'am.'

'None of that "ma'am" nonsense. I am Marianna. In any case, my bedroom is at the bottom of this set of stairs, and yours is at the top.' With that they reached the low-ceilinged landing, and Marianna unlocked the door to a plain little room.

Agnes followed her in, recognising at once that this was the dormer window she had seen from the street. The ceiling was sloped dramatically towards the window, which was framed with plain blue curtains. The bedspread was white and the pillows lacked frills or ruffles. A dresser and washstand, and a small oak chest made up the rest of the furniture.

'There is a servants' bathroom downstairs,' Marianna said. 'Daisy will show you. But make yourself very comfortable up here. And keep your door open at night in case I call out, won't you?'

'Aye, Marianna, that I will,' Agnes said, placing her purse on the dresser. No hiding it under a pillow or mattress here, because she had her very own room. *Her very own room.* For the first time in her life.

'What else are you good for? Julius will be anxious that you have plenty to do.'

'I'm a fine needlewoman, ma'am. I mean, Marianna. Mending and embroidery.'

'That is good, because Daisy stitches quite sloppily.'

'If I might say, Marianna, that dress hangs quite loose on you. I should be very happy to take it in.'

'You speak your mind,' Marianna said, absently glancing down at her dress. 'We shall see. Perhaps I'll fatten up again now I have company. Being lonely makes me sad, and being sad means I'm never hungry.'

The first nudge of guilt pushed against Agnes's ribs. Until that moment, she had viewed Marianna as nothing more than a way to get to the real prize – her mother – but now she saw in front of her a lonely middle-aged woman too afraid to venture out or even open her own front door. Impulsively, Agnes put her hand out and gave Marianna's fingers a gentle squeeze. 'I know we will be friends.'

'Well, then,' Marianna said, looking at their joined hands then carefully extricating her own, a light flush coming to her cheeks, 'I shall let you settle in, shall I? Come down when you're ready. Not before. Make yourself at home.'

Agnes watched her go, then closed the door quietly behind her. She fell on the bed on her back, arms and legs spread out. *My bed. My room.* She composed in her head the letter she would write to Gracie, and imagined how happy Gracie would be for her. Then she stood and went to the window, and looked down over parks and townhouses and trees bending gently in the afternoon breeze. For the first time it occurred to her that she needn't be in a hurry to ask about Genevieve, not if it put this position, this lovely little room that was *all hers*, at risk. But even such sensible thoughts couldn't extinguish the hot urge to know, to seek, to find.

'All in good time, Agnes,' she muttered. She pulled off the shawl and folded it away with her other meagre belongings in the dresser. She wondered if it would be too much to ask for a little of her wage in advance, for new clothes. A small oval mirror stood over the washstand, and she examined her reflection, pinched her cheeks for colour. Then she descended the stairs in search of her new mistress.

•

Agnes found Marianna in the same drawing room where Julius had first spoken to her. Marianna was on the chaise with a light blanket over her legs, her face turned away, gazing out the window, and Agnes took a moment to study her. She had a strong face, what Mrs Watford might have called 'good bones', with a long straight nose and remarkably few lines. Her eyes were slightly hooded, making her gaze seem sad. Or perhaps she was sad.

The wind had picked up and moved in the branches of the tree outside the window, making the sunlight disappear and appear again. Agnes could see beyond into a tiny garden, neat but unremarkable, as though nobody ever spent much time there. The room was quiet but for the tick of a clock and the occasional rattle of the window.

'I'm here,' Agnes said.

Marianna turned and smiled. 'Agnes, there you are. Pamela fetched me some new volumes from the library depot yesterday. They're over there by the fireplace in a box. Choose me one. Nothing frivolous.'

Nothing frivolous. There was no chance of finding anything frivolous in this collection of books. They all looked desperately 'improving' and reminded Agnes of the books she had been forced to read for lessons at Perdita Hall; and then the nights she had spent reading a battered volume of *East Lynne* to Gracie by candlelight, sitting on the floor between their beds. Unfortunately they only had volume two, so they never knew how the novel started or finished.

'What about *Recollections of a Missionary* by a Mister Marcus Cherrywell?' Agnes asked.

'Yes, that will do.'

Agnes sat in a wing-backed chair, opened the book, and began to read. Marianna turned her face back to the window and gave no indication that she was listening. She seemed, instead, lost in her thoughts. Agnes read on, and after about half an hour had passed, in the middle of a sentence, Marianna interrupted her.

'How did you have your trunk stolen? What happened?'

Agnes laid the ribbon at the page she was up to – dispiritingly close to the beginning – and closed the book. 'I was at the railway station—'

'Details. Which railway station?'

Agnes cleared her throat and paused a moment before she spoke. 'In York, ma'am. The one on Tanner Row. I had bought a ticket for a train to London without checking what time it left. I had to wait until after midnight to board.'

'I told you to call me Marianna.' But she wasn't staring out the window any more. Her eyes were fixed on Agnes and she nodded. 'Go on.'

'I was jiggered. So tired. I wanted to put my head down more than anything. There was nobody about except a well-dressed man. I nodded off and a few minutes later I woke up and my trunk was gone, and so was the gentleman.'

'Do you think he took it?'

'I don't know. Maybe. Maybe it was street urchins. There wasn't owt of value to a gentleman in it.'

Marianna wrinkled up her nose. 'Men,' she said, 'are not to be trusted.'

Agnes smiled. 'That's not allus true.'

'Allus? There's a Yorkshire term they beat out of me at boarding school. No, not *always* but . . . It was because he was handsome, wasn't it?'

'No, Marianna,' Agnes admitted. 'It was because he looked rich.'

She nodded slowly. 'Yes, yes, of course it was. The lower classes are always vulnerable to . . .' Marianna trailed off, then turned back to the window. 'I'm quite tired now, Agnes. Perhaps you can go and find Pamela and ask her to show you where the needle and thread are kept. I might have a little nap before supper.'

'Aye right, Marianna.' Agnes stood, unsure if she should offer some kind of curtsey or even a farewell, but Marianna was lost in her thoughts again, and didn't seem to notice when she left.

•

At supper time, Agnes met the other staff. Daisy she already knew. She was a sweet girl with a receding chin and mousy hair, and a gentle laugh. The cook, Annie, was as cheerful and ruddy as the head cook back at Perdita Hall, and Agnes wondered if there was something about working with food that made people merry. The older maid, sturdy steel-haired Pamela, was in charge of laundry and performed some of the duties of a housemaid: keeping things in order and organising a schedule of jobs. She'd been delighted to hear about Agnes's flair with a needle and thread and had quickly fetched a basket of mending for her.

The kitchen was roomy and warm, though lacking in windows. A lamp glowed on either side of the enormous cast-iron stove, where Annie was cooking them eggs and fried potatoes. Agnes sat with Daisy and Pamela at the round wooden table, sorting through the clothes in the basket.

'There's a few months' worth there,' Pamela said, and Agnes smiled at her broad accent, where the 'th' in months had become an 'f'. 'Daisy ain the much good at sewing.'

'Hush, now,' Daisy said. 'Nor are you, and you're in charge of the laundry.'

'It's me big meaty 'ands,' Pamela said, stretching out her hands. 'Can't do nuffing delicate like.'

'I'll enjoy it,' Agnes said. The pile was mostly socks and dresses, but there was one pair of Julius's long johns in there and it felt uncomfortably intimate to pick them up and inspect them.

'Under there,' Daisy said, pointing out a hole where the seam had come undone at the top of an inside seam.

Agnes folded them and put them back in the basket. 'I'll get on with this tomorrow.'

'Grub's up,' Annie said, and she began to fill their bowls with the fried eggs and crispy potatoes. It smelled so much more appetising than the celery soup and cold pork sandwiches that had been taken out to Marianna and Julius earlier.

They ate and chatted, Agnes answering their questions about Yorkshire and the long train ride, but there was only one question she wanted to ask them. As Daisy was clearing the plates, she finally asked it.

'Is there any other family that comes by regularly? Brothers? Sisters? Julius's mother?'

Pamela and Daisy exchanged a glance, and even merry Annie turned her mouth down in a frown of disapproval.

'You're not to mention Marianna's sister,' Daisy warned. 'She gets very upset by it.'

'Why?'

'Nobody really knows,' Daisy replied. 'Family secrets.'

'There's talk that Genevieve – that's her sister – stole Marianna's 'usband,' Pamela said.

'Husband-to-be,' Daisy corrected.

'Marianna's been a mother to Julius these past ten years,' Annie said, tucking a yellow-blonde curl behind her ear. 'I don't think he even considers Genevieve his mother any more.'

'Gave up his fiancée for Marianna, he did,' Pamela said.

'What? Why?'

'He was all set to marry Miss Georgina Bell, but Marianna didn't like Miss Bell and vice versa,' Daisy explained. 'When Miss Bell declared that when they were married she wouldn't live in the same house as Marianna, Julius told her the wedding was off.'

'Caused a right scandal,' Pamela said. 'Did he care? Not likely. He's a good boy is our Julius.'

'But did Genevieve ever live here?'

'Before my time,' Daisy said. 'Annie and Pamela knew her.'

'Nobody really knew that woman,' Annie muttered.

57

'Do you know where she's gone? Does she send letters? I should like to know if—'

'Ladies?'

Agnes turned sharply, and saw that Julius had descended the stairs and was now looking at them with a frown. How much had he heard? Her pulse flicked hard at her throat.

''Ow can we 'elp you, sir?' Pamela asked him.

'By curbing your gossip.' Now he looked pointedly at Agnes and her face grew warm. She glanced away. He must think her devilishly foolish. Though she wasn't sure why she cared so much what he thought. Was it because she longed for his good opinion, as her brother?

'Just a bit of harmless chelping, sir,' Agnes said.

He addressed Annie. 'I came to tell you that Marianna insists on advancing Agnes five shillings from her wage, as all of her things were stolen.'

Then his eyes were back on her and she knew he mistrusted her, but she couldn't bring herself to offer him her reassurances.

'Make us some cocoa too,' he said. 'And for yourselves.'

'Yes, cocoa,' Annie said. 'We'll bring that right up.'

He turned and headed back up the stairs, and everybody released their breath.

'Don't mention Genevieve to him either,' Daisy said, the moment he was out of earshot.

'Understood,' Agnes said, stopping herself from asking the million questions that leapt onto her tongue.

'I bet he knows where she is, though,' Daisy said.

'Knows. But doesn't care,' Pamela responded. 'He's a good lad. Wants nuffing to do with her.'

Agnes kept her head down, and suppressed further questions.

I bet he knows where she is, though.

How was Agnes to get him to part with that knowledge, without putting her position here at risk?

•

From her bedroom, later that evening, Agnes sat on her bed in her shift and watched people and horses and carriages move past on the street below. The flow of traffic seemed endless. For once her stomach wasn't howling with hunger. She had bathed and she looked forward to new dresses tomorrow; even now her grey dress was damp and hung by the fireplace downstairs, smelling of lye soap.

The room grew dark and she rose to light a candle, then noticed something outside her window. Light. She went to the window and stood with her nose against it, peering out. All along the street, the gas lamps had been lit. Never had she seen so many lamps. The light they produced rivalled the stars; spots of bright illumination in two graceful, curving rows, either side of the street, against the dark sky. Agnes found herself smiling. To see such a marvellous thing with her own eyes, eyes that had only ever imagined such wonders, it had surely been worth leaving behind everything she knew.

•

Agnes had been working at the townhouse on Belgrave Place for three days when Marianna first woke her in the deep of night.

At first the little voice calling 'Agnes' worked its way into a dream, and she was hiding in the woods behind Perdita Hall and Mrs Watford was looking for her. 'Agnes! Agnes!'

Then she came to wakefulness. It was inky dark, and the wind rattled at the windows. But the voice was still calling, and Agnes realised where she was and called back, in a croaky voice, 'Coming!'

She threw back the covers and pulled on her dressing gown. Her feet were bare because she hadn't enough to buy new slippers just yet, and the floor was cold beneath her toes. She made her way down the creaking, narrow stairs, hanging tightly onto the banister in the gloom. As her eyes adjusted to the dark, she saw that Marianna's bedroom door lay open.

'I'm here,' she said.

'Thank you. Get the lamp, won't you? It's on the dresser by the window. There's oil in it, and matches beside.'

Agnes did her best to feel her way to the dresser. A little weak moonlight from behind the curtains helped, and she lit the lamp and then could look around Marianna's bedroom. It was enormous, on the same side of the house as the drawing room, perhaps even the same size. Marianna sat up in a large brass bed with delicate hangings over the canopy and posts. There were three wardrobes and two dressers, a large chest, four small bookcases and two upholstered chairs. The floor was covered in thick woven rugs. The mantel over an ornate fireplace was crowded with ornaments. The wallpaper was pale green, gold flocked, and the walls were crammed with paintings and miniatures. She recognised one of the paintings as the church at Hatby, and moved over to it to look more closely.

'It's St Mary's,' Agnes said.

'Yes. I haven't been there in years. Does it still look the same?'

'The woods have grown denser around it. There's not so much sunlight.' She turned and smiled at Marianna. 'A little more mystery.'

'Silly girl,' Marianna said, but she was smiling too. 'My family live just beyond those woods.'

'Is that right?' Agnes said, lightly. 'Then you must mean the Breckby family, because Lord Caspian's house is up there on the hill.'

'He is my father.'

'Do you ever visit them?'

Marianna looked away. 'I can't sleep,' she said. 'A dream woke me and now I can't even close my eyes again. Open the curtains. It will be morning soon.'

Agnes glanced at the clock. It was five minutes after three and the sunrise was still a long way off, but she did as she was asked. From here, she could see down into the garden. The strange silhouettes of orange trees and the dark mouth of the fish pond.

'Will you read to me?' Marianna asked. 'There's a history of Rome on the bottom shelf of the closest bookcase to the door. I'm at volume four.'

Agnes held her tongue so she didn't point out that reading the history of Rome would likely put both of them back to sleep. She crouched by the bookcase and found the volume, then returned to sit in one of the upholstered chairs. The wind continued to wail outside and Agnes saw swinging branches, moonlight and gas-light flickering among the shadows.

'Your feet must be freezing,' Marianna said, and tossed her a knitted rug. 'Put this around them.'

Agnes tucked her feet up on the chair with the rug over her knees. 'Chapter eleven,' she read. Then curiosity got the better of her and she closed the book again. 'What was the dream? Was it really so awful that you couldn't go back to sleep?'

Marianna shook her head. 'It wasn't awful at all, dear. It was the kind of dream so unspeakably lovely that waking up makes one want to cry for disappointment.'

'An unspeakably lovely dream? What about?'

Marianna was having none of it. 'Go on. Chapter eleven.'

Agnes dropped her head and read. The wind slowly died down and pale pink appeared at the far edge of the sky, over the rooftops of London. Her voice hoarse, she finally looked up to see Marianna asleep once more. Agnes closed the book, extinguished the lamp, and drew the curtains. She left Marianna behind, sleeping in the grey morning light, and hoped she might have another of her unspeakably lovely dreams.

CHAPTER 5

At the end of the first week, Agnes, dressed in one of her two new pale blue serge dresses, had been to the library depot on the Strand to fetch more books for Marianna, and had chosen a few that were slightly less dry. Marianna liked history, so Agnes read Mr Carlyle's account of the French Revolution, which had quite a few sensational details and kept them both interested. By the second week, she had sneaked in a book of short ghost stories, overcoming Marianna's objections by assuring her there was no details of love and romance to contend with – and if there were, Agnes would simply skim over them. By the third week, Agnes had Marianna hooked on mystery novels, and they both gasped and squealed through Mr Collins' *The Woman in White*; Marianna didn't even complain about Walter and Laura's love affair.

Over those three weeks, Agnes felt she was swimming through the days. Marianna woke most nights and then slept late in the day while Agnes had to work on the mending and help with the rugs, all in a fog of tiredness. She saw the sun come up through Marianna's bedroom window more times than she cared to count and felt exhausted falling into bed most nights, sometimes skipping supper so she could have another hour or two of sleep before the inevitable early morning call.

That the time was spent mostly inside was starting to wear on her. There wasn't even a visit to church on Sundays to break the routine; instead, a vicar came to them, on account of Marianna being unable to leave the house. Agnes's contact with the outside world was a short walk with Daisy every afternoon for some fresh air. Mostly, though, she witnessed the world through thick window panes. She submitted to this routine, had been careful not to ask about Genevieve, to earn Marianna's and Julius's trust. But her spirit longed to roam and ramble, was not well suited to being cooped up in the locked house. She had escaped Perdita Hall, only to end up circumscribed again.

One fine spring afternoon, as she and Marianna settled in the drawing room for reading time, Agnes cast her gaze towards the window – the orange trees, the pansies all in bloom – and said impulsively, 'Let's sit in the garden for reading time.'

'I don't go outside,' Marianna said, her mouth turning down slightly at the corners.

Agnes put down the book and approached her, sank to her knees in front of her and said, 'Look, Marianna. Look outside.'

Marianna reluctantly turned to the window.

'The sunshine on the leaves as they move on the breeze. Do you not want to feel that breeze on your cheeks? Hear the birds?'

Marianna turned back to Agnes, then grasped her hand. 'Dear, you don't understand.'

'Help me understand.'

'The world is very big. Too big for me. Its bigness . . . gets inside me and I feel as though I am going to burst.' She glanced at the garden again, then dropped her head. 'I wasn't always like this.'

Agnes, whose dearest wish was to live beyond walls and windows, could not understand this fear. But she saw Marianna's pale hands tremble and was overcome with a wave of compassion so strong that she impulsively stood and took Marianna in her arms. 'I will stay with you. Very close by. And all you need do is listen to me read. You can even close your eyes if it frightens you to be out.'

She felt Marianna's tight shoulders ease a little. 'Close my eyes? Yes, I suppose I can.'

Agnes stood back and held out her hand. 'Close them now if you like. I will lead you, just as though you were blind.'

Marianna considered her for what seemed like a long time, and Agnes was sure she would say no. Indeed, Agnes felt her own pulse ticking hard at her throat in that long silence: had she gone too far, pushed too hard? Would Julius come to find her in the kitchen tonight to berate her?

But then Marianna closed her eyes, and stretched out her hand.

Agnes smiled, closed her fingers around Marianna's and pulled her to her feet. 'You won't regret this,' Agnes said, leading her out of the drawing room, grabbing the book on the way. 'I promise you.'

She led Marianna down the hallway, calling down the stairs to the kitchen for Daisy to fetch Marianna's hat and gloves and bring them to the garden. Then the garden door was open and they were stepping out into the warm, fresh air. Robins pipped in the hedges. The faraway sounds of hooves beat on the road. The breeze in her hair. She glanced back at Marianna, whose eyes were still closed and whose mouth was drawn into a straight line.

'This way,' Agnes said, leading her to a sunny stone bench beside a garden bed overgrown with lavender. She sat her down and then settled next to her, her hip against Marianna's. 'Can you feel the breeze on your face?' Agnes asked.

Marianna nodded, but there was still no smile. Agnes told herself to be patient.

Daisy emerged from the house with the hat and gloves, and approached them curiously. Agnes fixed the hat on Marianna's head and Daisy pulled on her gloves.

'What about you, Agnes?' Daisy asked. 'You're in the sun too.'

'I don't mind if my hands get a little brown,' Agnes said, shooing her away. 'We won't be here long. Just one chapter. What do you think, Marianna?'

Marianna's furrowed brow told Agnes she might be thinking, *A whole chapter?* But nonetheless she nodded. 'Just one.'

Daisy withdrew and Agnes began to read. Her fingers were tightly entwined with Marianna's, and halfway through the chapter she noticed her companion's grip loosen. She glanced up to see Marianna had cautiously opened one eye. Agnes put her head down and kept reading, becoming aware of the way Marianna's body was relaxing. At the end of the chapter she looked up again.

Marianna had removed her hat. The sun was in her hair, and she gazed around her with a look of wonder on her face.

•

After a chapter, Marianna declared the need to lie down, so Agnes accompanied her upstairs to her bedroom. Marianna handed Agnes her gloves and asked her to put them in the drawer, so Agnes turned to the nearest chest of drawers, a polished dark walnut piece of furniture behind the bedroom door. But the top drawer wouldn't budge. She was just about to say, 'It's locked,' when Marianna called out, 'Not that one.'

Agnes hesitated, looking over her shoulder. Marianna had hung up her hat and was striding towards her, then snatched the gloves out of her hand.

'This one,' she said, yanking open the top drawer of another chest, this one painted white beside a matching wardrobe.

'Sorry,' Agnes said.

Marianna caught herself. 'Just old clothes in there,' she explained in a gentler tone. 'Most of them not mine. Too good to throw away, though.'

Most of them not mine. 'I see,' Agnes said, and apologised again. But her brain was ticking over wildly. *Not mine.* Then whose? She knew the answer: Genevieve's clothes. And likely other things of Genevieve's. Even evidence, perhaps, of where Genevieve had gone.

Agnes helped Marianna to bed, but she couldn't keep her eyes off the chest of drawers.

•

After supper that night, Agnes sat in the kitchen with the other servants, working on a piece of embroidery. It was a handkerchief with a spray of lavender in the corner, and she intended to collect some lavender from the garden and dry it out and tie it into the handkerchief as a gift for Marianna. Daisy, Pamela and Annie were chatting merrily. It seemed Annie had taken a shine to the new butcher she had paid a call on today, and Daisy and Pamela could not stop themselves from making slightly lewd jokes about it. Agnes laughed along, but her eyes were on her sewing the whole time.

She became aware at one point that the other three had gone quiet, and when she looked up she realised why. Julius stood in the doorway in his shirt and waistcoat, and he had her in his gaze.

'Agnes. May I speak with you?'

Agnes had done a good job of avoiding Julius over the past three weeks. Given so much of her work was in the early hours of the morning, and that she retreated down here to the servants' section of the house to sew or write letters in the evenings, there hadn't been any need for her to say more than good morning or good evening to him. Her impression was he barely approved of her, and Agnes had spent enough time in her life enduring the disapproval of others.

'Certainly, sir,' she said, putting her sewing aside, wondering what she had done wrong to prompt his visit.

She stood and he led her back up the stairs and down along the hall that led towards the back door, then admitted her to a small but very tidy study. He did not ask her to sit down, so she waited, hands in front of her, to hear how she had failed him.

But as soon as the door closed behind him, he approached her and took her hands in his. She noticed that his sleeves were rolled up towards his elbows, and he had well-formed forearms. 'Thank you,' he said, and his hands were warm and there was such a light in his eyes that it quite transformed his face.

'Thank you?' she asked.

He withdrew his hands and her grasp was empty again. Emptier than before.

'How did you do it? How did you get my aunt outside?'

My aunt, too, she thought. 'Ah. Now I take your meaning. Well, sir, it was really quite simple in the end. I told her to close her eyes and I would lead her. She sat there on the bench with her eyes screwed shut for quite a time, but then she opened them and was happy.'

'Close her eyes? I had never thought of it. Mind you, I'm always trying to get her out the front door, to go to see a physician or a merchant. Never had a bit of luck.'

'I should think the crowds would frighten her terribly, sir. Why, they almost frighten me and I'm unfrightenable.'

He smiled, and suddenly she could imagine exactly what he looked like as a boy. There was something open and honest about his face. 'Are you, then? Unfrightenable. What a wonderful word, and what a wonderful way to be.'

She beamed at him and a moment passed and then he remembered himself, broke the mutual gaze and strode to behind his small, oak desk and stirred up some papers on it. 'Well, then,

I do believe I owe you an apology. I was less than friendly when you arrived and less than delighted that Marianna gave you the position. But I am a man who recognises his errors, and I was wrong. I am sorry, Agnes.'

Agnes felt keenly that there was much to admire about Julius, and for a moment she admired him very warmly; then she reminded herself that he was likely her brother and perhaps that was why she felt so warm. 'There is no need to apologise, sir,' she said.

'You may call me Julius,' he replied. 'Marianna refuses formality and so I must too, or seem pompous.'

'The last thing you seem is pompous,' she said, then finished her sentence with his name, said slowly, trying it out, 'Julius.'

The boyish smile again, the glance away again. Stirring the papers on his desk again. Then another glance up, under his eyebrows. Gently, 'You may go, Agnes.'

'Good evening,' she said, and reluctantly left.

•

The following day, at long last, she had a letter from Gracie. Gracie had always struggled with reading and writing, blaming it on her bad eye. Agnes didn't see how this was possible, given Gracie's lacemaking ability, and suspected instead that Gracie simply found it more difficult than the others at Perdita Hall. She had been teased for it, and Agnes had been hauled in front of Mrs Watford more than once for planting a fist into somebody who dared to call her Gormless Gracie. Agnes especially appreciated, then, the thick wad of pages. She excused herself from the kitchen, where she had been loosening the seams on one of Annie's dresses, and raced up the stairs to her own room. It was a grim grey afternoon, and she pulled a chair under the window for light, unpicked the seal and unfolded the pages. Gracie had written it, as every Perdita child must, on the back of paper already used for laundry lists and class schedules. Paper was scarce. It even smelled of Perdita Hall: a faintly citrus scent over old damp. Agnes was reminded sharply of the world she had left behind barely a month ago, and took a moment to breathe out gratefully for this new life she was living.

The first thing she noticed was the tiny letters jammed into the top margin, which said: *Sorry so long replying you know how hard I find writting. Did it over severall nights.* Agnes smiled, and continued to read.

Dearest Agnes,

How I loved receiving your letter! I will try to write quickly so you are not too long without the comfort of your dearest friend! I will tell you all that is exiting that has been happening here. Bernadett Challenger fell down the stairs and brock her arm and had to be sent to York to have it set by a sergone. Captain Forest has paid for it all because he does not want her to have a bent arm for life. A little boy of around 7 or 8 died in his sleep for we don't know why. They slopped out the boys dormertory and sprinkled carbolick everywhere, and we were all forced out to the churchyard to pray for him at his funeral. His coffin seemed so very small and I did cry a lot as it seemed so sad, espeshly on a dowly Yorkshire day. Is London very bright and sunny compaired with Hatby? I would reckon it to be very noysy. Mrs Cranbourne has arrived and told me they are locking away the ink wells now so I will write more later.

The letter picked up again in a different-coloured ink then, and Gracie scribbled on for a few pages with the lesser news. Who had become friends with whom, who had been in trouble for shirking, a description of a new young nurse in the nursery, and how Hannah Coromandel had been discovered eating 'sope'. Gracie was fierce in her defence of Hannah, apparently, while everybody else had laughed at her. Agnes missed her violently, then. Dear Gracie, who saw the good in everyone, even Hannah Coromandel who had been beastly to both of them in the past.

Eating *soap*. Good lord.

Gracie left and came back to the letter twice more, each time with a different ink. Mostly it was more trivia, but on the final page, her tone became more hesitant.

> Today I was in Hatby dropping off a parsel and picking up lemon polish when I saw Cole Briar. He asked after you and was very kind to me. Did you never think he was handsom, Agnes? He was very nice to me and said to come and see him again.

Agnes frowned.

> When I said that I should like to see him again in the village he smiled at me in such a way that made my heart quite flop over on itself. I expect you think me as gormless as the others. I shall send this now so you get it sooner. I am sorry it has taken me so long.
> I remain your most loving ally.
> Gracie.

Agnes put the letter down and turned her gaze to the window. Rain had begun to fall, and the view of the trees was distorted by rivulets of water. She didn't like Gracie writing of Cole Briar in such a way, and it aroused all her protective instincts. But Gracie was a long way away, and seventeen years old now. No longer that little red-haired, queer-eyed girl that Agnes had been defending as far back as she could remember.

As Agnes folded the letter and slid it into the top drawer of her dresser, she heard noise from downstairs. Julius had arrived home from the hospital and supper would soon be served. Everything would tick along as normal and soon she would be in the warm kitchen with the other servants, and Gracie would be just fine without her. She had to be.

For three days in a row, Agnes took Marianna into the garden to read, and for three nights Marianna didn't wake and need her. Agnes thought that perhaps she had discovered the secret to curing Marianna's sleeplessness, but on the fourth night she was proven wrong; the voice in the dark pulled her up from under the tide of sleep and she felt her tiredness all the way to her marrow.

Agnes rose and pulled on her dressing gown, slid her feet into her new slippers, and made her way down the stairs. She remembered the routine easily. Light the lamp, draw the curtains – all was still and dark outside – and make sure Marianna was propped up comfortably.

'What would you like me to read?' Agnes asked, kneeling next to the bookshelf.

'We haven't heard from Mister Cherrywell in a while.'

'Didn't we decide he was boring?'

'Precisely what I need to get back to sleep, dear.'

Agnes selected the volume, yawning widely, then settled herself in her chair and opened the book to read. From time to time, her eyes would flick towards the walnut chest of drawers, the one she suspected held Genevieve's things. It was locked, but Agnes knew that the key was in the drawer beside Marianna's bed. She had seen it once when looking for matches. So far, she hadn't dared to sneak about and look for it: not because she feared discovery and losing her position, but because she was so fond of Marianna and valued her good opinion. This surprised her enormously: that fondness could be a heavier brake on her impulses than reprimands and warnings.

She read on. The dark outside the window thinned and began to brighten from the east. Marianna had fallen very quiet and Agnes glanced up to see she was nodding off.

Now she couldn't stop thinking about it. About the key, the chest of drawers, what might be inside. Words kept appearing on her lips, but her brain had long ago stopped making sense or significance of them.

Dare she?

A little more grey light in the room. Now Marianna was sleeping. Agnes closed the book and put it aside. Sat silently for one minute. Two. Marianna didn't wake.

She stood and told herself she wouldn't do it. How crushing it would be to see Marianna's soft brow bewildered, disappointed. One step towards the door, another. But then she had switched direction and was creeping towards the bed. She told herself she was simply making sure that Marianna was resting comfortably, that her pillow wasn't too high or her covers too low. Agnes watched her hands as if they belonged to somebody else. Sliding open the drawer silently. Then the key was in her palm, just as quietly, and Marianna was still sleeping, her face soft and smooth in repose.

Agnes's heart thudded so hard she almost imagined she could hear it. She had the key now; she may as well finish the task. She hurried to the chest of drawers, took a quick glance over her shoulder to make sure Marianna was still asleep, then slotted the key into the lock on the top drawer.

Clothes, just as Marianna had said. Agnes pulled a nightdress out, shook it, held it against her own body. It would have been a perfect fit, and it gave her a little glow to know she was of the same dimensions as Genevieve. She folded it again, still checking nervously on Marianna, and placed it back. She hoped for more than clothes. Agnes rummaged in the drawer, her fingers touching silks and satins, cotton and wool, found only more clothes. She slid it closed, locked it, and went to the next drawer. No better luck. Only clothes, mostly underwear and nightwear. All of fine quality.

The last drawer, then. Agnes kneeled and realised she could no longer see if Marianna was awake or not. She took a deep breath and unlocked the drawer.

More clothes in a thin layer over . . . Agnes withdrew a flat wooden box with a Chinese pattern on the lid. She sat back on her heels and pulled it into her lap, felt about for the catch and it sprang open. Jewellery. Rings and brooches and necklaces. These must be Genevieve's; Marianna always went unadorned. She tried one of the rings on and it fit, so she tried on another. Agnes was aware that sitting here, going through drawers and trying on jewellery was a good way to lose her job, but she became so enamoured of the idea that she was wearing her mother's things that she couldn't stop herself. The jewels all sat in a silver tray inside the box, and Agnes lifted it expecting to find more jewels beneath.

Instead, she found a soft, once-white material, yellow with age and a little moth-eaten.

Marianna stirred in her sleep and Agnes craned up to see if her eyes were still closed. Heart beating hard, she withdrew the material and shook it out.

A tiny dress. A baby's dress.

Agnes's breath caught in her throat. She fingered the light fabric, then saw the rings on her hand and sense rushed back in. Working quickly, she folded the dress, placed it and the silver tray back in the box, and slipped off the rings. All of it went firmly back in the drawer. She stood and returned the key to its home, then took a moment to stroke the hair away from Marianna's brow. Her aunt. That baby dress among Genevieve's precious things was the proof, if any further was needed. Agnes smiled down at her aunt, then impulsively leaned in and kissed her forehead.

Dawn was nearly here. Agnes put out the lamp, drew the curtains and left.

Although she might have returned to bed and slept for a few more hours, Agnes's brain was far too busy with questions to sleep. Instead, she descended all the way to the kitchen, with the idea of warming some milk. But she became aware even before she hit the bottom step that there was somebody else awake and moving about in the kitchen. Warmth and soft clatter.

Annie was there, her apron clean and tied tightly. Usually Agnes saw her at the end of the day, when her apron was smeared with food and half falling off.

'Good morning, young miss,' Annie said. 'You're up early.'

'As are you.'

'I like to get ahead of the day,' she said. 'You?'

'Couldn't sleep.'

Annie indicated a pot on the range with a nod of her head. 'I'm making cocoa for meself. There ought to be enough for both of us if you'd like some.'

'Oh, thank you,' Agnes said, sinking into a chair at the kitchen table. 'I would like some. I'd love some.'

Annie fetched a second cup and then shared out the warm liquid. There wasn't quite enough for both: they ended up with two-thirds of a cup each, and Agnes was deeply grateful for Annie's generosity. The plump woman sat with her, tucking her unruly yellow curls behind her ears.

'Orright, then, why are you not sleeping, love? Is it Marianna having you up at all hours?'

'I think so.'

'She sure has grown fond of you, missy.'

'And I of her.' Agnes sipped the cocoa. It was hot and sweet, and she curled her hands around the cup to warm them. 'How long have you been here, Annie?'

'Must be fifteen years now.'

'Is that how long Marianna has lived here?'

'No, she's been here closer to twenty.'

'And she's allus stayed inside?'

'As long as I've known her, yes. The cook who was here before me told me that for a while she wouldn't even sit near a window.'

Agnes mused on this. 'I wonder what happened to her.' Then, when she realised that the whole house was asleep and nobody would interrupt them, especially not Julius, she asked, 'What was her sister like? Genevieve?'

Annie shook her head. 'She wasn't Marianna's equal. And that's all I'll say.'

Agnes felt a flare of irritation; this was her mother Annie spoke of. Not only did Agnes need to know about her, she needed to hear what was good about her. But then, she considered, a woman as unorthodox as Genevieve would perhaps always draw condemnation.

'Do you know where she went?'

'No idea. She left in a hurry. When was that . . . nine years ago? I swear, time is rushing past at such a rate. Julius was only twelve or thirteen, I remember that, and too proud a boy to cry over losing her. It was a good thing Marianna loved him so much, or else he might have become cold inside.'

Cold inside. Agnes had often wondered if a lack of love had made her so. 'So, Genevieve abandoned him?'

'It's complicated.'

Agnes spread her palms. 'There's time before breakfast. It's barely dawn. And I really ought to know all I can about Marianna if I'm to be a good companion to her. I don't want to say the wrong thing.'

'Well, the worst you can say is her sister's name, so simply know that much.'

'Because she abandoned Julius, or because she stole Marianna's fiancé?'

Annie narrowed her eyes. 'You are asking a lot of questions this morning, missy.'

'Go on.'

Annie drew breath, seemed to be considering whether or not to answer. 'Well,' she said at last, 'as I understand, Marianna was betrothed to Mister Ernest Shawe. But she didn't marry him in the end; Genevieve did. That's all I know.'

'Shawe? But Julius's surname is Halligan.'

'Oh, Mister Shawe wasn't Julius's father.'

Agnes felt the world spin. Was Julius the illegitimate child? Had Agnes placed herself at the centre of an elaborate self-deception? 'Then, who . . .'

'When Julius was a wee lad, maybe two or three years old, Genevieve adopted him. He was the son of her dearest friend from school, and both she and her husband died of typhus in Ireland.'

The fire in the stove popped softly, but all else was quiet. Two thoughts appeared in Agnes's mind at once: first, that Genevieve could not be such an awful person if she adopted Julius, and second, that Julius was not related to her. So, why did she feel such an intense sense of knowing him, in her body and her blood?

'Do you know why Genevieve left?' Agnes asked.

'I remember that day well,' Annie said with a raise of her eyebrows. 'Never forget it. The only time I ever heard Marianna raise her voice. Shrieked like a harpy, she did. Didn't know she had it in her.' She adjusted the apron strap on her left shoulder. 'They'd had their father here, visiting from Yorkshire, in the year their mother died. Bit of a stiff fellow. Nobody much liked him but back in those days we all kept below stairs. Marianna doesn't much stand on ceremony, but my word Genevieve did. Servants were servants and ought to remain so.

'After a few days of visiting, their father left and after that Marianna and Genevieve had an argument. Brutal, it was. Insults traded on both sides. We couldn't hear every word of it, but I did hear with my own ears, clear as you can hear me now, Marianna shrieking at Genevieve, "How am I to look at you now I know what you did?" Genevieve was gone within a week. Thought she was disappearing in the dawn but of course the servants were all awake and we saw and heard her but didn't stop her.' She sniffed archly. 'No great loss.'

Agnes's mind was bursting with questions, none of which Annie would know the answer to.

'Master Julius sat at the front window for a week, watching for her to come back,' Annie continued. 'Eventually Marianna drew the curtain and said he was to sit there no more. He was certain she'd come back, though; talked about it with us all the time. After a few months, he stopped talking about it. How long he kept thinking about it, I don't know.'

'Did anyone ever hear from her? Perhaps she met some mishap. Perhaps she is . . .' She couldn't bring herself to say *dead*. Didn't want to imagine that she had come so far only to find her adventure was already at an end.

'I don't know, missy. Pamela picked up the post once and said she saw a letter from Paris looked like Genevieve's hand, but we don't know for certain. We just try to do our best for Marianna and for Julius, who has grown into such a kind man. That's how you ought to know he's adopted – Genevieve didn't have a kind bone in her body.'

Not a kind bone in her body. Agnes let the words sink in, and she thought about Gracie and how kind she was and how it meant that people took advantage of her and could get away with any cruel behaviour. Perhaps a woman didn't have to be kind. Perhaps Genevieve was something else. Strong, determined, unconventional. These were all admirable qualities in men. Why not in women?

Agnes asked no further questions. She finished her cocoa and then helped Annie wash the pot and cups, and stayed a little longer to help roll the oats for Marianna's breakfast, which she always took in bed, and prepare Julius's poached eggs. But all the while, she was musing, asking herself how far she would go to find her mother. She'd already made it to London. Why not Paris?

CHAPTER 6

A weekend followed of glorious late spring weather. Agnes persuaded Marianna to stay in the garden until the afternoon shadows grew long. She no longer clung to the bench, but moved freely about from one side of the garden wall to the other, delighting at bees and blooms and soft breezes. Julius joined them for a while, pottering around pulling weeds and puffing about needing to hire a gardener if they were to spend so much time outside now.

On the Monday morning, Agnes met Marianna in the drawing room after breakfast as usual. She expected to sit and read, or chat while sewing, but Marianna was dressed as though to leave the house. Hat, gloves, coat. She had styled her own hair, and it fell loose at the back.

'The garden, Marianna?' Agnes asked.

'No. Today, I want to go to the library depot and choose my own books.'

Agnes blinked. 'You want to walk to the Strand?'

Marianna lifted her chin and nodded. 'Yes, why not? Why oughtn't I browse the books and see what's there?'

'No reason at all, if that is what you wish.' Agnes's mind worked quickly. Had Julius left yet? Ought she tell him? Ought she discourage Marianna? Walking in a walled garden was vastly different from taking to the crowded streets of London, especially on such a fine day when everyone would be about.

'You've helped me see there is life outside, Agnes.' Then she licked her lips quickly and said in a softer voice, 'I want to try.'

'Let's say we will go to the end of the street and no further today,' Agnes suggested.

Marianna nodded.

'Aye, then. Take my hand.'

With Marianna's hand in hers, Agnes led her up the corridor and across the entranceway then pulled open the door. Sunlight fell in, brighter than she'd expected. Marianna squinted, held back a little.

'Marianna? We can stay if it's easier.'

'Of course it's easier,' she said, but took a step forward anyway. They crossed the threshold, descended the three steps, and were a few yards from the house when Marianna stopped.

Agnes felt Marianna's hand become cold and clammy. Her breathing was coming in constricted wheezes.

'Turn around,' Agnes said gently. 'We will go back inside for now.'

'But . . . I want to . . .'

'Look how far you have come. Look! This was unimaginable just a few weeks ago.'

Marianna turned and surveyed the short distance they had travelled, then released Agnes's hand and scurried back to the house. Agnes followed, then closed the big door behind her. Marianna was already in the drawing room, pulling off her hat and coat and gloves roughly.

'What a fool I am,' she muttered. 'What a jolly fool.'

Agnes approached, taking her gloves and hat and putting them aside, enclosing her fingers over Marianna's. 'No, no, Marianna. Be kinder to th'self.'

'I wasn't always like this, you know,' she spluttered, and anger turned to sadness. Her eyes welled. 'I was normal. I could go out. If he hadn't . . . but it was so long ago. I can't still blame him. I can't keep hashing over what happened. It's me who's at fault.'

'Blame whom for what?' Agnes said, curiosity prickling.

'Don't listen to me, I'm talking nonsense,' Marianna muttered.

'You aren't at all.' Agnes considered her, among all the shining, beautiful things in the drawing room. A woman of middle years, with hair not quite pinned right, her eyes glassy and her jaw trembling. 'Help me understand. How does it feel to you, being outside?' Agnes asked. She had spent far too many years cooped up behind walls and couldn't imagine what would persuade Marianna to stay inside all the time.

'Feels as though . . .' She tapped her heart. 'As though I'll be crushed by how big the world is.'

'But you don't feel like that in the garden any more?'

Marianna shook her head.

'So, perhaps one day you will be just as comfortable walking to the corner. Or to the Strand for books. Imagine that.'

Marianna turned away, then slumped down on the sofa. 'You are very sweet, dear.'

Agnes sat with her, her curiosity refusing to abate. 'What happened to you, Marianna?' she asked gently. 'Was somebody cruel to you?'

'Few people get through life without being the victim of a little cruelty,' Marianna said with a bitter twist of her lips, dabbing at her eyes with her handkerchief. 'Only the weak never recover.'

'Give over, you're not weak. You're strong. Five minutes ago you faced your greatest fear.'

'And now I'm trembling like a ninny.' She grasped Agnes's wrist. 'I hate this. It isn't really me,' she said. 'But we are all of us the sum of what has happened to us.'

Agnes met her eyes steadily, wishing she could see all the way into her mind and memories. She reached up and lifted a strand of unsecured hair. 'Turn around, Marianna. Let me fix your hair.'

'Oh, let's just unpin it. One thing about a life spent indoors is that I've never had to worry too much about how I look.'

Agnes pulled out the pins and laid them on the couch beside her. Marianna dropped her head and her breathing returned to normal, her demeanour became calm again.

'I think I will spend the day in bed,' Marianna said. 'I feel quite drained by all of this.'

'Let me help you——' Agnes started, but Marianna held up her hand softly.

'No,' she said. 'I am happier with my own company. You're a good girl. I shan't need you today, so catch up on some mending. Tell Pamela I'll have my lunch in my room on the dot of twelve.' She rose, and Agnes watched her go, the depth of her concern for her aunt only matched by the relentless curiosity about what she had endured, and how that might mean something about Agnes's secret past.

•

Late in the afternoon that day, Agnes took herself out into the garden. Without Marianna to keep her busy, she had spent the day in the dim kitchen with the mending basket and now she felt cooped up and in need of some time by herself. Annie, Pamela and Daisy were good company, but the three of them at once meant lots of chatter and silly jokes.

Even though there was still light in the sky, the wall kept the garden entirely in deep shade. She could see, though, that Julius sat out here. His back was turned to her, and he was slumped slightly, as though the effort of remaining upright had become too much for him. She considered going back inside, but at that moment he turned and saw her.

He straightened, mock-brightened. 'Good evening, Agnes.'

'Good evening, Julius. You are home early.'

'Yes, rather a wretched day. Please, don't let me stop you enjoying the garden too.'

Agnes took a few tentative steps forward. She had been hoping to sit precisely where he was; the only other places to sit were the edging stones of the garden beds or the mildewed lip of the fish pond.

He made a show of moving over, and she sat on the bench, leaving space between them.

'Tell me, how is my aunt today?'

'She has been in her bedroom since morning.'

'Unwell?'

Agnes turned the word over in her head. 'Unwell in her heart, maybe. She insisted this morning that she would walk to the library depot. I do not know how long she had been preparing herself, sharpening her will. In any case, she made it only a few yards from the front door.'

Even in the gloom, she could see his face soften. 'Oh, poor Marianna.'

'She took those few steps outside, though, Julius,' Agnes said. 'She was so brave. But she felt no pride. Only disappointment.'

'Indeed. I could not imagine she would ever step outside the front door again,' he replied. 'You have been good for her, Agnes. I have done my best to keep her company, but she has been lonely for many years. She has kept no friends, has little contact with her family.' He chuckled. 'You know, it took me six months to convince her to hire a companion.'

'Is that so?'

'Yes, and the first girl we hired . . . Marianna scared her off almost instantly. The poor lass was trying to appear cheerful and friendly, and rabbited on about taking Marianna to Cheapside to look at dresses. Marianna shrilly told her that they would not set foot outside the house, *ever*. The lass decided not to take the position.'

'Aye, then. It's a good thing I turned up,' Agnes said lightly.

'With that Yorkshire accent, yes. Nobody else had a hope once Marianna had heard you speak. You northerners run in packs.'

They were both laughing now, but then Agnes said, 'So, you weren't born in the north?'

The mood sobered. Agnes became aware that the birds had grown quiet as afternoon slipped into evening. 'Indeed, no. I'm sure the servants haven't failed to tell you that I was an orphan, adopted at a very young age by Marianna's sister, Genevieve.' He shook his head. 'Though we don't say her name much around here any more.'

Agnes became aware that her heart was thudding. 'No?'

'No,' he said, with such a tone of finality that Agnes took it as a warning. Still, she had to swallow hard not to ask the questions that leapt to her tongue. And then, perhaps perceiving that he sounded fierce, he said again, 'You have been good for Marianna, and for that I am grateful.'

'She is . . . like family to me,' Agnes ventured.

'Is she so? I am glad. For if you love my aunt a tenth as much as I do, I know you will never let her down.'

The garden was dark now. His face was pale and his eyes black, and something about the quiet and the gloom emboldened her to say, 'And what of you? When I first stepped into the garden this evening you seemed weighed down by cares of your own.'

At first he didn't respond, and Agnes thought he might be angry at her for overstepping the boundaries that society had laid between them. Ordinarily, she wouldn't care if somebody thought she had behaved inappropriately, but the idea that he would have a low opinion of her stung. So, she was much heartened when he offered her a thin smile.

'Did I? Well.'

She waited, hoping the silence might do what a thousand questions wouldn't, and make him continue to speak.

'I studied for a very long time and worked very hard to become a doctor,' he said at last. 'And my most prized goal was the Hospital for Sick Children. Every day on the way home from my studies, I took the route via Great Ormond Street, to stand beneath it and admire it. It's a beautiful building, Agnes. Have you seen it?' Agnes shook her head but he didn't wait for her response before continuing. 'It has towers and turrets on it like a castle in a fairytale. I suppose I saw myself as though I were in a fairytale too: a magician who could heal and make people happy. But there is so much pain in the world, Agnes. For every child I save, another dies. We are all so fragile, so vulnerable to illness and injury. My dreams have become an endless parade of little bodies, still and cold.' His voice trailed off. From within the house, the bell for supper sounded.

Agnes had a strong impulse to reach for his hand and squeeze it, but she knew that even if it were welcome now, it would make them awkward with each other later. So, instead, she said, 'It takes a great man to feel so deeply.'

'Thank you, Agnes,' he replied, and their eyes met and held.

A moment passed, two. Then he took a deep breath and said, 'I ought not trouble you with such—'

'Please do not apologise,' she said, speaking over the top of him, reluctant to return to formalities. 'Let us go inside for supper. Light and warmth and food may yet cheer you.'

He seemed about to say something else, but then thought better of it. They returned to the house together, Agnes downstairs and Julius up to the dining room.

Rain moved in that evening and set in for a week. The kitchen became especially gloomy, but was nonetheless always warm and dry due to the coal-burning stove. When Marianna didn't need her, Agnes spent her time sitting at the scarred kitchen table, a lamp set up at her elbow, working on embroidering the collar and cuffs of one of her mistress's nightgowns. One wet afternoon, when she was alone, her thoughts turned, as they had often, to how she might get to Paris. She had walked to Victoria Station in the rain on her day off to enquire about a fare, but the boat train, which was the most convenient and direct way, was expensive. Once in Paris, she would barely have money left over for somewhere to stay and none at all for a return journey. The ticket master had suggested she could catch the train to Folkestone or Dover and then look for a cheap passage on a goods ship, then find another train at Calais. The thought filled her with doubt. She spoke no French, and her knowledge of how the world worked was so circumscribed. They used different money in France: how would she pay for things? How would she find her way around? She had spied a book about Paris in among Marianna's books in the drawing room, but hadn't yet been in there alone for long enough to search for a map or other kind of guide. But every day, her resolve grew harder. She would go to Paris, she would seek Genevieve, just as soon as she had an address to go to. As much as she loved Marianna, staying here as her companion was not Agnes's greatest desire. Her greatest desire was to find her mother, and she couldn't rest too long. Desires, if not tended, too easily dimmed and were forgotten.

Pamela came in, then, untying her scarf and shaking raindrops out of her hair. 'Letter for you, Agnes. Shall we have tea?'

'I would love tea,' Agnes said, taking the letter from Pamela's fingers. It was from Gracie, which was a surprise, as she'd had a letter from her a week ago. This one was thin. Agnes plucked it open and removed a single sheet. On one side was an old recipe. On the other, Gracie's handwriting.

Dear Agnes,

I have screwed up my currage to write, though I've had to perswade Charlotte Pelican to give me her month's stamp by promising to make her bed until August! That is the hardest-won Penny Black anyone has erned, I'd wager. There is a reason, though, dear friend. There isn't another person alive I can talk to about this. I have been seeing Cole Briar every day this week. Remember your old route out of the grounds? Yes, I've been climing your tree, Agnes! You would be proud of me. Perdita Hall is not the same withowt you. Everyone is always mean to me and Cole is not. I was wurried at first that he still pined after you, but he says that was just nonsense. We sat in the woods for hours and he made a chain of daisies for me. I was going to send it to you as a present but I am too selfish. It is under my pillo. Agnes, I think I love him.

Do you think me a gooseberry? I need your good advice!

Your friend and sister,
Gracie

Agnes refolded the letter, frowning. How had Gracie let herself be so swayed by the eel? Was she really so flighty that only Agnes's presence could keep her safe? She felt acutely her distance from Hatby, where she could put her hands around Gracie's shoulders and shake some sense into her. Pamela placed the teapot on the table, but Agnes pushed back her chair.

'I'm sorry,' she said. 'I have to go and write a letter.'

Pamela pursed her lips. 'That sounds urgent.'

'It may be.' Agnes headed for the stairs. She needed to let Gracie know, in no uncertain terms, that she was to stay well away from Cole Briar.

●

The damp weather got inside Marianna's lungs and she was bedridden with a streaming head cold, which Annie also managed to catch. Pamela took over the cooking, and Agnes spent her days by Marianna's bed, reading to her and keeping her supplied with hot broth and clean handkerchiefs. Agnes didn't catch the cold: growing up in a foundling hospital meant she had already caught every cold she was due in her life.

On the fourth day, Marianna waved her away after lunch and said she needed to sleep. Annie, too, was tucked up in her own little grey room below the stairs. Julius was at the hospital, and Pamela and Daisy had just closed the front door behind them to go to the market. Agnes heard the quiet descend on the house and knew she was, for all practical purposes, home alone.

She descended the stairs to the drawing room and made straight for the book about Paris. She sat on the rug, her skirts spread out around her, and opened the book. The first page was a fold-out map of Paris, and she traced the route of the Seine through its centre with wonder. The book was not as old as others Marianna kept, its spine still cracking as she turned the thick pages. History of Paris. Nature of the arrondissements. Famous landmarks. And here at the back, a guide to important phrases. Where is the railway station? *Où est la gare*. Agnes sounded it out, but it didn't seem like French. She still sounded as though she was from Yorkshire. *Est* rhymed with best, *gare* with stare. Still, she tried to commit some other phrases to memory. How much for a room? One night, two nights, three nights, four nights. Do you know Genevieve?

She closed the book, slid it back in its place. Perhaps she would borrow it when she went to Paris. Nobody would miss it. Marianna had never asked to be read it and Julius didn't touch the books in the drawing room, though he had some of his own fat books about medicine in his study.

Julius's study.

The thought was clear and bright. Somewhere in his study, she would find Genevieve's address. She knew it. And with nobody around, there might never be a better time to investigate.

Agnes hurried her steps lightly down the corridor, extra quiet past the staircases, and in a second had the door handle to Julius's study in her fingers.

It didn't move.

'Hell fire,' Agnes said, under her breath. She bent and looked through the keyhole. The room was bathed in soft grey light. The desk was closed, the chair tucked neatly beneath it.

Agnes pulled two pins out of her hair. A hank of golden hair fell beside her face, and she tucked it behind her ear. She had never picked a lock before, but Alexandra Orion had once picked the lock on the pantry while on dishwashing duty and stolen two biscuits. While she didn't share the biscuits back in the dormitory, she did explain the mechanics of tripping a lock. Agnes bent one pin to use as a lever in the bottom of the keyhole, and with the other began feeling around for the stiff barrels that kept the lock in place. 'Some will be loose, but others will be stiff,' Alexandra had said. 'Keep pushing on them gently while trying to turn the barrel with the bottom pin.' More difficult than it sounded, and she was just about to give up when an audible *snick* told her the lock had given way. She turned the handle and was in.

Agnes closed the door quietly behind her, and stood a moment looking around. If she were Julius, where would she keep information about Genevieve?

The desk, of course. She moved silently across the rug, her hip brushing a chest of drawers, and prayed that the desk would not be locked too. It wasn't. She opened it, revealing tidy stacks of paper and an intricate series of tiny cupboards and drawers. Her gaze lit on a leather-bound book and she flicked it open. It was a diary, and she quickly closed it. Yes, she had broken into his study and was rummaging among his belongings, but she had no desire to breach his privacy completely. Another, slimmer volume sat spine out between bottles of ink and a box of pens. She slid it out. This time it was an address book, and she hunted eagerly for G. No Genevieve. Not under M for Mother, or B for Breckby; although the rest of the Breckby family were there, the address in Hatby written in neat cursive. She slipped the address book back into place and tried one of the drawers. It wouldn't budge, but there was no lock on it that she could see. She felt around under it; right at the back was a tiny metal lever. She pulled it, and the drawer popped open.

Letters. She took them out in a bundle and sat in Julius's office chair, the letters in her lap. She leafed through them, and finally, near the bottom, she found it. A letter with a return address on the back from Genevieve Breckby, 22 Rue Cousineau, Paris. Her fingers fumbled to open it. At that exact moment, the door to the study opened, and there stood Julius. A hot, unpleasant feeling flashed through her blood. She could see his eyes, taking in the scene: his desk open, the drawer emptied, the letters in her lap, one half-open in her hands. And although she imagined he would be angry, the expression that arrived on his face was one of sadness. He was disappointed in her. His disappointment cut her a hundred times deeper than righteous anger ever could.

'I'm sorry,' she said.

'You'll have to leave,' he replied.

'I have a good reason. Really I do. Will you hear it?'

He wavered. She placed the letter among the others and left the bundle on the desk, then stood and walked towards him. 'Please, Julius. I ask only that you listen to my reason.' Her pulse was pounding hard at her throat. She kept telling herself that, if nothing else, she had Genevieve's last address.

'I will hear it,' he said. 'But you must swear to me that it will be the entire truth, Agnes, for I know you are hiding something. I have known it from the moment I first met you.'

Shame warmed her cheeks. 'It's true,' she said. 'I'm sorry. I am mortally sorry, but I swear to you, for the love I bear Marianna, I will tell you the entire truth. If you will but listen and try to forgive me.'

He strode past her, closed his desk. 'Come,' he said. 'We will go to the garden where nobody can hear us. You can tell me everything.'

•

The garden was damp, and no sun pierced the clouds. The stone bench was wet, so neither sat. Rather, they stood in the cool air, the door to the house shut behind them. Agnes crossed her arms defensively over her chest. Julius's hands were clasped together tightly.

'So,' he said. 'Let us start with this: Is Agnes Forest your real name?'

'No, my real name is Agnes Resolute.'

'You are one of Captain Forest's foundlings, then? I knew the name was suspicious. I know more about Hatby than you perhaps imagined. Captain Forest is known to my family.'

Agnes felt the flame of embarrassment on her cheeks again. How foolish she had been.

'Why are you here, then, Agnes Resolute?'

Agnes set her shoulders and said, 'Julius, I have reason to believe that I am Genevieve Breckby's daughter.'

She watched his face. Shock, but also recognition.

91

He sat heavily on the bench despite the wet, and Agnes kneeled before him.

'You came here looking for her?' he asked.

'Aye, at first. But I stayed because my love for Marianna is nowt but genuine. Truly, it is more so than you know, because I think of her as my aunt.'

'Why do you think yourself Genevieve's daughter?'

She quickly explained the story about the unicorn button, about Miss Candlewick's comment, and he nodded and showed no anger, from which she took heart.

'Do you believe me?' she asked him.

'That you are Genevieve's daughter? I can only say that I knew there was a scandal in the family, an illegitimate child, and I know that Genevieve would think little of abandoning a child; she abandoned me.'

The pronouncement stung, and words leapt onto her lips to defend her mother. She was different, unique, of course society would judge her. But Agnes sensed it was not the right time.

'I've never asked Marianna about it, of course,' he continued. 'She and Genevieve bear no love for each other.' He chuckled darkly. 'No love at all. And I wouldn't upset her by mentioning Genevieve's name and you must promise you won't either.'

'By my word,' she promised. 'I wouldn't want to cause her any pain.' But even as she said this, she wondered if it were true. If she found Genevieve, if they were reunited, Marianna would eventually have to know.

He ran a hand through his hair. A gust of wind shook raindrops out of a tree and onto them, but Agnes maintained her posture before him, knees growing damp and cold.

'And what is it you want from Genevieve?' he asked softly.

'Put your mind at rest. I desire no money, no elevation in society. I desire only to know . . . what it is I am. I spent nineteen years in an institution that was determined to make us all conform. Others around me accepted it, became biddable. I never could. That must come from somewhere. Bred into me, as surely as my fair hair.'

Julius nodded. 'I do understand. I am an orphan myself, with no memory of my parents. But, Agnes, Genevieve is not what you think she is. She abandoned you, she abandoned me. She does what she wants, yes, but cares little for how her wants may cause the unhappiness of others.'

'But she took you in, long before she abandoned you,' Agnes said boldly. 'And she left me with a token that led to her. Perhaps she is not so callous as you think.' Then quieter, she said, 'You keep her letters.'

He smiled ruefully. '*Kept* her letters. There haven't been any for many years.'

'No? Then how do you know she is not sick, or dead, and cannot write to you or come back for you?'

Julius shook his head. 'Ah, Agnes. How am I to explain to you?'

'With words. With the truth, as I have given you today.'

'Yes, reluctantly, and only today,' he said, and it was the closest he had yet come to expressing his anger over her betrayal.

She dropped her head. 'I'm so sorry,' she said.

'I know you are, but I also know you aren't, for you would have done it the same again, wouldn't you?'

'I . . . I suppose so. But I am not proud of it, nor do I think myself your superior for tricking you. I am driven by a savage engine, Julius.'

'Then perhaps you are a little like her,' he said. 'But I see more good in you than I saw in her, at the end.'

'At the end?'

'She left. I know she and Marianna had argued. I was a lad of eleven and I adored her. Of course I did; she was the only mother I ever knew.' He turned his eyes away, chewed on his bottom lip a moment as though reining in a strong feeling. 'She was good to me, for a while. Brought me to live with Marianna because her husband was awful, particularly to me. I don't remember much about him now, but he had violent moods, and I often caught the rough edge of his tongue.'

'She saved you from him?'

He shrugged. 'Perhaps she was saving herself. But yes, things were much more settled and happy with Marianna. For a while. Then Genevieve left. She crept into my room early one morning . . . I'll never forget it. Rousing me from the hard sleep that children sleep. Grey morning light. She kissed me and said she'd be back for me very soon. I folded it into my dreams and fell asleep again. When I woke up, in daylight, she was gone.'

Agnes waited. He turned his gaze back to her, his dark eyes sad. 'I waited. There is probably little more I can say without making myself sound pathetic. I waited. She sent letters . . . the ones you found. Short letters full of nothing: *How are you? I am well. Today I saw a monkey at the zoo.* I don't think any of the letters were more than a page long. The shortest was the last one, where she told me . . .' His voice caught. He cleared his throat, then said, 'I'll never forget the words: "I think it fair to tell you I don't intend to return."'

His hands were soft on his knees, and Agnes longed to put hers over his, to squeeze his fingers in her own.

'So, Agnes, if that is the kind of woman you look to for example, perhaps you are better looking elsewhere.'

Agnes turned this over in her mind, and still couldn't find it in her heart to condemn Genevieve. With only one side of the story, how could she? But she had no reason to dissuade Julius from his opinion, especially on the day she had been revealed as a liar and a sneak.

'Do you still want me to leave?' she asked him.

He shook his head. 'You are welcome to stay until we prove your presumption one way or another. I will go to see my aunt's family in Hatby at the end of the month, and I will try to elicit the truth from them. If it is true, I will do all I can to have you welcomed to the Breckby family, in a way that is sensitive to Marianna's feelings. There is no longer any need for you to pick locks and read old letters.'

Agnes dropped her head in shame. He didn't understand. She didn't want entrée into the Breckby family; she wanted to meet Genevieve. She *needed* to meet Genevieve.

Luckily, she already had the address.

•

Marianna lingered in bed for four more days. A persistent cough took hold of her and she slept worse than ever. On the fourth night, Agnes heard her name called seemingly seconds after she had fallen asleep. Reluctantly, she slid leaden feet into her slippers.

'Coming,' she mumbled, reaching for her dressing gown. 'I'm coming.'

In Marianna's room she lit the lamp and drew the curtains. Marianna sat up, coughing weakly.

'Can I fetch you some water, Marianna?' Agnes asked, kneeling by the bookshelf searching for the most boring book available.

'No, no. I'll catch my breath soon. What time is it?'

Agnes glanced up at the carriage clock on the dresser. 'It's just before eleven o'clock.'

'Oh, dear. That's early.' She coughed again, but then settled against her pillows. 'Come and sit with me, Agnes. I don't want books, I want company.'

Agnes stood, yawning and pulling her reading chair towards the bed.

'No, not the chair. Just you.' Marianna patted the bed next to her.

Agnes warily climbed up, sitting on top of the covers, holding her knees against her chest.

Marianna coughed again, lighter now. She looked pinker than she had for days. Agnes smiled at her. 'I know the cough is bothering you, but you look quite well.'

'Thank you, dear. I'm on the mend I suppose. I just . . .' Her brow knitted, and Agnes waited for her to finish. 'It's silly, really. But sometimes I'm afraid I'll die in my sleep, all alone.'

'It's just a cold, Marianna. You won't die, I promise.'

'I know. I know. But in the dark, when the cough has hold of my lungs, I can imagine it. Imagination can be a fierce thing, don't you think?' She considered Agnes's face. 'You are tired. I've tired you out this week with my silly worrying.'

'Aye, I'm jiggered,' Agnes admitted.

'Make yourself more comfortable. Come.'

Agnes settled on her side, propped up on her elbow. Marianna reached for her hand then sank back into her pillow with closed eyes. 'I feel calm when you're here,' she said.

Guilt stung Agnes's heart. For the past few days she had been planning her departure – at least in the short term – from Marianna. She had only waited for the older woman to recover from her illness.

'Why don't you go back to sleep,' Agnes yawned.

'Will you stay a little?'

'Aye, be right.'

Marianna sighed and, as the carriage clock ticked on in the softly lit room, her breathing became deep. Agnes blinked back sleep, her thoughts blurring against one another. The few phrases of French she'd learned from the book, the train schedule for Victoria to Folkestone, Genevieve's address.

When Marianna's voice came it seemed unnervingly loud and sudden. 'Why be afraid of death? It's living I've been afraid of.'

Agnes blinked, shook herself. 'Marianna?'

But Marianna settled into sleep again. Agnes watched her a while, Marianna's face soft in repose, her chest rising and falling quietly. Agnes considered their hands, interlinked on the bed covers. Her eyes fell closed . . .

Hours later Agnes woke. The lamp had burned down, but the soft summer dawn was at the window and her hand was still in Marianna's. Gently, she extricated her fingers. She rose, drew the curtains closed, made sure Marianna was warmly tucked in and kissed her soft cheek.

'Sweet dreams,' she said, turning away, and she meant it.

•

Within a week, Marianna was well again. She even slept a few nights in a row, giving Agnes some much-needed rest. It was a Thursday morning after Julius's departure, when Agnes waited in the drawing room, balanced on the edge of the sofa, Gracie's shawl folded in her lap.

Marianna came down after breakfast and sat in the wing-backed chair beside the window. 'Good morning, Agnes.'

Agnes stood and crossed the room, kneeled before Marianna, and carefully placed Gracie's shawl in her lap.

'Agnes? What is this?'

'It is the most valuable thing I own,' Agnes said. 'It is how you know I will come back.'

'Come . . . back?'

Agnes would have given everything she owned not to have seen Marianna's face in that moment: uncomprehending, desolate. 'I have to go,' Agnes continued quickly. 'It's a family thing. But I will be back. I don't know when and I hope it won't be long.' She hadn't enough money for it to be a long trip; indeed, if she ran out too fast, without sufficient for a return fare to London, she would be forced to stay and find work. 'But I promise I will be back. If you'll have me.'

Marianna considered the shawl in her lap, her mouth drawn into a line.

'I will need all the wages I am owed thus far,' Agnes said, keeping her voice neutral despite her high emotions.

'See Pamela,' Marianna said grudgingly.

'Please don't be angry with me,' Agnes begged, sick with guilt.

Marianna didn't say a word.

'Marianna?'

Nothing.

Agnes stood and left Marianna sitting there, face turned stubbornly away.

Within an hour Agnes had her things packed in an old fruit crate from the back of the pantry, the Paris book stolen and hidden among her clothes. They wouldn't miss it, and of course she intended to bring it back, so, she reasoned, it wasn't so much stolen as borrowed. She gave the staff the same story she had given Marianna, that she needed to see family unexpectedly; but she did not wait to see nor say goodbye to Julius. Easiest not to see his face, answer his questions. Easiest not to feel so keenly how much she'd miss him. As she left the house on Belgrave Place behind, her sadness at letting Marianna down began to balance out by her excitement about what came next. Crossing the Channel. Paris. Her mother.

The Present

Predictably, I wake at two-thirty in the morning. Wide awake, with misplaced morning energy surging through my blood. I keep my eyes resolutely closed for an hour, but sleep comes no closer and I open them with a sigh. A streetlight beyond the window sends a beam struggling in beside the blind. I hear rain. I rise and open the blind, and outside is dark and wet. A single car speeds past, tyres hissing on the wet road, its tail lights reflected red in black puddles. Then the road is empty. It's both too late and too early for traffic.

I pull on warm clothes and go to the kitchen. Mum has no coffee, only tea bags in a bent box. I drink a cup of weak tea and then take the keys and head out to the car. While I'm feeling energetic, I can make an early start on the mound of old papers in Mum's office and then be up at the clinic to see her when visiting hours begin. I hope that I might find the second page of that letter I was reading, but having seen the mess of her office I don't hold out much hope.

There's a smudge of light on the horizon when I arrive at the college. I let myself in through the front door, and it clangs shut and locks behind me. I pass a cleaner at the top of the stairs, wheeling his trolley along the corridor. He looks at me curiously but says, 'Good morning,' nonetheless.

'Morning,' I say, aware of how Australian my accent has become. Back in Sydney, I'm regularly ribbed for sounding like a pom; here, I'm practically the Crocodile Hunter. I let myself into Mum's office and switch on the light. By now, I am dying for coffee. Dying for it. I tell myself that in a couple of hours I'll have lots of things sorted, and the cafe across the courtyard behind Beech House will be open and might even sell something with bacon on it.

I start by pulling books out of the pile and sorting them into neat stacks. I shake each one before I stack it, to make sure nothing important has been filed between the pages. At one point, a photograph drops out and I bend to pick it up. It's Mum and me. I look about twelve or thirteen; awkward, skinny, smiling with closed lips. I sit on the floor and study it longer. Mum is wearing big sunglasses, her dark hair tumbling over her shoulders, and she is laughing so widely that I can see her back teeth. She is a picture of gorgeous vivacity. I don't remember this photo. I try to glean details of the surroundings but it looks as though we are sitting on a couch, belonging to somebody I've long forgotten. I stand and stretch, then tuck the photo into my handbag. I see my phone in there, lying dormant, and think about phoning Geoff. I haven't contacted him since a brief text message telling him I'd landed. But then, what will I say to him? Unburden my heart about Mum? He was tired of me unburdening my heart, I knew it. 'You used to be so happy.' He had said it so many times, in an accusatory tone, as though it was my fault and nothing to do with him, or with all the miscarriages.

No, I'm not going to phone him. I don't know what will happen next. I can't go back to Australia and leave Mum here doo-lally in a clinic, but nor can I stay: I have a life in Sydney. A husband, a job, friends.

I return to the pile as the clouds return and the rain deepens outside. Coldness has seeped into me and as I flick the override switch on the heating timer, there's a knock at the door. I open it curiously and see the cleaner standing on the other side.

'I need to vacuum in here,' he says.

'Come in,' I say. 'But please don't disturb the books and papers. Somebody has already dumped it all in the middle here.'

He comes in, hitching his backpack vacuum cleaner over his shoulders. He's a solid little nugget of a man with sandy curls. 'I did that,' he says.

I am shocked by how casual he sounds. 'What? Why?'

'There was a storm about two months ago. A branch came through the window and everything was sitting on the desk getting rained on. I was the only one here.' He shrugs. 'I didn't want her to lose anything. She's a nice lady. Where has she gone?'

'I . . . she's unwell. I'm her daughter.'

'Tell her I said hello.'

'I will . . . Did she know that's why you moved her things?'

'Yes, of course. She thanked me. Gave me a bottle of wine. I don't drink, so I gave it to my brother.'

I wait near the door while he vacuums. I can see now that one of the windows has new, modern glass; not the dimpled old glass in the other panes. The cleaner vacuums carefully around the mess in the middle of the room, then gives me a smile and closes the door behind him. I return to the work, despondent. By eight o'clock all the books are back on shelves and I stand among a dozen knee-high piles of papers. Some are photocopies of journal articles and book chapters, some are priceless Victorian documents, some are random to-do lists; but they are all so jumbled together that I feel hopeless. Where to start?

I pick up a wad of pages, stop the ones in the middle from slipping sideways, and sit at Mum's desk to sort.

An hour later, after coffee and a soggy bacon sandwich, I have imposed some kind of order on the chaos. Neat piles sit on Mum's desk, and I take the time to go through the old letters pile, hoping to find the rest of the letter I found yesterday; the one from the woman to the child she couldn't keep. But I have no luck and it's after nine and time to go to see Mum, to remind her that her things weren't thrown lovelessly into a pile; that somebody was saving them from water damage and that she has forgotten that too.

•

Mum is in good spirits when I arrive, keen to chat. She remembers very clearly the 'lovely cleaner' who saved her books after she'd left them piled on her desk while looking for something; the imaginary scoundrels who sullied her things have been forgotten. She sometimes repeats herself but seems mostly lucid, and she's out of bed for the time being and sitting at the little table and chair set beneath the window. The curtain is drawn, hiding the view of the brown brick building next door. Mum is impatient to be out of the clinic and back home; she asks every nurse who comes in about it. A doctor arrives, and I sit back and watch them interact, and wonder what will happen to Mum. Can she go home? Somebody ought to be with her. Should that somebody be me? I have wanted a baby for so long that I have read every book on the topic of birth and child-rearing, and it is clear that if one has a child one stays home to meet all its needs. The responsibility with one's parent is not so clear. Would Mum want me to give up my job? She has been a feminist trailblazer; has told me a thousand times that it's important for women to work, not to be consigned to the domestic sphere, helping others. But what do I do when she's the one who needs my help?

'You know,' she says to me as the doctor leaves, 'I think they mean for me to stay here. They think I'm all over.'

'You're not all over,' I say, stroking her hand soothingly. Then, thinking to distract her, I say, 'Mum, I found an old letter. Or a page of one, anyway.'

'I have lots of old letters,' she says. It sounds dismissive but I can tell she is glad to have something else to think about.

'"To my child whom I could not keep",' I say.

Her brow twitches and I can see she is thinking so hard that it's a physical effort. 'That one . . .' she says. 'That is . . .'

'It was only the first page. Is there more?'

'There's reams of it,' she says. 'It's not a letter so much as an essay. A story. I became quite obsessed with it, trying to verify the dates and the people involved.' Her eyes focus and refocus as she concentrates. 'Bah! It keeps slipping away from me. As if the ideas are there and when I reach for them they escape down a hole. The letter is in two or three chunks. If I got interrupted reading it I'd leave it and then forget it . . .' She smiles weakly. 'This is awful. My brain . . .'

'How about I try to find the pieces for you? Would that make you feel better?'

'Yes. Remind me of their names. Something about a sparrow. Oh, and I have a memory of some Chinoiserie.'

'What's Chinoiserie?'

'The Victorians loved Oriental art,' she says, as though that explains everything. 'Would you, Victoria? Would you find those pieces and put them back together? I wanted to write a paper about that letter, once I'd verified the people in it. Or publish it in my next book . . .' She trails off. 'I have notes towards a book somewhere.'

'I can find those too,' I say, understanding that what I am promising amounts to helping Mum find her memories, which are scattered and escaping from her. But Mum seems settled and happy, and so I don't dare withdraw the promise.

•

The following morning I return to Mum's office lighter in mood on account of a good night's sleep. I am determined to go through all the papers, and find the rest of that letter. An hour of work and I am flagging. I need music, or coffee, or both. Silent repetition. Pick up papers, leaf through and squint – Do I need glasses? Perhaps I'll follow that up back in Sydney . . . thoughts of Geoff. Sick regret. – then put them aside and go to the next wad. I rise and leave the office. There's a water bubbler in the hallway and as I approach I notice a tall man standing there, filling up a plastic water bottle. I stand nearby and wait, and then he realises I am there and smiles at me, making a show of hurrying up. 'Sorry,' he says.

He has a kind face, with pale blue eyes and soft, blond eyebrows. I think of Geoff, and how he doesn't smile, and never looks kind any more. Was it always like that? I seem to remember him being gruff even in the beginning, and me treating it like some thrilling game.

'Take your time,' I say, but the kind-faced man is already screwing the lid of his bottle back on and making a gesture towards the bubbler. 'It's all yours,' he says, and then paces off down the corridor.

I bend to drink, and realise my neck feels tight and crooked from sitting at Mum's desk bent over papers. When I return to the office, I go to Mum's reading chair and move aside the pile of folders that sits on it. I have to pull the chair out away from the wall so I can recline it, and then I sit back and sigh a little, closing my eyes. In my mind's eye, I see lines and lines of nineteenth-century handwriting. I take a moment to breathe and listen to my heart beat, try to relax my muscles.

Then I open my eyes and reach down for the handle to fold the footstool back in. Instead of a handle, my fingers brush a puckered pocket in the side of the chair, the kind of place one might store magazines or remote controls.

If I got interrupted reading it I'd leave it and then forget it.

My hand darts into the pocket. Papers. I pull them out and a quick glance tells me it's the same handwriting, the same letter. I flick to the end only to see that it is incomplete.

I hesitate about taking it from the college. The document might be a hundred and fifty years old. But it might cheer Mum up to see it, so I slip it into the back of a sturdy book, wrap the book with rubber bands, and tuck it into my bag to take to the clinic.

•

At the clinic, Mum's bed is empty and at first I'm alarmed, thinking about her wandering. But then the nurse tells me Mum is with one of the doctors, having some X-rays, and I should go and have a coffee and come back later.

'Not in the clinic cafeteria, though,' she says, with the hard conviction of a fellow coffee lover. 'Go to Ellie's down the road.'

I find the cafe one block from the clinic and sit in a quiet back corner with a double-strength latte and three sticks of sugar. One by one, I stir the sugar sticks into the liquid, then take a sip. Strong and sweet.

I glance at the clock and think about calling Geoff to kill time, then remember I have the old letter. I take it from the book, unfold it and straighten it on the table in front of me, peering at the handwriting. Once I get the hang of how the s's and the r's are different, it isn't too difficult to read. As I drink my coffee, and then another, I read.

105

CHAPTER 7
Moineau

—led to your birth and ultimately to me losing you. I offer these words not as excuses, but as explanations. I write it all down in as much detail as I can remember, so that you will understand. You will be a woman one day, and you will know the unrelenting force of passion. They say we are creatures of emotion, as though emotion were a trivial thing to be dismissed. But my heart and my body have known feelings so mighty that they have overridden even God's words. Men do poorly to imagine women weak. We have pounding oceans inside us.

It starts with my Aunt Harriet, my father's sister. I had always been fond of Aunt Harriet, and she of me. She was bold and bright, with wild brown curls and a laugh that could shake walls. Her husband, my Uncle Oswald, seemed small and pale beside her, like a male spider next to the large and busy female. But she loved him madly; her eyes shone every time she looked at him.

When he died suddenly, late in the spring of the year I met Emile, my father insisted I travel south to keep her company for the summer. And so I set out to Millthorne, a tiny village in Dorset, to offer what comfort I could. By this time, it was just past the solstice. Bright days turned into long, warm evenings. I took two trains to get to Dorchester and then hired a carriage the rest of the way. I was tired by the travel, but enchanted with the countryside. We rattled down steep hills crowded on all sides by wild foliage – chestnuts and sycamore and oak – and navigated through crooked laneways paved with wildflowers and alive with glistening insects. I was used to the flat moorlands around Hatby, the grey streets and inert stone of the village. Millthorne seemed more alive somehow, wrought in warm colours and crowned with glittering leaves. The coach drew to a stop on a straight, quiet street as the afternoon shadows grew long. The coachmaster handed me down and a smiling middle-aged man in black livery approached. I presumed from his mourning gear that he was Aunt Harriet's, and I was right. He introduced himself as Toby, Harriet's second man, then took my trunk and led me down the street a little way and around the corner to my Aunt Harriet's house.

I followed him inside to the entranceway. It was dim, the lamps not yet lit. Toby deposited my trunk and rang the bell for the maid, while I pulled off my gloves and unlaced my bonnet. 'Where will I find my aunt?' I asked.

'Jones will come for you in just a moment.' His eyes were kind, but sad. 'Your aunt has taken the loss . . . badly.'

I imagined Harriet under a veil, her light snuffed out. Perhaps I hadn't contemplated how difficult this visit might be until that moment. I had been fixed on getting out of Hatby, at stopping the endless discussion about whom my sister or I should marry, as though husbands could be meted out fairly to both of us the way cake is.

Jones arrived then. She had been a faithful servant to Aunt Harriet for nearly twenty years, and usually travelled with her. We knew each other well. I handed her my bonnet and gloves and she touched my hand with her gnarled and worn fingers. 'She's in the drawing room. Don't be surprised by what you see.'

I nodded, and followed her through the dark corridor. She paused outside the drawing-room door, nodded to me once, then knocked quietly and opened the door.

Don't be surprised by what you see.

Rather than my solitary aunt, slumped on the sofa all in black, I was greeted by a roomful of people. The curtains were drawn so it was too dark for a moment to find Harriet with my eyes, but she was most certainly not in black. Seven people in all sat in a circle around the table; all eyes were closed as a woman intoned strange sounds; soft moans.

Jones leaned into me, her breath tickling my ear. 'They are having a séance.' Then she backed away and I stepped into the room properly, hands clasped before me. No aspect of my good breeding had ever taught me the appropriate behaviour for entering a séance, so I waited.

At length, the moaning woman put up her head, almost as if she were sniffing the air. 'A new energy has entered the room.' Then she turned her gimlet eyes on me and my stomach chilled. 'Who are you?' she said.

'I am Harriet's niece.'

Harriet's eyes flew open then, and she called out, 'Hello there, Little Sparrow,' which was her favourite name for me, and she could not be persuaded to call me anything else. 'We'll be done in half an hour. Madame Azhkenazy is terribly close to making contact. Get Jones to show you your room and do close the door firmly as you go.' Then her eyes were closed again, and Madame Azhkenazy had turned her terrible stare away from me. I backed out of the room, closing the door as Harriet had asked, and called for Jones.

She led me up the stairs past at least five new portraits of Uncle Oswald, and then into a large room with a high wooden bed. The canopy and covers were all shades of white and cream, and at first I didn't see the creamy-coloured cat nestled on the foot of the bed.

'Off with you!' Jones shouted at it, but I stayed her hand and brushed my knuckles gently across the cat's head.

'What's her name?'

'*His* name is Basil. Thinks he owns the place.'

'I don't mind. He can stay in here. I like cats.' We'd had many dogs and cats at Breckby Manor. There was something lovely about the way they loved me, just as I was.

Basil rolled on his back and exposed his belly.

'Looks as though he likes you too, ma'am,' Jones said, plumping the pillows and making sure the curtains sat straight.

I walked to the window and looked down on the street. A shop across the road was closing, the shopkeeper bringing in the last of the fruit crates and bolting the door. The inn next door to it was still quiet. I could hear evening birds and the sky was washing to pale blue–pink. Thatched roofs lined each side of the street, and a man walked an enormous dog along towards the millstream.

'I shall leave you be, then, ma'am,' Jones said. 'Toby will bring up your trunk shortly. Supper at seven. Your aunt's . . . friends should be gone by then.' Jones left and closed the door, and I sat on the bed with Basil, rubbing his head until he purred loudly.

I flopped onto my back and stared up at the canopy. I didn't need to ask whom Aunt Harriet was trying to contact through the séance. Even though she must be feeling such terrible grief, I couldn't help thinking how lucky she was to have loved the man she married. I was certain that neither my sister nor I would be so fortunate.

In the end, I didn't see Harriet until breakfast the next morning. Jones brought me a supper tray when it transpired that Madame Azhkenazy needed the séance to continue until late, and I fell asleep while there was still light in the sky, so tired was I from travelling.

The breakfast room was in the conservatory at the back of the house, lit through crowding trees by the morning sun. Harriet was there already, wearing a green house dress, her hair tied up under a yellow scarf.

'Good morning, my dear. Would you like Cook to poach an egg for you?'

'Yes, please,' I said, pulling out the wooden seat and sitting down. Sunlight fell on the table in front of me.

Harriet rang a bell, spread some marmalade on her roll, and fixed her gaze on me with a smile. 'It is so *good* to see you, Little Sparrow.'

'I share your feeling,' I said. 'I must say, I hadn't thought to find you in such good spirits.'

'Ha!' she said, flapping her hand at me. 'And I know you are not saying that with any judgement, which is why I like you, my dear. We understand each other.'

A maid came in then with a fresh pot of tea, and Harriet asked for two poached eggs and some grilled ham for me. The maid took her time setting my place, during which Harriet and I remained silent. Like Harriet, I had never mastered the art of not caring what servants heard me say. I picked up a roll and buttered it while Harriet poured me tea. The first sip was heaven: hot and strong and malty.

'Well,' she said as the maid withdrew. 'I am in good spirits. I am. As you can see, I am not wearing black. I refused to wear it at all. Black would mean he was gone, and he is not gone.'

110

My smile froze a little on my face. 'No?'

'Yes, he is dead in the ground, and I will not hold his dear hand again . . .' At this, her voice caught and she wobbled almost imperceptibly, but then she brightened again. 'But his spirit is very close, Little Sparrow. I dream about him every night, you know. He says not to forget him. As if I could forget him!'

I didn't know then that dreaming about someone you have lost is very common, and not to do with ghosts at all. Then, I was even a little convinced that Uncle Oswald was making a connection from the other side. 'I am glad you are having sweet dreams.'

'See? You know the right thing to say. Not like that awful Doctor Mortensen who is convinced I have lost my mind. I have not!' She refilled her own cup. 'Madame Azhkenazy may be a Russian, but she is not a crook. She is helping me contact Oswald. He is still around, you know. I can feel him.'

I didn't know how to respond. I knew, of course, that many people were interested in spiritualism. And I knew that my vicar back in Hatby was very opposed to such practices. But all I could see was that my aunt, whom I'd expected to find horizontal with grief, was her usual bright self. 'If Madame Azhkenazy is providing you comfort,' I said, 'then I am glad she is helping you.'

She reached out to pat my hand. Her skin was thin and pale. I could see the veins blue beneath the surface.

'She does look rather fearsome, though,' I continued.

'Oh, do not be frightened of her, my dear. She will not harm you in any way. But you must understand that she has seen things that none of us shall ever see, and we should be horribly changed and fearsome ourselves if we had. I doubt that talking with the dead is a pleasant pastime, and she has rather a lurid history herself.' Harriet launched into a summary of Madame Azhkenazy's background as a poor child from Novgorod who was ostracised for having visions. While she spoke, my breakfast

111

arrived and extreme hunger made me graceless, but Harriet either didn't notice or didn't care. I always had such an appetite in summer. Perhaps it was due to the long days of rambling outside getting, as my mother cautioned me on the rare occasions she noticed me, 'ruined with freckles'.

'Now, you must forgive me,' Harriet said at length. 'I have the drapers coming in this morning to take measurements for the drawing room and the bedrooms. I am rather bored of the curtains we have now and I intend to have them all in shades of green. It was Oswald's favourite colour, you know. Can you entertain yourself?'

'Gladly,' I said. 'I'll take a walk.'

'Good girl. There's a lovely old well down past the church. All sorts of superstitions attached to it, but such a pretty place. They call it the Hawthorn Well, and the old pagans used to worship there. You'll miss it if you don't know to look for it. You'll see the procession of hazel trees in the near corner of the churchyard. They say if you drop a buttercup in the well, it will show you the face of the man you'll marry.' Again, her voice caught and she seemed shaken by something deep within.

'That sounds like a very silly superstition, aunt,' I said to her.

Her smile was restored. 'Yes. It is. I never liked buttercups anyway. Common as muck, they are. You'll do better than buttercups, my Little Sparrow.'

She rang the bell for the maid to clear away, and we went our separate ways.

•

What a warm, cloudless day it was. The sun was in the leaves and the birds all sang as though they knew what was going to happen, whom I was going to meet.

112

I followed the road down towards the millstream, then took the path along beside it. The rushing water emptied into a pool between the trees, where ducks swam and dragonflies darted. I kept following the trickle through the woods, and up to a tree-lined gully where a row of giant sycamore trees bent their branches to the ground. On the other side of the gully, farmland opened out and sheep grazed up a green hill. I was invigorated by the clear weather and decided to walk up the hill to see what was on the other side.

I didn't realise until I was halfway up that I'd underestimated how steep the hill was, nor how hot it would make me. My legs were burning when I finally reached the summit, and there was no shade. I sat down on the far side of the hill, from where I could see all the way to the next village, nestled in a wooded valley, and a carriage travelling on a distant ridge. The only sound was the shushing of the breeze and a buzzing bumblebee at a patch of wildflowers.

Such quiet bliss. But I was so warm!

So, I retraced my steps back down and followed the signs to the churchyard, meaning to find the Hawthorn Well. By the time I got to the churchyard, though, I was sticky and red-faced and hot. The sun was moving towards noon in the sky, and all I wanted was to get somewhere cool and have a drink of water.

And that is why I went into the church that day. Outside, a cart sat beside the path and an unhitched horse wandered about the grass siding, nibbling on long tender grass. The Church of St Thomas was more than five hundred years old, and was in the process of having all the old box pews removed and bench pews fitted. I knew this, because last time Aunt Harriet and I spoke, she had told me about how she'd led the Parish Society's fundraising efforts. Inside, I was unsurprised to see long planks of timber stacked up against the walls, and find a large section of the nave empty of seats: just a bare stone floor. I relished the cool as I closed the bright sunshine out behind me. In the chancel was a man with his back to me, doing something near the altar. I presumed it to be the vicar, who Harriet had told me was a young man with thick hair, as this man appeared to be.

I called out, 'Excuse me, Vicar, could I trouble you for a drink of water?'

He turned, and I saw immediately that he was not a vicar. He wore brown pants, a pale blue shirt with the sleeves rolled up to his elbows, and a dirty apron. Behind him was a saw-horse, and a collection of tools.

'I am sorry—' I started, at precisely the same time he said, 'I am no vicar.'

'I can see that,' I said, then wondered if I sounded as though I was judging him. I thought about telling him that Aunt Harriet thought the vicar quite a silly young man and there was no shame in being identified as different from him.

But he smiled and said, 'I can still fetch you a drink of water.' His accent was French, only slightly, as though he had been in England many years.

'Thank you,' I said. 'It's a terribly hot day.'

'I went to the pump just half an hour ago,' he said. I watched him as he moved to the south aisle to a tall pail. Hung on the side was a tin cup, which he dipped in the water and then brought back for me.

It was cool in my hands, and the water tasted sweeter than water had ever tasted. Now he was close, I could see his face more clearly. He had wide, flat cheeks and chestnut sideburns at odds with his dark curls. His nose was straight, but not thin, his nostrils slightly flared. His mouth was full and wide. He had a day or two's worth of beard stubble. It was his eyes that I would remember later, though. They were a shade between green and grey, with heavy lids that folded to an exotic angle at the outside corner, and thick black lashes. I became aware I was staring and handed him back his cup. '*Merci*,' I said.

He responded with a long line of French that I hadn't a hope of understanding and I laughed lightly and shook my head. 'I have the French of a schoolgirl, a careless one at that.'

'Well. Lucky my English is so good.'

I stood there, smiling at him, with him smiling back at me, and it might have gone on like that for quite a while had not the real vicar appeared then to interrupt us.

'May I help?'

His words broke the spell. How Aunt Harriet had ever thought the vicar young was beyond my understanding, but then she was sixty, so perhaps anyone below that age was young to her. He was a steel-haired middle-aged man with a limp. He peered at me, then at the carpenter, and back again at me suspiciously.

I introduced myself and told him I was Harriet's niece, and his suspicion melted away on hearing my aunt's name. The carpenter had moved back to his saw-horse and I made five minutes of polite conversation with the vicar, my eyes sliding back to the carpenter a few times, before finally having the courage to say, 'Your man there provided me with a drink when I came in.'

'Emile? Did he?'

Emile.

'He's a fine man as well as a fine carpenter, then,' the vicar continued. 'And now, I'm sure your aunt must be expecting you home for lunch.'

I understood the vicar was stopping me from being alone with Emile again, and this thought both annoyed and chastened me. I nodded. 'Good day, then.' I called out, 'Thank you again, Emile.'

He lifted a hand but didn't turn around. 'Good day, my lady.'

I left the church, and returned to the bright street.

I suppose you think me a silly young fool, so perhaps it will surprise you to know that that day, when I met Emile, I was not young by anyone's definition. At six-and-twenty, I was in danger of being thought 'left on the shelf', but the truth was that my parents were prevaricating over which of their daughters – my sister or me – should marry Mr Ernest Shawe (who, it should be remarked, never struck me as earnest but was always very sure of himself), and Mr Shawe's regular journeys to the Far East for trade meant that a deal had taken a long time to strike. Of course, my sister and I both knew that, had Mr Shawe been keen on either of us, it would have been decided a long time ago. Moreover, there was another fellow waiting in the wings, a Mr Wilburforce Peacock, who was nearly forty; and I had been threatened with him too. I did realise, of course, that I would become either Mrs Shawe or Mrs Peacock in the next year or so. I knew and accepted my fate, as all women of my breeding do because they must. But perhaps knowledge and acceptance in the mind do not translate to knowledge and acceptance in the body, and it seemed to be my body that had the strongest reaction to Emile the carpenter. Indeed, it barely let me sleep that night. A restlessness infected all my muscles. I could not be comfortable. I tossed and turned, and whenever I dozed off, I thought of him again and it was like tasting something sweet and cool.

The next morning, Harriet and I agreed over breakfast that we would take a picnic lunch to the Hawthorn Well at noon. I spent the morning in my room reading with Basil on my lap, and went downstairs only when I heard the doorbell ring. Aunt Harriet had not said anything about expecting visitors, especially this close to our planned departure. I paused at the bottom of the stairs and listened into the entranceway.

'Madame is not expecting you,' Jones was saying.

'She will see me,' a voice said in return, and I recognised the accent as Madame Azhkenazy's.

Jones was silent a half a moment, then said, 'Do come in,' and led her to the drawing room.

Curious, I followed in their wake. I arrived at the drawing room just as Jones was leaving, closing the door.

'Madame Azhkenazy?' I asked.

Jones's mouth pulled into a tight line. 'She has been turning up unannounced rather a lot of late.'

'She gives my aunt comfort,' I said reassuringly.

'Your aunt gives her money,' Jones countered, then realised she had said too much and bowed her head. 'Sorry, ma'am,' she muttered and slipped past me.

I opened the door to the drawing room. The curtains had been taken down and the sun dazzled through the window panes. Aunt Harriet sat on the sofa. I had her profile. Madame Azhkenazy kneeled on the floor in front of her, and held her hands.

'Aunt?' I said, interrupting them.

Madame Azhkenazy leapt up, her hands still around Harriet's, and gave me her chilling stare, but this time I didn't flinch from it.

'Oh, there you are, Little Sparrow,' Harriet said. 'Madame Azhkenazy had a prophetic dream last night and she has come to tell me about it. Would you mind if I skipped our picnic?'

I thought about saying yes, I would mind. I thought about dragging her out of Madame Azhkenazy's clawed fingers, but then I changed my mind. Harriet trusted her, and Harriet certainly had plenty of money. She would hardly be ruined by a fortune teller.

'Of course not,' I said. 'I hope you gain some comfort from your . . . friend.' I nodded at Madame Azhkenazy and offered

117

her a smile; she blinked back at me warily. She must have been quite beautiful as a young woman, with her thick straight hair and her round cheeks. 'Good day to you both.'

I left the drawing room and was crossing the entranceway to go back upstairs when Toby emerged from below stairs with a basket. 'Here you are, ma'am. Your picnic.'

'Oh,' I said. 'We aren't going. Can you—' I was going to ask him to save it for the next day, but then I said, 'Actually, I will take it, thank you, Toby. I'll go by myself.'

He smiled and offered me the basket. 'Splendid idea, ma'am. It's not a day for being inside.'

So, I struck out on my own to find the Hawthorn Well, the basket over my right arm. I walked up the street towards the church, wondering if Emile was in there today, wondering if he had slept poorly last night thinking of me, then telling myself not to be such a ninny. For all I knew he was married, or not interested in red-faced, sweaty blonde women who mistook him for the vicar. I kept my head down as I walked past his horse and cart, past the church, and through the arch into the churchyard. It was walled by grey stone, with a large yew tree in its centre. A wooded slope came up on my right and I walked right past it, forgetting that Harriet had said the well was hidden. I walked instead to the far side of the churchyard and back, and was about to let myself through the gate on the north side and out into the fields when a voice behind me called my name.

I turned. It was Emile, in his shirt sleeves and apron, waving to me from the gate through to the church. I waved back, then stood awkwardly, wondering what to do next. He seemed to be doing the same.

I took the first step, and when he saw me move towards him, he also uprooted himself and we met under the yew tree.

'Good afternoon, Emile.'

'And to you, ma'am. What brings you back to the church today?'

'I'm looking for the Hawthorn Well,' I said. 'My aunt says it's a lovely place for a summer picnic.'

'It's back that way.' He inclined his head. 'Would you like me to show you?'

'I would like that very much,' I said. 'Kindly lead the way.'

He turned and I followed him, stealing glances at his strong shoulders and back. 'You must look for the hazel trees,' he said, as we approached the wooded slope. I peered at the profusion of leaves and branches in front of me, and discerned the round hazel leaves. Two tall trees, their foliage almost grown together, stood side by side. He parted the leaves and I stepped between them, and found myself in a dark procession of hazels, even spaced and overgrown, leading down a slope for thirty yards.

'Down there,' he said.

When we emerged on the other side, we stood in a walled space, paved with ancient stones that surrounded a bubbling spring.

I think I might have gasped with delight. 'This is *beautiful*,' I said, placing the basket on the ground and kneeling on the stone. I reached into the well. It was cool and clear. 'If I'd known this was here yesterday I needn't have bothered you for a drink,' I said. Then I turned to smile at him.

Emile gave a little bow and said, 'I shall leave you be, my lady.'

My body shouted no, but thankfully the word didn't make it out of my mouth. 'I have a picnic,' I blurted instead. 'There's more than enough for two. Will you join me?'

He wavered, clearly as full of doubts as I was. We both knew that Harriet, the vicar, everybody would find the idea of me sharing my picnic with the village carpenter highly incongruous if not improper.

But it was a warm summer's day. The well was secluded and shady. And we both wanted it.

'I will,' he said, with another incline of his head.

'Good show,' I said, and I set about spreading out the rug on the paving stones and laying out the jars and unwrapping the treats Cook had packed up for me. He untied his apron and hung it over a low tree branch, and sat on the opposite edge of the rug. I passed him a wooden plate and a spoon, and we began to sample the food. Cold lamb and pigeon pies, dressed salads, rolls and cheese, tiny fragile fruit tarts. There was also a bottle of lemonade and two tin cups. I filled my plate and then sat back, trying to eat delicately even though I was ravenous.

'What marvellous food,' he said, spearing some lamb on his fork. 'I haven't eaten this well in . . .' He trailed off, but I didn't ask him to finish.

'It's my Aunt Harriet's cook,' I said. 'She's very good. She's been in service to my aunt for nearly fifteen years.' I took a too-big bite out of a pie, and had to put my hand over my mouth while I chewed.

He smiled at me. 'Steady now.'

I flushed with embarrassment, then managed to swallow it and say, 'I have rather an appetite for a woman. Aunt Harriet has had to caution me twice already since I arrived. "Slow down, Little Sparrow, there's plenty of food and plenty of time."'

He seemed to be trying not to laugh. 'Little Sparrow?'

'It's what she has always called me. When I was very small, she visited one miserable November when it rained forever. I was desperate to get into the garden, but my mother wouldn't let me. Aunt Harriet said I reminded her of a little sparrow, trapped in the house and always trying to be free. Clearly it wasn't about how I ate.'

We laughed together. I was delighted by the way the skin around his eyes creased, the way I could see his back teeth. But mostly I was delighted that I'd made him laugh. 'What's the French word for sparrow?' I asked him.

'*Moineau*,' he said.

'That's pretty. Everything sounds prettier in French.'

'Not necessarily,' he said. Then, 'Actually you are right. I was only being polite.'

'Well. Don't be polite. Be yourself,' I said.

'If that is what you wish, ma'am.'

'And don't call me ma'am.'

'If that is what you wish, *Moineau*,' he said, grinning.

A lovely bubbling happiness welled up in me. My smile seemed too big for my face. 'Yes,' I said, 'that is what I wish.'

'Here is a good location to wish anything,' he said, gesturing behind him with one of his big, square hands. 'You see?'

I noticed then that, tied to the branches of an untamed hawthorn bush on the other side of the well, were dozens of ribbons. Some bright, some faded and ragged as though they'd been there for years.

'What are they?' I asked.

'It is a wishing tree. Some of these old places have superstitions attached to them. People have come here for centuries to talk to the fairy folk, and have a wish granted. They tie a ribbon in the branches as a gift.'

I was utterly delighted by this thought. 'Fairy folk? Nobody believes in fairy folk.'

'Even good church citizens do it,' he said. 'One doesn't have to believe in fairy folk to make a wish.'

'And what wish would you have granted, Emile, if the fairy folk were listening?'

He thought for a minute, then said, 'More fine days like this one, in good company.'

'Me too,' I said.

I asked him a million questions about himself. Where he was from (the Loire Valley), why he had come to England ('family reasons' with no further explanation offered), why he had become a carpenter ('timber speaks to me'). He, in turn, asked me very little. Our mismatched classes wouldn't allow him to interrogate me the way I had interrogated him. He asked about my aunt, about where I had grown up, and little else. When an hour had passed and the food was mostly eaten, and he started looking back in the direction of the church, I did not want to let him go.

'Are you expected back soon?'

'I was expected back a little while ago, I think,' he said. 'I haven't a pocket watch.'

'Go, then. I will pack this up. I did enjoy your company, Emile.'

'And I yours.' He offered a sad smile.

'Tomorrow,' I said impulsively. 'If I should bring a picnic tomorrow to the well at the same time . . .'

He stood, didn't answer. 'Good day, *Moineau*.'

'Good day.'

I watched him pick up his apron and head up the slope, then disappear behind the veil of green.

•

I admit I did not expect him to come back the following day. His reluctance to accept my invitation had cut me deeply, but I was vain enough to believe it due to the difference in our social standing rather than any indifference to me. I had Cook pack me a picnic anyway, and she packed enough for one and a half because my appetite's reputation had preceded me. Aunt Harriet was meeting with her reading circle in the next village over, and nobody expected me to be anywhere, so I was completely free to sit by the well all afternoon and pine for Emile.

But he was there. He was standing there, his back turned away from the path, waiting for me, and my heart nearly burst from my chest to see him.

'Emile.'

He turned. '*Moineau*,' he said, and handed me a posy of wild roses. 'For you.'

We had only an hour, and it went in a blink. But we had an hour the next day, too, and we fitted into that brief wedge of time a thousand conversations. By the third day, I knew everything about him and he about me. Well, not precisely everything. I still had not told him about my pending marriage to either Mr Shawe or Mr Peacock, telling myself that these things were not yet set, and there was no point in introducing a refrain of misery to our lovely summer rhapsody. Besides, he had neatly sidestepped a half a dozen times the full story of what family circumstances had brought him from the Loire Valley to Millthorne, so I reckoned that we were even.

On the third day we overstayed our hour because we were lying side by side on the picnic rug watching fast-moving clouds overhead and calling out the shapes we saw. His arm was only a half an inch from mine, and I imagined I could feel the warmth from his skin leaping across the space between us. My night-time imaginings of him had become quite wild, quite improper, and although I told myself that they were just imaginings, they were a kindling wind on flames that had no right to burn.

His proximity, his heat, his strong hard body. I ached from my centre to my extremities; a sweet violent ache that made every other sensation I'd ever felt seem painted in watercolour. I knew the moment couldn't last, but I held on to it hard; but not too hard to crush it.

'It's time to go,' he sighed, at length.

'I know. Tomorrow?'

'I'm sorry, I cannot. I have . . . family to visit.' His gaze slid sideward and I wanted very badly to know who his family was and why he would not speak of them.

'I shall look for you on Monday, then,' I said.

'I will be here on Monday, yes.'

We packed our things and headed up the path, emerging into the churchyard just as the vicar opened the gate and strode under the arch. He took one look at us, walking slowly together, dreamy-eyed, and he said, 'Emile, I presume I am still paying you to work for me?'

'Of course, sir,' he said, hurrying away from my side.

Then the vicar turned on me. The wind was high and it whipped at his silver-streaked hair, fanning it out like a bird's tail. 'And you, Miss Breckby? I shall be telling your aunt about this . . . dalliance.'

'There is no dalliance,' I said, my pulse thundering sickly in my throat. How I hated the vicar then, with his angry red face and his ridiculous flighty hair. 'You ought not to speak to me like that.'

He turned on his heel and walked away, leaving me alone in the churchyard, the wind causing the branches of the yew tree to make shifting shadows on the silent graves.

•

Harriet came to my bedroom just before supper. Her peremptory knock told me I was in for a lecture, and I was right. Even though Harriet adored me, even though she didn't believe women should be so constrained as we are, she used all the words I expected. 'Improper' and 'unsuitable'; even 'shocking' and 'indecent'. I cried silently as she spoke, tears running down my cheeks and off my chin, but still she didn't soften.

'Emile Venson is a carpenter,' she said to me at the end. 'You cannot fall in love with a carpenter.'

'It is a decent profession. He's not a footman, or a pauper. Besides, I am not in love.'

'The vicar noted a besotted expression on your face.'

'The vicar is a narrow-minded fool. You have said it yourself many times.'

'Still. You cannot see that man again. Understood?' She reached out to brush a tear away from my cheek, stern but sympathetic. 'I'm afraid, Little Sparrow, that is the end of it.'

She turned and left me there, weeping silently, sitting on the edge of the bed while Basil slept on heedlessly.

But Harriet was wrong. That wasn't the end of it at all.

CHAPTER 8
Moineau

So, now I must tell you about my sister, your aunt, because it is here that she enters the story of your conception and birth, and it is she who is wound almost as tightly into it as Emile and me. I love my sister. But I also know my sister better than I know any person other than myself. We are close in age and grew up in such physical and emotional proximity that her faults, invisible as they may be to others, are easy for me to see. She has two chief failings. The first is that she cannot bear for the eye of attention to fall anywhere but on her. She is canny, though, and knows how to draw attention without ever seeming to deliberately try. For certain, she is tall and blonde and striking; we both are. But she does not use her striking looks for attention. Rather, she has a wide selection of little nuanced tricks to get people to attend her and like her, and nothing is beneath her. She exaggerates illnesses, adds drama to injuries, seeks special consideration for her very delicate emotional states, thickly layers humility over real achievements,

126

and refuses to ever accept a compliment until it has been offered at least four times.

The second failing is that she listens with her own heart but speaks with the mouth of our family. That is, no matter what she might be feeling – and she has strong feelings; I know because I can see them in her eyes and hear them in the tone of her voice – she will parrot exactly what my father or mother would say in almost every situation. It isn't that she cannot think for herself, I'm sure; it's simply that she is determined to be a good girl for Papa and Mama, even at the cost of her own convictions. I do not know if she is aware she does it, but I am certain that one day she will either explode like a coiled spring kept under too much pressure, or be forever damaged of spirit.

She arrived without warning the day after Harriet had lectured me. A carriage brought her direct to the door, even though the street was narrow. There was much rattling and jingling, shouting and neighing, and insistent knocking at the door in the late afternoon. I peered curiously out my window but didn't see who it was until I had descended the stairs.

'Sister!' she exclaimed and I found myself wrapped up in a hug that smelled of lavender and soap flakes.

Harriet was in a foam, ordering servants about and exclaiming apologies that were really reproaches: 'You should have told us you were coming, dear, we might have had your room aired.' 'I don't know who stops by without saying they will. How am I supposed to feed you?'

But my sister brushed her complaints off airily, saying, 'I couldn't eat a thing and I'm happy to share a bed if I must. You are to go to no trouble, Aunt. I know I am an inconvenience.'

'No, dear, no. Not an inconvenience—'

'I won't hear you say otherwise! I'm a dreadful girl, and I promise I will make it up to you. Only I am tired and a little

127

ill from my long day of travel and require somewhere to sit and catch my breath.' She pulled off her gloves and handed them to Toby, who laid them on top of her trunk and put his hand out for her bonnet.

'Jones, take my nieces to the parlour and make sure they are comfortable. Off you go, girls. I'll be along shortly.' Then she turned away and was muttering to Toby, and even Basil had come down and was sniffing at the luggage as if to see what all the fuss was about.

We followed Jones around behind the staircase and down a dimly lit corridor, where she opened the door to the formal parlour. She lit the lamps, arranged the cushions, cracked the window to release the stuffy air, and straightened a painting. I could tell from her glances at us that she was most displeased with this unexpected arrival. My sister stood very still with a straight back by the mantelpiece, hands folded together. I pulled out an upholstered chair from beneath the polished table, and sat. Jones took her time, but neither of us said a word until, at length, she left us alone, closing the door behind her.

My sister threw herself on the sofa, stretched out and laid her hand over her head. 'I really am so terribly unwell. Travelling is *awful*.'

'I quite like it.'

She opened one eye and fixed it on me. 'You are contrary.'

'Quite the opposite,' I joked and she laughed too.

I rose and went over to the deep green, floral rug next to the sofa, then sank to my knees beside her. We joined hands. 'So,' I asked, 'why have you come?'

'To keep you company.'

I prickled warily. My sister did not care whether or not I had company. 'Aunt Harriet is company enough,' I said. 'She's in good spirits.'

'Yes I can see that. She's taken off her mourning attire already.'

'Didn't even wear it.'

'No!' she said in a mock-scandalised tone. 'In any case, I thought you must be dying of boredom and would welcome my arrival, but . . .' Here she sat up and looked towards the door to ensure we were still alone. 'I'm here for another reason really and you aren't to mention it to Harriet. Or anyone. In fact, perhaps I oughtn't tell you.'

'You must now.' My curiosity was a little piqued but, again, this was my sister's way. Stories were never told, they were *revealed.*

'Well, I have come to see if Mister Ernest Shawe will follow.'

'What?' I had been so eager to leave that conversation behind and, in the company of Emile especially, it had receded into the dim-lit parts of my mind. Now here was my sister, hauling it into the bright light again. I am sure I wilted a little.

'I am tired of his indecision, Sister. And you must be too. He has been hanging around at the manor and hemming and hawing about his choice and I have had enough. I believe if I can draw him out, without our mother and father dancing about him nervously, he will make his choice and you and I can get on with marrying him or dear Mister Peacock, who has been terribly patient.'

'*Dear* Mister Peacock? Have you feelings for him?'

'I like him enough, but I'm no fool. Shawe owns seven factories and three houses; Peacock only one business and two houses. Shawe would be the better husband.'

I squirmed, gently extricating my hand from hers. 'How can you speak so? Ought there not be more between a man and a woman than expedience?'

'What do you think Shawe says about us? Which of us will bear the bonniest sons? Which will run the household most

129

efficiently? Which will look the handsomest on his arm if he meets the Queen? Of course he does. It is an exchange; no more or less. Along with the great freedoms we have been given, we have obligations.'

'Now you sound like Papa.'

'Papa is wise.'

I couldn't say aloud the other thoughts I had, because they were most improper. But in order to bear 'bonny sons' it meant that one of us would have to lie with Shawe, and one with Peacock. It seemed so intimate a thing to be so publicly decided, and I felt suddenly revolted by it. I remembered the warm charge of energy I felt with Emile and despaired of ever feeling it with anyone else, especially not either of our designated husbands. Misery descended on me.

'Oh, don't look so downcast,' she said to me, stroking my hair. 'You'll make me miserable too.'

The door opened and Harriet came in. At her appearance, my sister immediately slumped back on the couch again.

'You poor dear,' my aunt said. 'Are you very unwell? I am a terrible aunt for making you feel unwelcome.'

'You made me feel quite perfectly welcome,' my sister replied. 'I have a headache, Aunt.'

'Jones swears by soaking brown paper in vinegar and leaving it on your forehead; would you like me to ask her to prepare that for you?'

She recoiled almost imperceptibly. 'No, I think I shall just go to bed. Perhaps Cook can send something light up? Some broth or bread . . . or both? And perhaps something sweet for after.'

'I will have a full supper tray sent up to you within half an hour,' Harriet said, helping my sister to her feet. 'Jones is even now airing the bedroom facing the garden. Let me show you the way.'

I watched them leave, then I stood and made my way to the window, and sat in the sill looking out into the garden through the little diamond-shaped panes. Wild pink roses bloomed in profusion on a bush under the window. Emile had given me wild roses. I have always loved wild roses; there is something pretty and unassuming about them.

Had I been allowed to keep you, I would have called you Rose. I do not know what your name is now.

The evening was approaching fast, and it had been a whole day without Emile. Tomorrow was Sunday, and I hoped I would surely see him at church. Harriet couldn't scold me for greeting him politely.

I knocked my head lightly against the glass. It was hopeless. What did it matter if I saw him? I was being foolish, so foolish. The sooner I adopted my sister's practicality, the better. There was no future with Emile.

•

I rose early the next morning, and chose a dress that was pretty but not too frivolous for church – pale blue with gold buttons – and took particular care to brush my hair into golden waves, then rolled up the back loosely and plaited and pinned the sides. I watched myself in the mirror, turning my face from one angle to another, wondering how he saw me. Were my cheeks round enough? My lips arched enough? Quite clearly they were not, and I despaired, then cheered myself by remembering that Emile seemed to like me as I was, then despaired again because whether we liked each other or not made no difference to our fates. I was quite exhausted by the time I descended the stairs to look for my aunt and sister to go to church.

I found them in the drawing room. Harriet was bustling around, and bossing Jones too, while my sister lay on the sofa still in her nightgown with her hair loose.

'Aren't we going to church?' I asked.

'Your sister is too unwell,' Harriet said.

'I am!' she averred from the sofa. 'This monstrous headache simply will not go away.'

'And so I have sent a message to the vicar that he must come here after the service and give us our own. You needn't go to church either, my dear.'

I hesitated a moment, furious with my sister who was no less well than I, then said, 'But I want to go to church. I want to go out. It's a fine day, Aunt. I don't want to stay inside.'

'Release yourself then, Little Sparrow. I shall stay and play nursemaid. Why, only two days ago Madame Azhkenazy said I would be called upon by somebody younger than me, in their hour of need. I had thought it might be you, but here it is your sister. Fancy that!'

I met Jones's eyes across the room and could see she and I shared an opinion on this nonsense. Luckily for me, I did not have to be pulled into it. 'I wish you all well, then. But I am going out to church.'

I don't think my aunt noticed me leave.

The bells on the church rang out between the houses and the shops and the inns, and the folk of the village in their Sunday best meandered along the same route as me towards the church. Inside, the seating arrangement was mixed: some families had occupied the remaining box pews, some sat on mismatched chairs that had been brought in until the new pews were finished. I made my way to the front to one of Emile's pews, running my hand along the beam at the back of it as I found a seat. He had carved the back of each one with a pattern of wild roses and I sat, fingers tracing the carving in front of me, until the gentleman who sat in that pew turned and glared at me.

I tried not to look around too eagerly for Emile as the church filled up. I tried not to turn my head every time I heard the door open. But when the vicar stepped up to the pulpit and opened his book of prayers, Emile was not there and my heart felt like a stone.

The vicar was not a charismatic man. I ordinarily love the homilies but he read them as though he had never seen them before, stilted and without meaning. Some of my favourite lines I said under my breath along with him to keep me interested, but truthfully it was quite the most boring service that I had ever sat through, and someone as mighty and good as God should never be boring. I knew that I could not return home after the service because the vicar would be there and I didn't want to have to listen to him mangle any more beautiful words. I also didn't want to see him looking at me with his judging eye.

So, I struggled through the service, then found my way out into the sunshine again. I thought about going to the Hawthorn Well, but that was far too sad without Emile, so instead I headed north and was a quarter of a mile from home before I realised that I was trying to find Emile's house.

He had told me he lived at the northern end of the village. I regretted not asking for further details, but at the time I thought I could find him easily at the well every day. The vicar and my aunt had put paid to that; at least now they were together, keeping each other occupied, while I hunted for Emile.

Eventually, the village ran out to the north and the dirt road continued on through dense woodlands, so I turned and walked back, eyes open for any narrow siding or a gate that I'd missed. Sure enough, an overgrown laneway I'd walked past was actually the head of a narrow, rutted road. I made my way down it, past one tumbledown house and then another. Then I saw Emile's cart out the front of a third house, which was small and plain but beautifully kept. Of course, he was a carpenter, so I need never have feared that one of the ramshackle places was his. I approached the carved wooden gateposts and stopped, not sure what to do next. Did I really think I would go up and knock on his door? A long, lean dog loped up to the gate and barked at me, and it shook me out of my reverie. I turned on my heel, face warm with embarrassment, only to hear the sound of approaching hoofbeats. Emile appeared, on horseback, and he had already seen me.

I waited, my hand on the gatepost, as he cantered up towards me then dismounted.

'*Moineau*? Is everything well with you?' he asked with a concerned expression.

'I was out walking and I saw your cart and was admiring your . . . gateposts.'

He smiled, and it undid all my knots and I smiled in return. 'Thank you. I am very proud of them.' He reached over and unlatched the gate, and the dog shot out and began leaping all over him, bathing him with his tongue. 'Now, now, Marin,' Emile said to the dog. 'Calm, please. Meet my friend, *Moineau*.'

'Very pleased, sir,' I said to Marin, rubbing his head.

Emile had led his horse into the yard and left the gate open behind him, so I followed him around to the back of the house to a tidy stable.

'Did you build this?' I asked.

'Yes, of course.' He removed the horse's saddle and bridle and led it to the water trough. As the horse drank, Emile eyed me. 'Are you not worried what the vicar or your aunt might think of you coming by?'

134

I didn't tell him that they were otherwise occupied, because I wanted him to think me brave. 'No,' I said. 'I am not worried.'

'Then come in. Poor Marin has been alone overnight and will need feeding and lots of affection. Perhaps you can give that to him while I make us tea.'

And even though my good breeding told me that I *should not*, I thought about my sister and the potential arrival of Mr Shawe (and along with him the closing down of all my heart's own choices) and I went inside with Emile.

While he fed Marin, lit the range and scooped tea from a battered tin, I looked around me. His house was very plain. This room was both kitchen and sitting room. The walls were not papered like Harriet's, but lime-washed. The beams were visible in the low ceiling. His rugs were thin and plain, but his furniture was beautiful, clearly all made by him. Tables and chairs and a long settee with hand-sewn cushions in faded blues and greens.

'I adore your carvings,' I said, sitting on the settee and touching the carved wood.

'I very much enjoy making patterns in the wood,' he said.

'And you sew as well? These cushions are very neatly done. Better than I could do, I expect.'

He didn't answer, and the first prickle of suspicion touched my heart. I turned my head to the narrow window, its glass so thick and warped that the hedge on the other side was just a green blur. Marin had come over and put his head in my lap, and I patted him idly until Emile joined us, placing a wooden tea tray on the low table in front of us. A plain china pot and two cups were accompanied by a plate of sliced bread and cheese.

I met his eyes and saw sadness.

'My wife,' he said. 'My wife sewed the cushions.'

'You have a—'

'There was an accident,' he said quickly. 'Seven years ago. I lost her.'

A dead wife, then. I wasn't sure what the right facial expression was for the occasion, so I settled for a solemn nod. 'I am sorry.' Seven years was a long time. 'Did you have any . . .'

'Children? No. We hoped for children, but the accident came in the first year of our marriage. I was twenty-two, she just twenty. Her horse threw her and then brought its front hooves down on her . . .' He touched his own skull, unable to say the word.

'I see. That is very sad. To die so young with so much ahead of her.'

'I came here from France to be with her. Her family live at Harper's Hill, a little way from here. I have been visiting with them this weekend. This is what I do now for seven years. I go to see her mother and father. It makes them happy.'

What a good man he was to continue to see her family after all these years, when he probably had family of his own back in France.

He sat opposite me and reached over to pour the tea. I felt intimidated by the magnitude of what he had just told me. I didn't know what to say and so I said nothing, keeping one hand firmly on Marin's head. Finally, I managed, 'What was her name?'

'Eleanor. She was a good woman, but I have now been without her for three times as long as I was with her. It's hard to remember what she was like . . .' He shrugged. 'But she was here for a time, and she sewed those cushions.'

'Well,' I said. 'Her needlework is very fine.' I sipped my tea.

There was a brief, awkward silence and then he said, 'Marin likes you.'

'I like him,' I said. 'Why do you not bring him with you to the church while you work?'

'The vicar doesn't like dogs.'

'Really? I think that says a lot about him, don't you?'

He nodded. 'Agreed. But I daren't upset him as the job I am doing is a long and well-paying one. Poor Marin will have to get used to his own company.'

I hesitated, wondering why I was about to say aloud the thought that came to my mind. 'I can come by and keep him company.'

He smiled, but shook his head. 'There is no need.'

'But you wouldn't object if I did come by and take him for a walk? I do love animals and my aunt's cat isn't anywhere near as affectionate as dear Marin.' It was a simple way to feel connected to Emile, perhaps a silly idea and yet I clung to it.

Emile placed his cup back in his saucer. 'I would not object,' he said. 'But do be careful that your aunt does not object.'

'My aunt is preoccupied at the moment with my sister,' I said. 'Not to mention the Russian medium who is in her house most days, peddling prophetic dreams about my dead uncle. She will hardly notice I'm gone.'

'Not noticing isn't the same as not objecting,' he said.

We both fell quiet. We had strayed into difficult territory. Were we, even now, declaring an attraction for each other in acknowledging those who would oppose it? It seemed our easy conversation by the well would not come to us here, in his house. Even though the well was secluded, it was still public. Now, we were truly in a private space, hidden from the eyes of the village. I felt a warm shiver at the thought. What happened here, nobody would ever know. His gaze met mine across the table.

'I should go,' I said, feeling like a sailor who has suddenly noticed how far off course he has strayed. I shot to my feet. 'I should . . .'

He stood too and reached for my fingers. My vision turned bright, watching as he drew my hand towards him, gently pushed up the edge of my sleeve with his thumb, then pressed his mouth against the inside of my wrist with warm, insistent lips. I gasped as desire bloomed deep in my body.

Then he released me and I hesitated a moment, head swimming.

'Goodbye, *Moineau*,' he said, as though nothing had just passed between us.

'I'm sorry,' I muttered, although I wasn't sure why, as I hurried away.

I didn't breathe again until I was outside his gate, and then my breath turned into laughter. He'd kissed me. *He'd kissed me!*

We had passed a waypoint, Emile and I. From here, there was no clear path back.

•

I did not see Emile for a week, though every night he was in my thoughts as I slipped off to sleep. In fact, throughout the day if my aunt and my sister were making small talk in the drawing room, I would often drift off in my imagination and replay that kiss on my wrist over and over until I grew flushed and warm. My sister became curious about Madame Azhkenazy, and even joined in on one of the séances, though she said it was only to keep Harriet company. They invited me too, but I used the quiet in the house as an occasion to sit at my windowsill and gaze out at the dark village, wondering what he was doing.

I saw his dog every day, which probably sounds more amusing than romantic. Every morning I walked to his house, and Marin would come to sniff me at the gate. I released him and we rambled together in the woods and fields. At first he was unsure, but he grew more sure of me as the days passed, and by Thursday he was waiting at the gate for me.

'Come on, my friend,' I said, opening the gate for him. He loped ahead of me, and the sun shone on us both, and I felt close to Emile and wondered if he knew that I had been by every day. If only Marin could talk. I would rub his ears and make him promise to tell Emile that I thought of him every waking moment.

•

It was upon my arrival home on the Saturday that I saw the liveried coachmen unloading trunks outside the New Inn, which was around the corner from Harriet's house. The coach was gleaming, painted with a fancy crest, and the horses were tacked up in matching harness. It looked as though somebody important had come to the village, and so I hurried home to see if anyone there knew who it was. I banged the door shut behind me, pulling off my hat and gloves and slinging them onto the sideboard, and hurried down to the drawing room calling, 'Hoy! Have you seen the fancy coach outside the—'

I stopped as I burst through the door. The room was empty, but I could see through the bare windows out into the garden, and it was apparent, now, which wealthy and important man had brought his coach to the village; Mr Ernest Shawe stood with my aunt and my sister in the garden. They were talking among themselves, and Mr Shawe's golden head was bent over a lavender bush, examining the leaves as though he were passing on some great lesson about horticulture to the ladies. I could hear my heartbeat over every other sound in the room. *Thud, thud, thud.* For here it was, that destiny I had thus far evaded. I knew I should go outside and join them, but I couldn't. Not after a day in the woods with Marin, dreaming about Emile. Instead, I ran upstairs to hide in my room.

•

And so exactly one week after I had last looked for Emile during church service, I saw him. But what different circumstances I found myself in. I was bracketed on one side by my aunt and sister, on the other by Mr Shawe, who was being overbearingly attentive to me. We sat in a row of chairs near the back because we arrived late and Emile's hand-carved pews were already full. Rain fell heavily outside, and the hem of my dress was damp. I recognised Emile's back in a pew near the front, his thick dark hair, the noble set of his shoulders. My eyes never left him throughout the whole service. My heart, just a few yards from his, felt a million miles distant. He did not turn around and so did not see—

The Present

The letter runs out here, unfinished. I look up and notice that the cafe has filled and I am hogging a table while other patrons wait. There's a group of women with babies, the high chairs and strollers crowding out the front of the cafe. Mothers' groups always give me such mixed feelings. On the one hand, I love to see babies and small children; I love their poreless skin and liquid eyes. On the other hand, these women seem so casual about the miracle they have sitting in front of them, a miracle I can't conjure no matter how much I bend my brain and body to the task. Sometimes, I even hear them complain about their babies. *He had me up all night. I just want to take a shower in peace.*

I carefully fold away the letter and sling my bag over my shoulder as I leave, hoping Mum is back from the X-rays.

•

Mum is back in her bed, happy to see me, and proud to say that what they thought was a fractured rib is actually perfectly fine.

Thinking about fractured ribs reminds me powerfully that Mum had a nasty fall in traffic and even though she didn't break anything, she is bruised and sore and healing and so vulnerable. I sit with her and show her the letter and we talk about where the other parts of it might be, and finally I say to her, 'Emile, Mum. When I first arrived, you said you had your accident because you thought you saw him.'

'Saw who, dear?'

'Emile. You walked into traffic because you thought you saw Emile.'

Her eyes cloud over, but her expression otherwise remains the same. 'Nonsense. I'm not that far gone.'

I do not push the point, but I am more determined to find the rest of the letter for her. And for me. 'Do they end up together happily?' I ask her.

'I can't remember, dear,' she says lightly, but I can tell she's tired of talking about her memory and its failings. 'How is Geoff getting on without you there?' she says, somewhat too brightly.

I shrug. 'He's fine, I'm sure. I haven't called him.'

'No?'

'I will soon. He's . . . he'll be busy.'

Her eyes grow silvery, the way they always have when she is looking inside my brain. 'Is everything all right with you two?'

'Not really,' I say. It's easier than lying.

She pats my hand. 'My poor Victoria. Don't worry too much. Every marriage has its ups and downs.'

I laugh and say, so gently, 'Mum, you've never been married.'

She laughs now too, and we are still laughing when the wardsman comes around with some mail for her. By the stiff, blue envelope, I guess it's a get-well card and Mum does too. It immediately irritates her: the shame of her incapacity has so far been private.

'What's this nonsense?' she asks. She hands it to me. 'Go on, you open it.'

I open the envelope. It is, indeed, a get-well card, a very pretty one: a photograph of the sun rising over a lavender field. I open it and read aloud the message inside: *I am so sorry to hear you are unwell, Margaret. You have my best regards and support. Andrew Garr.*

At the mention of this name, Mum immediately begins to wind up. 'How dare he?' she says, under her breath, shifting and flapping her sheets. 'How dare he?'

'Mum? What's wrong? Who's Andrew Garr?'

'The Dean. The fellow who has been pressuring me and pressuring me to retire. The fellow who had my books junked into the middle of the room. He's *happy* I'm in here. This is everything he wants. I wonder which traitor at the college told him. I'd happily wring their neck!'

Mum's agitation has caught the attention of a passing nurse, who bustles in and admonishes in a loud voice as though Mum is a child. 'Mrs Camber, settle yourself,' she says, smoothing the bed covers down again. 'This is no way to act when your daughter has come all the way from Australia to visit.'

'*Professor* Camber,' I mutter under my breath, and I reach across to stop the nurse's hand. 'We'll be fine,' I say to her. 'Please. Leave us be.'

The nurse harrumphs at me, and Mum settles again, looking at the photograph of the lavender field. 'I used to love lavender,' she says. 'He's ruined it for me now.'

I try to think of a way to distract her, and so I say, 'Would you like me to read to you?'

'I am perfectly capable of reading myself,' she says.

'It's nice being read to, though,' I say. 'You can just lie back and close your eyes. I saw there are some books in the recreation room. Shall I go and fetch you one?'

Mum looks at me, and her eyes tell me that her soul has wandered a little distance from me. 'Perhaps. Yes. See if they've got some George Eliot.'

'I'll be right back,' I say, and kiss her cheek.

The moment I leave the room, I am thumbing through my phone for the number of the Dean, this Andrew Garr. I'd like to say it's because I want to leap in and defend my mother to him, but I suspect there is another truth lurking here, and I need to know it if I'm to decide what to do about Mum.

•

I have to wait three days for an appointment with the Dean of Mum's department. His administrative assistant tells me he has just left for Amsterdam for a conference. I spend time with Mum every day, but in the clinic we are forced into awkward extended time together. I can't talk to Mum for hours on end, especially when she has become vague and fearful. She always knows who I am, but sometimes she speaks to me about things I don't know anything about, or repeats herself, or talks in circles. We are most relaxed when I read to her. I've brought some of her George Eliot books from home, but Mum and I will always disagree about George Eliot. I find reading her so dull and slow. Minutes creep by, both of us under the window with the view of the bricks next door. This isn't a happy life, and we both know it.

So, I spend time at home, too; at Mum's home, that is. My childhood bedroom was long ago turned into an office, and the smaller of the three rooms has been converted to a guest bedroom. This is where I sleep, waking every morning to the smell of my mother, even though she isn't there. I begin to sort through her office too, but I haven't found the rest of the letter and I've looked at everything in the piles.

Professor Andrew Garr's office is one floor below my mother's at Locksley College. There are renovations going on in the waiting room, half of which is hidden from view behind a paint-splattered drop sheet. But I can hear men talking on the other side as they drill and hammer and plaster. Their accent is so different from the tradies back in Australia, and I have a momentary pang of homesickness for good old Aussie working-class voices. It is the first time since arriving that I miss anything from home.

When Andrew emerges from his office and strides across the worn carpet to greet me, I recognise him immediately as the man from the water bubbler. I cannot put these two versions of him together: my mother's account of a tyrant, and this open-faced and young man. Surely nobody my age (younger?) should be in such a position of power over my mother.

'Oh, hello,' he says. 'You're Margaret's daughter? I wish I'd known that day I saw you. I assumed you were a student.'

'I'm a little old to be a student.'

'Never,' he says. 'I should have recognised you. You look like your mother.'

Nobody has said this to me, ever, so I am a bit speechless as I follow him into a modest office, where we sit in armchairs shaped like buckets and he offers me tea.

'No, thank you,' I say, but his assistant comes in and puts a jug of iced water and two glasses on the coffee table between us.

As he pours us a glass of water each, I look him over. He's tall – perhaps six foot five – and has brown hair that is starting to thin at the front. He is dressed in a dark blue suit and gold tie, and his hands are big and ungainly. He passes me my glass of water and I take a polite sip and return it to the table.

'So, Victoria. It's a pleasure to meet you properly.'

'It's Tori,' I say. 'Only Mum calls me Victoria.'

'Well, then. It's a pleasure to meet you, Tori. Your mother has spoken about you often and fondly.'

She has? I am stupidly blindsided by this. I have long harboured a suspicion that Mum is faintly embarrassed to have such an ordinary child. 'She has spoken about you, too,' I say. 'Not much of it is complimentary.'

He smiles ruefully. 'We were not always at odds, your mother and I.'

'I would be so grateful if you could give me your side of the story.' I realise as I say this, that I will believe his side without question. He has a face and an aspect that I cannot imagine being untrue.

He steeples his fingers and rests his chin on them. 'Margaret is an incredible scholar. She has been an asset to Locksley for many, many years. Do you know, my interest in history comes from seeing her on the telly in my late teens?'

'Really?'

'She can make history come alive. I know it's a terrible cliché, but . . .' He trails off, seems to be choosing his words carefully. 'In the past two or three years, Margaret has found it . . .'

He pauses, and I realise he is worried about upsetting or offending me. 'Go on,' I say. 'I need to know the whole truth so that I can make a decision about what to do next.'

He nods, and there is such empathy in his eyes that I worry I'm going to cry when he starts to speak again. 'It started with complaints from the students. She rambled off topic, lost exam papers, had angry outbursts in class. It escalated. It was clear to me what was happening, and I was . . . I was *desperate* to get her out of the classroom so she could preserve her reputation.'

My tears prick. I nod. 'I see.'

'I put her on research leave. Nearly lost my job over it from the Chancellor. She hasn't published in a very long time. I don't know if you knew that.'

'I knew she hadn't written a book in a while. I thought she was working on one.'

'She hasn't written anything now for five or six years.'

This fact floors me.

'When I spoke to her about her research,' he continues, 'she . . . the ideas she had were beneath her. Rambling, unsupported . . . Margaret is a scholar from another age, but she had always been fiercely bright. She managed the transition to our new systems – which are unforgiving, I'm the first to admit that – with ease and good grace. To see her start to fall apart like this was difficult for me to watch.' He leans back in his bucket chair and sighs. 'By this stage she was two years past retirement age. She has a lovely package to retire on. I tried to encourage her to take it and go but . . . your mother's sense of self, I think, is very tied up in her work.'

Part of me is irritated with him for making such a pronouncement; I want to shout at him, *You don't know her!* But of course he's right.

'I wanted her to go gracefully,' he continues. 'Unfortunately, she has stayed and . . . this is very hard to say, especially to you. She has become a bit of a . . .'

'A joke?' I offer.

He sighs. 'It sounds more cruel than it is, but yes I suppose that's the word. Her colleagues say things about her. Fondly at the moment. But the longer she stays . . .'

'She can't stay,' I say. 'She has a diagnosis. There is no escaping that.'

He nods. 'I am sorry to hear that. It's good you could come to be with her. She's too proud to accept visitors from work.'

The sadness is like lead in my heart, lead in my blood. I feel tired and heavy. We are silent for a few moments.

'If I may,' he says. 'My own mother went through something similar. It was an acquired brain injury from a car accident. A young lad – one of our students at Locksley, as it happens, though he

147

left afterwards – had had a few too many pints and backed his car into a bus stop where Mum was sitting.' His voice is very even now, as though he is controlling his feelings carefully. 'She couldn't speak and I'm sure she barely recognised my sister and me, and she succumbed to pneumonia about eight months after the accident. In any case, I knew when we were with her – no matter that she didn't know who we were – I could tell that something inside her relaxed. That whatever she was experiencing inside, our presence calmed her, on the level of her soul.' He patted his pocket, rattling his keys, and glanced away, embarrassed. 'I expect that sounds nothing like rigorous scholarship. But I knew it to be true. Mothers and their children bond through body and mind, but also through soul. When body and mind are gone, that still remains.'

I drop my head and sniff back tears, then raise my eyes again and apply a smile. 'Thank you very much, Andrew,' I say.

'My pleasure,' he replies. 'If there's anything I can help you with while you are in town . . . How long are you staying?'

I don't answer. I can't think about how long I'll be 'in town' because I am not sure at all any more that Mum can be left here alone.

CHAPTER 9
Agnes

'*Mademoiselle? Mademoiselle?*'

Agnes's eyes flickered open. Her neck hurt. A man in a crisp uniform was shaking her awake and speaking to her in long streams of incomprehensible language. Her heart started. She remembered where she was: on the train.

'Gare du Nord?' she croaked.

'*Oui, mademoiselle. Gare du Nord.*'

She blinked the sleep out of her eyes. The train was stationary, empty. She wondered how long she had been asleep here before the guard found her. He was speaking to her again, and when she managed to tell him that she didn't speak much French he recoiled at her thick accent. She knew nothing about pronunciation: she had only read the words, never heard them.

'*Oui, mademoiselle,*' he said again, then in very broken English, 'The train is terminate.' Then he turned away and walked back down to the other end of the carriage. Agnes stood and retrieved her crate of belongings from the rack above her, relieved to find it all still there. She ached from her toes to her crown. She had been travelling since dawn: two trains from London to Folkestone, and then a two-hour wait for a crusty fisherman's boat to take her across the Channel. The joy of seeing the sea, of breathing the fresh salty air, was soon ruined by the slow, unsteady passage, which left her slightly damp and unable to banish the smell of fish guts from her nostrils. In Calais, she had used enough broken French to exchange her English money and board the first of two French trains, punctuated by an alarmingly long wait at a tiny rural station, where she saw no other soul the whole time until the train at last, mercifully, arrived.

Sometime after settling in to the long, hard seat, she must have been exhausted enough to fall asleep. She felt groggy as she stepped out of the train and onto the platform, then walked the length of the concourse and out into Paris.

The shadows were growing long, but the city was still all movement and colour. Agnes had learned the route from the station to her mother's address by heart, but took a few moments outside the station to admire the mighty arch and the statues on the cornices. Then she turned and began her walk.

The first thing that struck her about Paris was that it lacked the grime and grit of London. Everything seemed to be in good repair, shining and polished, even the street lamps. Coloured awnings were open above shops and cafes, and people drank and ate at tables on the footpaths. Many of the buildings had balconies, decorated with wrought iron. And everywhere there were trees: shady sycamores enclosed in iron grates. Agnes let the sounds of the city wash over her: chatter in French, dogs barking, children playing, hooves of horses, a distant street vendor. She followed the route she had learned, and if she had not been so exhausted perhaps she would have enjoyed more of the sights and sounds; but for now she put one foot in front of the other down wide boulevards, then further towards the river where the streets grew less ostentatiously wide and pretty, quieter and duller somehow, until more than two miles of walking were behind her and she had found Rue Cousineau.

This street was narrow, with room for few trees and no awnings. Apartment buildings in varying states of good and poor repair loomed close on either side. Agnes walked along, concentrating hard on reading the numbers to take her mind off the fact that night was coming and the crate grew more awkward to carry and she spoke hardly any French and she had only forty-three francs and no idea of where she would sleep tonight. Because any moment now she would find number 22 Rue Cousineau, and Genevieve would answer the door, and then everything would be all right.

Everything will be all right.

As the building numbers dwindled from three figures to two, she hurried her steps. Here was 38. Here 30. Here 26. And here . . .

Agnes stopped, staring. Number 22 Rue Cousineau was not an apartment building at all. It was a warehouse with large letters painted across the front: *Valentine et Valois*, and under that in smaller letters: *Marchand de thé.*

Tea merchant? But where was Genevieve?

The warehouse had two wooden doors, painted brown, and they were closed. Agnes glanced around. It had grown late, but perhaps somebody was still inside. She walked up and placed her crate at her feet, then thumped on the door three times and waited. The street was quiet. No lamps. She leaned her ear against the door and thought she could hear voices inside. She thumped again, and called out, 'Hello? Hello? Open the door, please!'

Footsteps and then one of the doors creaked open on a large, dim space lit feebly by oil lamps. A young man wearing a flat cap and rough, grey clothes peered out at her.

'*Excusez-moi,*' she said, a line rehearsed repeatedly, '*où est Genevieve?*'

The man answered her with a curious cock of his head, and she didn't know if she hadn't made herself understood clearly or if the mention of Genevieve's name had prompted it.

'Genevieve Breckby,' she said. 'I need to see her.'

The man turned and called over his shoulder in French. The only word Agnes could make out was 'Genevieve'. From within, a plump woman rumbled out. She had hair pinned loosely, a stained apron over a grey dress, and was flushed and clearly irritable. She pulled the door open wide, and Agnes could see inside the warehouse more clearly. Shelves and barrels and crates, an unpolished wooden floor and counter, the strong smell of dried leaves.

'What is it?' the woman said, clearly a native English speaker.

'Please, I've come all the way from London to find Genevieve Breckby.'

'Then you've wasted your time,' the woman said.

'But she did live here?'

'She worked here. She's gone.'

'Do you know where she's gone? Is she still in Paris? Did she leave an address?'

The woman shook her head all through Agnes's questions, then finally said, 'Don't ask me. I know nothing.'

'How long ago did she—'

The woman held up her hand. 'Don't ask me. I do not know, and I do not care. Now, excuse us. We have a few small jobs to do before we can go home. I have nothing else to say about Genevieve.'

The door closed in Agnes's face, and she stood there for a moment with her heart thudding. Genevieve wasn't here. But Agnes didn't believe for a moment that the woman knew nothing, as she had said. She had seen the way her eyes flicked, the move of the liar's gaze. Agnes knew because she had trained herself not to do it at Perdita Hall, and it had saved her many a time. But more than that, the woman had seemed angry at Genevieve. She had said she didn't care, but everything about her tone and demeanour said the opposite.

Agnes thumped on the wooden doors again, calling out, 'Hoy! Please, let me in. Please. I need to find her!' Banging and shouting, her voice echoing down the quiet street. But the doors did not open, and the street grew darker, and her crate with everything she owned was at her feet.

Exhausted, overwhelmed, Agnes sat on the ground next to her crate, with her back against the doors of the warehouse, and she put her head on her knees and held her breath hard. She hardly ever cried, and was not about to start. She held that pose for a long time, and perhaps would have continued to hold it until she curled up and slept on the ground outside the warehouse, but a woman's voice nearby startled her.

Agnes looked up, her hand going out protectively to her crate. Across the road stood a petite woman who looked to be in her thirties with dark hair piled elaborately on her head, and a deep blue dress with a jangling belt around her hips. She was calling to her in French. Every word of the language Agnes knew – which wasn't many – had now slid from her mind in her weariness and misery, so she simply called back, 'I don't speak French.'

The woman crossed the road and bent in front of her. She was incredibly beautiful, with high prominent cheeks and huge blue eyes, skin as smooth and white as a porcelain doll's. 'You are English, yes?'

'Aye.'

'I said, do you need a room to stay?'

Agnes nodded enthusiastically, even as doubt crept in.

The woman held out her hand, Agnes thought to shake it. But when the woman's fingers closed around hers, she hauled her to her feet, then brushed off Agnes's skirt for her. 'I hear you shouting for miles,' the woman chuckled. 'What is your name?'

'Agnes, ma'am.'

'I am Madame Beaulieu. Many girls stay with me when they are not welcome elsewhere. I have many rooms. You work a little for your keep, until you are ready to go. Follow.'

Agnes thought about not following her, but right now it was dark, she was tired, she had no idea where else she might get accommodation in Paris with the meagre amount of money she had, and at the very least it seemed Madame Beaulieu's rooms were near the warehouse, where Agnes intended to return tomorrow. So, she picked up her crate and walked up the street after Madame Beaulieu, who had an easy, languorous pace. The street was dark and quiet. They approached an apartment building that Agnes must have passed on her way to the warehouse. It was unremarkable except for the tall sycamore that stood at its side, and the shingle that hung over the door, which read *Maison de Cygnes*.

Madame Beaulieu withdrew a key from the belt around her hips and unlocked the front door. The foyer was, again, unremarkable. Gloomy, modestly furnished, with a staircase curling around to upper floors. 'Here we are. Your first night is free, and tomorrow we will discuss how you earn your keep.' She closed the door behind them and walked to a bureau to light an oil lamp, which she brought to the bottom of the staircase leading up into the dark. 'Many lovely girls here. You will like them.'

'I think I'd rather pay a little money for the night,' Agnes said. 'I can afford two francs.'

Madame Beaulieu waved her away with her free hand. 'No. You keep your money. I have never seen anyone look so sad. Tomorrow, we will discuss the details.'

Agnes followed Madame Beaulieu up the stairs with trepidation. 'What kind of work do the girls here do?' she asked.

'Oh, many thing,' she said airily. 'Helping with cleaning and cooking and sewing. You can choose.'

'I sew,' Agnes said. 'I am a seamstress.'

'We have no trouble in finding you something tomorrow, but for tonight somewhere to put your head and forget your trouble.' Another flight of stairs, and another. 'You share a room with Molly. She is English too and she is here now for many month. She is very happy. Ask her.'

They arrived at a landing with a low ceiling, and a pleasant smell of old perfume and fresh flowers. The corridor continued for a few yards, but Madame Beaulieu knocked on the first door at the top of the stairs, then opened it without waiting for an answer.

Two beds sat side by side under a window with a thick blind drawn down. 'Ah, Molly is not here. She will be along soon. This is your bed.' She indicated the one on the left. 'Bathroom is along the hall. I will see you in the morning.'

'Thank you,' Agnes said, dropping her crate on the bed.

Madame Beaulieu smiled, but there was something hard about her smile. 'The morning,' she said. 'Come downstairs when you wake.'

She left, closing the door softly.

Agnes kneeled on the bed and lifted the corner of the blind. From here, she could see down to the street all the way to the tea merchant where her mother had worked. Worked? Genevieve Breckby? In a warehouse? What hard times had she fallen on? Knowing her mother had faced hard times made Agnes believe she would survive her own. She curled up around her crate, not intending to sleep; intending rather to think and plan and solve. But her thoughts began to blur against each other, and she drifted off in the lamp-lit room.

•

When she woke, it was because somebody had entered the room. It took her a moment to remember where she was. A tiny-boned girl with loose dark hair was standing at the chest of drawers, her back to Agnes.

'Molly?' Agnes asked.

The girl turned, a hairbrush in her hand, and smiled at Agnes. 'And who might you be?'

Not English at all. Molly was Irish.

'I'm Agnes. I'm . . . new. What time is it?'

'It's after eleven.'

Agnes noticed that Molly wore a pretty dressing gown, rather than a dress. 'Do you allus come to bed this late?'

'I've been working,' Molly said, sitting on her own bed and brushing her hair.

'Working? For Madame Beaulieu?'

'Yah, of course.'

Agnes was about to ask, what kind of work does a girl do until eleven in the evening, dressed in nothing but a robe? But she knew. She had known, at some level, since the moment Madame Beaulieu had found her. Now, more than ever, she needed to be canny.

'I'm sorry. Am I keeping you from going to sleep?' Agnes said, shifting the crate off her bed and onto the floor.

'No, it always takes me a little while to relax after . . . So, you arrived today?'

'Aye. It seems a million years since I left London, but it was only this morning.' Agnes's head swam with tiredness. She unlaced her shoes, unbuttoned her dress and let it drop to the floor, and climbed into the bed. 'How long have you been here?'

'Going on five months.'

'And when did you start . . . working?'

Molly smiled, and she had a sweet face. There was nothing hard at all in it, which surprised Agnes. 'Ah. Well, Madame Beaulieu will give you five or six days to see things her way. And you will; we all do eventually. Until then, she might make you wash dishes every night until your hands are raw, and beat carpets every day until your arms ache.' Molly shrugged. 'In the end, it's easier to entertain her clients, and it pays much, much more.'

'Much more?'

'Oh, yes. This is a fine establishment with a good reputation. You can make twenty-five francs a night, with your room included.'

Agnes's mind whirled, thinking about that kind of money. But then she remembered how it would be earned, and she recoiled from it. She pulled her covers up to her chin. She did not want to insult sweet-faced Molly by saying she'd rather wash dishes forever, so she said nothing.

Molly extinguished the lamp and slid into bed. 'Goodnight, then, Agnes. I'm glad to have a roommate again.'

'Goodnight,' Agnes said.

Within moments, Molly was breathing peacefully and deeply. Far more peacefully than Agnes imagined she would sleep.

If Molly was right, Agnes had a week to find some clue of Genevieve's next move. She was on the right street, and she wasn't afraid of a few days of menial work in a bordello. But she would not lie with men she didn't know, no matter what.

You will; we all do eventually.

'Not me,' Agnes said under her breath, but she lulled herself to sleep by imagining what twenty-five francs a night might buy her.

•

Agnes woke in the morning, unsure of the time. She kneeled on the bed, lifting the corner of the blind to gaze across at the tea merchant. The front doors were open now, but she couldn't see anybody going in or out. She watched for a few minutes, when she was startled by a loud voice saying, 'Don't do that!'

The blind was snatched out of her hand and wrenched back down by Molly, whose hair was a sleep-snarled cloud.

'What? Why? It's morning.'

'We aren't allowed to have the blinds open during the day. And not just by Madame Beaulieu. It's a law.'

'A law?'

Molly's voice grew gentle. 'Oh, Agnes. You know where you are, don't you? You know what Maison de Cygnes is? We are a good establishment, with wealthy clients. We must abide by the will of the *gendarmerie* if we want to keep our good reputation. Blinds drawn, all the time.' She yawned, then brushed at her hair with her fingers. 'Come along. I'll show you where the bathroom is and the dining room, and perhaps we will meet some of the other girls. Do you know any French?'

'Hardly any.'

'Well, then. I can teach you. My grandfather was French. That is why I came to Paris, to stay with him when he was ill and dying. Unfortunately, he had many debts and left me nothing, and while I was gone my mother died and my father sailed to Australia. I had no home to go back to in Dublin.' Her eyes grew wistful, but soon she cheered herself up. 'Ah, it's not so bad. I'm alive. Look at me. Come on, let's show you around.'

Molly took her to a tiny bathroom at the end of the corridor, with a water closet and a small round tub. After she had washed up, they returned to their room to dress and descended the stairs to the dining room, where a skinny, spot-faced girl was handing out sweet rolls and pouring hot chocolate from a white china pot. Agnes sat with Molly and another two girls whose names she forgot immediately, at a long table of dark wood. All the blinds were drawn, which meant the room was illuminated only dimly by the bright cracks of light around the blinds. The room was large, with a bare wooden floor, and the lime-washed walls were decorated with paintings and postcards. Molly chattered away with the other two girls in rapid-fire French while they ate. The spot-faced girl served her breakfast, then moved to the other end of the table to collect empty dishes and disappeared through a dark doorway, presumably into a kitchen. Agnes supposed she did the menial work because she was resisting doing the other work, which Molly and the equally pretty, coquettish girls she conversed with were willing to do. Or perhaps she was not considered pretty and coquettish enough.

Agnes wolfed down her food, then was itching to move. Madame Beaulieu was nowhere to be seen, and Agnes, keen to set the terms of her employment, asked Molly where she might find her.

'Oh, she'll be around. You can't go a day without seeing her,' Molly said airily. 'She'll find you when she needs you. Come back upstairs and tell me a little about yourself and I'll teach you a few good French phrases.'

The other girls looked at them curiously as they spoke English. One, a creamy-skinned beauty with silky hair almost the colour of silver, giggled behind her hand and whispered something to the other girl. Agnes immediately took a dislike to both of them.

As she followed Molly back upstairs they paused on the first landing and Molly pointed down the corridor. 'These are the rooms where we meet our clients. They are beautiful rooms. Would you like to see one?'

Agnes shook her head, although she was curious. One room's door stood open, and she could see a glimpse of dark red furnishings.

'Very well,' Molly said, and up they went another floor. 'This is Madame Beaulieu's apartment. If you are *desperate* to see her, you can come up here. But she's always very busy.'

Then up one more flight and they were back at their own room. Agnes saw immediately that her crate of belongings had been moved. She had left it on the floor, but now it sat on her bed. 'Somebody has moved my things,' she said.

Molly seemed unconcerned. 'Perhaps Suzette has been sweeping the floor and—'

But Agnes was already diving through her belongings, and found that her purse – with her money and her identity papers – was missing. 'My money's gone!' she said. 'Somebody has stolen it!'

Molly grasped her hand with her own cool fingers. 'Hush now. Quiet now. We will find whoever took it. There are only eight of us living here and—'

At that moment, the door opened and Madame Beaulieu stood in the threshold. 'Good morning, Agnes. I trust you have eaten?'

'My purse is gone. All my money. My papers,' Agnes blurted out. 'You have to find who took it.'

'Darling girl, *I* took it. I came up to look for you, and there it was sitting out in the open. I do trust my girls, but it is best I look after your precious things. It is locked safely in the strongbox, in my office. You have nothing to worry about.'

Her reassurance did not bring Agnes much relief. She had assumed that she could slip out and never look back, whenever she wanted. Now Madame Beaulieu had her purse, that would not be so easy.

She tried not to let Madame Beaulieu see her mind ticking over. 'Thank you. That is most kind. Now, I am willing to do some chores for you to earn my keep. Shall I start in the kitchen?'

'You may start in the laundry,' Madame Beaulieu said, and Molly, whose hand was still in Agnes's, stiffened. 'All the sheets must be boiled and hung today. You do know how to wash sheets, I take it?'

She did. And she hated it. On those irregular occasions at Perdita Hall when she had to leave the quiet mending room and fill in for somebody at the copper, she had learned to light the fire, boil the water, stir in the soap, wrestle the hot wet sheets into the cold rinsing water and then through the mangle, then pin them outside with raw fingers. 'I would be very happy to,' Agnes replied evenly. 'Only this afternoon, may I have an hour to myself for a walk? I do like to walk every day.'

'Of course. But I will mind your purse. There are . . . how do you Londoners say it . . . pickpocket.' Her emphasis fell on the last syllable, and it sounded like a sweet French word for a flower. But her meaning was not sweet at all. It was dark. She would not let Agnes escape; not yet. 'You won't need it. As long as you are willing to work, we will feed you and give you all you need, right here.'

'Thank you, Madame,' Agnes said. 'Kindly show me the way to the laundry.'

●

By two o'clock, Agnes was exhausted in both body and mind. Nobody had told her to come to the dining room for lunch, so she had missed it, shut up in the dark, steaming laundry with raw hands and aching back. Her brief glimpses of the outside world were taken through the back door as she went to hang sheets on a crisscross of rope lines stretched from high fence to high fence, in a garden devoid of grass or flowers. When she dropped one of the sheets in the dirt and knew she had to wash it again, she nearly dissolved into frustrated curses. But she endured, because she would not lie with a man for money. She would *not*.

Her mind ticked over and over, working out how to get her purse back from Madame Beaulieu. Sneak in and steal it back? Go to the *gendarmerie*? Maybe all she had to do was ask nicely, on the day she was ready to leave. But when would she be ready to leave? When would she give up on finding Genevieve here? Somebody at the tea merchant knew something; how could she make them speak to her?

And of all of the things they had taught her at Perdita Hall, why hadn't they taught her French? She knew why. Captain Forest presumed the foundlings would never leave the north, let alone the country. She took a few moments to feel proud of herself, getting this far. Then she tried to say over and over in her head the few phrases Molly had made her memorise, sitting right there on the folding table, before she'd been called away to see a gentleman client. *Where is? I am. How much? With, from, to. Man, woman, child, cat, dog, husband, wife. Slower, I don't understand. Help! Leave me alone.*

But by four it was all over. Nobody was in the kitchen to tell her not to slice herself a hunk of bread and cheese, but she gobbled it down before anyone caught her, just in case. Her hands were bright red and her hair was probably a mess of semi-damp fluff, but Madame Beaulieu had said she could go walking after she'd finished the sheets, and Agnes wasn't about to double-check on that ruling. She strode towards the front door without a backward glance, and threw it open.

Madame Beaulieu was there in an instant, and Agnes wondered where she had been lurking.

'Agnes?' she said, just as Agnes was about to close the door behind her.

'You said I could go walking.'

Madame Beaulieu applied a smile, approached her with that languorous gait. 'But of course. You aren't a prisoner.' She indicated the bell on the door. 'Ring it twice. That's how I'll know it's one of my girls. I'll let you back in myself.'

Agnes nodded and went to pull the door closed, but Madame Beaulieu held it. 'Don't be too long now, my English rose. You'll be helping Suzette with the dinner preparations.'

'Right then, madame,' Agnes said deferentially, even though she had hoped to do nothing more than collapse into bed when she returned.

All of this fell away from her mind as the door to Maison de Cygnes closed behind her and she was outside in fresh air and clear daylight. She took a moment to inhale deeply, then set her sights

162

on the tea merchant. It was a fine, warm day, and she saw a stocky man in a white apron stacking empty crates in front of the shop. He saw her as she approached and watched her go inside, but said nothing to her.

With the doors and windows open, the shop didn't seem so shadowy and grim. All the shelves and the long counter were made of unfinished, honey-coloured wood. Large barrels and boxes were organised along the walls, and behind the counter smaller containers were stacked on narrow shelves. A woman of about twenty-five years was behind the counter, her back to Agnes, organising canisters on shelves. Agnes said, '*Excusez-moi*,' and she turned, gave a bright smile, and said something in French. Agnes caught the '*bonjour*' but not the rest of the sentence. She pressed on anyway.

'*Où est Genevieve?*'

The young woman clearly understood her, and very quickly returned fire, in an incomprehensible sentence that most definitely used Genevieve's name.

'I'm sorry. My French is very bad.' What was the phrase for *Slower, I don't understand*?

She shrugged. No English.

'*Où est Genevieve?*' Agnes asked again.

This time the woman spoke slowly, and Agnes made out a few distinguishable words. *Madame Valentine. Boulevard des Italiens. Genevieve. Avec Monsieur Valentine.* Agnes took a moment to process. Valentine was one of the names on the door. The owner. She was framing her next question when a heavily accented, blustering voice behind her said, 'What is all this?'

Agnes turned to see the stocky man. The armpits of his shirt were sodden with sweat, as was his forehead. His thick, brown moustache was waxed into an immovable shape that covered his mouth almost entirely.

'Good day, sir. I am looking for Genevieve.'

'Genevieve doesn't work here any more.'

'Does anyone know where she is? Is Monsieur Valentine available to talk to?'

He puffed up like a toad. 'Monsieur Valentine,' he spat, his voice unctuous with dark sarcasm, 'doesn't work here either.'

'Then may I speak with Monsieur Valois? Would he know where I could find her?'

'I am Monsieur Valois,' he said. 'And I can't tell you a thing about Genevieve. She is gone.' Then he switched to French and gave the girl behind the counter a tongue-lashing; for what Agnes did not know, but she hoped it wasn't on her behalf.

Agnes tried to charm him. 'Thank you. Thank you, Monsieur. While I am here, perhaps I could ask you if you have any positions vacant? I am looking for work in Paris.'

'You don't even speak French,' he said, with a dark laugh.

'I am not afraid of hard work. I—'

'Get out.'

Agnes gave the young woman behind the counter an apologetic smile, and made to leave. Monsieur Valois followed her onto the street and followed her a little way. Her spine prickled.

She stopped walking, then turned to face him. 'Monsieur?'

'I saw where you came from.'

'I assure you I am only staying there until I find good honest work.'

To her horror and shock, he grabbed her and pulled her hard against his hot, sweaty body. 'Maybe I will tell you where that woman is, if you come to me willingly. No money.'

Agnes's body went stiff, she leaned away from him as far as she could. 'Let me go,' she said. 'You would tell me nowt of use, and my honour is still worth something to me.'

'Even better,' he said, leaning his face into her ear. He licked her neck.

She shuddered, fought to get away, but then he released her willingly. 'Goodbye, silly English girl. I am tired of silly English girls.' He turned and walked back to the tea merchant, and Agnes stood in the street, wiping his saliva off her skin with her sleeve.

CHAPTER 10

Agnes was elbow-deep in scummy dishwater just a few hours later, in the steamy and dank kitchen below stairs at Maison de Cygnes. She didn't mind. After her encounter with Monsieur Valois, she was more certain than ever that she would not sell her body as Madame Beaulieu wanted her to, and no amount of vile menial work would have her change her mind. She could endure it; it wasn't forever. Here she had a bed in the short term, and every afternoon to roam. The moment she got upstairs, she would open Marianna's book on Paris, and find Boulevard des Italiens and plot her route. The young woman at the tea merchant had said only a little that Agnes could understand, but enough to lead her to where she should start looking.

Madame Valentine. Boulevard des Italiens. Genevieve. Avec Monsieur Valentine.

Did she mean that Genevieve had married Monsieur Valentine, the other owner of the business, and was now Madame Valentine? It would explain why she had worked there. Was it worth returning

166

when Valois was not there to see if she could find out anything about Monsieur Valentine? But on her first visit, the English-speaking woman had told her Genevieve was gone. Very definitely gone, as though she had never been welcome.

Agnes was accustomed to this mystery about Genevieve by now, and even counted herself lucky to have a mother with such an interesting and unconventional life. She could feel the same blood surge in her own veins. Genevieve had refused to be constrained, and so now Agnes was emboldened to do the same.

And she had an address. Well, a street name. That was a start.

Suzette, the spotty lass who served the food, entered the kitchen at that moment with more dishes and a few sharp words in French. Perhaps a lifetime of being bullied for her feeble looks had turned her sour. Agnes had no idea what she said, so she kept her head down and continued working.

After the kitchen was cleaned and swept, Agnes and Suzette sat down together at a small wooden table and ate the food the other girls had left. Suzette chewed and swallowed like a hungry dog, but Agnes had little appetite, and was first to excuse herself and trudge upstairs into the main house. It smelled of perfume, cloying and trapped in the lightless walkways of the house. Upstairs she went, hurrying past the floor where the girls worked, and arriving at the floor where Madame Beaulieu kept her rooms. She hesitated there, thinking about how difficult or easy it might be to snoop about and liberate her purse and papers; but before she could formulate a plan, a door opened and Madame Beaulieu appeared.

She spotted Agnes instantly, and startled. Agnes could see in the dim lamp-light that she drew her eyebrows together. 'What is it? Why are you standing there like a ghost?'

'I'm sorry, I didn't mean to alarm you.' Agnes smiled. 'I wanted to talk to you. Do you have a few moments for me?'

Madame Beaulieu beckoned, her irritation melting away. 'Of course. Come.'

Agnes realised the older woman probably expected her to capitulate now, and agree to entertain the male clients. She moved down the gloomy hallway after Madame Beaulieu, who used a key to unlock the door to a corner room. 'Here,' she said. 'Make yourself comfortable.'

Agnes stepped into a spacious sitting room, with four windows – all of them covered, the last of the evening light edging the blinds. Madame Beaulieu lit lamps, and a soft glow illuminated dark patterned wallpaper, intricate gold and silver frames on small paintings of naked women, a delicately carved carriage clock and two deep sofas. A chaise under one of the windows.

'Go on, sit,' Madame Beaulieu said.

Agnes sat. She expected Madame Beaulieu to sit opposite, but instead she sat directly next to Agnes, so close that Agnes could feel her breath as she said, 'Have you decided to work for me?'

'I *am* working for you,' Agnes said. 'I have worked very hard for you today.'

'Don't play innocent. Few things provoke me more than a woman who is deliberately naïve. You know what I mean.'

'I will need more time. Will you give me a week? I will do any chores you ask and never complain.' A week was enough time to find Genevieve on Boulevard des Italiens, she was sure of it. Almost.

Agnes could see Madame Beaulieu's face working. She was annoyed, but her mind was turning over.

'I can't afford to support you if you will not work for me,' Madame Beaulieu said at last. 'A girl like you, an English rose . . . We have many men who would pay a high price for your company.'

'Then I will leave tonight. If you give me my purse, I will go immediately.'

'Don't be hasty!' she said. 'Of course I will not throw you out tonight.' Clearly, Madame Beaulieu still hoped she might change her mind. She held up four fingers. 'Four more nights. Talk to Molly. She will tell you. It isn't so bad.'

Agnes nodded. 'Four more nights and I will talk to Molly.' And in the meantime, she would find her mother or somewhere else to stay or perhaps both if Genevieve welcomed her.

'Good girl.' Madame Beaulieu was all smiles now. 'This business, we need new girls all the time. My clients, they grow tired of the same pair of arms.' She shrugged. 'Some of my girls, they come work for me for a season, then go and marry good husbands who are . . . What do you English say? Never the wiser. As long as you don't tell him.'

Agnes grew curious. 'And your husband?'

'I have no husband.'

'You're called Madame.'

'I tell people I am widowed. But I am never married.' She leaned back in the sofa, growing pensive. 'Though I did love. Many times. Too many times.'

Agnes dropped her gaze. 'I didn't mean to pry.'

'I am not offended by your questions. I am happy to tell you that when I was young and beautiful, like you, I fell in love with a man. He was a student, the son of a very wealthy family in England, and he came to study here in Paris. We met and we fell in love and he gave me a flower every day, and rented me an upper-floor apartment, and gave me money for beautiful clothes, and made me promises . . . ah, they made my head swim. But he finished his studies, and returned to his family, and he married the virgin he'd been promised to since his birth.' Her eyes were sad for a moment, but that was soon banished. A grim set came to her mouth. 'Then I met another young man, another student. I knew now how it would go. I took the gifts, I lived the life, and when

169

he was gone I was no longer in the flush of my youth. So, the next time, I did not fall in love. I found the richest, ugliest fool I could, and I took everything given by him and I invested it with care, because I knew my looks would not last. Money, though; money lasts if you know what to do with it.'

Agnes tried not to let her shock show. 'You took enough from him to buy this house?'

'To buy one apartment, where I set up my business. And because I am clever and because I only hire the best girls . . .' Here she nodded towards Agnes. 'And also because I knew important people who would prefer their business kept private, I thrived.' She opened her palms. 'I used what I could. Nobody can blame me for that.'

The loud ring of the doorbell interrupted them, and Madame Beaulieu stood. 'Who is that? All my clients are here this evening already.' She scurried out of the room and Agnes followed her down a flight of stairs, but then stopped and let her go ahead. She wanted to watch from up here, if she could; to see what kind of person came to a bordello.

The moment the door opened, she shrank back into the shadows – for the caller was Monsieur Valois. Madame Beaulieu was speaking with him in rapid French, and Agnes hadn't a hope of understanding what they were saying. The conversation was soon over. Agnes heard the door close, and leaned out of hiding to see, with relief, that Madame Beaulieu was alone.

'Well, Agnes,' she said, ascending the stairs, holding her skirts so she didn't trip on them, 'you have made quite an impression on Alain.'

Agnes didn't want to know Monsieur Valois had a name, or that Madame Beaulieu knew him. She stood, still as a stone, wondering what was coming next.

'In all these years, he has never once come to my door. But tonight, he says he wants the English girl.'

Agnes's heart picked up its rhythm. 'What did you say?'

'I said no, of course. But not simply because you have not yet come to your decision about working for me. I would never give a girl to a man with that expression on his face.' She made a spitting noise.

'What expression?'

'I have seen desire in many forms, Agnes. But when it looks that hungry and that angry, it never ends well for my girls.' She reached out and patted Agnes's head. 'You see? I do look after you.' Then she withdrew her hand. 'You look tired. Best to go to bed now. You will have to help Suzette with breakfast in the morning.' Then she turned on her heel and departed back up the stairs, returning down the corridor to her rooms. Agnes heard the door to the sitting room shut, and thought about Madame Beaulieu sitting there alone in the lamp-lit room, among her beautiful things.

•

Finally upstairs in her bed, Agnes opened the Paris book and searched for Boulevard des Italiens. She unfolded the map and followed the index, and her heart leapt when she saw it was only half a mile long. Surely she could find Genevieve in four days. It looked to be one of those boulevards she had seen when she first arrived in Paris, on that wide sunny day before she had slunk into this narrow street and her horizons had contracted. She lay back on her pillow and imagined where Genevieve might live. An apartment with big windows where the blinds were never drawn, where light and air filled the rooms, where Agnes might sit with her while the sounds of the city rattled and hummed outside. What would she ask her mother first? Not, *Why did you abandon me?* Agnes did not feel abandoned in life. She believed life probably felt the same for everyone: ultimately every man and woman was alone in their own mind. Perhaps, instead, she would ask, *How do we get on in life, women like you and me?* Agnes smiled, thinking of

171

what Genevieve might say, and without realising it she drifted off to sleep with the lamp on and the map unfolded in the book on her lap. She was dimly aware that Molly came in much later, put her book away and extinguished the light, then remembered nothing else until morning.

•

Standing on Boulevard des Italiens the following afternoon, Agnes realised this job would not be as simple as she thought. The Parisians lived vertically. On both sides of the road, above shops, apartments stacked up four and five storeys; some floors with arched windows, some with square, and some little more than attic peep-holes. It had rained all day, and the tree branches were weighed down with water, the footpaths were wet and slick. Agnes stood outside a bookstore with an elaborate clock mounted over the door, and practised in her mind the sentence she'd had Molly teach her that morning: *Je cherche Genevieve Breckby, ou Genevieve Valentine.* I am looking for Genevieve Breckby, or Genevieve Valentine. Of course, she would struggle to understand their answers, but so far she had managed. And she also knew how to ask to please write it down, so she could show Molly later that evening. She took a deep breath and went in.

Within an hour, she certainly knew the French word for 'no'. Nobody knew Genevieve, under either surname, but one kind man had told her in broken English that not every shopkeeper knew the names of the people who lived above him, and that she would be better off knocking on every door.

Knocking on every door? There were hundreds.

She returned to the first building and crossed the chequerboard floor to the stairwell. She paused a moment, her foot on the bottom step and her hand on the wrought-iron balustrade, and it seemed she could hear her own heart loudly in the echoing space. Then she took a step and another and another, and began knocking on apartment doors. In and out of buildings she went, up and down curving staircases. In some buildings wary concierges would stop her before she could get to a single apartment, utter a declamatory '*non*' at Agnes's question about Genevieve, and gesture towards the street. In others, the stairs were in poor repair and no light fell. She stood at the thresholds of apartments with high ceilings and white light gleaming on precious objects with the intensity of Heaven; and at the thresholds of apartments where the floors were rough and bare, the beds were broken or the chairs were non-existent; and at thresholds where the door simply never opened. She asked her question thirty or forty times, '*Je cherche Genevieve Breckby, ou Genevieve Valentine*'; and a hundred times she was greeted with shrugs, shaken heads, or a '*Je ne la connais pas*', which she came to understand meant something like, I don't know her.

Nobody knew her. And when Agnes realised she had spent nearly two hours and had not moved far down the street at all, she felt overwhelmed and tiny. She returned to Maison de Cygnes, to more back-breaking work, to more memorising French words with Molly, and this she repeated day after day. Four days passed and Madame Beaulieu said nothing about their agreement, and so Agnes stayed. In two more days, she might have finished the whole street. But then there were the apartments where nobody had opened the door, or where the concierge had refused to answer her question. She was barely closer to finding Genevieve, and she had to decide whether to stay in Paris, or go back to Marianna and Julius, to the quiet house and the easier life.

No. She would not retrace her steps, not yet. Surely those who retraced their steps would end up trapped in the same place forever.

On the fifth day, on her return to the bordello in the late-afternoon light, she passed coming the other way the young woman who had spoken to her at the tea merchant, on the day that Monsieur

Valois had been so vile to her. At first, Agnes didn't take much notice of her, but the young woman stopped and touched Agnes's shoulder.

Agnes turned around and said, 'Good afternoon.'

'Agnes?' she said.

'*Oui.*'

Then the young woman said a long sentence in French; her voice was urgent, and Agnes's pulse prickled.

'Wait, slow down. *Parle lentement. Je ne comprends pas,*' Agnes said.

The young woman took a deep breath, glanced over her shoulder at the tea merchant, then back to Agnes. 'A man look for you.'

'What man?'

More French. Agnes willed herself to understand, but couldn't.

'Not Monsieur Valois?' Agnes asked.

The young woman shook her head. 'A man look for you,' she said again, then spread her hands as if to say she couldn't help any more than that, and went on her way.

A man look for you.

What man? Had Madame Beaulieu been bragging about her virginal English rose to her clients? Agnes checked all around her. The buildings were so close together the street had grown dark early. She felt a long way from the wide, well-lit boulevards. She shivered, and went inside.

•

Later, an hour or so after Agnes had fallen into an exhausted sleep, her shoulders aching from moving trunks of crockery in the basement, the door to her room opened and Molly came in and lit the lamp. Agnes was used to her late arrivals, so rolled over to go back to sleep, but then she heard Molly sniffing softly as she brushed her hair on the edge of the bed.

Agnes sat up. 'Molly?'

174

Molly turned to face Agnes, and she sported a swollen cheek with a cut across it. Tears dripped off her chin.

Agnes threw back her covers. 'What happened to you?' She touched Molly's face, and Molly winced.

'That was his ring,' she said. 'The cut. The rest was his fist.'

'One of the clients hit you?'

Molly nodded. 'And worse. He threw me across the room. Everything went dark. I woke up and he was . . .' She shook her head. 'He didn't pay me, and he kicked me in the stomach.' She parted her robe and lifted her nightgown, and Agnes could see an angry red mark.

'Have you told Madame Beaulieu?'

'No. She'll be asleep. All will be well. It isn't the first time I've been hit, but it's certainly the worst. My head is so sore. My face . . .' She trailed off into big, open-mouthed sobs that made her look like a little girl.

Agnes gathered her in her arms and held her tight, rubbing her back. She felt as fragile as a bird. 'Sh, Molly. Sh. Don't cry. He's gone now and he can't hurt you any more. Madame Beaulieu will make sure he never comes back. I'm going to fetch her right now.'

Molly extracted herself. 'I don't want to wake her or be a bother.'

'It's her job to protect you.'

Molly sniffed dubiously. 'It's her job to make money. We used to have a man, a big Russian fellow named Oleg, and he guarded the door all night and if one of the clients got rough or didn't pay, he'd come and sort them out. But he left and she said it wasn't worth hiring anyone new, as things hardly ever went wrong.' She wiped her nose on her sleeve. 'Madame Beaulieu does hate to be woken.'

'Then let her be angry at me. You need to see a physician.' Agnes pulled on her dressing gown and went to the door. 'Don't go to sleep. Once at . . . where I grew up, there was a girl who fell down a staircase and couldn't be roused for nearly a minute. Then she sat up and seemed perfectly fine until she went to sleep that night. She never woke up the next morning.'

Molly nodded, her face drawn and solemn. 'I'm too sore to sleep anyway.'

Agnes opened the door and felt her way down the staircase in the dark. She knew which was Madame Beaulieu's office and which her sitting room, so one of the remaining rooms must be her bedroom. Agnes knocked on each in turn, trying the doors. The first opened on a dark bathroom, the second didn't open at all. But by then, Madame Beaulieu had woken and was standing at the door of her bedroom. In the gloom, her eyes looked almost black. 'What is that racket?' she hissed. 'Is that you, Agnes? What a lot of trouble you are.'

'Molly's hurt,' Agnes said. 'Badly. She'll need a physician. She's taken a blow to the head and a kick to the stomach.' At this last, Agnes's voice began to tremble as the full horror of the situation sunk in. She had never been safe here. 'She may have broken bones or bleeding in her skull.'

'So, you're a nurse now, are you?' Madame Beaulieu said icily, but nonetheless she closed her bedroom door and said, 'Come. Take me to her.'

Agnes led her back up the dark stairs and into the tiny lamp-lit room. Molly sat on the bed. She had her tears under control but the swelling on her face was worse, distorting her eyelid. It was with an odd gratification that Agnes noticed Madame Beaulieu take a sharp intake of breath.

'Who did this to you?' she asked, sitting next to Molly and gently turning her face to the light.

'Monsieur Bergeron.'

'Did he pay you?'

'No, madame.'

'I will get Sergeant Vermette to apprehend him. Do you need a physician?'

'I don't want to be a bother.'

'She needs a physician,' Agnes said emphatically. 'Look at her. Molly, show her your middle.'

'No, no, I don't need to see,' Madame Beaulieu said.

'I can go out and find one,' Agnes said. 'Just tell me where to look.'

'We have a physician that we use,' Madame Beaulieu said, rising to her feet. 'Molly, get dressed. I shall do the same and meet you at the front door. We shall go to see Doctor Lemaître. He looks after my girls.' She swept out of the room, and Agnes helped Molly to her feet.

'Will you help me dress?' Molly asked. 'I can't wear a corset.'

'Right you are.' Agnes turned to her crate. 'Here, this old house dress of mine will suit. I used to wear it at my last position, in London. I never left the house much.'

Molly disrobed, without shame. She winced as she lifted her arms over her head for the dress to be put on her, and Agnes had to sit at her feet and help her into her shoes. 'There you are. Perfectly respectable for a trip to the doctor.'

'Doctor Lemaître,' she said with a grimace. 'He's awful. We go to him for help keeping us out of the family way, or getting us out of the family way if we're already in it. But he's also one of our clients. He's been with all the girls here.'

Agnes hid her distaste. 'But he's still a physician, Molly. He will be able to tell if your injuries are serious. He'll stitch up your face if you need it.'

Molly smiled weakly. 'But he won't mend my heart or make me feel safe again,' she said, her voice almost a whisper. 'Lordy, Agnes. I thought I could endure anything.' She gulped, took a deep breath, then said, 'Help me down the stairs?'

Agnes did as she asked. The lights in the entranceway were lit and Madame Beaulieu was waiting. The older woman put an arm around Molly's shoulder and leaned in to kiss her forehead. She said something to her in French, in a soft, reassuring voice, and her hold of Molly was gentle.

'Good luck,' Agnes said as they left. She made her way back up the stairs and slid into her bed. She closed her eyes, but sleep wouldn't come. She kept thinking about her belongings, locked in a strongbox inside Madame Beaulieu's apartment: which was probably also locked. How she wanted to take her things and run. She'd been a fool to be here for so long. This was an awful place, where awful things happened. She had never been safe here. Tomorrow, she would retrieve her purse and be away for good.

•

Suzette woke her at dawn and shouted something at her in French. Agnes blinked into awareness. She looked across at her roommate's empty bed and said to Suzette, 'Molly?'

Suzette gave an exaggerated shrug and barked another order, then disappeared back down the stairs. Agnes rose and dressed, slipped her shoes on, and went down to start her kitchen and laundry work until Madame was awake.

She was on high alert, looking for Madame Beaulieu, eavesdropping on the other girls' conversations to hear if they mentioned Molly's name. Not that she would have been able to understand them if they had. Suzette kept her busy with cooking and cleaning until nine, then managed to say in English, 'Linen. Second floor.'

Second floor. The rooms where the girls met their clients. Agnes had not set foot on that floor yet, and she recoiled. She didn't want to see Molly's blood on the sheets. She was tired of waiting for Madame Beaulieu to appear, so, instead of stopping on the second floor, she continued to the third, and went along to the large room at the end of the corridor. She knocked briskly. Madame Beaulieu called out, '*Entrez*,' and Agnes opened the door.

'Agnes,' Madame Beaulieu said. 'Again.' She sat on the chaise drawn up under the window, where she had drawn the blind up half an inch to look into the branches of the sycamore tree outside. The rest of the curtains and blinds were drawn. Like the rest of the house, in perpetual gloom.

'I beg your pardon, Madame. But I came to ask after Molly.'

'That cad Bergeron will have to pay for everything. Molly is in the hospital,' she said, her accent intensifying and her h's disappearing as she grew angry. 'A broken rib. Doctor Lemaître has got her in with a surgeon he knows. Don't worry. You will see her again soon.'

'Actually, Madame, no. I won't. I intend to leave. My four days are up.'

'Five,' she said, with a slight smile. 'You have been here five.'

'Five, then,' Agnes said, refusing to waver from her goal. 'I have given you the agreed-upon period of service and I have decided that I do not wish to stay. If you would be so kind as to return to me my money and my papers.'

Madame Beaulieu stood slowly, and began to cross the room, her skirts rustling. 'Are you sure? I have had a very good offer for you, my English rose.'

'From whom? Nobody knows I'm here.'

'Valois.'

Agnes's skin seemed to shrink around her muscles. 'What? No. You said you wouldn't—'

'He has offered four times more than usual. You could have one hundred francs in your purse tomorrow morning when you leave.'

One hundred francs! She could rent a room for a month with that. 'No. I am leaving today. As per our agreement—'

'Our agreement that you did not honour. For you did not leave after four days.'

'You didn't ask me to.'

'The responsibility was yours. Our agreement is invalid.' She narrowed her pretty eyes. 'I could make you.'

Agnes felt fire in her veins. 'I will *never* lie with a man for money,' she spat, pulling her spine erect. She stood a full three inches taller than Madame Beaulieu and would not be intimidated into conceding to such a repugnant demand. 'Certainly never with a man like Valois. Give me my things and let me go.'

Madame Beaulieu's pretty face closed up. Her mouth a tight line, her chin set, her brow unyielding. A moment passed, and another. They glared at each other. Agnes's heart thumped with anger and fear.

Finally, Madame Beaulieu forced a little smile. 'Fine. I will get you your things. Go upstairs and pack your bag . . . your *box* . . . and I will bring you your purse.'

Agnes relaxed. 'Good. Thank you.'

Madame Beaulieu strode back to the window, and Agnes left her there, drumming her fingers on the sill in the small strip of daylight.

She was upstairs, folding her nightgown, regretting a little the loss of the house dress she had given Molly, wondering where she was going to sleep tonight, when she heard Madame Beaulieu's footsteps on the stairs. She expected next the sound of the door opening, but it did not come. Instead, there was a rattle and a clunk.

Agnes turned, her eyes on the door, fear blooming warm in her chest.

Footsteps again, this time descending.

'Madame Beaulieu!' she cried, hurrying to the door. She rattled the handle, but it was locked. 'Madame Beaulieu!' she called again. 'No! You can't lock me in! You can't do this to me! Let me go! *Let me go!*'

But Madame Beaulieu did not return.

CHAPTER 11

Agnes's over-inflated certainty that she could pick the lock led to an hour of panicked fiddling with pins, during which she cut her fingers and finally gave up and started shouting instead. Her voice grew hoarse and eventually she came to sit on her bed, fingers laced tightly together. The morning turned towards midday and the dark room became stuffy. Impulsively, she stood and opened the blind. If they saw the rule broken, the *gendarmerie* might come by and she would call out to them. She opened the window too, letting in a breeze that swished lazily in the high branches of the sycamore but didn't do much to cool the heat in her face. She thought about calling out the window, but the tea merchant was close by and she didn't want to alert Valois. The tree branches obscured her view down to the street, but she watched for hours, hoping to see somebody walk by to whom she could appeal. The street was quiet and narrow, and the solitary set of footsteps she heard belonged to somebody she couldn't see, and therefore couldn't trust. She laid her forehead on the sill and listened to her own pulse, her own breath. *What am I going to do?*

Wait until Madame Beaulieu brought her to Valois then run for her life? Madame would have already thought of that, and put some kind of measures in place, even if it involved allowing Valois himself to physically restrain her. She shuddered so violently at the thought that her teeth rattled once against each other.

Allow it to happen, take her hundred francs and forget it? No, this could not be her story. She had not come all this way, bent so many truths and worked so hard, to be forced to relinquish control of her body. The idea made her want to scream, *I am my own.*

I am my own.

What would her mother do? She thought about Genevieve, working at the tea merchant. Why had she left? Perhaps Valois had treated her despicably too. In the very moment she had the thought, she became utterly convinced of it. Of course that was what happened. She and Genevieve had a common enemy in Valois, and Agnes would make sure that he would not win with either of them.

She lifted her head and leaned out the window. The branches of the sycamore were too fine up here to hold her, but one level down she saw a sturdy branch that would take her weight. A narrow window arch jutted below her, and below that the tiny balcony on Madame Beaulieu's floor. She would be seen; no, wait. The blinds were always closed. She could do it silently, reach for the branch and, from there, shinny down the trunk, using branches for footholds.

Agnes shook herself. It was too dangerous and she would have to leave everything behind. Perhaps Madame Beaulieu would come along soon and set her free. Perhaps Molly would come home from the hospital and let herself in. Perhaps it would all work itself out sometime in the next few hours, before the evening came and her appointment with Valois became inescapable.

She sat on her bed and waited as the afternoon wound out and the shadows outside grew longer, and all the while two awful scenarios played out in her head. In one, Madame Beaulieu gave her to Valois. In the other, Agnes fell to her death escaping out the window.

One after the other, over and over. Until she made her decision. If she stayed, a night with Valois was inevitable; if she left, a fall to her death was only a possibility. She wouldn't have her belongings or her money, but she would still be able to find somebody to help her or some honest work for a bed somewhere.

Agnes went to the window. She slipped off her shoes and held them in her hand a second; she needed bare feet in order to feel her way down to the arch, but she didn't want to escape shoeless. The street was quiet; no footsteps, no traffic. Agnes cast her shoes out the window and onto the street. There. Now she had to follow.

She hoisted herself up on the windowsill and sat for a moment, feet dangling. The breeze stirred the hem of her skirts, and this made her feel inexplicably heartened. She turned from the hips, grasped the sill and let herself out the window. Her upper body still held her weight, while her feet stretched out to find the arch beneath her. Slowly, she lowered herself further, terrified of the moment when she had to shift her weight to her feet on the curve of the arch. A little further, and her shoulders began to burn. Toes extending, only finding air. She clung to the sill with her hands and the last drop to the arch made her stomach flop over. But then she was on it, her hands sliding down, finding thin purchase in the gaps between the brickwork. She stood for a moment, fingers splayed on the wall, shifting her desperate feet so they felt more secure, and trying not to feel the distance between her soft body and the hard paving stones below.

When she had found her point of balance, she slowly crouched, knees turning sideways, one hand supporting her down the wall. She half-jumped, half-slid onto the balcony below, striking her elbow hard on the railing. The thud and the clang of her landing rang out through the street. If Madame Beaulieu was nearby, she would have heard. Now, there was no time for fearfulness. Agnes climbed onto the top of the railing and reached for the branch of the sycamore tree that grew closest to the balcony. She locked both her arms around it and heaved herself onto it, desperation infusing her body with strength she didn't recognise. She held the branch and wormed her way towards the tree trunk, where she sat in a fork for half a moment assessing the other branches. Agnes was an experienced tree-climber – she had used trees to climb over Perdita Hall's wall and back many times – and she knew that the trick was to plan the route up or down. She quickly assessed the tree, then began to descend. Down, one branch to another, until she was in the lowest fork, which was still at least seven feet from the ground. She could see her shoes – one upright, one overturned – waiting for her.

The only way now was to jump. Agnes lowered herself as far as she could, arms twisted behind her still holding the branch, but then her muscles gave way suddenly and she slid and tumbled to the ground, rolling over her ankle to land on her hip, her shoulder, head striking the ground. The thud juddered up through her skeleton. The world flickered and dimmed a moment before roaring back to life. Her ears rang and her head swam, but she sat up.

'Agnes!'

Somebody was calling her from down the street. A man. Despite her grogginess, she knew to run.

But my shoes . . .

No time for shoes. She ran unevenly. The pain in her rolled ankle was excruciating but she wouldn't be caught. Not now. Footsteps behind her, gaining on her.

'Agnes, wait!'

In her addled state she couldn't place the voice. It was male; but apart from that, she was in no rational frame of mind to figure out who it was. Valois. Or perhaps it was Madame Beaulieu's crooked doctor who frightened Molly so. It didn't matter. Only escape mattered. In her tiny French vocabulary, she found the words for 'Leave me alone' and 'Help' and she yelped them to the sky before ducking down a narrow alley, only to find she was facing a dead end. Fifty feet ahead she saw a stack of old crates and she ran to them, skidded to a halt beside them and sank down to hide. The man's shadow fell ahead of him, his top hat, arms and legs grown long from the afternoon sun behind him.

'Agnes?'

Her heart thundered, her throat closed up. She was a wild animal, trapped. She looked around for a weapon she could use against him, whoever he was; found a short plank of thin wood from a broken crate. A nail stuck out the end. She clutched it in her desperate fingers.

Then he was upon her hiding place, and his face appeared. She blinked, trying to make sense of what she saw.

He held out his hand. In it, were her shoes. 'You forgot these,' he said.

'Julius!' she gasped.

•

The grim, dark rooms of Maison de Cygnes could not have been more different from Julius's rooms at Hotel Londres on Rue de Rivoli. The windows ran almost to the floor, and no blinds or curtains had been drawn to block the warm afternoon sun. It shone a healing light on everything she could see: the polished wood, the plump upholstery, the deep crimson wallpaper, and her own white ankle, which rested in Julius's firm, warm hands.

'Nothing is broken,' he declared, his fingers feeling up and down. 'Can you point your toes?'

She did as he asked, and winced.

'Turn it this way . . . good, now that way. Which hurts the most?'

185

'It all hurts,' she said.

'But which the most?' he insisted.

'That way.'

'I see. Well, it appears you have damaged some of the smaller ligaments, but it should heal in about a week with rest.' He gently lowered her leg onto a footstool and smoothed down her skirts. 'Best to keep it up and don't walk on it.'

How was she to obey that command? She had to find a job, somewhere to live, keep looking for her mother. 'But, I—'

'No,' Julius said. 'No complaining. Agnes, you climbed out of a fourth-floor window. You are lucky you didn't die.'

Heat flushed her cheeks. She wondered if Julius knew what kind of establishment Maison de Cygnes was. Of course he did. He was no fool.

'I didn't work for her,' she blurted. 'Madame Beaulieu. I mean, I did work for her, but not . . . not with the men. I cleaned things, I shifted boxes. Owt I could to keep me away from *that kind* of work.'

Julius smiled. 'Agnes, the fact that you climbed out of a fourth-floor window,' he said again. 'Only somebody who is desperate would do that. I know what you were escaping from.'

She sagged a little, feeling exposed and ashamed. 'I suppose you think me a fool.'

'That's the last thing I think of you,' he said, rising and going to the door. 'Now wait here. I will be back directly.'

He closed the door of the apartment behind him, and Agnes looked around. It was small, but the light made it feel bright and airy. Over the carved mantel hung a gigantic mirror, and from the ceiling a polished chandelier. The cornices around the ceiling were elaborately patterned, and a large, thick rug covered most of the floor. Beyond another door were, presumably, his bedroom and bathroom. She couldn't stay here with him. It wouldn't be proper, and she knew Julius worried about what was proper.

He had helped her hobble away from Rue Cousineau, then hailed down a horse and carriage travelling past. His good clothes and money convinced the owner of the carriage to help, despite Agnes's dishevelled appearance. There had been time only to speak in snatches. When she disappeared from Belgrave Place, he had deduced immediately where she had gone. As soon as he could, he had followed her and was surprised, just as she had been, not to find a house but rather a tea merchant at his last address for Genevieve. He had been back three times, and a worker there had told him about the young blonde woman who had come to ask about Genevieve. On his fourth visit, from near the tea merchant, he had seen her tumble from the tree and come after her.

That was all they had managed to exchange. Once they were in his rooms, he became the gentleman physician, dressing the graze on her elbow she didn't know she had, making certain she hadn't a concussion, and tending to her injured ankle.

Agnes wanted to go to the window and look down at the busy street, but Julius had told her to keep her leg up and so she stayed where she was. Shortly, Julius returned. He sat in the chair opposite her and placed a key on the brocade footstool next to her.

'I have rented you your own room,' he said. 'It is down one floor, and I shall take you there in a little while.'

'Oh, you mustn't go to any expense for me.'

'Nonsense. If you are who we think you are, it is only right that you stay in a good hotel.' His mouth twitched with a suppressed smile. 'Not a bordello.'

'I wouldn't have stayed there if I had any other choice,' she responded heatedly.

'Clearly,' he said. 'Now you have choice.'

Although she felt guilty, Agnes was relieved and delighted to have somewhere comfortable and safe to stay.

Julius shifted in his chair, resting his hands on the upholstered arms. 'You didn't find Genevieve, I take it? I looked for her at the tea merchant too.'

'They said she had worked there but left. My French is very bad, but one of the workers told me to look for Madame Valentine on Boulevard des Italiens. So, I've been there several times, asking at every apartment.'

'You believe this Madame Valentine knows where Genevieve is?'

'Or perhaps Madame Valentine *is* Genevieve. Perhaps she married one of the owners of the tea merchant and that is why she was working there.'

Julius drummed his fingers. 'Hm.'

Agnes waited while he turned this information over in his mind.

'Julius, why are you here?' she asked at length.

He locked his eyes on hers, and something passed between them. A charge of heat and energy that she had never felt before, as though this moment were brighter and sharper than all the moments leading up to it or away from it. Her breath caught a little in her throat.

'I came to find you,' he said tenderly. 'Marianna was worried about you.'

'Does she know why I came to Paris?'

'She has no idea. She just wants you to come back to London. I don't think you understand how fond she has become of you.'

Agnes's stomach turned over with guilt. 'I did know,' she said, 'for I was equally fond of her.'

'And yet you left?'

'I need to see Genevieve with my own eyes. I need to know her. I need to see where I fit in the world, where I belong, and she is the key. Do you not wish to find her too? She is your mother. In a sense.'

'In a sense. She was the only mother I knew until she abandoned me.' His gaze slid away from hers, and he shrugged lightly. 'Perhaps, if finding Genevieve and learning the truth is important to you, then it's important to me.' Then he straightened and leaned forward. 'I know people who might help. We will find her, but first you must rest for a few days and make sure your ankle repairs.'

We will find her.

Agnes closed her eyes and sighed heavily. She heard him stand and opened her eyes to see he was reaching his hand down to her.

'Come along,' Julius said. 'I'll show you to your room.'

It seemed almost unbearably intimate to have his arm so tightly around her as he helped her down the stairs. She insisted she could walk herself; he insisted he should carry her, and so they settled on this assisted descent. Her ankle yowled with pain. He released his grip in the long, carpeted hallway and she missed it instantly, then told herself she was being a silly fool and he was a physician and that was the only reason he held her so closely.

'Here we are, then,' he said as they arrived at the dark wooden door of her room. 'I will come to check on you tomorrow, but it's important you have a proper night's sleep. I'll have them bring you up some supper.'

He turned to go, but then turned back. 'Ah. Almost forgot.' Out of his pocket he pulled a bent envelope. 'A letter arrived for you the day after you left.'

Agnes took it, recognised Gracie's handwriting. Then she boldly grasped his wrist. Neither of them moved for a few long moments. She said, 'Thank you, Julius.'

He nodded once, then gently pulled himself from her grasp, and left.

189

Agnes fitted the key in the lock and pushed the door open. Light from the tall window hit polished objects, and she would have wept with relief, had she been the type to weep at all. So much space and air. So many soft places to sit. She hobbled directly to the window and lifted the sash, letting in the mingled odours of food and flowers and horse dung. She perched on the sill for a while watching the traffic on the street below, relishing the stark contrast to her accommodations just this morning. Then she made her way back towards the large, soft brass bed and eased herself down among the pillows to open the letter.

> *Dear Agnes,*
> *You will be angry but please don't be too angry. I know you said that Cole Briar was no good and I should not see him any more but really he is not as bad as you say. He says he loves me and I know I do love him. You never knew becos he was always mithering you and I never said, but I alwus liked him. Don't bother writting back, not to this address, Agnes, becos I am going to be like you and run away from Yorkshire! It's true! Cole has received an offer of a job in India where he will make lots of money so I am going with him to Calcutta! By the time you receeve this I will already be on my way. I wish I could see your face when you read this and no weather you are happy for me or angry with me. Please don't be angry, Agnes. I will send you a letter the minit we are in our new town and maybe even one day you will come and see me. We are named after ships, Agnes. It is time we got upon them!*
>
> *With much love and exitment,*
> *Gracie Badger*

Agnes flung the letter away from her in frustration. Running away to India with Cole Briar? Agnes should never have left her behind. Agnes didn't like to acknowledge it, but she had always suspected that Gracie was a touch simple. It was just like that slippery eel Cole to convince her to do something foolish. Agnes sighed. Perhaps her own journey was foolish, too. She was just more capable of fending for herself than Gracie ever could be.

She lay a while thinking about Gracie, about how far she would travel, and her mind filled with pictures of warm skies and wide seas. She didn't intend to but, while the sun was falling close to the horizon, she fell into a deep sleep. If somebody came with her supper, she didn't hear them.

•

In the morning, when a bright wedge of yellow light fell into the room, a maid in a white apron bustled in. She carried a silver tray, which she set down on the end of Agnes's bed, where Agnes lay reading. On it was an enormous breakfast of pastries and meats, with a steaming pot of what smelled like coffee.

'Thank you,' Agnes said, arranging herself so she was sitting.

The maid spoke to her in French and Agnes shook her head.

'Sorry, I don't understand . . .'

'Meester Julius says me not to get you out of bed. He leaves you a letter.' She tapped a folded note on the tray, then backed out and left the room.

Agnes flipped back the covers and stretched out towards the tray, bringing it back to sit on her lap. She unfolded the letter.

Agnes, I have some business to attend to. Stay in your room and rest. I will see you before lunch. Julius.

She admired his handwriting, the loops and the lines flowed tidily but with flair. There was so much about him to admire, and she told herself she ought to stop it immediately. Putting aside the letter, she fell on the food.

As the morning went by, servants came and attended to her. One to collect the tray, another to bring her the English newspapers, another to help her dress and fix her hair, another to make the bed and clean the little bathroom. She had nothing to do except rest – a pale bruise had started to spread from her ankle bone – and read. She imagined what she might be doing if she was still at Maison de Cygnes, then decided she wouldn't imagine that ever again. That book was closed. She felt a twinge thinking about Molly, but then told herself Molly was surely sensible enough to get herself out of the bordello now she had been injured by one of the gentlemen.

Gentlemen. A rather loose application of the word.

Julius came, as promised, just before noon. He knocked and opened the door, but had his hand theatrically over his eyes. 'Do forgive me just barging in, Agnes,' he said. 'Are you fit for company?'

Agnes laughed. 'As you see,' she said, and he uncovered his eyes.

'I didn't want you to have to walk on that ankle to open the door,' he explained. 'May I see how it looks?'

Agnes nodded, and he approached the chaise on which she sat, under the window. He sat beside her ankle, slipped her shoe off, and inched up the hem of her skirt. Agnes's heart thudded a little harder, and her skin felt warmer than usual. She pointedly turned away, her gaze going to the window. Across the street was another building, and she traced the lines of the wrought-iron balconies with her eyes, while Julius's firm hands gently manipulated her joint.

'That bruise is not too bad,' he said. 'The swelling has definitely subsided. I think we will have you up and about in a few days.' He smoothed her skirt and she bent to re-shoe herself, feeling the loss of his touch.

'I can't suppose upon your generosity for so long,' she said. 'I should look after myself.'

'With what?' he said with a smile. 'I've been to see your Madame Beaulieu this morning and have in my rooms a fruit crate with your belongings in it, yes including your purse. I didn't need to open it to hear there are no coins in it.'

'Then she has taken my last few francs.'

'It would seem so, Agnes. I will bring your clothes to you later, but I have also drawn in a favour from the wife of an old friend, who will come to see you this week and make you some new clothes.'

'You cannot—'

'I can and I will. Agnes, if you are right and we are family, I cannot leave you to fend for yourself. If you are wrong about Genevieve, then helping you is a small price to pay for doing the right thing, as a gentleman should do. Please, no more protests. You are staying here until you are well.'

'And after that?'

'We go to find Genevieve. Together. My same old friend is already asking about this mysterious Madame Valentine on Boulevard des Italiens. By the time your ankle is healed, we should have an address to visit.'

'You would come with me?'

'I'll have to.' His jaw twitched with repressed amusement. 'Your French is . . .'

'I know,' she said, laughing. 'It's abominable.'

'I'd never heard French spoken with a Yorkshire accent before yesterday,' he said, smiling at her fondly. 'What *were* you shouting at me?'

'Leave me alone,' she said. 'One of the girls taught me some French.'

His face grew serious. 'What an awful place that was, Agnes. How fortunate I found you.'

'I saved myself,' she reminded him. 'I would have survived one way or another.'

Julius locked his gaze on hers. The sun found ginger highlights in his sideburns, and she could see faint stubble on his jawline 'I believe you, Agnes, for you do seem a little invincible to me.' He patted her knee. 'I should leave you to rest.'

'No, stay,' she said impulsively. 'Perhaps we can share our lunch and you can tell me what Marianna has been doing. I miss her.'

He wavered a moment, and Agnes knew he was battling between what was proper, and what was pleasant. Perhaps being in Paris helped him decide. 'Very well,' he said. 'I'll have a tray sent up.'

Despite the pain and bruising in her ankle, Agnes enjoyed the next few days more than any since she'd left Perdita Hall. A dressmaker came and took her measurements and asked her to choose fabrics. With Julius's urging, she chose gorgeous colours and textures, and awaited her first fitting. He arrived, too, with the gift of two proper leather trunks with handles. In the larger one, he had tipped all her belongings from the old crate. 'That horrid thing, I asked to have burned,' he told her. She spent her mornings reading, then took lunch with Julius, falling into long conversations with him. They always started with Marianna, then ranged out across topics from family to religion to history and the stars. She told him a little about growing up at Perdita Hall, how she had been saved from material poverty but had emotional poverty in its place, and how Gracie Badger had always been the sister of her heart, the only person she had loved and who had loved her in all her life. Julius told her how he had left the hospital, how the suffering of the little ones had become too much for him, and his great shame at not being stronger because he knew that they needed him. He now wondered if he even wanted to be a physician at all. More than once, they were still talking at supper time, though Julius never stayed for supper or into the evening. On the Monday following her escape from the bordello, when she was able to walk without much pain, Julius came to her room with a grin on his face.

'I have an address,' he said simply, as she opened the door to him.

'An address?'

'Madame Valentine.'

'Is it Genevieve?'

194

'I don't know. I have the address secondhand from a member of the *gendarmerie* who is familiar with her. The only way to know is to go and knock on the door, I expect.'

Agnes's excitement rose, like fizzing bubbles in her blood. 'Can we go now?'

Julius shook his head. 'Tomorrow, Agnes. I wanted you to rest for a few more days, but I can see I won't be able to keep you still much longer. But tomorrow, I promise you, I will take you there.'

•

Agnes wore the Sunday dress she had bought while working for Marianna; the pale blue cotton with the white buttons and collar. If she was about to meet her mother, she wanted to look neither drab nor showy (not that she had much to wear that was showy). Julius blanched at her suggestion that they walk to Boulevard des Italiens, telling her that her ankle would swell up and then take even longer to heal. Instead, she was able to experience the noise and colour of the wide boulevards of Paris from the inside of a well-appointed carriage. While Julius paid the driver, Agnes stood in front of the building where Madame Valentine lived. Grey clouds covered the sun and a rough wind, laden with the scent of coming rain, shook the branches of the sycamores, dislodging a few tired leaves and sending them spinning down the street.

Julius joined her and took her elbow. 'Are you ready?'

'Aye,' Agnes said.

They stepped inside the building and were halfway across the parquetry floor to the staircase when an elderly woman emerged from a ground-floor room and accosted them with a sharp phrase of French.

Julius glanced at Agnes. 'The concierge,' he said. 'Let me take care of it.'

Julius applied a smile and, in mellifluous French, addressed the concierge. Agnes had no idea what he was saying, but heard the words, 'Madame Valentine'.

The concierge did not respond to his smile or his pleasantness, and returned fire with more sharp words.

Julius turned to Agnes. 'She says we cannot simply walk up and see Madame Valentine without invitation. We can leave a message with the concierge and hope that Madame Valentine responds.'

'Ask her if Madame Valentine's name is Genevieve.'

Julius turned to the concierge and asked the question in French. He was met with glaring silence.

'I don't think she's going to tell us that, Agnes,' Julius said.

Agnes sighed. This morning she had been so sure that today would be the day. She'd felt her hope all through her body, like some golden liquid making her shine from within. But now she felt like the sky outside. Clouded. Cold. 'Leave a message then,' she said. 'Tell her it's urgent we speak with her.'

Julius nodded, then gave his name and address. As Agnes noticed the concierge neither write it down nor even repeat it back, she began to think of other ways she could contact Madame Valentine.

The door opened and a fist of cold air entered the building. A dark-haired woman of about forty came in, pulling off her gloves. She greeted the concierge in French, but her accent was decidedly English. Agnes noticed the concierge's gaze flick from the woman to Julius and back again, and instantly knew that this was the woman they sought.

It was not Genevieve.

'Are you Madame Valentine?' Agnes asked.

Madame Valentine, whose foot was on the bottom stair, paused and turned around. 'Yes. Who are you?'

The concierge began to speak, but Agnes spoke over the top of her. 'I am Agnes Resolute, and I am looking for Genevieve Breckby. Do you know where she is?'

The woman's face crumpled with fury. Her dark eyes narrowed, and she managed to spit, 'Yes, I know where she is.'

'Would you be able to tell us?' Julius asked. 'We are her . . . children. We have lost her.'

'And you should be glad for it. I'll tell you where she is: she's with my husband.'

The concierge grasped Julius by the shoulder and turned him towards the door, shouting at him.

'Please,' Agnes said, pulse thick in her throat. 'Can you not give me an address? I would do anything to find her.'

But Madame Valentine was stomping up the stairs, and the concierge was wrestling Julius towards the doorway.

Genevieve had once more slipped beyond her reach.

CHAPTER 12

Agnes had walked past the Parisian cafes many times and longed to sit at one of the outside tables with coffee and cake. Today, however, the rain was setting in and she and Julius found themselves jammed in a cramped back corner of a cafe, surrounded by the smell of damp coats and cigar smoke.

Agnes sipped her coffee disconsolately. A slice of some sticky delight with pastry and icing sat in front of her untouched.

'I know you're disappointed,' Julius said, not for the first time.

'Why must Madame Valentine be so cruel? Why could she not just tell us where Genevieve is?' Agnes mused, also not for the first time.

Julius's hand reached across and stopped her fingers from drumming the tabletop. 'Take heart. I gave the concierge our address at Hotel Londres. Madame Valentine may soften her view and contact us.'

Agnes felt this possibility so unlikely that her disappointment was fresh and sharp again. She withdrew her hand from under

Julius's, irritated with him for being so naïve. 'She is not going to contact us.'

'One never knows.'

Agnes was also disappointed that Genevieve's list of sins was growing. Along with abandoning children – both Agnes and Julius – she also, apparently, stole other women's husbands. 'Julius,' she said impulsively, 'tell me something nice about Genevieve. Something good that she did.'

'Well, she took me in when her friend died.'

'Yes, yes, but I mean a memory you have of her that is good. Something specific.'

Julius steepled his fingers and rested them against his chin for a moment, thinking. Then he said, 'She sang to me every night before I went to sleep. Old folk songs she had learned when she was a child.'

'Anything else?'

He furrowed his brow, then said, 'When I was eight or nine, I fell out of a tree in our garden.'

'At Belgrave Place?' Agnes remembered no trees big enough to climb in the garden there.

'Yes, there was an old ash tree there at the time. I wasn't allowed to climb it, but climb it I did. When I fell, I was sure I'd be for it. Genevieve couldn't bear it when I disobeyed her, and would sometimes not speak to me for days if I was naughty.'

'Julius,' Agnes said lightly, 'something nice, remember? Something good?'

He smiled. 'Of course. That day, when I fell from the tree, I tried not to cry, so she wouldn't hear me and tell me off. But I was just a little boy and so I did cry, and my nurse came and she saw that I had cut my knees, so she called for Genevieve, which made me cry harder and louder. By the time she arrived in the garden, I was utterly undone. Sobbing and shouting not to tell Genevieve and that I was sorry and wouldn't do it again.' He dropped his eyes, picked up a fork and prodded his cake, but didn't eat any. 'Genevieve was not at all angry,' he continued. 'She put her arm around me and sat me up, and used her sleeve to wipe my face and she began to sing.' He shook his head, almost as though he were disbelieving of his own story. 'It was like a siren's song. I was mesmerised by it, and my tears dried and my heart found its own rhythm again. Once I had stopped crying, she handed me back to my nurse and told her to take me to Doctor Farraday to clean up my knees. Within a week, she'd had the tree cut down. I always thought she did that to protect me.'

'I reckon she did at that,' Agnes said.

He shrugged. 'Perhaps she did it so I wouldn't climb it again and cause her so much trouble.'

'No, she loved you. In her way. She's an unconventional woman, isn't she?'

'That's one way of saying it.'

Agnes reminded herself that Julius's views were conservative and proper, and didn't find him wanting for it. He had a strong moral compass and there was a nobility in that; for all that he espoused the views of his class and sex, he had been kind to her and didn't judge her.

'Will you go back to London now?' Agnes asked.

'Will you come with me?'

Agnes shook her head. 'Not yet.'

He sighed, shifted in his seat. 'I suppose we have to wait for the dressmaker to come back anyway. Shall we stay another week? Then I should get back to Marianna, and decide what it is I'm going to do with my life.'

Agnes didn't answer. She did not want to commit to a time to leave. Julius spoke as though it would be the easiest thing in the world for her to return to London, to tend to Marianna and sew his long johns. To be circumscribed by the walls of the house and the garden for the rest of her life. No, there was more ahead for her yet. She knew it.

Instead, she said to him, 'When you told Madame Valentine we were Genevieve's children . . .'

'Yes?' he said, after she had paused for a few moments.

'Why, she will think we are siblings.'

'I suppose so. That is the usual way of things. As you said, though, Genevieve is unconventional.'

She held his gaze for a little while then said, 'Do you think of me as you would think of a sister?'

'I . . .' Words eluded him. His face grew pink.

Agnes almost laughed. 'No, then?'

Julius recovered his composure. 'You are dear to Marianna and always welcome in our home,' he said. 'In that sense, you are like family to me. To us.' Again, his hand stole across to cover hers and this time she allowed it to rest there. 'I know you think you want to meet Genevieve. I know you think that she will unlock for you the mysteries of your own heart, your own place in the world. Where you belong, as you say.'

Agnes felt her heart pierced by his acute knowledge of her.

'But Agnes, what if where you belong is somewhere you've already been and left behind?'

Agnes twisted her wrist so her hand faced up, then Julius locked his fingers between hers and squeezed firmly. 'It is for me to say where I belong, Julius,' she said. 'I still want to find Genevieve.'

He nodded. 'I understand, and I will help if I can. We may yet hear from Madame Valentine. We will wait, and we will see.'

Agnes smiled at him, because he was lovely and with her hand in his she felt a strange sort of shifting feeling that was both pleasant and full of promise.

But she didn't tell him that she wasn't the type of woman to wait and see.

•

The rain set in. Agnes had only ever experienced Paris under a blue summer sky, but now that the grey clouds hung low, the city seemed crowded and suffocating. She was glad to return to her room at Hotel Londres, where she spent the afternoon thinking about ways she could make Madame Valentine tell her where Genevieve was. After supper with Julius, she read – a supernatural tale by Mrs Oliphant that Julius had bought for her – until her eyes felt heavy, then extinguished her lamp.

Sleep would not come. Her thoughts chased themselves through the alleyways of her brain. She would doze and then start, doze and start, until finally, after midnight, she found herself wide awake, listening to the rain hammer on the window.

Agnes rose, pulled on her robe, and drew the curtain to look down on the street. The insistent traffic had stopped. The bars and dance halls were all closed. Gas lamps shone in puddles. The whole city was asleep. She thought of Julius, sleeping in the room upstairs; of Molly, sleeping somewhere in a hospital; Madame Valentine, sleeping in her apartment on Boulevard des Italiens. All of them asleep, while she was awake with a raging brain.

The concierge. The concierge at Madame Valentine's apartment was also asleep. A plan began to form.

Agnes dressed and pulled on her shoes. The opening and closing of the door to her room seemed impossibly loud in the dark hallway, amplified by her apprehension. She made her way down the stairs and across the chequerboard floor of the foyer, then out into the rainy Paris night.

She had been so fixated on leaving that she had brought no umbrella; in fact, she didn't own one. The last umbrella she'd had was the ragged one Julius had lent her, and she wasn't about to alert him to her need for one now. Rather, she decided that the empty wet streets would work in her favour. A pair of drunk, laughing men stumbled past, but otherwise the rain had kept everyone inside. Even the street-sweeping machine sat, without horse and rider, on the side of the road. Agnes ducked under trees and overhangs where she could, but was soon thoroughly wet. A trickle ran down the back of her collar and her shoes squelched in puddles. The discomfort would be worth it. She could sneak right past the concierge, wake up Madame Valentine and refuse to leave until she told Agnes where Genevieve had gone. Agnes didn't think too closely about the details. Details were for the timid. She marched on. In the distance, she heard a bell strike three. Apart from that, the city was so quiet that she could hear the hollow hiss of the lamps that lit her way.

Up ahead on the corner, she saw a man, standing like a statue under the awning of a shop. She hesitated, dropped back. From his outline, including his large cavalry sword, she identified him as a member of the *gendarmerie*. Agnes crossed the street and ducked through an alley to avoid him. She arrived on a wide boulevard with shops lit from inside. She passed a jeweller and a dry-goods store, a book binder and a seamstress. Then finally found herself on Boulevard des Italiens. The rain thinned a little, and she palmed water off her face. She made her way down to Madame Valentine's apartment building and reached for one of the handles on the big double doors.

They were locked. Of course.

Agnes wanted to kick herself. How had she been so naïve as to think that people's houses would be open at three in the morning? If she rang the bell, she would wake the concierge, and get no closer to Madame Valentine.

She backed up and stopped beneath the same tree she had stood under earlier that day, looking up. Which window was Madame Valentine's?

She counted the floors. Flat three was surely the third one. She bent to the ground and scooped up a pebble, aimed and flung it at the window. It fell well short, bouncing off the brickwork on the second floor.

Agnes glanced around. A vendor's cart was parked nearby. It rested on a slant, its high roof at an angle. But still . . . Agnes found a handful of pebbles then climbed up the running board of the cart. Her ankle twinged, so she found her balance before climbing onto the cart's roof. She planted her feet wide and counted the windows again. When she was certain she had found one that was Madame Valentine's, she began pelting it with pebbles. The first two missed, but three and four found their mark. She waited. Nothing. More pebbles. Five, six, seven.

A light went on. Agnes tossed another pebble, just to be sure. It bounced off the wall and clattered softly to the footpath. The window opened and Madame Valentine leaned out.

'You?' she said. 'Go away. I'll send for the police.'

'Tell me where Genevieve is,' Agnes called up to her.

'Be quiet. You'll wake my daughter. Go away.'

'I won't go away. I'll stay and I'll make more noise. All you have to do is tell me where—'

'Sh!' she hissed. Then, 'You're soaked.'

'I need to know where she is.'

Agnes could not see her face clearly, but detected a change in her posture; she was thinking about capitulating. A moment passed. Another.

'Wait there. I'm coming,' she said. The window closed.

Agnes gingerly climbed down from the vendor's cart and waited at the door to the apartment building. It seemed to take a long time and she was considering pelting all the other windows with stones when she heard the lock clunk. The doors opened, and Madame Valentine stood there in a dressing gown, a lamp in her hand. 'Come in, then,' she said. 'What was your name again?'

'Agnes.'

'How old are you?'

'Nineteen, ma'am.'

'Who wasn't a fool at nineteen, I suppose,' Madame Valentine muttered, leading her up the wrought-iron stairs, Agnes dripping all the way. She pushed open a door on the third floor and let Agnes in ahead of her.

While Madame Valentine placed her lamp on a side table, Agnes looked around. The room was tidy, but gloomy and small. The rug was thin, the upholstery worn, the brass unpolished. It spoke of a family that had fallen on hard times. Madame Valentine gestured Agnes to a small sofa, then sat next to her, pulling her dressing gown tight over her chest and holding the collar together.

'Thank you, Madame Valentine,' Agnes said. She was damp and cold, but excited.

'My name is Rashmi. That is what you should call me.'

Agnes nodded.

'So, you insist on knowing where your mother is?' Rashmi asked.

'Aye, I do. I've met her but once, and she didn't know me. We are . . . estranged. It is my dearest wish to know her.'

'You have heard the expression, "Be careful what you wish for"?'

Agnes nodded. 'I have.'

'If you want me to tell you where Genevieve is, first you must allow me to tell you *who* she is.'

Agnes tried not to sigh or show impatience. 'Certainly. If you feel you must.'

'Well, you are a most demanding girl. There is no doubt you are related to her.'

Agnes could not repress a small shine of pride.

At that moment a door opened, and a girl emerged, rubbing her eyes. She had dark hair like her mother, but pale, milky skin. Agnes guessed her to be about twelve.

'Mama?' she said.

'Go back to bed, darling. I have to talk to this lady, but she will be gone before you wake up.'

The girl looked at Agnes. Agnes remembered being twelve, in a body that grew in all directions at once, and she smiled gently at the girl. 'I promise I won't stay long,' she said.

Rashmi rose and put an arm around the girl's shoulders, said a few quiet words to her, and then dispatched her to her bedroom before rejoining Agnes on the sofa.

'Are you ready?'

Agnes nodded.

Rashmi turned her eyes towards the lamp and began. 'My family have been tea merchants for eighty years. My mother was born in Darjeeling but I was born in London, to an English father. Like you, I never knew my mother. She died while giving birth to me. I was the only child of the marriage and my father was very protective of me. He did not remarry, and he made certain I had the best of everything, and that included finding me the best husband when I turned twenty. One of his colleagues had a son, Saul. Saul Valentine. We were married a week after my twenty-first birthday. He and my father immediately began to do business: Saul believed that Ceylon could be as good a producer of tea as India. Up in the highlands, where it is cool and rainy. Father invested money in Saul to travel and plant tea. He bought land in the Kandy district – just twenty acres – and built a factory. At first, nobody believed he would succeed. Ceylon was for cinnamon, India for tea. But within two years his first export arrived in London: one hundred pounds of Ceylon tea. He bought more land, grew more tea. Others were quick to move in and plant tea as well, but Valentine Tea enjoyed five good years. We did very well.

'I didn't see him, of course. He was always in Ceylon. He had a house at the plantation, another in Colombo. I asked to travel with him, but he always said no. I did love him, in my own way. I saw so little of him that I built in my imagination a version of him that perhaps was not quite true. Hardworking, committed, loyal. He was none of those things, really. We saw each other so rarely that it took six years before our daughter came along. When she was born, he stayed home for six whole months. I thought perhaps it was to be with us, but I see now that this was the time when his business fell apart. I lost my father that year and I was always grateful that he didn't live to be ruined by Saul's business dealings.' Rashmi, who had been looking away the whole time, now shifted on the sofa and turned her gaze towards Agnes. 'My poor father. Did you know your father, Agnes?'

'No. And while I've wondered, I have no image of him in my mind to pin my dreams on,' Agnes said.

'I have no doubt Genevieve might have known many men. I wonder if your father is Saul. There is nothing of him in your countenance. I suppose if you meet her you can ask her. She doesn't strike me as the type to mind if she's exposed as a woman who has loved many.

'In any case, back to my story. There were many debtors after us in London, and that's when Saul took up with Valois, who's a cad.'

Agnes nodded vigorously. 'Oh yes. I have met him.'

'I am still not sure quite how Saul got into so much trouble with money, but I assume it was a combination of poor management, bad speculation, and the fact that he couldn't be sober for more than a few hours at a time. If there was claret nearby, Saul didn't stop drinking until it was gone.

207

'We moved to Paris. Saul bought us a beautiful apartment and I convinced myself we would be happy. He continued to travel and Valois built the other end of the business here. We sold tea to a few of the big hotels in the city and things went well for a while. I was in the store with my daughter several days a week, doing what I could to reduce our costs. I helped weigh the tea and package it, read over invoices and so on. Then Saul returned from a trip to London and said we needed to hire more staff so I could return to raising our child. That's when Genevieve started working for us.

'I had no idea then who she was. She certainly didn't present as a woman who came from a noble family. She had no airs and graces, and she worked hard. Very hard. She became indispensable very quickly. She visited all the hotels and charmed the management sufficiently that they began to order from us, or increased their existing orders. Valois had installed her in an apartment on Rue du Temple and in four months we became the most successful tea merchant in Paris. Genevieve ruled everyone with an iron will. The staff despised her, but my word she got results. When Saul was home, he couldn't stop talking about her. He stayed late at work with her in business discussions. Or so he said.' She pursed her lips and fell silent for a moment, then continued.

'In fact, he had known Genevieve for years. At least since around the time our daughter was born. I have no clue when their acquaintance warmed from friendship to love, but hiring her to work at Valentine and Valois was not a business decision, for all that it turned out to be good for our business.

'I was blissful in my ignorance. I only rarely went to the store because I despised Valois so much. When I went there, Genevieve was sickeningly nice to me. For a while, she came by my house a few nights a week when Saul was away. I found her odd, but endured her company because of her importance to our business. She ate dinner with us, and sometimes played with my daughter, who adored her of course. Genevieve was beautiful and fair and *shone* somehow, as though the rest of us were all a little dull and lightless by comparison. But I knew her niceties were not her real self, because I knew how she treated the other staff at the store, and I heard how sharply she spoke to my servants, even the nurse who was the sweetest, warmest woman one could know. I sensed there was a cruel edge to Genevieve, and I still do not know what those regular visits were about, unless they were a way of being in Saul's life while he was far away.' Here she sighed and paused for a little while. The rain outside was easing, but Agnes was still very damp and cold, and she willed Rashmi to keep going.

'She was in my house, in my life, in my daughter's life,' Rashmi said. 'I feel as though she has been everywhere that was precious and private to me. But soon enough, she disappeared for a long time. I did not know why and nor did I ask. I assumed she was gone forever and for that I was a little relieved.' Rashmi shrugged. 'Fool that I was. Eight months later, Saul returned from Ceylon and I overheard him mention Genevieve to Valois. He had taken her there! She was turning her iron will to the business in Kandy, but this time it wasn't working quite as well. Saul had been insightful enough to take the risk on growing tea in Ceylon, but his success had inspired many, many others. He had to share the market.

'I had to live with the knowledge that when my husband went overseas, he was spending his time with her. When he was in Paris, he became distant from me. I would find him sitting in the armchair by the fire, a faraway look in his eye, and I knew he was thinking of her and not me.

'I saw Genevieve only once or twice after that. She stayed well clear of me. No more visits. Things went downhill rapidly. Saul had invested in a tea plantation in another part of Ceylon but it didn't produce anywhere near enough tea to cover its costs. He began to sell things, including our beautiful apartment. The day

I moved in here, he promised me it wouldn't be forever. I rather suspect I am going to be here forever now, because my husband is gone and I guarantee you Genevieve is with him. The business continues to limp along, and Valois sends me a little money every week and for that I stay in Paris. But we do not live as we once did, and none of my family back in England will help. They are all angry that so much of my father's money was sunk into Saul's businesses, and that Saul mismanaged it so badly.' She spread her hands, and her voice was weary. 'What am I to do? I have a daughter to introduce to the world, but I am too far from anyone who can help us find her a husband, and too poor to make her attractive anyway. I rather fear she will have to work for her living. She is so young and so tender, and I despair for her future.

'Not that Genevieve ever thought about my daughter's future. She simply took what she wanted. That is the kind of woman she is.'

Rashmi paused here and Agnes took a few moments to let the details sink in, forming her own opinions in the shadow of Rashmi's. Finally, she said, 'Where is she now?'

'So, I have not convinced you that you are better off without her in your life?'

Agnes shook her head.

'Very well,' Rashmi said. 'She is in Ceylon. Either at the plantation at Kandy, or in the house in Colombo. I can give you the addresses.'

Agnes's heart sank. She had feared this answer. 'So, she is not in Paris?'

'She wouldn't dare show her face here again, just as Saul hasn't in several years. I imagine they are living a merry life over there, and good luck to them. No, she is not in Paris.' Rashmi smiled bitterly. 'How far are you prepared to go to find her?'

CHAPTER 13

How far are you prepared to go to find her?

Agnes turned this question over and over in her mind as she lay in her bed. She had peeled off her wet clothes and drawn on a dry nightdress, but she still felt cold and shivery in her belly. The rain eased and light began to glow from beyond the window, and she considered her answer.

Her heart leapt to say, *Any distance!* To tell her that even meek and simple Gracie Badger was in Calcutta. But she was also full of doubt. Gracie had Cole to provide for her and protect her, but such a distant journey alone might be too risky for Agnes. So far she had been from York to London and then to Paris and, if she were honest, had barely survived it. How was she to find a passage to the warm middle of the world? How was she to feed herself and shelter herself if she got there? And if she did all this, and still didn't find Genevieve, what then?

Genevieve. With every story told to her, Agnes's picture of her mother became more detailed. Rashmi had no kind words to say about Genevieve, of course, but why would she? She believed that Genevieve had destroyed her marriage, when it was clear her wretched husband was to blame. He had borrowed too much money, he drank too much claret, he treated the world as though it were his and had been ruined when he found it wasn't. Was it not always the way, that the woman was to blame for the particular, even when it was evident the man was responsible for the whole?

In fact, Genevieve's story rose in the cracks of Rashmi's account. Having run away from London and her oppressive husband, she had found work with a tea merchant and turned around their fortunes, tried to be a good companion to her employer's wife and child, travelled across the seas to use her mind and her will in the public world – as women were so rarely allowed to do – and perhaps she did fall in love with Saul Valentine, but surely a heart could not be turned that was not already turning away. Perhaps it was more than business that kept Saul apart from Rashmi.

Once again, beneath the condemnations of Genevieve, Agnes found small truths that indicated some good in her mother; larger truths that indicated Genevieve resisted every attempt to shape and control her. Whatever else happened, it seemed, Genevieve remained Genevieve. That was something worth admiring. Poor Marianna, whose life had been the opposite: shut in deeper and deeper, while Genevieve's life expanded.

Agnes closed her eyes and thought about Ceylon. All she knew about it she had learned in her lessons at Perdita Hall. Cinnamon and snakes.

She drifted off as the sun moved into the sky.

•

At mid-morning, the little grey-haired dressmaker who had helped her choose fabrics flounced in with an armful of dresses.

'Mademoiselle Agnes,' she said. 'Are you ready?'

212

Until lunchtime, Agnes tried on dresses and allowed the dressmaker to gather and pin while she stood, still as a statue. Her other troubles were temporarily forgotten in her luxurious immersion in silk, satin and lace. One was a red silk basque that sat long over a frilly white underskirt; another, a pale pink taffeta and lace with a narrow skirt to be worn over a frilled bustle; and yet another, a striped grey-and-black travel dress. There were dresses for the house and one startling sapphire blue evening gown that sat just on the edge of her shoulders and gathered there with bows and lace, with a train gathered in soft folds that fell gently behind her. There were also bonnets and gloves and even pairs of shoes to choose from. The dressmaker pulled petticoats and dresses off and on Agnes, tutting and muttering in French. She left four of the dresses behind, declaring they were a 'perfect fit', and said she would have the rest to Agnes by the end of the week.

Alone at last, Agnes wriggled into a soft blue summer dress of Czech silk and cotton. Her own dresses had been plain and cheaply made; now she could feel the weight of good fabric, and could appreciate the tiny, neat stitching. She walked from one side of the room to the other, noticing her ankle felt much worse after her night-time outing and clambering, and wondered if she looked as elegant as she felt. When Julius sent a message for her that afternoon, asking her to dress for an evening out in Paris, she lovingly withdrew the sapphire gown from the wardrobe.

•

As Julius handed her up into the carriage that evening, he noticed her favouring her ankle.

'What have you done?' he asked, somewhere between irritation and fondness.

'It's a little swollen again. Aye, don't look so mithered.'

'I'm not mithered. At least I don't think so as I'm not sure what it means.' He climbed into the carriage and sat next to her. 'Do you want me to examine it?'

'You can hardly do that in an open carriage in the middle of traffic,' she laughed, batting him with her fan. 'Besides, I was rather hoping you'd notice my bonny new gown rather than my wobbly ankle.'

The carriage jolted forward and joined the traffic on the wide boulevard. Julius met her gaze evenly. 'Of course I noticed,' he said. 'But I hadn't words to express how beautiful you look in it.'

Agnes glanced away, hiding a smile.

The rain had cleared and the streets of Paris were bursting. The long summer evening was not yet growing dark.

'Where are we going?' she asked Julius.

'To an early performance of the opera, and then to dinner. I trust you are happy with that?'

'I've never seen an opera,' she said.

'Then I am very pleased to be the man who opens a door to that world for you,' he said.

They made their way through the streets of Paris, down boulevards, past shops and cafes and hotels. Eventually, they arrived outside a theatre in the second arrondissement, and Julius helped her down, taking care with her injured ankle. They joined a queue of well-dressed folk, slowly making their way under a huge arch and into the building. Julius guided her with his hand on her elbow, towards a set of stairs. 'Up here,' he said. 'The pit is no place for a lady.'

The foyer of the theatre was dim, brass fittings gleaming softly in the lamp-light. They queued again through another door, and then were inside the theatre itself.

Agnes gasped. The vaulted ceiling was the colour of cream, and covered in patterns of gold. They were on the topmost level of the theatre, and Agnes could see down over layers of balconies, each decorated in gold carvings, all the way to the pit at the bottom. She took her seat, soft and richly upholstered in crimson fabric, and gazed at the decoration over the proscenium arch. An angel either side, perhaps ten feet tall with wings spread, appeared to hold up part of the arch. Between them a curtain of richly embroidered gold fell to the stage floor. Gas lamps lit each balcony, glowing against the deep red wallpaper. She felt very small in comparison to such grandeur, but it wasn't an unpleasant feeling. Rather, she was glad that such things existed in the world.

'I have never seen such a beautiful thing,' she said to Julius.

'Wait until you've seen the opera,' he replied. 'Even more sublime than the view.'

But the opera was the least interesting thing about her visit to the theatre. Agnes quite liked the costumes, but could hardly bear the warbling voices and the deafening crescendos. She spent most of the performance looking at other people in the other stalls, imagining who they might be and what they might do. Julius clearly loved the music. His eyes shone as he glanced from the stage to her and back again. At one point, during a slow melodious song, he reached for her wrist and lay his fingers there a moment, a look of transport on his face. The hot touch of his skin against hers transported her too, but for different reasons. She might have sat like that forever, but then her belly started to rumble with hunger and although she felt the cold on her wrist when he withdrew his hand, she was glad that the opera was over.

They queued again to leave, but not for long, because patrons of the upper levels were allowed to leave first. They emerged into the fresh air and evening dark. All the gas lamps were lit, and the streets were nearly as bright as day. Agnes could smell food cooking, and swallowed hard over her hunger.

'Is it far to where we are going to eat?' she asked.

Julius pointed across the road. 'Just over there,' he said. 'Do you think you will survive it?'

'Perhaps,' she said, smiling.

They waited for a break in the traffic then picked their way across the road, and opened the door to a restaurant with high ceilings and walls covered in pretty murals. A small counter stood near the entryway, with a lamp glowing brightly on top. Here, a gentleman greeted Julius in French and then showed them to a table near the back corner of the room. Here it was a little dimmer and quieter. Agnes took the seat against the wall, on a long upholstered bench, and Julius sat opposite on a chair. A waiter came for their order, and Agnes allowed Julius to order for her. Her French was so bad she had no idea what was on offer anyway.

They talked about the opera and the theatre, and about Paris and how different and shining and merry it was, compared to London. Their food arrived and Agnes tasted the most tender beef she had ever eaten. They were brought a bottle of wine, and Julius was astonished that Agnes had never tasted it. After her first sip she was quite happy to keep it that way.

Finally, they left the restaurant and climbed into their waiting carriage.

'I propose a carriage ride around Paris by gas-light,' Julius said as they settled next to each other. 'I would have suggested a walk, but your ankle is clearly in need of more rest.' He leaned forward and told the driver to drive on, then returned his attention to Agnes. 'You haven't told me how you hurt it again.'

'Ah, well,' said Agnes. 'I didn't want to worry you.'

'I understand you well enough to know that to care for you is to worry about you,' he said.

Agnes turned his words over in her head. *To care for you. To care for you.* She had known, of course, but to have him state it so boldly gave her a sweet, hard feeling that she did not know how to name.

Julius was still looking at her expectantly, his knees turned towards her and his back turned to the Paris cityscape flashing past in a whirl of light and colour.

'I went back to see Madame Valentine.'

'When?'

'Early this morning. Around three.'

'Agnes! It poured all night!'

'Aye, it was siling down. I was sodden, but she let me in and she told me where Genevieve is now.'

'And where is that?'

'Ceylon.'

Julius pressed his lips together tightly. Agnes waited. At length he said, 'You are not thinking of going to Ceylon?'

'Well, it's obvious I am thinking of going to Ceylon. According to Rashmi – that's Madame Valentine's name – Genevieve is living with Saul Valentine, either at the tea plantation or in his house in Colombo.'

Julius grew agitated. 'This is nonsense! How would you get there? What would you do to support yourself or keep yourself safe? Agnes, you must remove this idea from your head immediately. I forbid you from even considering it.'

Confronted with this demand, Agnes's intention to take the journey was immediately cemented. 'Who are you to forbid me from owt?' she said quickly, lightly.

Instantly, his demeanour changed. He grasped her hands and drew them up against his chest. 'Forgive me. Forgive me, Agnes. I had no right to speak to you so sharply. I simply cannot bear the thought of you travelling such a great distance.'

'As for how I would support myself and keep myself safe; well, I would take a position on a ship and seek the protection of the captain and his crew. I am not afraid of menial work, as Madame Beaulieu would have to admit.'

At the mention of the bordello he winced.

'You cannot stop me, Julius.'

He gently returned her hands to her lap and withdrew his own. 'I am coming to understand this better every minute I know you,' he conceded. 'Will you listen to any reason?'

'Maybe.'

'When Genevieve wrote me letters, she included only the return address of the tea merchant. I presume she did not live there.'

'No. Rashmi told me she had an apartment on Rue du Temple.'

Julius nodded. 'And yet, she did not send her letters from that address.'

'I don't know what you are implying,' Agnes said, though she thought she might and she didn't like it.

'Genevieve didn't want to be found. Not by me. Not by anyone, perhaps. The facts as they stand are that she abandoned you, she abandoned me, she hasn't written to me for years, and even those letters concealed her location. If you go to Colombo, you must accept that Genevieve desires no reunion with you.'

Agnes shook her head. 'She left the button with me when she surrendered me to Perdita Hall. She would not have left that clue if she didn't, somewhere in her soul, desire to know me one day.' In that heated moment she believed it more powerfully than she ever had, and she was prepared to go on a ship to Ceylon to prove it to Julius and show him how wrong he was.

Julius looked at Agnes, and Agnes at Julius. Over the noises of hoof falls and carriage wheels, church bells rang out in the distance.

'Well,' Julius said at last, 'this evening turned out quite differently from how I'd hoped.'

'What did you hope for?' she asked.

218

'Never mind that,' he said. 'I can't let you go to Ceylon in the bowels of steerage. It would not do, if you are indeed my . . . family.'

'Don't tell me—'

'Agnes, shush and listen. We will . . . I will cover all of your costs. I will send you by steamer, which is faster, through the Suez Canal, which is also faster. You will have a first-class cabin and you will be safe.'

Agnes's heart sped with excitement. 'I cannot agree to such generosity.'

'I'm afraid I will not, under any persuasions, withdraw my offer. If you must go, you go for both of us. And for that, I will ensure you go on a good British ship and have a return passage so that you are not so long away from . . . from us.'

Relief surged through her. 'I will accept your offer then, with warmest regard.'

'Yes, I'd rather hoped you'd say that,' he replied, glancing away. 'Sometime tonight, in any case.'

She watched him for a few moments, puzzled; he soon returned his attention to her and said, 'It's decided then. We will return to London tomorrow so that I may book your passage. I think it best we do not go back to Belgrave Place yet, as Marianna will have too many questions and it would upset her to lose you twice. But can I extract from you a promise that, on your return from Ceylon, you will come directly to our house? I will ensure you money for the train.'

'Aye, by my word. I'll be longing to see Marianna by then, and I will have so much to tell you, Julius.'

He nodded once. 'Very well,' he said, and leaned forward to tell the driver to take them back to Hotel Londres.

•

Their plans unfolded quickly after that, too quickly for Agnes to ponder whether she ought to change her mind. Of course it had occurred to her that the journey might be fruitless, but now the excitement of going on a ship out into the ocean had gripped her and all her imagination was fixed on it.

The dressmaker called in with her new clothes, which Agnes lovingly folded into her leather trunks. The porter then conveyed them out to the carriage for her. She and Julius chatted on the short ride to the station, and then boarded for London. The first-class experience of train travel was certainly different from her earlier journey: comfortable seats, food in the dining car, and patterned carpet on the floor. She and Julius drank coffee and played cards under the lamp on the little table between them. From the train, they boarded the ferry. The ride was tempestuous and Julius grew a little green, but Agnes didn't feel in the slightest indisposed and presumed from this that she would have no trouble on the open ocean. The train from Dover to London was next, and then Agnes was compelled to wait in the busy concourse of Victoria Station, on account of her still-healing ankle, while Julius organised and paid for their onward journeys and her passage to Ceylon. After the clean, bright streets of Paris, London looked quite grim.

As she waited, watching the ebb and flow of people around the pillars and arches, she cursed herself for her curiosity in asking Julius how much the journey would cost. Upwards of fifty pounds in first class! She had demanded he book her second class, and he finally agreed when she pointed out she would be happier with a companion in her cabin. Even so, the amounts of money he could part with so casually stupefied her, and left her with the lingering suspicion that a gift of such value would curb her freedom somehow.

It was two hours before he returned, and the afternoon had begun to cool. He strode down the concourse with a merry smile on his face, waving a short piece of paper.

'Here,' he said, presenting it to her. 'One second-class passage to Ceylon, and return, aboard the Royal Mail Ship *Udolpho*. It departs Saturday afternoon from Victoria Dock.'

'Saturday? But it's Thursday today.'

'The next one isn't for three weeks, so I thought you would prefer to get away sooner.'

'Where shall I stay until then?'

'*We* shall stay in a guesthouse that I know of, about eight miles out of town, but directly north of the docks. I intend to be with you, Agnes, until you board that ship.'

She clutched the ticket in her hand, her palm moist with perspiration. 'Thank you,' she breathed. 'Thank you with all my heart. I've never been so excited.'

'All the more reason to have a quiet evening. Come along. Let's find the porter and collect our luggage.'

•

It was evening by the time they arrived. An old friend of Julius's owned the guesthouse, a thirteenth-century building with jettied overhangs that sat across the narrow road from the village green. Julius introduced Agnes to his friend, Hugh, in the small entranceway. He had an open face and round eyes, and Agnes would have taken to him immediately if she wasn't so tired from travel, and made to feel so awkward by his curious stares. He clearly wondered what relationship existed between Julius and Agnes, and his questions were all designed to unlock that mystery.

Julius interrupted him and said, 'Agnes is very tired. Can she have supper sent to her room?'

'Of course,' Hugh said, with a wide grin. 'Allow me to show you to your room, ma'am. Julius, meet me at the pub.'

Agnes followed Hugh up narrow, uneven stairs and then out onto a landing whose floor leaned dramatically to the left.

'This is the ladies floor,' Hugh was saying. 'The bathroom is at the end of the hallway. Your key will open it. Here is your room.' He unlocked the door and handed her the key. 'I'll have someone bring up your trunks and some food in a little while.'

'Thank you. I'm very grateful.'

He gave her one last curious look, then left, his feet squeaking on the floorboards.

Agnes closed the door behind her. The room was small but cosy, with a four-poster bed, a thick rug and lace curtains. She made her way to the window – this floor, too, was old and uneven – and peeled aside the curtain to look out over the green. The ankle injury had trapped her inside again. It seemed half her life was spent gazing out of windows. The view outside was much quieter than Paris, but still not as quiet as the village where she had grown up. Agnes supposed no place was truly quiet this close to London. Two ladies in dark grey riding habits cantered past, and Agnes watched them enviously. One day, perhaps, she would learn to ride a horse. Across the other side of the green, a team of horses driven by a young man in a very high carriage with huge wheels sped by. A mother played with two chubby children – identical twins, by the look – and a rangy dog on the green.

Agnes sat on the edge of her bed and found herself wondering, just like Hugh, about her relationship with Julius. She admired him so greatly, and sometimes being near him made her imagination flare and her reason dim. She developed, on such occasions, a strong desire to touch him, or to feel him pressed hard against her. She remembered the feel of his fingers on her wrist at the opera, and imagined them elsewhere on her body. On the curve of her hip, her breast. For his part, he had hinted enough times now that he cared for her and had spent a large sum of money on her, but perhaps she misunderstood his intentions. Men like Julius could spend large sums of money and never notice them. Perhaps all that drove him was familial care. That thought deflated her so much that she had to stand up and stride about her tiny room, driving her fingernails into her palm. *You mustn't be such a fool, Agnes.*

When she had calmed down she returned to her window. In just two days she would be on a ship, on the ocean. She was equally frightened and excited as she watched the world and imagined her reunion with Genevieve, and let all other unsettling thoughts float away.

•

The following morning Julius insisted she rest her ankle and gather her energy for her journey, and so she was cooped up in the little room most of the day while he went out riding in the woods with Hugh. Agnes read, but could barely focus on the lines in front of her. Time crawled, and she grew irritated with Julius for leaving her without his company for so long.

Late in the morning, she moved her chair next to the tiny window and pushed it open to let in some fresh air. She saw Julius, then, with Hugh, returning from the stables, still in riding breeches but their horses nowhere in sight. They were joking about something inaudible and Agnes could see that Julius's cheeks were flushed from exercise and merriment, and she had the feeling of a soft clunk in her heart, as though something important had finally made sense to her. She wondered if perhaps she loved him. To see him happy and carefree, after the difficulties he had experienced working with the children's hospital, made her feel happy and carefree. Agnes may not have known much about love, but if his happiness was hers, that was a clear sign, was it not? She watched him approach but he didn't see her; it was a powerful thing to study somebody who didn't know they were being studied. They disappeared under the first storey of the house, and Agnes returned to her chair and realised she was smiling.

223

Agnes was invited downstairs to Hugh's cosy lodgings for a lunch of roasted chicken with potatoes and the most divine gravy she had ever tasted. He apologised that his wife was visiting her cousin in Woodbridge, that it was 'dashed inconvenient', but 'he had to let her off the leash every now and again'. Agnes didn't reward his joke with even the smallest laugh.

The afternoon was spent in Hugh's lodgings, and Agnes taught them to play an old Yorkshire card game called Four'n'Switch, beating them both soundly many times. Hugh laughed about it, but Agnes could tell he was annoyed at losing repeatedly. He began to gulp his brandy faster and his jokes became crueller. After supper, Agnes had had enough of being cooped up inside.

'Julius, I want to go for a walk around the green.'

'Your ankle,' he said, as though it explained everything.

'My ankle is fine. I will have plenty time to rest it on the ship. I feel like a trapped bird.'

Hugh raised an eyebrow at Julius, and a glance passed between them.

'Go on, old man,' Hugh said. 'Take the lady for a walk. You told me yourself this one is a malcontent in the parlour.'

Agnes didn't know whether to be proud or irritated with this pronouncement, but Julius soon smoothed it over. 'What I actually said was that Agnes's spirit is too adventurous for the ordinary pursuits of women,' he said to Hugh, although his eyes were on Agnes. 'And that I admire that about her.'

Hugh waved dismissively. 'Either way. Take the lady for a walk.'

'Sir,' Agnes said before Julius could reply. 'I am not a dog in want of exercise. I am quite capable of taking myself for a walk.'

Hugh found her retort amusing, but Julius rose quickly and said, 'I'd be delighted if you'd let me accompany you, though.'

'I'll fetch my coat.'

They met at the bottom of the stairs. The evening had grown unseasonably cool. The sky was pale watercolour blue streaked with gold. Together, Agnes and Julius crossed the road and began to slowly circle the green. On the far side, a tall stone monument stood and they made their way around to it. Here, Julius insisted she sit and rest, which she did. It was enough to be in fresh air. They sat together on the plinth of the monument, a statue of some local figure in the clothes of an old dandy: ruffled cravat and tricorn hat.

Agnes leaned back and looked at the sky. The silhouettes of birds arrowed overhead. All grew quiet; the air was cool on her cheeks. She sighed softly and closed her eyes.

'Agnes, there is something I must say to you.'

Agnes opened her eyes. Julius sounded so serious and now she grew worried. Was this about the money he had spent? Or had he guessed her feelings and needed to let her down? 'What is it?' she asked, heart ticking a little faster.

'I do not know how to . . .' He took a deep breath, set his jaw. 'When you return, I would . . .'

Agnes gazed at him, puzzled and apprehensive.

He tried again. 'While you are away, I intend to travel north to see Lord Breckby in Yorkshire. While there, I will ask him if he has any objections to our marriage.' Then, having finally got it out, Julius nodded once, decisively. 'There.'

Agnes's brain whirled. Words from his declaration flashed up before her. *Marriage*. Julius wanted to marry her. The thought amazed and excited her. But then there was that other word, a shadow. *Objections*.

'Objections?' she said. 'And what if he has them?'

'Agnes, I'm sure he will not. When he finds out who you are—'

'A lass from the local foundling hospital? Give over! You know he will object! And why do you speak of marriage in this way, as if it is decided between you and Lord Breckby? Were either of you, at any stage, going to ask me if *I* have feelings on the matter?'

A look of horror and embarrassment came over Julius's face, and if Agnes had been thinking clearly she might have felt sorry for him. But her pride had been so bruised that her head overheated.

'My apologies, Agnes. I misspoke. I am so nervous in speaking to you of this matter—'

'*This matter*? Is that how men speak of love? Do you love me, Julius? Is that what you are trying to say? Or are you trying to say that now you have spent so much money on my improvement—' Here she flapped the skirt of her dress violently. '—I am a chattel that can be installed somewhere as long as your grandfather doesn't think it looks too cheap among his things?'

'Agnes, no. I never meant for you to infer such insults from my words.'

'Because you and your family have money and I do not, did you assume my assent? Do you think all poor girls moon about after rich men, and so the only person whose permission must be sought is his Lordship, so he can decide whether I am worth the social embarrassment?'

'Please understand. I was tongue-tied by the moment. Of course I love you. I fell in love with you watching you with Marianna. I love your will and your fire but also your kindness, I love your voice and your eyes and . . . I love everything about you, and I want to make you my wife.'

But now Agnes was not so sure. Love confused her. Perhaps growing up without family as she did meant that she could only love crookedly or distantly. She doubted herself, and she didn't like the way he spoke. *Make you my wife* sounded like he would own her. She wasn't sure if she loved him, and Hugh's words about letting his wife 'off the leash' echoed in her head.

'Ask me when I return,' she said; she immediately regretted it but didn't take it back. Instead she stated it more boldly. 'Ask me on the day I come back, when I have had a chance to meet Genevieve and know better who I am in this world. I promise you that if you ask me then, I will give you a swift and decisive answer either way. But for now, I am not certain enough to say yes.'

Julius's entire posture softened. He smiled weakly. 'I am such a fool.'

Agnes wanted to comfort him, to say *Don't be sad* or take his hand in hers and squeeze it gently; but now she felt awkward and exposed and it was easier to think of other things. A journey by sea to the middle of the world. Yes, that's what she would think about.

Julius stood and straightened his waistcoat, then pulled his coat tighter. 'It's quite cold out. Perhaps we should return to our lodgings.'

'It is cold,' she agreed, glad to be on firmer ground in their conversation.

'Colder than I expected,' he said pointedly. 'I thought it was the middle of summer.'

Agnes didn't answer, and they returned to the guesthouse in silence.

•

Victoria Dock on the Plaistow Marshes was a wonder of modern construction, and Julius happily explained to Agnes the swing bridges and hydraulic machinery on the way down in the train. Agnes barely heard any of what he said. Everything was muffled through the sound of her thumping pulse. As the train slowed through the sprawling docklands, Agnes saw huge, black objects made of metal jutting into the grey sky like monstrous trees; she saw wide wooden decks and jetties teeming with men of all colours, who loaded and unloaded freight in and out of iron warehouses, and tall silos, and belching steamships; she saw a sea of train carriages in sidings, filled with coal. It all made her feel very small and soft.

The train left them at Custom House Station and, as they alighted, Agnes was struck by the sour, ancient smell of the river, and the steam and smoke that lingered in the air. The ships were now in full view, and Julius pointed out one to her: it seemed impossibly large, with two masts and a black funnel in the middle. 'There she is,' he said. 'The RMS *Udolpho*.'

Agnes fought the feeling that she was simply one more commodity, being loaded onto a ship and exported out into the vast, sun-soaked empire. She drew a little closer to Julius. 'Where do I go now?'

He stopped, turned her to face him. 'All the way across the world, my dear Agnes.'

•

Other passengers were taking their friends on board to show them their cabins, but Agnes said goodbye to Julius at the bottom of the gangplank. His failed proposal lingered between them awkwardly, and as people pushed past and around them, he took her hand and kissed it through her glove. He reminded her of her promise to return to him the moment she arrived in London, and handed to her an envelope. 'You will need this. Don't open it until the ship has left port.'

Agnes nodded, her heart in her throat. 'Goodbye, Julius,' she said, tucking the envelope into her purse.

'Farewell, Agnes,' he said, and he was gazing curiously at her. 'What is it?'

'I expected tears.'

'Not me. I hardly ever cry.'

He smiled. 'Of course you don't.' He gave her a gentle push towards the gangplank, to show that he was letting her go.

She found her way into the queue and ascended onto the ship. As her foot struck the wooden deck, she realised what an enormous step it was and excitement fired up inside her once again, burning away her fear. All around the edges of the deck, protected by metal rails, were wooden bench seats. She kneeled on one and looked back towards the dock, trying to find Julius. There he was, his tall top hat disappearing into the crowd towards the station. Her heart twinged, and she pressed her lips together hard so she wouldn't let out a little moan of regret.

She withdrew the envelope and picked away the seal to peek inside. Money. She'd known it would be. Julius wouldn't send her out into the empire without means. She kissed the envelope and tucked it away again. The deck was busy, noisy, but she had a sense of stillness and quiet inside her, thinking about Julius. At length, a steward found her and asked if he could take her to her cabin, but she refused.

'If I may, I will sit here and take my last few breaths of English air.'

'The ship won't move for another hour,' he said.

'All the same,' she replied.

The steward nodded and smiled. 'As you wish, madam.'

Agnes settled in her seat and cast her eyes back towards the dock. Julius had left long ago, but her gaze sought out the direction he had disappeared. Then, finally, she turned her gaze away and over the gleaming river, out towards the east.

CHAPTER 14

Once the ship was clear of the Thames and out into the open waters, Agnes decided to see her cabin. The ship would make her way through the English Channel then out into the Bay of Biscay sometime in the evening. The trip to Colombo was said to take three weeks: she would have plenty of time to look at the sea, and she was curious about what a second-class cabin on a Royal Mail Ship looked like.

She found a steward, a very tall man with round spectacles, who read over her ticket and smiled down at her. 'I will take you directly there, Miss Resolute. I am bound by the rules of the company to remind you about your return journey.' He pointed at small writing at the bottom of the ticket. 'You'll see the date here.'

'The date?' She peered at it. 'You mean my return passage is already booked?'

'Yes, ma'am.'

The date was two weeks after her arrival. Two weeks? Even if that were enough time to find Genevieve, it wasn't enough time to get to know her. 'Is that able to be changed?'

'I'm afraid not, ma'am. It is one of your conditions of passage. We do like to know how many guests we will be carrying on any journey.' He smiled. 'But they would have told you all this when you booked it.'

'It was booked for me,' she said, taking the ticket and folding it away.

'Ah, of course.'

'Are you telling me that the person who paid for this ticket chose the return date?'

'That is right, ma'am.'

Now she knew for certain the money was not freely given by Julius. It had conditions: her return on a date of his choosing.

Agnes softened as she thought of what Julius might say, were she to question him sharply. He would say he didn't want to be parted from her so long, that he was only trying to protect her. She supposed she understood; the problem was that his care and protection resembled restraints and control, just the way she had been treated for nineteen years at Perdita Hall, where nobody had cared for her.

She followed the steward along the deck and then through a door and down a narrow flight of stairs. The air here seemed stale and trapped. They arrived on a long corridor, barely more than a shoulder span across, with brass railings running the length of both walls between a series of numbered doors. He pointed out the two bathrooms at the end of the corridor, but then stopped at room twelve.

'This is yours, ma'am. The keys will be inside, but . . .' He paused and listened, and Agnes could hear it too: raucous laughter. 'It sounds as though your roommate is already here.'

'I was led to believe I had just one roommate,' she said.

'Yes, that is correct. It sounds as though she may have some friends with her.'

Agnes steeled herself. The steward backed away and strode off down the wooden corridor, his white suit bright in the gloom. Agnes turned back to the door and pushed it open.

All at once the laughter stopped, and four pairs of eyes were looking at her. Three young women and an older one, presumably their mother, who sat on a long couch with her feet up on Agnes's trunks.

'Hello,' Agnes said.

'Well, here is your roommate, Tempie,' the mother said, lazily removing her feet. She was a large woman, corpulent and ruddy, dressed in a grey taffeta gown that strained at the seams.

One of the daughters, a plump girl with mousy hair, ducked out of the bunk where she had been sitting and came to take Agnes's hand. 'I'm Tempie,' she said.

'Agnes,' Agnes replied, noticing how very soft Tempie's hand was.

'Don't be alarmed by my sisters and my mother. They don't intend to stay. They are sharing cabin number seven. It's quite a large one.'

'I'm not alarmed at all,' Agnes said, though she was spectacularly relieved. Tempie had a kind, soft face, but the two other girls were studying every inch of her from shoes to bonnet. 'Pray, introduce me to your family.'

'My mother, Mrs Dartforth; my sister, Mercy.' Here, Tempie gestured to a dark-haired, sharp-eyed young woman who barely raised a smile. 'And my other sister, Constance.'

'Or you can call me Connie; I don't mind,' Constance said. Her hair was white-blonde and tightly curly. 'It's lovely to meet you.' Nothing about her voice or her posture suggested this was the truth.

'Well,' said Mrs Dartforth. 'I suppose we should leave you to unpack. Tempie, will you come with us?'

'I would rather like some quiet time to unpack too,' Tempie said.

232

Agnes went to her trunks and kneeled on the rug to unclip the clasps, listening but not watching them.

'Quiet time?' Constance sniffed. Agnes could identify her by her sharp voice. 'Lord, but you are boring, Temperance Dartforth.'

'Leave the poor girl be,' Mrs Dartforth said. 'You know she'll never be the equal of either of you.'

There was the sound of taffeta rustling, the air next to cheeks being kissed, and then the door closed and it was quiet.

'Sorry,' Tempie said.

'What for?' Agnes asked, turning to her.

'My family.'

Agnes held her tongue, although she wanted to say, *They should apologise to you.* Instead she said, 'Be right, Tempie.'

Now that the cabin was emptier, Agnes could take in all its detail. It was a small room, with wood-panelled walls and a lamp mounted on a brass fitting. On one side was the couch, built into the wall but lushly upholstered. Opposite was a set of bunk beds with white covers and pillows. Between, stood a dresser with four drawers and a large mirror. Behind the cabin door was a narrow wardrobe, built into the wall. The ceiling was painted iron, with rivets and girders visible. Light came from a round window above the couch.

'It isn't bad, is it?' Tempie said.

'Very comfortable.' Agnes pulled out her nightgown and undergarments and began to fold them away in a drawer. 'Will you miss your family down here?'

'No. I volunteered to take a separate room from them.'

'With a stranger,' Agnes said, trying not to laugh.

Tempie smiled, her cheeks flushing. 'Quite. Look, Agnes, I know we've only just met but could I prevail upon you to let me sleep in the bottom bunk? Only, I've a dreadful fear of falling out in my sleep.'

'I would prefer the top, so you see we are already perfectly compatible.'

'I'm so glad. Are you going to Calcutta too?'

'No, I am travelling all the way to Colombo,' Agnes said, as she began to hang her dresses.

'Colombo! On your own? Do you have family waiting there for you?'

It was easier to say yes, then Tempie offered that she too was meeting family. Her father, in fact, who had been living in India for two years and had at last asked the rest of the family to join him.

'I rather hope that Mother won't be so difficult when she has her husband by her side again,' Tempie said. 'But that may be a silly thing to hope for.'

Agnes finished unpacking, set her hairbrush on top of the dresser, and slid her trunks under the bottom bunk next to Tempie's. She reached up to tuck her purse under her pillow.

Tempie said, 'I am not good at conversation.'

'I need none,' Agnes said.

'I like to read and think quietly. Would you be offended if I did that until dinnertime?'

'I would be delighted,' Agnes replied.

Tempie smiled. 'You're right. Perfectly compatible.'

Agnes climbed the ladder at the end of the bunk and flopped down on the bed. It was deep and soft, and the boat rocked gently. She breathed out slowly. She was on her way.

•

The first- and second-class passengers shared a dining room and saloon, and it was into this first room that Agnes and Tempie entered together, after having spent an afternoon in perfectly blissful silence and then helping each other to dress. There were twenty-eight passengers in all at this end of the ship, many already seated at two long dining tables that, Agnes noted, were bolted to the floor. A glistening chandelier hung from the ceiling, but the same rather grim wood panelling made the room seem dim and small. Tempie's mother beckoned them grandly, and Tempie leaned into Agnes and said, 'I'm afraid I must join my family, but you are free to sit where you please.'

'Come along!' Mrs Dartforth called. 'You too, Agnes. It won't do for a young woman to be sitting among strangers.'

'Well, that's settled then,' Agnes said lightly.

Two long upholstered seats sat either side of the dining table, and Agnes followed Tempie and Constance down one side, and ended up sitting opposite Mrs Dartforth and sharp-eyed Mercy, who gazed haughtily around the room as the ship rolled softly beneath them.

'Ugh,' Mrs Dartforth said as the ship lurched. 'I have been quite ill all afternoon.'

'Wait until we reach the Bay of Biscay later this evening,' Tempie said. 'We shall all be sick as cats eating rats!'

'Delightful,' Mercy sneered.

'Temperance likes to read about ships,' Constance offered, as though it explained all her sister's failings.

The table slowly filled up. Introductions were passed between people who were close enough to offer them. Agnes met the ship's Reverend and his daughter, a gap-toothed girl of about fourteen. Across from the Reverend sat a missionary and his wife, who were on their way to Colombo. Beside Mrs Dartforth sat a pair of young gentlemen who simpered at them blushingly. Mercy looked fed up before the food was even served, and Constance threw another casual, careless insult at Tempie. Agnes had already had quite enough of the Dartforth family.

'Is it true you like reading about ships?' Agnes said quietly, so that only Tempie could hear.

Tempie kept her voice low too. 'Oh yes. I have books and books. I know all of the different types and I even have a whole book of route maps that my uncle gave me. I love them so much. I wanted so badly to go to India on a real sailing ship, but Mother wouldn't have it. Steamships are not real ships, you see. Steamships are changing the way men connect with the sea. The thrill of it is dissipating.' Then Tempie stopped, blushed. 'I suppose you think me a fool.'

Agnes smiled. 'Quite the opposite. What an *interesting* girl you are.'

'It's just when I think about ships and the way they travel, it makes me feel as though the world is vast and beckoning. My family say it's a silly thing for a girl to be interested in.'

'They don't know everything.'

Tempie smiled shyly.

Their meals began to arrive, and Agnes learned to eat with the sea moving under her. At one stage, a great lurch sent everyone's plates sliding, and it was only with quick reflexes and a lot of laughter that they were saved from ending up in laps or on the floor. Mrs Dartforth found out the names of the young gentlemen and introduced them to her daughters as the Misters Glynn, brothers though they resembled each other not at all. The mousy nondescript one was named Leonard and the sad-eyed one with dark hair was named Peter. Agnes was more interested in chatting with Tempie or the missionaries.

After dinner, they were invited through to the gallery saloon for the evening's entertainment.

By contrast to the cramped dining room, the saloon was open and gleaming with gas-lights that hung on each huge pillar. The cornices were elaborately moulded, the floor covered in patterned carpet, and all along the walls and around the pillars were positioned thick, padded chairs. At one end, a wide staircase led back up to the quarterdeck. Behind it, a long, dim corridor ran off, presumably towards more cabins and down to the mail rooms and lower-class decks. At the other end, just to the side of the entrance to the dining room, was a wooden dance floor and a stage, where a heavily rouged lady and a weary-browed man were arguing softly over the grand piano.

'Let us sit at the other end,' Mrs Dartforth said. 'I simply cannot bear music. It is always too loud and too insistent.'

Agnes thought about sitting with the missionary couple, but she couldn't leave Tempie at the mercy of her family, so she followed them to the other end of the saloon, where they sat in an alcove. The young gentlemen, much to Mrs Dartforth's evident delight, joined them. Piano music started, and the rouged woman sang. At first, they played a few sad folk tunes, but then the tempo picked up and a waltz began. Mrs Dartforth, her eagle eyes on the young gentlemen, said, 'My daughters love to dance.'

Immediately, Mousy Leonard Glynn stood and asked Constance to dance. Agnes could see in Constance's eyes the flicker of disappointment. Clearly she'd had her sights set on his mopey brother, Peter. Nonetheless, she went with him, and then Peter stood and offered his hand to Agnes.

'No, no, not me,' Agnes said quickly. Quite apart from the fact she had no interest in Mister Glynn, she had never learned to dance and did not desire to make a fool of herself.

'Yes, not her,' Mrs Dartforth interjected. 'What about my other daughter, Mercy?'

Mercy smiled, but even her smile was cruel. Peter Glynn was reluctantly redirected and took Mercy to the dance floor.

'It's a pity they haven't another brother for you,' Mrs Dartforth said to Tempie, almost as an afterthought.

'I am much happier not dancing,' Tempie said.

'Yes, that's very wise. A girl of your size looks foolish dancing. It's a pity you must eat everything you see, Tempie.'

Tempie's shoulders sagged forward, and Agnes grew enraged with the vile Mrs Dartforth, who was easily one-and-a-half times Tempie's size.

'I think you are very bonny,' Agnes said to Tempie, quietly so Mrs Dartforth wouldn't hear.

'Thank you, Agnes, but I know I am not. My sisters got all the beauty, but I like to think I got a good mind.'

'So you did. And a good heart, which counts for something too.'

The dancers returned and Peter Glynn asked Agnes to dance again, and she was forced to say that as she was lately recovering from an injury she would not be dancing tonight or any night on the journey. It was partly true; Julius had told her not to exert herself lest her ankle swell up again. Peter declared that then he wouldn't dance either, and both Constance and Mercy protested loudly and Mrs Dartforth gave Agnes an icy stare. The young men sat with them and Agnes tried to lean away from the conversation, but Peter was insistent in his attention to her, and so the other girls pulled their chairs closer and Agnes was trapped among them.

'I rather think the singer has a nasty voice,' Constance said. 'You know *I* can sing. Like a bird.'

'That's hardly true, Connie,' Mercy said. 'You are too imaginative with the truth.'

'Don't be beastly,' Constance replied. 'You know that I sang for Mister Hammersmith's party and everybody loved it.'

'I have no doubt you sing like an angel,' Leonard told Constance, and she smiled at him tightly without meeting his eye.

'Do you sing, Agnes?' Peter asked.

'I do not.'

'Surely this is modesty. You must have many accomplishments.'

'I do not,' Agnes repeated.

Mrs Dartforth's eye took a magpie glint. 'Why, we know nothing about you; not even your surname.'

'Resolute,' Agnes replied.

'Unusual! Who was your father? What kind of name is that?'

Agnes was tired of Mrs Dartforth, and the three weeks ahead seemed very long. 'It's Hungarian,' she lied. 'My father was a Hungarian bearskin trader. He is now in the grave, along with my mother, who was the last daughter of a dissolute noble family from the north of England. I travel to Ceylon to live with an uncle whom I've never met, who owns an enormous cinnamon plantation and is obscenely wealthy. But I have only ever seen a portrait of him and he has no pity in his eyes.'

There was a moment of perplexed silence, and then Mrs Dartforth said, 'Well, then,' with a loud puff, and Peter exclaimed at the same time, 'Poor orphaned girl!' and it all became too much for Agnes. She stood and excused herself, and made for the staircase, up and out through the panelled alcove and through the door to the deck.

It was drizzling, and clouds covered the stars. She sank down on the very same bench where she had sat and watched London disappear behind her that morning, heedless of the wet. The air was fresh and salty, and she took huge gulps of it. She thought about Julius, and compared him to Leonard and Peter Glynn, and wondered why she hadn't agreed to marry him. The ship steamed on into the night, leaving England, and Julius, further and further behind.

•

Agnes woke in the night to a hacking, choking noise. She took a moment to orient herself, eyes running over the girders above her. The ship. That's where the pitch and sway came from: she was out on the ocean, somewhere between England and Ceylon. The sea was fierce; rain thundered overhead. And in the bunk below, Tempie was vomiting.

'Tempie?' Agnes asked, sitting up.

'Oh, Agnes, I'm so sick,' Tempie managed, before coughing wetly again.

Agnes folded back her covers and put her bare feet on the cold rungs of the iron ladder. The ship yawed dramatically, and she clung tightly to the rails on the way down.

'It must be a storm,' Agnes said, inching in beside Tempie. The sour smell of vomit was strong in the air.

'I had nothing to vomit into, so I used this hatbox,' Tempie said. She sat up, dishevelled in the dark. 'But I think I have it in my hair.'

Agnes patted her shoulder. 'I will go to the bathroom and fetch you some water and a cloth.'

'Would you? I'm so wretched, and I don't think I'd make it all the way down the hallway without being sick again.'

'Wait here.'

Agnes climbed off the bed and opened the door to their cabin. The lamps all along the way were lit, a gentle golden glow in the stormy night. The ship seemed to rise and slap down on the sea hard, and Agnes had to hold the rail all the way up the corridor so she didn't fall over. But she didn't feel sick, not at all. She'd known she wouldn't. She'd known she and the sea would get along just fine.

The rug was soft under her bare feet. She staggered down the hall and then opened the door to the bathroom. A bureau by the bathtub had dozens of folded towels and washers in it; on the stand were four china jugs of water. Agnes doused two washers in water and then made her way back down the corridor, the whole world rolling beneath her. The cabin door creaked shut behind her

240

on its own. Tempie had lit the lamp, and Agnes could see she was pale and shaking. The hatbox sat on the ground beside the bunks.

'That will have to be thrown over the side,' Agnes said, pushing it aside with her toe. 'Here.' She wiped Tempie's face and chest. 'Your nightgown is all soiled. Do you have another?'

Tempie nodded and indicated the drawer. Agnes found a cotton nightgown and helped Tempie out of her dirty one. Her big soft body was as white as a lily. Agnes helped her dress, tied the ribbons at her cuffs and collar for her, then sponged the vomit out of her hair.

'Thank you, Agnes,' Tempie said. 'I can't think what I've done to deserve such kindness.'

'Everyone deserves such kindness,' Agnes said. 'Lie down. I think it's fighting the rolling that makes you sick. Lie down and roll with it.'

Tempie did as she was told and Agnes found a spot on the side of the bed, from where she could stroke Tempie's hair. 'You have to imagine that you're an infant, and this is a big cradle. Let it soothe you.'

'My belly does *not* feel soothed,' Tempie protested. 'Why are you not seasick, Agnes? Have you been on the ocean before?'

'Never,' Agnes said. 'I crossed the Channel. That is all.'

'I don't like it. I worry that we will sink. Do you know how many steamers have sunk since 1840?'

'I'm sure I don't, but you must stop worrying. The ship won't sink while I am on it. I believe this with all my heart.'

'Why so?'

'Because I am specially charmed.' She hung the damp washcloths over the rungs of the bunk ladder. 'Close your eyes and I'll tell you a story.'

Tempie closed her eyes. 'Go on.'

'Once there was a girl who had no mother and no father. She was left at a foundling hospital in the cold, grey north when she

241

was only a week old. When it came time to name her, they called her after a ship. Her name was Agnes Resolute.'

Tempie's eyes flew open. 'Agnes! No!'

'And she was called that because she was born with sea legs and charmed that no ship she sailed on would ever sink.'

'Agnes, is it true you are an orphan?'

'Sh,' Agnes said. 'Let me finish the story.'

Agnes began to recount her adventures so far: learning about her mother, having her luggage stolen, living with the paupers, growing to love Marianna, escaping from the bordello, turning down Julius's marriage proposal. Tempie gazed at her wide-eyed through the whole story, and the rain hammered and the wind blew and the ocean roared. But Tempie stopped vomiting.

'My goodness, Agnes, you must be the most courageous woman in the world!' Tempie said when Agnes had finished.

'Don't tell your mother or sisters a word of it,' Agnes said.

'Of course I shan't, because look: your story has cured me. I am not ill any more.'

'Then close your eyes and sleep, and the storm will pass and morning will come.'

'Will you stay down here with me?'

Agnes longed for her own bed, away from the stench of vomit. But Tempie was such a gentle, sad lump of a thing, and Agnes felt nothing but pity for her. 'Aye, then. Move th'self over.'

Agnes slid into the bed next to Tempie, and put an arm over her waist. Tempie was asleep in just a few minutes, and Agnes listened to her breathe awhile. But then the ship's rocking did its work, and Agnes, like an infant in a cradle, drifted into a deep and soothing sleep.

CHAPTER 15

As the days went by on the ship, Agnes and Tempie became firm friends. Through the rough seas of the Bay of Biscay, they learned to eat their meals over the little railings called 'fiddles' that were erected on the table. When the ship steamed past Gibraltar, they stood together on the foredeck and gazed at the fortifications and the open mouth of St Michael's Cave, so taken with the sight that they missed the Divine Service given by the kindly Reverend Dunbar in the saloon. Along the coast of Spain they shared secrets and spotted porpoises, and Tempie told Agnes all she knew about ships and sailing routes. They were the triumphant egg-and-spoon team in the afternoon sports on deck, when the *Udolpho* moored in Marseilles to put off dozens of bags of mail. As the weather grew warmer, the cabin became the last place they wanted to be: hot and cramped. They abandoned their corsets and found a place in the shade of the quarterdeck to hide from Tempie's family and lift their skirts to their knees so their skin could feel the slight breeze that the movement of the ship created. They read to each other, and

Agnes showed Tempie how to improve her long-and-short stitch. Their hands grew tanned and their faces always shone. In the Strait of Bonifacio, the earnest and melancholy Peter Glynn followed Agnes out on deck one evening while everyone was singing 'God Save the Queen' in the saloon. He declared Agnes his queen, and Agnes put him off gently. Tempie later told her that Mercy now hated her with all her heart but that she, Tempie, would always remain loyal. To say Mrs Dartforth was growing to dislike Agnes was an understatement, but perhaps she allowed the friendship to flourish because she was embarrassed by Tempie's size and plainness, which were, to Agnes's mind, the least important things about her. In fact, now Leonard Glynn had been definitively rejected by both Constance and Mercy, he had turned his eye to Temperance without a hint of shame.

One night, in the Strait of Messina, they were woken by shouts and commotion from above, and left behind their stuffy cabin for the cool evening air. The captain and the Reverend and some of the stewards and the Orientals in their beautiful vests were pointing and gasping, and Agnes followed their gaze to see bright orange light against the sky.

'Oh, my Lord!' Agnes breathed, hastening to join them all at the port side of the ship, which was passing an erupting volcano. Down towards the aft, a line of third-class passengers were likewise hanging off the railings, applauding and shouting with excitement every time a flame shot into the night sky.

'What is it?' Tempie asked.

'Mount Stromboli,' said the captain. 'She's always on fire, that one.'

'There's a village at the bottom of the mountain,' one of the stewards said. 'I could do without the excitement of living there.'

Agnes gazed as hard as she could, until the fiery shapes were burned to the back of her eyes, in the hope she might remember it forever. The flames were as bright as the sun, the orange sparks shooting up fast and drifting down slowly, and long rivers of bright orange lava flowed down the black sides of the mountain. Tempie squeezed Agnes's hand and said, 'Oh, the things we've seen, Agnes.'

Agnes squeezed her hand in return, speechless for the first time in her life.

•

Ten days after they left London, they approached Port Said and the entrance to the Suez Canal, which would take them into the Red Sea. The heat had grown increasingly unbearable, and the Glynn brothers bragged about 'dossing' on the deck at night, which was much cooler. Agnes said she would like to do that too, which scandalised Mrs Dartforth beyond words. She was further scandalised when the young men said at lunchtime that they intended to go ashore when the *Udolpho* reached the port, even though they weren't predicted to arrive before ten in the evening.

'I hear Port Said is quite, quite dangerous,' Mrs Dartforth said, banging her fork on the table for emphasis. 'You'll have broken heads and rifled pockets when you return. *If* you return.'

'Ah well, ma'am,' said doughy Leonard, 'a pair of lads like us can certainly contend with any street bandit. Besides, I hear tell that the town is never asleep. We will not change our plans for any persuasion.'

'Take Tempie with you,' Constance joked. 'If somebody tries to rob you, she can sit on them.'

The only people who laughed were Tempie's mother and sisters. Everyone around, including the young men themselves, were mortified by such a cruel joke. Tempie pushed her chair back and hurried out of the dining room, and Agnes tore off after her with Mrs Dartforth calling in her wake, 'Oh leave her be, Miss Resolute. She's far too sensitive.'

Agnes caught up with Tempie outside their cabin, and held her in her arms while she cried.

'What a beastly thing to say,' Tempie declared. Her face was flushed and tear-stained.

'I know.'

'How could you know?' Tempie bit back. 'You are beautiful and . . . and slim and . . .'

Agnes held back her own sharp retort. 'I have been teased for other things, Tempie. I know how it hurts, but I also know that the wound goes only as deep as you let it, and if you distract th'self with some terribly wicked plan, it usually goes away altogether.'

Tempie sniffed, blinking her tears away. 'What terribly wicked plan?'

'I want to go ashore with the lads.'

'To Port Said? To broken heads and stolen purses?'

'We have stayed aboard at every other port. Imagine, an exotic town, all lit up at night.'

Tempie shook her head. 'Mother would never let me.'

'Aye, too right she wouldn't, which is why we won't tell her. We don't reach port until ten this evening. She will be in her cabin by then, as she is every other night.'

'But how can I show my face again to the Misters Glynn, after they laughed at Constance's terrible joke about me? What if they *do* want me to sit on a thief?'

Agnes giggled, but it was kindly and Tempie giggled too.

'Oh, Agnes, I am so sorry for snapping at you.'

'I don't mind. I will tell you something: the lads did not laugh at the joke. Rather they looked scandalised *and* I'll have you know that Leonard seems very interested in anything you say at dinner.'

Tempie blushed furiously, her neck going almost the colour of beet. 'I don't know if I dare.'

'I'm afraid you are going to have to dare, dear friend, for I am taking you with me.' Agnes imitated Leonard's very posh London accent as she said, 'I will not change my plans for any persuasion.'

Tempie looked terrified, but even so she said yes.

•

'Really, Agnes, this is scandalous,' Tempie said as they crept down the corridor of the men's saloon. It was one floor above the ladies' area, and much wider and grander, Agnes noted.

'Hush now. Do you remember their room number?'

'Six.'

The ship's engine was quiet, and made only a small lulling movement. Agnes found the right door and knocked softly and swiftly. The door opened, and Peter Glynn's face lit up when he saw Agnes.

'Agnes!'

'We're coming with you.'

Leonard joined them, a dubious expression on his face. 'Tempie? Has your mother approved this excursion?'

'I . . .' Tempie blushed.

'She hasn't,' Agnes replied. 'But we are still coming with you.'

Leonard and Peter exchanged glances, then Leonard sighed. 'You must stay close to us. The locals in Port Said are thought to be quite brutal with travellers. They'll extort you if they can, and rob you if they can't.'

Agnes had left all but a little of her money under her pillow in their cabin. 'Aye, aye,' she said. 'Come along. Before we are heard or seen by Mrs Dartforth.'

The boys locked their cabin door and together the four of them climbed up to the deck. A few others from the second class were whistling for the little ferry boats that darted between the ship and the wharf. Tempie shrank against Agnes while they waited their turn, but soon enough they were down the ladder and into a small, shallow skiff. A dark-skinned man demanded sixpence, and Leonard paid him. Then they too were darting away from the ship. Agnes could see all the other ships in the port, the town on one side and on the other flat desert. A lighthouse blazed at the mouth of the port. The wharf smelled salty and fishy, and the scent of coal hung in the air. Leonard helped Tempie ashore and Peter put his hand out for Agnes. She wanted to brush his hand away but realised she would need it as she climbed out of the shallow boat, holding her skirts up with one hand.

'Lord!' Tempie said. 'I've forgotten how to walk on land.'

Agnes laughed. It was the same for her. As they made their way along the wharf, the unmoving ground felt odd and jolting against her feet. She noticed Leonard take Tempie's arm and draw her in close. Peter tried to do the same with Agnes, but she pulled away.

'For safety,' he said, and Agnes reluctantly agreed.

'Just for this evening,' she replied.

They emerged into a well-lit thoroughfare. Rather than stone buildings, these were made of wood, three or four storeys high, with wrought-iron balconies. White canvas awnings were set up, gas lamps hanging off their corners, and tables of wares laid out. The shouting of hawkers intensified as they walked past. Agnes saw a fine-looking Egyptian couple – he in loose white clothing with a little brimless hat, she dressed in layers of white and black, with a diadem in her hair holding a veil – buying water from a black man with a tank on his back. He offered them a cup, then bent to fill it, and waited for them to drink and return it. A large store with lamps all lit in its windows declared itself an ENGLISH STORE in large writing across the awning. They went in and Agnes couldn't make sense of the profusion of objects for sale, none of which seemed English at all. She browsed the postcards, and dearly would have loved to send some to the people she missed. But she didn't know Gracie Badger's address, and if she sent one for Julius, then Marianna might see it and worry that she was so far away.

Tempie held a beautiful Arabian-looking crown on her head. 'What do you think, Agnes?' she asked.

'I think it's beaten iron that's painted gold,' Leonard huffed, examining the price. An Egyptian man hurried over and started talking about how his merchandise was 'all good quality' and 'real Arabian gold', and he and Leonard engaged in some good-hearted haggling until Tempie had her crown and the merchant had his still-inflated price met. Up and down the street, swarms of people moved about, as though it were midday and not approaching midnight. Many English and French, many dark-skinned, some in suits and dresses, some in loose white robes; beggars and street vendors and gangs of children running about, all of whom, Tempie said, should long ago have been in bed. Agnes soaked up the noise and the smells, the heat and even the company. They wandered the thoroughfare for an hour, then wound up inside a concert hall. A dark man in white clothes had ushered them in, promising them the entry was free, but of course once inside they were compelled to take a table and order food or drinks. Leonard and Peter were very gentlemanly and ordered coffees and cakes for everyone, and they sat in the crowded gas-lit room, choking on thick tobacco smoke, and watching a tall, thin woman on a tiny stage sing quite poorly in French.

Their coffee and cake arrived and they shouted over the entertainment and the noise of the crowd, sharing their observations and declaring that everybody was wrong about Port Said and it was a very friendly and enticing place. The singer finished and while the stage was being set up for a band, they were finally able to hear each other properly.

Leonard called over a waiter and directed him to bring them more coffee. The waiter had difficulty understanding him and

Leonard began to rant at him. Agnes's face flushed to be associated with him, and she tried to smile at the waiter kindly as he darted off to fetch their order.

'Dashed idiots, these natives,' he muttered and Peter agreed with his brother.

'I am so glad you brought me on your adventure, my dear friend,' Tempie said, giddy and silly with excitement, slinging her arm around Agnes's shoulders. 'I have never been so happy.'

'I like an adventurous spirit in a woman,' Peter said.

'You wouldn't believe her adventures!' Tempie exclaimed. 'Will all that end when you find your mother, Agnes?'

Peter's eyebrows shot up. 'Your mother? I thought she was dead.'

Tempie pressed her hand to her lips. 'Oh,' she said. 'I'm sorry.'

Leonard leaned forward. 'Go on. Spill it.'

Agnes was mildly annoyed with Tempie for letting loose her secret to these buffoons, but she smiled nonetheless. 'Aye, it's true. My father was not a Hungarian bearskin trader and I never knew my mother. I'm going to Colombo to find her. It is the last place she was seen or heard of.'

'She's a foundling!' Tempie added flightily. 'Left on a doorstep!' She rattled on a little longer until Agnes reached out and pressed a finger over her lips.

'Oh! Sorry, Agnes,' Tempie said.

Agnes withdrew her finger. 'Be right, Tempie. We don't want to bore the lads with my history.'

Peter had narrowed his eyes. 'How then, Miss Resolute, are you so well dressed?'

Agnes noted he didn't use her first name, and certainly all the mooning passion had left his voice. 'I have been lucky enough to have a benefactor,' she said, hoping it was vague enough.

'A man?' Leonard asked.

Agnes did not answer, not wanting to drag Julius's name into it. 'There are surely more interesting things to talk about than me,' she said. 'Tempie, why don't you tell us about—'

'I am interested,' Peter said. 'I am *very* interested.'

Agnes stood. 'Thank you, sirs. I am tired and will make my own way back to the ship.'

'Agnes?' Tempie said uncertainly.

'Enjoy your evening, Tempie,' Agnes said, and hurried away from the table and out into the balmy evening air.

Tempie joined her on the street a few moments later. 'I'm sorry!' she cried. 'Oh, what a terrible friend I am!'

'I blame you for nothing, Tempie. The sirs oughtn't have been asking questions about money. Even I know it's vulgar.' But her heart was still ticking briskly. She didn't mind for her reputation, but she did mind for Julius's.

'But it's all perfectly fine,' Tempie said. 'You're going to marry Julius. It's not at all grubby.'

Agnes stopped and turned to Tempie, who looked at her with big soft eyes. 'To some people, us poor folk *always* look grubby,' Agnes said.

'Not you.'

'Aye. Well, I imagine the young sirs will have things to say about me, and I'd rather not be around when they did. Shall we get along to the ship?'

Tempie agreed, taking her hand.

At the wharf, Agnes saw the *Udolpho* on her anchor out in the channel. All the little boats moored along the jetty bobbed and swayed gently. There were men in some of them, chatting in their strange language, the bright ends of their cigarettes flaring in the dark. The sky had clouded over, covering the stars and the crescent moon. The air was warm.

251

Agnes found a sixpence for a boatman, and as they rowed out across the water, Agnes thought of the expression on Peter's face when he realised she wasn't the lady he'd thought she was. It turned her mind to Julius, to his goodness and his kindness. Poor Julius, awkwardly tripping his way through the proposal, only to have her rain fury down on his noble head. The regret was like nausea, burning inside her, turning her stomach over. She fiercely longed to be in the quiet house on Belgrave Place with Julius and Marianna, and not half a world away.

•

Agnes was dressing the next morning when the door to their cabin banged open and a shrill voice called, 'Tempie!'

Agnes hurriedly gathered her clothes to her chest and looked up, to see Mrs Dartforth blocking the doorway. Tempie, who had been reading in bed, made a little moaning sound of fear.

'What is it, Mrs Dartforth?' Agnes asked.

'Don't you even speak to me,' Mrs Dartforth said. 'Come along, Tempie. Up and away. I know what you did last night, and now I know who *she* is.'

Tempie was on her feet, pulling on her dressing gown. 'What? But how?'

'Luckily for you the Misters Glynn have apprised me of the entire situation. Poor Tempie. You fell under her spell. Now pack your things. You are not staying another moment in this room with that . . .' Mrs Dartforth's hostile gaze was on Agnes. 'That *foundling.*'

'I'm sorry, Mother. I won't leave the ship without your permission again. Only don't take me away from Agnes.'

'I said, pack your things!' Mrs Dartforth cried. 'I'll not have you or anyone I love stay a moment longer with a liar, a woman of questionable background and no future!' Then she shook her head. 'Hungarian? Hmph.'

Tempie began to wail, and so Mrs Dartforth strode forth and began pulling her things out of drawers and stuffing them in her trunk. Agnes watched them leave, numb.

'I'll never forget you, Agnes,' Tempie said tearfully as her mother dragged her from the room.

Agnes didn't answer. The door closed and all was quiet.

•

All that day Agnes sat up on deck in the hot sun, watching as they passed through the canal to Suez. The ship crawled, its movement not enough to create a breeze and cool the oppressive heat. Agnes had only seen the Suez Canal on maps, and it was far narrower than she could have imagined. On one side, nothing but sand. On the other, buildings and camel traffic, and half a dozen urchins who ran along the side calling out to passengers, offering to dive for money. One or two of the passengers threw coins in the water and the urchins dived in and swam right under the ship looking for them. It seemed much too risky for Agnes's liking, and she held her breath as much as the skinny-limbed children did until they popped up, coins held triumphantly in their dark fingers.

On one occasion, a plain-faced girl of about Agnes's age, whom Agnes recognised as one of the first-class passengers, threw in a coin that nobody dived for.

'Well, that's a waste,' she muttered.

'Do you not worry that a child will be drowned?' Agnes asked her.

The young woman looked at her witheringly. 'I suppose it only fitting that a foundling would worry herself about wretched heathen children whose parents don't care for them.' Then she smiled cruelly. 'Would you like me to throw some money in for you to dive for?'

253

Agnes opened her mouth to offer an insult, but changed her mind. Such coarseness would only confirm the woman's opinion of her. Instead, she chose to be silent and rise above it. As the young woman moved off, she called her a mardy cow under her breath.

So, Tempie's tale of Agnes's past had started to circulate. Agnes found she didn't mind so much. She wasn't ashamed of who she was. If anything, she was proud of how far she had come, given her poor origins. At Ismailia, when they were moored for a little while letting another ship pass, a silk dealer came onboard and Agnes made a show of buying some at a high price, right in front of the first-class lady, who looked on astonished and scandalised all at once.

They still weren't at Suez by nightfall, and Agnes retired to her cabin, skipping dinner and the hostile stares of the Dartforths and whoever else they had drawn to their cause. When she woke in the morning, they had entered the Red Sea.

•

Any pleasure Agnes took in having a cabin all to herself was immediately taken from her. The heat was crushing, and three times as bad in the airless spaces below deck. She sat up on deck, in the quiet shady spot she and Tempie used to share, and read a little and sewed a little and longed to have a cold bath. She could not imagine such heat was survivable. It seemed to scald her lungs. The sea was very flat and the ship steamed on quickly, but even the breeze it whipped up was hot, like the blast from a furnace when the door is opened. Land had disappeared behind them and was too hazed by distance and heat to be seen either side. The ship seemed the only thing between the brazen blue sky and the wide warm water. Agnes gazed at it, hollow and exhausted by the heat, and understood for the first time how Marianna could feel oppressed by the outside world. Only sea and sky, in the shimmering heat, and she a tiny beating heart between them.

●

The dining room was stuffy and the smells of food were trapped within it. Agnes sat as far as she could from the Dartforths, but Mrs Dartforth's voice and haughty gaze kept finding her. It was clear now that she had turned a dozen or so of the other passengers against Agnes. So, she sat with the Reverend and his daughter, and they were kind to her and asked her no difficult questions. From time to time, she saw Tempie glance at her, and tried to offer an encouraging smile, only to see Mercy smack Tempie's hand with a spoon. Agnes looked away, not wanting to make life more difficult for her erstwhile friend.

When talk turned to how anybody would sleep that night in the heat, the Reverend declared his intention to sleep on the deck that night. A dark mutter arose from the Dartforths' end of the table, and Agnes smiled to herself.

'Would you allow me to join you?' she asked the Reverend, in a voice loud enough to be heard at the end of the table.

'Of course, Miss Resolute,' he said, a twinkle in his eye.

All entertainment in the saloon was cancelled due to the heat, so after dinner Agnes went directly downstairs for a cold bath. Then she pulled on her loosest house dress, slid a pillow under her arm, and climbed up on deck. At the aft of the ship, the deck was covered in prone bodies, quietly chattering to each other. It seemed the entire third class was up there. But here at the wealthy end of the ship, there were only the Reverend and his daughter, and the missionary couple.

'We have saved you a spot, Miss Resolute,' said the Reverend's daughter, indicating a space between her and the missionary's wife, where a blanket was doubled over.

Agnes lay down on the blanket. She could still feel the hard wood of the deck beneath her, but the air was clear and fresh and warm. Above her, a million stars glowed: some fierce and bright, others small and dim. The sky was cloudless.

'Are you comfortable?' the Reverend asked, sitting up and leaning over his daughter.

'Aye. Thank you. Thank you for not . . . thank you for remaining kind.'

'I have spent many years studying the teachings of God, Miss Resolute. I feel God's love for all His children and I will not judge. But tell me, does their unkindness hurt you and make you sad?'

Agnes propped herself up on her elbow and shook her head. 'No, Reverend. I have been judged before, and no doubt will be again.' She smiled, remembering a detail from his last sermon, one she hadn't missed. 'Only God can judge me.'

'That is right.'

'What are they saying about me? Have you heard?'

The Reverend sighed, and his daughter took up the story. 'That you are a poor foundling but you have somehow ensnared a rich man to pay for your adventure.'

Agnes winced. 'Do they say this man's name?'

'I haven't heard it,' the Reverend's daughter said.

Perhaps Tempie had held out, despite pressure from her awful family.

'Take heart.' This was the missionary's wife, a warm-faced woman with her long straight hair in a tight plait. 'All this will be behind you, just as the sea continues to move behind you.'

Agnes lay down again, eyes on the stars. Only God could judge her, and only God could judge Genevieve. The thought made her smile. She watched the stars and listened to the gentle conversations of the kind folk around her, and slept eventually with the sky for a blanket.

Three days later, the Dartforths were due to disembark at Aden to meet their steamship to Calcutta. When the *Udolpho* was mooring, Agnes decided she must say goodbye to Tempie, who had been a good friend to her if only for a short time. She did not fear the Dartforths' opinions so much as she feared not having bid farewell to a friend.

Agnes knocked on the door of their cabin before breakfast on their final morning. Mercy answered the door.

'What do you want?' she said with a sneer.

Agnes could see that Tempie had been forced to sleep on the floor. She sat up and said, 'Agnes?'

'I wanted to say goodbye,' Agnes said, over Mercy's shoulder.

Mrs Dartforth bustled Mercy out of the way and took Agnes by the shoulder, manoeuvring her roughly into the hallway and closing the door. Agnes had to grab the brass rail to stop herself from falling. She could hear Tempie's muffled, 'Goodbye, Agnes,' through the door.

Mrs Dartforth set her firmly on her feet and took a step back. 'Please leave my family be. I know you have no mother and that is why you have run wild, but my daughters – especially Tempie – will do better without you around.'

'I am very fond of Tempie. I wanted only what was good for her.'

'You do not know what is good for her,' Mrs Dartforth said, and for the first time she dropped her haughty tone and seemed to speak from the heart. 'It is my duty to protect her. To make sure she grows into a woman who is safe in the world. Everything I do for her, I do out of love. I can't expect you to understand, motherless and without means as you are.'

Agnes was dumbstruck. She *loved* Tempie? She insulted her and constrained her, and yet she called this love? Perhaps it made

257

a twisted kind of sense: in Mrs Dartforth's world, shame was a way to make Tempie stop eating so much. Constraint was a way to make her navigate more easily in a world so difficult for women. Moving her away from Agnes was a way to protect her, not punish her. Agnes was floored by this knowledge, that maternal love could look so ugly and yet still be love.

Mrs Dartforth nodded once, as though the conversation was at an end, and turned towards the door.

'Be kind to her,' Agnes said.

Mrs Dartforth didn't answer.

●

Agnes went up on deck and watched them leave, glad when Tempie sneaked in a wave and a blown kiss, despite the obvious disapproval of other well-dressed folk. Agnes didn't care. In less than a week, she would be in Colombo, and she could tell Genevieve how it felt to be ostracised. She knew – she *knew* – that her mother would understand. If Mrs Dartforth had taught her anything, it was that mothers always loved.

CHAPTER 16

The RMS *Udolpho* steamed into harbour at Colombo during the night, and Agnes woke to find the ship at anchor. She had packed everything the night before, added some trim to her broadest-brimmed hat, and barely been able to sleep.

Now they were here. At last.

She queued up on deck behind other passengers, her luggage at her feet. A launch was making its way to and from the ship to transfer people to the docks, and the mail – a score of sacks of it – was being unloaded at the other end of the ship. Agnes jiggled her leg as she waited, eager to be off and away. Across the water, she could see low roofs and a profusion of palm trees. The heat was damp, sticky, and she longed for a breeze. She pulled her fan from her purse and fanned herself, but it barely cooled her at all.

Finally, she was passing her trunks down to a man wearing nothing but what appeared to be a twist of linen around his loins. Agnes longed to be able to wear so little; far more sensible in this heat. She climbed into the launch along with the Reverend and his daughter, and two elderly gentlemen who had joined them in Aden, and they made their way to the wharf.

Once they were on land, the Reverend turned to her and fixed her in his wise, grey gaze. 'Goodbye, Miss Resolute. I hope you find what you are looking for.'

'So do I,' Agnes said, impulsively squeezing him in a brief hug, then offering the same to his daughter.

'There is much that is good in you,' the Reverend said as she pulled away. 'I see it.'

Agnes looked around at the hazy sky, the bright sunshine, the lush foliage, the chatter and sweep of people. She felt alive and hopeful. 'There is much that is good in the world,' she replied. 'Thank you.'

At a small shop on the wharf she bought a map for a penny, examined the hotel names, and settled on the Victoria Hotel, hoping that anything named after the Queen would be suitable for an English girl travelling alone.

She struggled along on busy streets, where bullocks instead of horses pulled thatched carriages, and barely dressed locals ran about barefoot carrying rickshaws. She passed rows of small wooden houses, taller buildings with elaborately curved gables, and market sheds with low roofs and rough unfinished beams, packed with fruit and rice and coconuts and bundles of kindling. The women's clothes captivated Agnes: their shoulders were bare and they wore loose, flowing cloth decorated with elaborate lace borders. Finally, she approached the hotel, a building that wouldn't have been out of place in London: white stone, arched windows and a neat enclosed garden with rigidly trimmed trees. Under a tree, a group of white women in layers of linen sat on the grass with a picnic. Agnes felt hot, sweaty and red-faced as she huffed past them with her trunks, and finally into the cool interior of the building. Long chandeliers hung suspended from the high ceiling, the walls were pale green and the floor gleaming stone. All of the staff looked to be local; all of the guests were white.

Agnes engaged a room, but it would not be empty until later that afternoon. They held her trunks and changed some of her money for her, and then she was back on the busy Colombo street. Her heart tapped an insistent rhythm. There was no value in waiting. She hailed down a rickshaw to take her to Genevieve's Colombo address.

Agnes felt the distance she had travelled like an ocean in her heart. Stretching back across the miles, to cold grey England, where she had started this journey. How far she was from everything she knew, but how close to the one thing that mattered most. The rickshaw bounced along, though she felt very sorry for the man who had to carry it. They moved away from the main thoroughfares to shadier streets with trees not so neatly planted. Dogs and cats roamed the streets, looking as though they belonged to nobody and everybody at once. The rickshaw came to a halt outside a wooden building with peeling paint and boarded windows.

'Here?' she asked the driver.

He nodded, then repeated back to her the address she'd given.

She climbed out of the rickshaw and looked up at the house. It looked as though nobody lived there and her hope evaporated. She thought about climbing back into the rickshaw and returning to the hotel, but she had to be certain.

'Madam?'

She turned to the rickshaw driver, who held out his hand. She smiled and paid him, then he lifted the vehicle and ran off to find another passenger.

Agnes returned her attention to the house, then walked up the two front steps and knocked at the door. It was painted red, the knocker tarnished brass. Nobody came, as she'd feared they wouldn't.

Impulsively, she tried the door. It opened.

Agnes glanced behind her, then back to the house. Tentatively she pushed the door in. 'Hello?'

She was greeted by nothing but the smell of animal droppings. A wide entryway with a chequerboard floor lay ahead of her. Agnes stepped in, closing the door behind her. 'Hello?' she called again. This time she heard the scurry of clawed feet, and assumed she'd disturbed whatever creature had made its home in here. She moved into the next room. No furniture. The back windows weren't boarded and one was broken. Leaves covered the floor. A rug was rolled in a corner, sagging and mouldy. Chains that chandeliers had once hung on swung freely from the ceiling. From room to room she went, finding no furniture, no evidence of who had lived here, and when or why they had left. She ascended creaking wooden stairs, the carpet nails in place but the carpet long gone, and wandered through lightless rooms where dust and heat choked her. Nothing, nothing, and nothing.

Agnes returned to the lower floor, then out into the street. A breeze was stirring off the water, bringing with it the smell of salt and the first hint that the day might cool. Despondently, she made her way back to her hotel.

•

Later in the evening, in her room looking over the gardens to the busy markets, Agnes sat in the window seat and let the soft balmy breeze caress her face. The smell of spices and smoke rose and fell. She had taken a cold bath and dressed only in a linen shift, her fair hair loose about her shoulders. The sea inside her, after weeks, had not yet stilled, but she didn't mind the sensation. It would pass soon enough, here on the land again.

Tomorrow she would travel further: a hundred miles or more into the mountains to find the Valentine tea plantation. She cheered herself with the knowledge that there must be *someone* there, because

Valentine's name was still on the shopfront in Paris. She hoped, of course, that the someone was Genevieve, but her history of disappointments stopped Agnes from hoping too fervently. Tonight, for the first time, the flush of heat that had driven her this far was beginning to cool. She felt it and she feared it, because now she was half a world away from England, and from Julius and Marianna whom she had come to love, and she was small and soft and the world was big and brutal. Yes, tomorrow she would take the train to Kandy, and perhaps . . . perhaps she would find Genevieve and say to her the words she had rehearsed in her imagination for so long: *I am your daughter. You are my mother.*

She said these words aloud now, alone in her cavernous hotel room. But they sounded thin and unconvincing to her own ears.

How might Genevieve react? With a delighted laugh, a warm hug, a gaze that said, *Yes, yes, I know you. I* know *you.* Or would she be dismissive, tell Agnes she was abandoned for a reason, that tracking her down had been a waste of everyone's time and resources?

Agnes sighed, leaned her head against the cool brick of the windowsill and closed her eyes. If Genevieve wasn't there this time, how much further would she go? Another address to find, another door to knock on, another see-saw between hope and disappointment.

'I am in Ceylon,' she said, because she couldn't quite believe it herself. Not even in her wildest imaginings of adventures had she thought she would find herself here. This, then, was enough. She had travelled far enough from Perdita Hall now. No matter what she found tomorrow, she had come as far as she could.

Agnes tried to make her peace with the idea, but it kept her awake until long after midnight.

•

It was with gritty eyes and tired limbs that Agnes boarded the train the following morning, in the cool before the sun had risen far in the sky. The hotel manager had helped her plan her route: Colombo to Kandy, Kandy to the new railway station at Nawalapitiya, and then she would have to engage a carriage to take her to Valentine Estate. She left one trunk behind, and took her light one with her. She had no need for fancy gowns and she couldn't bear to wear corsets in this heat. Sensible, lightweight clothes, gloves and a broad-brimmed hat were all she needed. She slid her trunk into the baggage rack and found her place aboard the train. The seat was hard, and the table too far from her to be comfortable, but she had a window. Through it she could see the elaborate ironwork around the roof beams of the station and the local attendants in their calf-length pants and white sashes. A large-framed man with big hands took the seat beside her, inching into her space. Agnes leaned against the window. A half-dozen other passengers found their places in her carriage, including a pair of rosy-cheeked twin girls, who chattered animatedly to their mother in a language Agnes didn't recognise. The train let off a hoot, steam hissed and clouded around them, and they began to move.

Agnes had planned to read or to doze on the journey to Kandy. After all, it was longer than four hours. But the scenery was so spectacular and lovely that she didn't want to miss a second of it. They chugged out through the town and surrounding villages, across thundering bridges over wide rivers, through densely wooded expanses of land where the bright green branches and leaves scratched against the train windows, up through hills and around dramatic rocky brows, through tunnels so deep and long that she began to wonder if they would ever see the other side. She changed trains at Kandy, too quickly to take in the sights and sounds. She glimpsed a man riding an elephant as the train pulled away, and regretted heartily not being able to see it up close. This was a much smaller train with only one other person in her carriage, a man with a huge ginger beard who spent the journey scribbling in an accounts book and swearing every time the train jolted him and made him blot his ink. They travelled up and up, and the scenery dropped away on either side: steep hillsides with terraced fields of bright, brilliant green. By the time they reached the tiny village of Nawalapitiya, the air had grown misty and grey. She alighted and looked around the deserted platform, then a sense of panic gripped her. She had thought she would see porters, a ticket office where she could ask about a carriage, but there was nothing but the platform. She was walking towards the front of the train to ask the driver, when the bearded man who had been sitting in her carriage swept past her.

'Excuse me, sir,' she called. 'What is the best way to travel to the Valentine Estate?'

He turned, frowning. 'Does Saul know you are coming?'

'Aye, be right,' she lied. 'I'm his niece. Though the timing may be . . . unexpected.'

He tapped his hat. 'I have business dealings with Saul. My driver knows the way. I would be pleased to offer you his service and my carriage, given you are family.'

'My good fortune to meet you, sir!' she said. 'What name do you go by?'

'I am Daniel Fitzpatrick. I have a business up here hiring natives for work on plantations.' Here he frowned again. 'Not that I've sent any up to Saul for quite some time.'

'Truly, Mister Fitzpatrick, you have made a very long day much more bearable.'

'Come along, then.'

She followed him to his bullock-drawn carriage, where he spoke quickly in the native language to his driver, a dark-skinned man in crisp white. Her trunk was loaded on the back, and Fitzpatrick handed her up himself and settled in beside her. The driver dropped him at his own house – an enormous sprawling mansion with a garden that looked almost impenetrable – and took more instructions from Fitzpatrick about where to take her next.

'Give my best to Saul,' he said, leaning in the window. 'Haven't clapped eyes on him for months.'

She wanted to ask if Genevieve was there at the Valentine Estate, but thought it might give away that she wasn't his niece at all. 'I shall, Mister Fitzpatrick. And thank you.'

She settled back in the carriage, and it began to jolt along the rough road. Soon, she was surrounded on all sides by bushes and branches. A bug flew in the window and landed on her dress and she shrieked and brushed it off, then felt embarrassed. She had simply never seen a bug that big, and longed for tiny, English bugs. The sun fell lower in the sky; there was no way she would be at Valentine Estate before four in the afternoon. She was tired, mortally tired, and uncertain, and afraid, and the journey seemed to be taking forever.

At length, the road ahead of them opened up and they descended towards a towering stone-and-iron gate, with a wall running off in either direction. From here, she could see miles of green hills, the sun falling towards them. The air had cooled rapidly. In among the hills and trees sat buildings and houses dotted far apart from each other. The carriage rattled down the road and slowed in a large clearing in front of the gate. It steered around until it was facing back the way they had come, then stopped. She heard the driver climb down and walk to the back to fetch her trunk.

Agnes had hoped she might be let off at the front door, and as she stepped down from the carriage she said to the driver, 'Where is the house?'

'Valentine Estate,' he said.

'In there?' She pointed through the wrought-iron bars.

He nodded, and pointed too. 'Valentine Estate.'

'Aye that's all well, but will you wait for me here, please? Just in case there's nobody home?'

He smiled and nodded.

'Wait here.'

'We here,' he said.

'No . . . *wait* here. You stay here? Just for a few minutes.'

He nodded vigorously.

Agnes left her trunk by the side of the road and unlatched the gate. She walked no more than a hundred feet before she heard the carriage rattling away.

She spun round. 'Hoy! Wait!' she cried, but the driver had already thundered off up the hill. She ran after him for a few moments, but the hill was steep and she was weary to her marrow. She turned back to the gate, scooped up her trunk and trudged along the long, overgrown driveway, hoping to see a house soon.

It came into view around the next bend. Wide and white, stone and plaster, with broad front stairs and a verandah that looked as though it ran all the way around. Fruit trees that clearly hadn't been pruned in a long time grew either side of the stairs. Wooden railings, carved with Ceylonese designs, had been left unpainted and now swelled with moisture; some had rotted right through. Weeds flooded the garden.

Agnes's heart fell all the way to her toes. This house did not look inhabited, just like the house in Colombo. That meant she was miles and miles from anywhere, without means to return to the village – and, quite honestly, barely any idea which way the village lay – and evening was approaching. She took a deep breath. If the house was deserted, then so be it. She would find a place to sleep on the verandah; it would be just like sleeping on the deck of the ship. Tomorrow she could find her way back. She told herself not to think about the bugs. Or the wild animals.

Her shadow was long at her feet as she trudged towards the house, then up the stairs where she lay down her trunk and knocked loudly. Above the large wooden doors was an intricately carved wooden fanlight. She could see only darkness inside, but outside was still daylight, so she took heart.

Then she heard footsteps, and relief flooded her. She braced, wondering if she was about to come face to face with Genevieve.

The door swung in. A curiously handsome man, perhaps late in his forties, glowered down at her. His black hair was liberally streaked grey, and had grown almost to his shoulders in messy curls. He looked as though a razor hadn't been near his chin in a week. 'Who are you? What is it?'

'Are you Saul Valentine, sir?' she asked.

'Yes, I am. What do you want from me?'

'I have come to find Genevieve Breckby.'

He laughed without smiling, then stopped abruptly, his jaw pulling tight. 'Genevieve isn't here. She left me two years, five months and twelve days ago.'

Agnes forced her knees not to give under her. 'Can you tell me then, sir, where she is now?'

'Australia. Who are you?'

Australia. *Australia*. Agnes fought to breathe. She had crossed the ocean for nothing.

'Well, lass? What is your name?'

Her words spilled out, almost beyond her control. 'I am Agnes Resolute. I am a foundling. But I believe myself to be her daughter and I have come all this way . . . all this way . . .'

At this, he softened. His hazel gaze moved over her face, as if looking for Genevieve's resemblance in her lips and eyes. 'Genevieve's daughter, eh?' he said, almost tenderly. 'Well, then. You'd better come in.'

CHAPTER 17

Agnes followed Saul Valentine inside the house. One large room greeted them, with round pillars that held up a high ceiling. Doors folded open on the wide verandah, which faced the setting sun, and a cool breeze came in from across the green hills. The floors were stone, without rugs or mats. In fact, the house seemed curiously empty, with furniture grouped in little islands here and there. He led her to one of the islands: two chairs and a low table, beside a wooden cabinet. Here he poured himself a whiskey and offered one to her.

'No thank you, sir,' she said, as she sat. 'But I would be so grateful for tea.'

'Tea,' he said, deadpan. 'Huh. Very well. I can't stand the stuff myself. Given that it's nearly ruined me.' He smiled, a baring of wolfish teeth. 'Nearly. Not completely.' He rang a bell and a few moments later a painfully thin servant appeared.

'Mahesh, tea for the lady. Do we have any food in the house? Give her some. I don't know.' He waved Mahesh away. 'You know what to do.'

'Yes, my lord,' Mahesh said, and disappeared further into the house.

'He's my last man,' Saul said. 'I expect you feel sorry for me, to find me in such a dissipated state. I assume Valois told you all about me and that's why you are here.'

Agnes shuddered at the mention of Valois's name. 'No, sir. Rashmi told me where you are.'

'Ha! Did she send you to stab me or poison me?'

'Neither, sir.'

'Stop calling me sir. My name is Saul.' He swallowed his whiskey and poured another. Agnes noticed for the first time that his vest was dirty, as though he had dropped food on it and not bothered to wipe it off. She watched him for a little while, an idea forming in her mind.

'What is it?' he asked. 'You have that look on you. I know that look on a woman. You are judging me.'

'Far from it, sir. I mean Saul. Far from it. I am wondering if there is any possibility you are my father.'

He drew his brow down. 'Huh. Well, there's a question I didn't see coming. Tell me, Agnes Resolute, how old are you?'

'Nineteen.'

He performed calculations in his head, then said, 'No, I am not your father. Your father must be Ernest Shawe or Wilburforce Peacock. Let's hope, for your sake, it's the latter. Shawe is quite an unpleasant fellow. He once punched me in the jaw. Loosened one of my teeth.' Then, quieter. 'Though, I suppose, I did steal his wife.'

Agnes bit back disappointment. Finding her father might have been a small consolation for not finding her mother. 'How do you know that one of them is my father?' she probed.

'Because the two of them were quite mad for your mother twenty years ago, and I'm led to believe she strung them both along for a time. Her marriage to Shawe was forced upon her by her parents.' He laughed bitterly. 'Their folly.' He lapsed into surly silence.

270

Agnes considered him in the dying light of the day. Having met Valois, and having heard Rashmi's account of Saul, she had expected him to be quite different. More like the awful Glynn brothers, who thought the world belonged to them. Saul Valentine seemed rather more convinced that the world had fled his grasp.

Tea arrived, served with nothing more than bread and treacle. She ate it carefully, still managing to get sticky fingers. The tea revived her a little. Saul asked her to explain how she had come so far, and she did so through mouthfuls of food. He smiled at her admiringly, interjecting laughter and expressions of surprise. When she finished, he told her she had Genevieve's spirit, and this cheered her more than she could express.

'I need to hear good things about her,' she said. 'Everywhere I have gone, I have heard only of her faults.'

'Good things about Genevieve, eh?' he said, rubbing his chin. 'Well, then. Everything about her is good. What am I to choose?'

Agnes's spirit lifted. 'What did you love best about her?' she asked, then regretted it instantly when his expression became pained.

'What *do* I love best about her? For I haven't stopped loving her.'

'Aye, then, sir.'

'Her fierce intellect. Her snowy skin. Her refusal to be constrained—' Here his voice caught in his throat. 'Oh, away with you. I am too drunk and too melancholy for this.'

'I am sorry to cause you pain,' she said.

'You didn't cause my pain,' he replied. 'She did. Now, it is too far back to the village and I wouldn't trust anyone who offered you a room there anyway. You will stay here this night, but ask me no more questions. I will sit here and watch the sun sink behind the hills, and drink myself into a stupor again. Tomorrow, when I am sober and can trust my voice not to break, I will tell you about Genevieve.'

'Thank you, Saul,' she said, relieved. 'I am so very tired.'

'I'll get Mahesh to take you to Genevieve's room.' Again, the sad expression. 'I haven't touched it. It is exactly as she left it, the day she . . .' He gulped some more whiskey, then called, 'Mahesh!'

Mahesh came and picked up her trunk. 'This way,' he said.

'Goodnight, Saul,' Agnes said.

He nodded, waved her away, and she followed Mahesh out of the huge room and down a short corridor that hooked to the left, opening ahead of her into a low-roofed bed chamber.

Mahesh dropped her trunk on the ground and bowed to her. She noted his clothes, like Saul's, were unwashed.

'Thank you, Mahesh,' she said. 'You are a good man to stay with your master through difficult times.'

He smiled wearily. 'He has been good to me. Not all I have served have been so kind.' He gave her a pointed look, and she supposed he meant Genevieve. 'I stay to look after him. He has nobody else.'

Mahesh withdrew, pulling the door closed behind him. Agnes looked around the room. The bed lay under a heavy mosquito net. A rug was spread between bed and dresser. A large mirror framed in carved wood hung from the wall, and an empty bookshelf sat beside the window. The roof beams were visible, as was the dust on them. When Saul said he hadn't touched it, he was telling the truth. Agnes went to Genevieve's dresser, her pulse speeding guiltily. Genevieve's hairbrush. Agnes unpinned her hair then stood in front of *her mother's* mirror, brushing her hair with *her mother's* hairbrush. 'My mother's hairbrush,' she said. She picked up a little perfume bottle, glass wrapped in filigree, and squeezed the puffer. A spray of soft floral scent dampened her wrist, though a little stale from heat and time. Still, she inhaled it deeply. So, this what Genevieve smelled like. Agnes opened Genevieve's long wooden jewellery box and saw strings of beads, rings and bracelets. In the very bottom she found a tarnished locket, and sprung it open to

272

see two miniature portraits facing each other. One was Genevieve, perhaps a little younger than when Agnes had seen her in Hatby, with her golden curls and a merry pink glow on her cheeks. The other looked familiar, and it took a few seconds of concentration to realise that this was a young Marianna. Her hair a shade paler than Genevieve's, her nose thinner and longer, her expression more serious.

A twinge of regret passed through Agnes, then. Marianna had once been a young, beautiful woman with a serene and level gaze. Now she was trapped inside her own home by her fears, couldn't sleep for nightmares. No, that wasn't right. The dreams that woke her were 'so unspeakably lovely that waking up makes one want to cry for disappointment'. Agnes would never forget her saying that, never forget the gentle compassion it had aroused in her heart.

Agnes snapped the locket shut. Her weariness was making her sentimental, perhaps, but she longed to be back in the house at Belgrave Place. With Julius and Marianna, and even Annie, Daisy and Pamela. She allowed herself to imagine it. Would they think it strange if she returned as Julius's wife? Would Marianna? No, she would be delighted. Agnes wouldn't have to get up in the middle of the night to read to her any more. Or maybe she would, out of love instead of obligation.

These thoughts were getting her nowhere. It seemed as though the bread and tea was all the sustenance she was going to be offered, and she had travelled many miles today on so little sleep that she was dead on her feet. She took the locket and fastened it around her neck. Saul wouldn't miss it. He was too drunk to know what was here and what wasn't.

Agnes shed her dress and crawled into her mother's bed. The sheets smelled musty, and dust itched her nose. She closed her eyes, even though it was only six o'clock. *Genevieve slept here*, she thought as she burrowed under the silky covers. She closed her hand

273

around the locket, and willed herself to feel close to Genevieve, close to her mother.

But as she drifted off to sleep, it was Marianna who was in her thoughts.

•

In the morning, Agnes rose before the others. The weather had turned gloomy, with thick grey clouds gathering on the horizon and a sticky heat enveloping everything. She opened the doors from the main living area, and stepped out onto the verandah in search of cool air. Rain spat down lightly, and the distant hills were shrouded in a humid haze of mist. The tea plants stood out bright green against the grey. Agnes followed the verandah along and down four steps to an outbuilding. She pushed open the door and found the laundry, hung heavily with spider webs. She backed out, returned up the stairs and into the house, then found her way to the kitchen. Something rotten made the air thick, and she noticed a layer of muck over the range and sink. There was bread in the breadbox and a kettle on the range for tea. She made herself breakfast, and got out of the stinking kitchen as quickly as she could. She took her breakfast on a chair on the verandah, watching the rainclouds roll in. Nobody came.

Agnes thought she may as well put herself to use while she waited. She returned to the kitchen and hunted in the cupboard for scrubbing brushes, scouring soap, waxes and polishes, and got on with the job. It was no worse than she had done for her keep at Madame Beaulieu's bordello. She scrubbed the range and the sink, scoured the pots, waxed the table and benches, swept the floor, cleaned the copper and polished the silver. The smell emanated from an old pot full of food that had been left behind the pantry for what seemed like centuries. She marched the pot out of the house and threw the food over the garden fence, then scrubbed the pot until it looked new. The ice box was empty of both ice and food, and she rinsed it out with boiling water and left it open to dry.

It took hours, but finally the kitchen smelled like lemons and everything shone dully. Rain had moved in and thundered against the roof. Still, Saul wasn't awake, and she had no idea where Mahesh kept his quarters.

She was growing hungry again, and wasn't keen to eat bread and tea for a third meal in a row. She searched the pantry and found potatoes and rice. She cut the eyes out of the potatoes and washed the weevils from the rice and set both to boil. The only other edibles she could find were boxes of spice and salt, so she added some of those to the boiled potatoes and made a rudimentary kind of potato curry, whose aroma filled the house and eventually drew out Saul.

'What are you doing, woman?' he said, irritably.

She turned. It seemed he had slept in the same clothes he'd been wearing the previous day. They were crumpled and stained, his cravat hanging loose and his shirt untucked on one side.

'I'm making food. Where is your servant?'

'Mahesh? He doesn't work Sundays. Is it Sunday?'

Agnes thought about it. 'Aye, it is. You are right. Do you go to church?'

His answer was nothing but a bitter laugh. He pulled out his pocket watch and glanced at it. 'Well,' he said. 'It is nearly noon. I expect you'll want me to eat some of this mess you've made for my luncheon. Or my breakfast.'

'Aye, then. Come on. Sit down.'

He pulled out a chair at the kitchen table and she laid out two bowls and spoons, and served them each some of the food. Even though the dish was bland, it was thick and hearty and filled her up. As they ate, she stole glances at him. His eyes were bloodshot, his hair and beard wilder than the day before.

'Did you sleep poorly?' she asked him.

275

'A girl came along and roused up my ghosts,' he said.

'I won't stay. I will leave this afternoon, once you have told me about Genevieve.'

'You'll stay. It's Sunday, a terrible day to travel. Mahesh will return in the morning after visiting the markets. There will be food and ice for the box.' He pointed at his bowl. 'We won't have to eat this.'

She smiled. 'I learned to cook at Perdita Hall. I soon worked out that the girls who were good at it were usually made to work in the kitchen forever. I tried not to be too good at it.'

'You succeeded,' he said, with neither a smile nor cruelty in his tone. 'What were you good at?'

'Sewing. Mending and embroidery mainly.'

'Genevieve liked to embroider,' he said.

'Did she?' She bit her lip to stop herself from smiling too broadly.

'Yes. She said it made time stand still.'

'That's exactly how I feel,' Agnes said. 'The world is whirling about, but with needle and thread in my fingers I am quiet in the middle of it all.'

He smiled his wolfish grin. 'You are her girl, then.'

'Do you think she will want to know me?' Agnes asked, and was embarrassed by how small and uncertain her voice sounded.

'I should think so,' he said. 'Why wouldn't she?'

'Because she gave me up. She didn't want me.'

'You can't say that. Her father is a bloody fool. Pardon my language, but it's true. Perhaps your father was Peacock after all, and they had to have her give you up so Shawe would marry her. They did well out of the deal.' Then he sniffed, and stared down at his bowl. 'Who's to say who else it might have been? More have lain with her before me, more after. I suppose that's a scandalous thing to say around a lady.'

'I'm hardly a lady,' Agnes said. 'And as I know Genevieve bore me out of wedlock, then I know that she was neither innocent nor virtuous.'

'No, Genevieve is neither of those things. When Pepperman lured her away from me, I expect he knew that too, and that he is being led on as merry a dance as I was.'

'Who is Pepperman?'

'George Pepperman. Her husband. I don't know if she's told him she's already married, or if Ernest Shawe still thinks of himself as her husband. What a line of blockheads we all are. Where is my whiskey?'

'Sir, you only just woke up.'

'I told you not to call me sir. If we are finished with this nondescript meal, can we please return to the living room? I rather fancy a glass of single malt. In fact, I insist on it if I am to lay bare my pain.'

'As you wish, Saul,' Agnes said. She rose and followed him to the living room and they sat in the same place as they had the night before. The rain was bucketing down now, and thunder banged about between the hills. The cool air it brought was welcome, after so many days on end of heat and perspiration.

He poured himself a generous splash of whiskey, took a gulp, and then began.

'I met Genevieve on a journey away from Paris. We were in England. In London. What year is it?'

'1874.'

'Well, there you are. Ten years ago. My daughter was only beginning to talk, and Genevieve was living with her sister in Belgrave Place.'

'Marianna,' Agnes offered.

'That's right. And the lad, Julius. He wasn't even hers. She certainly hadn't wanted to be a mother. That was the reason she fled from her husband in the first place.'

'I thought you were the reason she fled from her husband?'

'Ah. Not so simple. When we met, he was engaged in a very forceful campaign to woo her back. In fact, it was through Shawe that I met Genevieve. Shawe and I were at Cambridge together. I was in London, raising money for a business venture. Shawe was there at the time, mooning after your mother, telling me all about how she was a horse that needed to be broken and by jingo he was going to break her and make her return to him. I met her at a party at his home. He was introducing her about as his wife, the poor fool, and she looked mortified and furious all at once. From the moment I laid my eyes upon her, I knew she wasn't a horse that could be broken. She had to be given the reins.

'Over several chance meetings and then a few that were carefully organised, Genevieve and I fell in love. I travelled a great deal, but I started every journey to Colombo from London so I could see her. The distance caused us too much pain, so I brought her to Paris and she worked for me for a time. Rashmi despised her, of course. Rashmi, who didn't want me, and didn't want my advances once we'd had our child, but, like the dog in the manger, couldn't bear for anyone else to have me. Eventually things became so tense between them, and I was away in Ceylon so much, that we decided Genevieve should come here. I felt as though I was living two lives: the proper life of a gentleman with his wife and child in Paris, and my real life with Genevieve.

'You asked me to tell you about her, give you something to admire.' He gulped more whiskey, seeming to steel himself. 'I will sound like a sentimental blockhead, no doubt, but every aspect of her was admirable. She was striking, of course. Her expression moved from imperious to merry to carnal and in every mode she was a woman beyond compare for beauty. She lived without restraints. To be with her was dangerous, thrilling. She followed all her appetites and cared nothing for the opinions of others. She once told me she had spent her girlhood being good, but all that had got her was marriage to Mister Ernest Shawe and him grumbling constantly that she should give him a son. I was more than in love with her; I was intoxicated by her. Life without her is . . .' He trailed off, jaw set tight.

'The people who have told me she was selfish—'

'Of course she was selfish. She was a devil for getting her own way. But men who can only love a weakling are not fit to call themselves men, in my view. Once you have known the wild, the sweet . . . Ah, more whiskey, Agnes. I need more whiskey.'

He refilled his glass, took a sip and then said to her, 'She isn't coming back to me.'

'You said she was in Australia.'

'Yes, Melbourne or some damnable place. Met George Pepperman in Colombo while I was back in Paris trying to clear my debts with Valois. She was gone when I returned.'

'You didn't go after her?'

'Of course I didn't. I'm not as pathetic as Ernest Shawe. The more I clung to her, the harder she would resist. My best hope is to let her go and believe she might remember me fondly.'

Agnes turned this over in her mind as the rain hammered down outside. The overgrown hedges in the garden heaved under the weight of the water. 'And is this Mister Pepperman also a wealthy businessman?'

'She doesn't care for wealth, Agnes. Put that out of your mind. She longs for experience. That is where she sees the value in life.'

Agnes closed her eyes for a moment and let the thought wash over her. This was her own truth, too. They were connected, she and Genevieve, and she was surer than ever that Genevieve would welcome her, want to know her. But Genevieve was in Australia.

'If Pepperman is wealthy, it is precariously so. He's in the theatre business. No wonder Genevieve was drawn to him. She lives life as though it were a drama. He and a business partner were over here looking to set up musical theatre for visiting passengers on the long run between England and Australia. They thought they could fleece them good, while they were glad to be on solid ground.'

Agnes thought about the music hall in Port Said, where the Glynn brothers had paid exorbitant prices for coffees and cakes.

'I have my suspicions that Genevieve might have gone to meet him to audition,' he continued. 'She liked to sing, and Lord knows she liked to be looked at. As her face grew lined and her waist grew thick, it became more important than ever to her that she was admired.' Here he shrugged. 'There. A portrait of your mother.'

'Was she kind?'

'Hardly ever.'

'Tender? Loving?'

'She loved fiercely, not tenderly. Oh, God, I miss her. I miss her. The deuce take me. I cannot bear this pain.' He hung his head in his hands, and Agnes waited while he composed himself. Finally, he raised his gaze and said, 'I am sorry I couldn't help you. You have come a long way. When does your return voyage depart?'

'Twelve days.'

'Then stay here. Be among her things. Take her clothes for your own if they fit you. They are of no use to me. Just, please leave her perfume. I spray it on my pillow from time to time and dream I am sleeping alongside her.' He cleared his throat. 'In some ways, I am like a stepfather to you. Allow me to play that role, even for a little while.'

Agnes smiled. Staying here would be a fitting way to end this journey in search of her mother. She could sort Genevieve's belongings, and find some small tokens to take home. The only problem was that she didn't want this to be the end of her journey. She wanted, more than ever, to meet Genevieve in the flesh.

'That is a kind offer,' she said to Saul. 'I will take it.'

Agnes thought to make herself useful in the time she spent at Valentine Estate. There had been no housekeeper in a long time, and so she set about putting the house in order. She swept out the laundry and washed all her own clothes, then Saul's and Mahesh's, keeping them to secure buttons and repair seams. She dusted and polished and sorted and laundered. Mahesh did what he could, but he spent much of his time managing the overgrown tea fields. It seemed Saul had sold off much of his estate to neighbours, and in his misery over the loss of Genevieve had missed several harvests. There was no money for workers in the fields as there had been in the first years of the estate, Mahesh told her. He was hoping to convince some relatives to come for the autumn flush, and in the meantime was simply trying to keep the weeds from ruining the crop.

Saul rose at noon every day. He was lucid for a few hours, during which time he thanked Agnes profusely and told her that she inspired him, that today he would go out in the fields and help Mahesh and plan for the recovery of Valentine Estate. But by four o'clock – after he had mooned about between the living room and the verandah, dispiritedly forced down some lunch, pulled on his shoes then taken them off again – he was back in his chair with his whiskey in his hand. Then he said he didn't want to go near the tea fields, that they terrified him, that Valois would come to recover debts and find nothing and probably cut his throat, and nobody would care and perhaps even the world would be better off. When he was drunk and in such a black mood, Agnes would retreat to her bedroom and sort through Genevieve's things. She polished jewellery and took in gowns so that she could wear them; dressed up in her mother's clothes and accessories, she studied herself in the mirror for hours, until her own face became unfamiliar to her, and she felt lost in the world.

Mahesh offered to take her back to the railway station at Nawalapitiya, and had been out that morning to borrow a neighbour's bullock and cart. Her trunk was waiting in the cart, she was dressed in one of Genevieve's cool cotton dresses, and Saul stood on the stairs watching her with sad eyes.

'You are so like your mother,' he said. 'I am sorry you didn't find her here.'

Agnes pulled on her gloves. 'Aye, but I am grateful that I found you, and found some stories about her in which she wasn't a monster.'

'She is so far from it. Oh, the devil take me! I miss her. If you ever do find her, tell her to come back to me.' He shook his head. 'She won't. She won't.'

Agnes leaned in impulsively and hugged him, and he clung to her tightly, then released her and strode up the stairs and inside. Agnes climbed onto the seat next to Mahesh.

'The long journey home begins,' he said with a smile, urging the bullock forward.

Agnes's heart felt hard and cold. 'I suppose it does,' she said.

•

Agnes returned to Colombo late in the evening, the day before she was due to board the ship home. After securing a room for the night at the Victoria Hotel, and dropping off her luggage, she walked directly to the wharfs. A brisk breeze off the sea cooled the humid stickiness. She could see the *Udolpho* out in the harbour at anchor, among the other steamers and a handful of clipper ships. Her return ticket did not tell her what time she would leave, so she searched in vain for somebody handling mail bags at the dock to tell her, but was finally directed to a wooden building standing at the end of the wharf.

Inside smelled like fish and ink. Agnes wrinkled her nose. A gentleman with salt-and-pepper hair stood at a wide oak table, a map laid out between him and an elderly couple who were asking many questions. While she waited, Agnes looked around the office. On the wall were pinned nautical maps with sea routes marked on them, and handwritten posters advertising positions aboard ships. She scanned them idly.

Then she stopped.

Wanted. A single woman without encumbrance to assist Ship's Surgeon as Nurse Assistant, aboard the clipper ship Persephone, *bound for Melbourne 9th of September. She must be of sober and steady disposition, English speaking, and well acquainted with the work of Nurse. Wage £3 payable in Melbourne. All living expenses aboard included. Apply to Dr Angel at The Grand Alfred Hotel.*

'Madam? May I help you?' This was the gentleman behind the counter, finished now with the elderly couple.

She turned, then tried to remember why she was here.

'Madam?' he said again, eyebrows drawing down curiously.

She may not have ever been a nurse, but she had spent time in the infirmary at Perdita Hall and was unafraid to embellish this small truth.

'Never mind,' she said to the gentleman. She pulled down the poster so nobody else would see it, and took it with her as she hurried off.

•

Late that evening, she wrote to Julius.

My dear Julius,
I am sorry that you will receive this letter instead of receiving me. The Udolpho *will steam away to England tomorrow without me. I have found a passage to Melbourne, Australia, instead. I do not know*

how long I will be away. I have heard fresh tales of Genevieve, and could not give up after coming so far already. I know I want to meet her and I believe, now, that she will want to meet me.

Please do not be angry with me. My feelings for you will not change and I trust yours for me will also remain constant. It simply isn't time for me to return yet. Please be patient, and if you cannot be patient, be forgiving. I seek a missing piece of myself, and trust I will return to you whole.

Give my love to Marianna and, yes, tell her I am indeed on the far side of the ocean, but that I intend to cross it one more time as soon as ever I can, to be with you both again.

With love,
Agnes

The Present

Life takes on a rhythm, even though nothing is settled. I can see that Mum is growing depressed, that she is tired of the clinic now her injuries are healing. I know we are avoiding the questions that need to be asked, but the ordinary relentlessness of life – sleep, meals, and so on – keeps me from falling into despair. I am returning from the supermarket with two bags of frozen meals-for-one in the back seat of my rental car when I decide to stop in briefly at the college and find the next volume of *Middlemarch*, which I've been reading to Mum. Because she collects old Victorian books, there are no convenient paperbacks that contain a whole story; everything is in dusty volumes. As I come up the stairs, I see that Mum's office door stands open and I hurry along, protective of her things.

I stop in the threshold 'Mum?'

She looks up. She has changed out of her hospital gown into what I presume she was wearing the day she had her accident. A pale pink wool top with dark brown blood stains, and a long grey skirt. Her feet are bare. She sits at the desk where I have made organised piles, but the piles are gone. There is chaos again. 'Hello, darling. I thought I'd come and find the rest of Moineau's letter.'

I move towards her and put my hand over her shoulder. 'Did a doctor say it was okay for you to leave the clinic? How did you get here?'

'No, and a taxi,' she answers, turning her attention back to the papers in front of her. 'What's happened here?' she asks. 'It's all out of order.'

'It was in order.'

'What kind of order? See . . . 1840s, 1850s, 1860s . . .'

I had never thought of ordering things by decades, because it makes no sense. I had organised by categories: articles, journals, letters, pamphlets . . . but here she is mixing them all up again.

'Mum, you shouldn't be here. You should be in the clinic.'

She glares up at me, suddenly defiant. 'Oh, should I? And would you? If you were me, would you be in the clinic? Or would you rail against the nurses treating you as though you were a child? And despise those doctors who speak to you as though they know you better than you know yourself?'

'All right, but then let me take you home. You oughtn't be here. I'll take you home, and I'll call Doctor Chaudry and we'll sort all this out later, okay? I saw the Dean yesterday, and he isn't going to empty your office. He's not, I promise.'

'Then why are all my things in disarray?' she cries.

I open my mouth to tell her about the storm, the cleaner, about the fact that I've been in here reorganising things as she asked, but I don't know if I can talk reason to her any more. I don't know if the words will fall just beside her, rather than making their way into her mind. I don't know if I will sound as though I am part of her imagined conspiracy of villains. So, I say, 'Let me take you home now. You haven't been home in ages. You can have a cup of tea and your own sofa and your own bed. How does that sound?'

Mum smiles weakly. 'It does sound nice. And my own bath. Not that hideous little shower at the clinic.'

'Wonderful idea. I'll draw you a bath and I'll cook for us too.'

Mum stretches out her hand to me, and I help her up and for the first time I notice she has shrunk. Perhaps only a centimetre or so, but she seems small to me.

As soon as I have her home, I am happier. Mum has her bath and we eat dinner together, and soon she is reading in her own bed, a little yellow light visible under the door. I sit on the sofa. The television is on. It's a real-estate show about people so rich they can afford a house in the country and a 'crash-pad' in London: the kind of show that makes poor people despair and middle-class people feel they have failed. I am not really watching, because I am thinking about Professor Garr. Andrew. I wonder if he has any idea where the rest of the letter is. Maybe there are depositories for papers around the college that Mum has forgotten about. I pull out his business card and look at it, put it down, pick it up again. He did say I could call.

I pick up my phone. There is a missed call from my work. I frown, thumb it aside, and call Andrew.

My heart is beating hard until he says, 'Tori, how lovely to hear from you,' and I feel reassured that I'm not overstepping some boundary I didn't see him put in place. 'How can I help?'

'My mother is looking for some papers, an old letter, a rather long one. In her . . . confusion, it's become separated into chunks and she can't remember where they are. But it gives her a lot of joy, so I think it's worth me trying to locate the rest of it.'

'It's not in her office?'

'Not that I've been able to find.'

287

He is silent for a moment, then he says, 'She left some papers on an outside table at the refectory one day, perhaps six months ago. A cleaner found them and returned them to one of her colleagues. I wonder if he still has them. I remember him being quite distressed that priceless old documents were left out in the open. Anything could have happened to them. Would you like me to check with him?'

'Could you?'

'I'd be happy to.' A short silence, but before I can say thank you and goodbye he says, 'Why don't you meet me for lunch tomorrow, and I can tell you if I've tracked them down?'

'I . . . yes. That would be . . . nice.' Lunch. The least sexy of all the meals. Surely I needn't tell him I'm married, that I don't wear a wedding ring because I lost it at the beach months ago and Geoff still hasn't noticed. I can't mention Geoff at all. That will just make things awkward.

•

I arrive at his office the next day at one o'clock and I'm shown through to a boardroom where a platter of sandwiches waits. My fear (hope?) that the lunch will be intimate or romantic is quickly quashed. This is a straight-up business lunch, and I sit alone for three minutes – long enough for condensation to form on the orange-juice jug – before Andrew comes in. He has a folder under his arm and apologies on his lips.

'I am so sorry,' he says, and indicates the sandwiches with a sweep of his hand. 'For this.'

'It's fine. The sandwiches look very nice.'

'Yes, but the point is . . .' He turns and shuts the door behind him. 'I have a new PA and I asked him to book a lunch meeting for two at the Chancellor's Club, and he got it mixed up with a board meeting this time next week. Electronic calendars . . . you know.'

'I honestly don't mind,' I say, helping myself to a ham sandwich.

He sits across from me and slides the folder onto the table. 'It's here.'

'Really?' I put the sandwich down and dust crumbs off my fingers, then open the folder. Familiar handwriting. I leaf through to the end. 'Ah, still incomplete.'

'Is it? These are the only papers she left behind.'

'I'm sure the rest of it is somewhere,' I say. 'Perhaps she'll remember.'

He pours himself an orange juice and offers me one and we sit in awkward quiet for a few moments, eating. Then he says, 'Let me make it up to you.'

'Make it . . .'

'Let me take you to dinner to make up for messing up the lunch.'

'There's really no need—' *Tell him you're married.*

'I insist. I really do want to take you to the Chancellor's Club as there's a wonderful museum attached that your mother was instrumental in setting up. I . . . I don't want to raise your hopes but I'm in the process of applying for it to be renamed the Margaret Camber Gallery.'

The wind is knocked out of me.

'No guarantees, you understand,' he says quickly. 'Bureaucracy being what it is.'

'I won't hold you to anything. But I would love to see the collection.'

'While you are in town?'

'Yes, while I am in town. I expect that eventually I have to return home to Sydney. Geoff will . . .'

'Geoff?'

'My husband. Geoff. He's a solicitor.' Conveyancing law. Nothing interesting. Nothing he's passionate about.

The awkward moment that I feared passes. He rallies. 'Well, perhaps you can take some photographs of the gallery to show him,' he says.

289

'He wouldn't be interested,' I reply, smiling tightly.

'Nonetheless.' Another moment passes, and he is looking at me but I can't read his expression. But I like the way he looks at me. There is patience there. I am not used to patience.

'I would love to have dinner with you,' I say, and I am pleased by how warm and sincere my voice is. 'What night would suit you?'

'Next Friday?' he says. 'Seven o'clock?'

'Absolutely,' I say.

●

I am in a daze of sorts as I drive home. I miss a green light and the Peugeot behind me honks furiously. Not as bad as running a red light, I suppose. I would love to be able to tell Mum about Andrew and ask her opinion, but she hates him; or at least, a version of him that she has created in her mind.

Mum is in the sunroom, dozing. I take a moment to watch her. Asleep, she looks old. My heart pinches. I am acutely aware that I won't have her forever. She opens her eyes, sees me, pulls focus, then smiles.

'Victoria.'

'I have the next part of the letter.'

She sits up, excited. 'Do you now? Where did you find it?'

'Andrew Garr found it for me.'

Her face closes up. 'He was hiding it from me.'

'No, you left it outside the refectory and one of your colleagues has been taking care of it.'

She frowns, deep vertical lines drawing themselves between her eyebrows. I can tell there is a glimmer of memory there, and I let her take her time. It's important to me that she doesn't think ill of Andrew.

'Well, then,' she says. 'Perhaps I did. It was kind of him to hunt it down for me.'

I want to say more, that Andrew is kind and patient and admires her greatly; but I know not to test her patience. 'Shall I read it?' I say, dropping into the brocade chair opposite her.

'Oh yes. Please do.'

CHAPTER 18
Moineau

—me or know I was there. So, I sat through the whole service, yearning and in misery. My future, ever more certain, was rushing towards me now and I had never been so desperate to escape it.

I managed to slip away from my family and Mr Shawe when Aunt Harriet stopped to talk to the vicar and all eyes were away from me. I smuggled myself out of the church with the departing crowd and turned towards the churchyard, even though it was teeming with rain by now. The hazel branches that hid the pathway to the Hawthorn Well were bent under the weight of water, and as I pushed through them my dress became instantly soaked. How I managed my way down that slippery, muddy path without misadventure, I do not know. But I had my mind bent on a strategy, and I was determined to see it through.

At the wishing tree, I pulled free the red ribbon from my hair, letting it fall loose about my shoulders. I wasn't sure how the wishing tree worked, so I pressed the ribbon against my lips and said, 'Let me be with Emile.' I reached up to the highest branch I could and tied it tightly, reverently. Then I hurried home, soaked through.

•

The rain kept me away from Emile's dog, Marin, the next day and the next, and of course my good breeding and Harriet's eagle eye kept me away from Emile. Harriet was particularly keen to see that I stay in. 'Even little sparrows like you must roost from time to time, dear,' she said. I sat inside and did little. I had my sister to distract me, and we played cards together and pinned each other's hair in increasingly elaborate and silly styles. Mr Shawe didn't visit, on account of the rain, and for that I was glad. But being still did not agree with me, not when I had so many wild feelings inside my body. I thought about my red ribbon, out there in the hawthorn bush in the wind and the rain, and it made me sad, as though I had left something precious to chance.

I could not leave this to chance. I could not trust in wishes. Should not a woman, if she desires something so greatly, take the reins?

I heard the rain ease on the Wednesday morning, very early, when I woke from a dream that dissolved upon waking. I closed my eyes but didn't sleep well after that, composing letters to Emile in my head. Before breakfast I rose and sat at the little writing desk, fumbling around with tired fingers for ink and paper. Marin wore a collar, and I planned to leave a note folded under it, for Emile to find.

Dear Master, your sparrow took me walking today. She told me she has missed me very much. There is a sad gleam in her eye, though, and I think she is missing somebody else. Love and licks, from Marin.

I read it, laughed at myself, scolded myself, told myself I was bold, told myself I was silly, changed my mind a score of

293

times. Finally, I folded the note and tied it with a little ribbon, and slid it under my pillow for the moment I could get away.

'Good morning, Aunt. It's fine today,' I said as I sat down at the breakfast table next to my sister, who grunted at me in greeting. She is not fond of mornings.

'I see that with my own eyes,' Harriet said, and slid a piece of paper across the table. 'Mister Shawe sent a note around not ten minutes ago. He's invited us to dinner tonight. Do you have something splendid to wear?'

My heart sank, but I managed to smile. 'I am sure I can find something.'

'The green velvet suits you well,' said my sister. 'The one with the brocade on the bodice.'

'It is too warm for velvet.'

'How you look is more important than how you feel,' she said with a smile, over the top of her teacup. 'You don't know the first thing about catching a husband.'

'What a lot of nonsense you girls go on with,' Harriet said, but fondly. 'I'm sure I wasn't such a ninny at your age. Mind you, by your age I had been married four years. It's a terrible thing your parents have done, making you wait so long. Perhaps one of you can force Mister Shawe to make a decision tonight. So, yes, Little Sparrow, the green velvet if it makes you beautiful.'

I ate dispiritedly, but tried not to show it. My sister, more animated after a boiled egg and three cups of tea, asked if I wanted to take a carriage to the next village, where there was a famed milliner; but I told her I had a delicate stomach and would stay in. Once she was gone, and Harriet had retreated to the drawing room with Madame Azhkenazy, I was free to slip away.

Marin wasn't waiting for me, but one call of his name and he came galloping out of his kennel and had his paws on the top of the gate, wagging his tail furiously. 'Hello there, my friend,' I said. 'Let's go roaming.'

We headed out of town and up the hill, all around past a chestnut grove, and finally back down. I was flushed and warm, and Marin's tongue was hanging from his mouth, when we returned to Emile's house. My heart ticked hard as I pulled the note out of my bodice and tucked it under Marin's collar. It instantly fell out, so I loosed the ribbon and tied it on. It slid around his collar and hung from the bottom, and I wondered if the note might fall off or be spoiled before Emile saw it. Perhaps that would be for the best.

I latched the gate behind me, called goodbye to Marin and made my way home to prepare myself for dinner at Mr Shawe's rooms at the New Inn.

•

I did not wear the green velvet. I wore grey silk, with a modest bustle, and my hair scooped directly back without any rolls or curls. I thought if I could be plain, then Mr Shawe would set his heart on my sister and I should be afforded a respite.

We made our way to the New Inn shortly after six, our spindly afternoon shadows walking beside us. Aunt Harriet seemed quite distracted by something, but she would not say what. My sister was beautiful in a pink satin gown, and was very pleased to notice the villagers who turned their eyes her way as she walked past. The New Inn was actually a very old building – six hundred years old, according to Harriet – built of wattle and daub and featuring very uneven floors. My sister rushed to hold Harriet's elbow as they made their way up the narrow staircase to Mr Shawe's rooms. I followed behind them. Perhaps I was sullen; I know my sister whispered that accusation sharply to me at some point during the evening. Shawe's man stood at the door and opened it to let us in. We stepped inside a large, low-roofed room, where several people stood about chatting, Mr Shawe among them. Everyone was very well dressed. Only I looked as though I might be a vicar's wife. A long dining table was set for dinner, candles burning.

'Oh,' Aunt Harriet said to us, her tone disappointed. 'I had hoped it would just be us.'

'Who are these people?' my sister said. Clearly she had made the same assumption as my aunt.

'The Clovelys and the Lamberts,' she said. 'And their daughters. Oh, blast. We must make sure we rule that dining table.'

But she could say no more because then Mr Shawe approached with his hand extended and greeted us.

I suppose I should tell you what Mr Shawe looked like, lest you think him some kind of monster. In fact, he was a handsome fellow indeed, with thick golden hair and blue eyes that were almost girlish in their roundness and long-lashedness. He wore tidy sideburns that ended on the sharp angle of his jaw, and a thin moustache. He was dressed in a dark coat and a brocade waistcoat, a white cravat tied about his neck. He had the best teeth I had ever seen: white and even. He was above thirty but below forty, and his fortune was as much earned as inherited. He was a very fine suitor indeed, but for his lack of a title and for his northern manner, which some in the south still found vulgar.

'Mrs Parsons,' he said to Harriet, then to me and my sister, 'Miss Breckby and Miss Breckby.'

'I am quite tired,' Harriet said. 'Would you be so kind as to seat me at the table? Directly across from you, sir, if I may. As the oldest in the room,' here she glanced around, 'do not deny me the conversation of a lovely young man such as yourself.'

'Of course, Mrs Parsons,' he said.

He led her off and sat her at the table, and my sister hooked her arm through mine and said, 'Stay close.' So, we did. We greeted my aunt's neighbours and made small talk. My sister mentioned her visit to the next village and was told she simply must get to Raven's Head, which was one village further along the stream, because there was a very talented glove maker there. I had once enjoyed such social events, but tonight I felt outside of it all. Had Emile arrived home yet? Had he found my note? What did he think of it? How I longed to see him again, have his hot lips on my wrist again. I fanned myself without thinking of it, and somebody said yes, wasn't it abominably hot and somebody else opened a window.

Harriet's ploy worked. With my sister and me either side of her, we were in Mr Shawe's circle at dinner, while the Lambert girls were relegated to the end of the table. I was away in my own world a little at first. The candlelight and the laughter and chatter and the ladies' glistening jewels were a bright blur around me, but I slowly became aware of Mr Shawe's determination to draw me into conversation. At first, he asked me how I liked the weather, given we were both from the north and hadn't these kind of warm days. I answered him and so did my sister, but I did it perfunctorily, while she leaned in and told him a story about the warmest day she had ever experienced at Hatby. Then when the food came – roasted pigeon and wild mushrooms – he asked me if I had ever been shooting. I shook my head, but my sister, again, pushed herself forward and told a little story. So it went. My sister only slightly to the south of flirting; me answering questions in monosyllables.

Just as the dessert arrived, the older gentleman sitting next to Mr Shawe – I think he was Mr Clovely – turned away from the conversation he had been having and fixed me in his gaze.

My apple snow pudding arrived at precisely the moment he said to me, 'Aha! I have remembered!'

I looked at him curiously. Conversation had softened as the puddings were served, and so I found a dozen pairs of eyes on me suddenly.

'I beg your pardon, sir?' I said.

'I have been wondering all evening where I have seen you before. Out on the hill today, with a big brown dog.'

My sister kicked me under the table. Harriet gave me a glare.

'Ah, yes, sir. I did go walking today. I was poorly in the morning but recovered and was keen to get out and walk. It's been a terrible few days of rain.'

'Whose dog was it though, lass? Big ugly thing, it was.'

My pulse was thick in my throat. 'He was a stray, sir. He followed me for a while on the hill. I don't know where he went after that.'

'You were uncommonly kind to him, given he was a stray,' he said, with an admiring smile. 'I saw you giving him a thorough rub. He must have smelled like the very devil.'

'There's no need to curse, my love,' said the woman across from him, presumably his wife.

The attention turned away from me and I relaxed a little. Mr Shawe was beaming at me. 'You like dogs? I have two, you know.'

'Really? What are their names?'

'Bonnie and Heather. Bitches. I find the female dogs always do what they're told. Have you ever been hunting with dogs?'

Here I shook my head again and my sister offered her own anecdote and in that little space when Mr Shawe's attention was off me, Harriet leaned on my shoulder and said, 'You didn't say you were going walking.'

'Madame Azhkenazy was there. I didn't want to disturb you.'

'Mind yourself,' Harriet said. 'Hurtling about the countryside like a pagan, attracting stray dogs.'

'You know I can't bear to be cooped up, Aunt.'

'Stay in the village. It won't do for a girl to be tramping about by herself.'

I ate a spoonful of my pudding. It was so sweet it made my teeth ache. I had had enough of food, enough of company. My imagination roamed to Emile's house, where it would not be so busy nor so bright. I longed to be there and knew at that moment that I would trade Mr Shawe and all his riches, for a quiet life with Emile.

•

Harriet warned me again at breakfast that I should not leave the village on my walk. My sister said she would come with me, but changed her mind after we dressed because it had become hot and she does not like the sun at all. I was relieved, of course, because this meant I could walk with Marin. How absurd to look forward so much to seeing a dog.

'Marin!' I called from the gate, and out he pounded and yes, there was something hanging from his collar, but I saw in a second it was my own note. I removed it and unfolded it, and my disappointment dissolved as I saw Emile's reply on the back.

Dear Moineau, my master must have been so pleased to receive your note! He read it over and over, and even admired the dear lines of your lovely hand with his eyes. I think he would very much like another one. Be gentle with me today because I have a sore paw. Your faithful friend, Marin.

How I glowed! I read it again and was so lost in my elation that I forgot that poor Marin was expecting a walk.

'Have you a sore paw then, my lovely fellow?' I said as I let him out of the gate. He didn't seem too troubled, but I kept the walk short nonetheless. I slipped home after without Harriet seeing me, scribbled down a few lines and returned it to a curious Marin, tying it onto his collar.

So we continued for over a week. It seemed Marin was comfortable telling us things we dared not tell each other. He started quite innocently. *Moineau thinks you the kindest man she has met. Master was pleased to see your face in church on Sunday, even though you were busy with your aunt.* But over time they became more intimate and more dangerous. *Moineau told me the last thought she has at night is the kiss you laid upon her wrist. Master has noticed his house feels very lonely in the evenings, and his bed very cold.*

One fine day, when I decided I would ignore Harriet's advice and take Marin for a long walk across the fields, I was surprised to see Mr Shawe coming in the other direction. We had not spoken since the dinner at the New Inn, but I knew my sister had called on him several times along with one of the Lambert girls, with whom she had become firm friends. I kept my head down and hoped he would not notice me, but that was fruitless of course. He jogged over, calling out, 'Miss Breckby!' and I was obliged to stop and wait, and tell Marin to sit and not growl at him.

'Well met, Miss Breckby!' he said, a high colour in his cheeks. 'Is this the stray Mr Clovely saw you with? Why, he has become very attached to you, I see.'

I didn't answer. Instead I said, 'Is it not a lovely day for a walk?'

'I do admire a woman who isn't afraid of the outdoors,' he said. 'Shall we walk together a while?'

'I was heading up the hill,' I said, hoping it would discourage him, but of course it didn't. Marin trotted along beside me and we made our way through the fields and then trudged up the slope to the crest of the hill.

Here, exhausted, Mr Shawe sat down. I sat with him and Marin beside me, and we looked out over the village. I could see the church and I knew Emile was in there, among his timber and his tools.

'I rather think that dog belongs to somebody,' Mr Shawe said. 'He is well groomed. Perhaps he escapes when he hears you coming.'

'Perhaps. He's a good boy.' I patted Marin's head, and he licked my hand lovingly.

'I wonder does he fetch. Here.' Mr Shawe found a stick and cast it along the path. Marin raced off and brought it back, dropping it at Mr Shawe's feet. 'Oh, I don't think so, good fellow,' Mr Shawe said to the dog. 'It's all covered in your slobber now.'

I took pity and picked up the stick and threw it again. Marin ran back and forth while Mr Shawe and I conversed about nature and animals, Millthorne compared with Hatby, and at every turn Mr Shawe tried to draw me out, tried to connect me more deeply with him; and I was quiet and did not elaborate and remained perfectly polite but aloof.

'Would you like to remain in Hatby?' he asked me at one stage.

'I would like to travel,' I said carefully. 'I think there are many fine places to see.'

'You ought to travel to the east, as I do,' he said. 'Perhaps you may get to do so one day.' He added pointedly, 'When you are married.'

'I do not think often of marriage,' I said lightly.

'I thought it was what every woman wanted,' he laughed.

'I'm not sure what I want.'

'You can have anything you want, if you marry well.'

The air between us had grown uncomfortable. 'Well,' I said. 'It's surely time for me to return to my aunt.'

'I shall walk you home.'

All I could think was I needed to return Marin to Emile's garden. 'If you do not mind, Mister Shawe, I have a great deal to think about and would appreciate my independence.'

He looked at me, his eyes narrowed slightly, and I could almost feel him trying to get inside my head, to measure me up. 'You do have a great deal to think about, I imagine,' he said. 'I shall leave you be.'

He rose and strode off. I watched him until he disappeared down the slope, and only then did I breathe easily again. Why on earth had he fixated on me? My sister was practically throwing herself at him. Perhaps that was it. Perhaps he liked me because my resistance made me seem more decorous. I would have to explain this to my sister, before she made a fool of herself.

A breeze lifted my hair off my neck, cooling me. Marin had laid his head on his front paws and was sleeping soundly, the way only dogs can. I thought about what Mr Shawe had said: *You can have anything you want, if you marry well.* In fact, the thing I wanted most of all would be forbidden me if I married Mr Shawe.

I allowed myself to imagine that I could marry Emile, that my parents wouldn't disown me, my aunt wouldn't faint in shock, the vicar wouldn't refuse to marry us in his church, and so on. Why shouldn't I marry him? He was not rich, but neither was he a pauper. Yes, I was used to a very different kind of life, but what did I really care for the trappings of wealth? In all of my life as a wealthy woman, I had known no greater happiness than Emile's company. I could learn to cook and to clean. Perhaps my father would buy us a house and give us a small staff.

I laughed out loud. Now I was well into the realms of make-believe.

I rose, told Marin to follow, and started back down the hill.

•

302

It was clear to me that something was troubling Aunt Harriet. Her happy spirit, which had not diminished with Uncle Oswald's death, seemed to have dimmed. Madame Azhkenazy came by every second day, and held a séance once a week in Harriet's drawing room. But even these moments of hope, where she might be able to contact Oswald again, did not sustain her the way they once had.

I tried to give her comfort, but she was determined to pretend there was nothing wrong, and she often had Madame there, which made it impossible for me to talk to her.

One evening, after dinner when her séance group were arriving, hanging up coats and ordering Toby and Jones about, I returned to my room and opened my door to see my sister standing there.

Her back was to me, her blonde head bent over something she had found. My heart pounded.

'Sister?'

She turned, her face flushed with guilt. I could see in her hand the notes between me and Emile. I reached out and snatched them from her, my ears ringing with fear and anger so that I could barely hear her excuses.

'I came to borrow a hairbrush. I can't find mine anywhere. They were just there in the drawer. I don't understand: who are Master and Moineau, and why do you have their correspondence?'

I thought about lying to her then, making up some wild story about letters I'd found, or a novel I was writing, or *anything* but the truth. But I could not rely on myself to do so, and my sister is very astute at detecting lies. So, I simply stood there, the letters in my hand, and said nothing, until the realisation flickered across her face and she took a step towards me and asked, 'Who is he?'

'A carpenter,' I said. 'The carpenter who is working in the church. His name is Emile. I think I love him.'

'Does he love you?' Then she shook her head. 'Of course he does, I've read his notes to you. You don't want to marry Mister Shawe, then?'

I shook my head. 'It's the last thing I want to do.'

'And here I have been certain you've been charming him away from me. You're all he ever talks about. But if you don't want him . . .'

I sat heavily on my bed. Basil looked up from his customary spot and miaowed at me. 'I don't want to marry anyone chosen by Father,' I said. 'He chooses terrible husbands.'

'It would be Mother's choice, too.'

'Even worse.'

'You would marry for love? And be poor?'

I nodded.

'Then why are you here now, with me? Why are you bothering leaving him little notes? Why do you not just go to him?'

'Because Harriet has forbidden it.'

She sat with me, took my hand in hers. 'Harriet is in a locked room downstairs trying to contact the dead. She'll never know.' Then in a whisper. 'I'll never tell her.'

I realised, in some deeper and wiser part of me, that my sister's encouragement was self-serving. All she really cared about was securing Mr Shawe's affections, along with his seven factories and three houses. Perhaps she even wanted me to be discovered, wind up disgraced; because then Mr Shawe would think me a liability as a potential wife. But all I heard was my sister telling me to creep out now, in the evening gloom, and see Emile. I felt like a bird in a cage, who sees that the door lies open.

'You really wouldn't tell?'

'Never. As God is my witness. It's summer and we're a long way from home, dear sister. I would have you pursue happiness, even if it is only for a little while.'

My heart pounding, I pulled on a light coat and my sister tidied my hair. Jones saw me near the front door, but pointedly looked away as I sneaked out. Then I was on the street, head down and hoping not to be recognised. Only a glimmer of light was left in the sky, enough to see my way and be seen. All the birds had gone to bed. Yellow light glowed from behind windows; the shops were silent and dark. Emile's lane was shadowy, but I knew the way well from my many visits to Marin. In fact, the dog was there at the gate to greet me.

'Hello, my friend,' I said softly, and realised my throat was dry. What on earth was I doing? I had not been raised to sneak about to men's houses in the dark. But neither had I ever been in love. No wonder poets wrote about it so rapturously.

Marin whined softly as I shut the gate behind me and it became apparent we weren't going walking, but he soon joined me as I crossed the grass to the front door of Emile's house. I knocked once, then stood and waited, heart thundering.

He opened the door. All the time that had passed, where I had only caught glimpses of him in church or had to make do with his little notes to me, had made us hungry to see each other. He grasped my hand and pulled me inside, slamming the door closed.

'*Moineau*? Is everything well? Why have you come to see me?'

If I am truthful, I barely heard what he said. He was shirtless, you see. I had only seen a shirtless man once or twice before, and they were doughy fellows working on the rail lines. The presence of him, in this state of undress, erased all thoughts from my mind for a number of seconds too long to be graceful. His arms and shoulders were well formed and muscular, his chest was broad with curling black hair growing over hard muscles. The hair grew in a line down across his flat belly, and disappeared into the top of his trousers. I registered all this in a few seconds and then he was pulling on a shirt and buttoning it up, and I was suddenly able to speak again.

'I'm sorry, I . . .'

'I wouldn't have answered the door that way if I'd known it was you. There have been some local boys around who come and knock to irritate Marin. I expected to give them a hiding.' I realised from the flush of his cheeks that he was embarrassed. 'But why have you come?'

'My sister said I should.'

'Is she the woman who has been at church with you the last few Sundays? I wondered if you were related. You look very similar.'

'I believe my sister is probably prettier than me.'

'Not possible,' he said, then remembered himself. 'Come in. Sit down. I'm making my supper. Would you like anything?'

I followed him into the living room and sat on the settee, while he moved behind the kitchen bench and stirred a pot on the range. I watched his back for a little while, and felt keenly the disappointment that I hadn't seen him shirtless from this view.

By now, I should confess, I was quite wild with passion. As these feelings were new, and I hadn't experience to temper them, they overwhelmed me completely. It seemed my whole body and mind was solely fixed on the idea of touching him and having him touch me. I tucked my hands under my legs and took deep breaths. Marin rested his head on my lap and looked at me with sad eyes.

'Away with you, Marin,' Emile said as he turned and saw the dog. He scooped a bowlful of stew out of the pot and came to sit opposite me.

'That smells good,' I said.

'It's a *tatouiller*. My mother taught me to make it. Would you care to try some?'

I was about to refuse, but then he held out a spoon to me and I leaned in and he tipped it gently into my mouth. 'Oh,' I said. 'That's delicious.'

'It's stewed vegetables and a few secret herbs,' he said smiling. 'I can only afford meat two or three times a week, but this manages to satisfy me after a long day working.' He ate a spoonful then said, 'I expect you eat meat every night of the week.'

I hadn't thought about what I ate before now. Food appeared in front of me and was cleared away. As money was not scarce among my family and acquaintances, he was right: meat was always on the menu. He didn't wait for an answer but instead asked me again about my sister and how I had entertained myself these past few weeks since we had spoken in person. We had grown shy with each other somehow. Now I was here, a clear declaration that I longed to be with him, it seemed we could talk about little more than trivial things. Finally – after a pause in conversation where I thought, *It is dark, I should go* – he said, 'So, you have told your sister about me?'

'Yes. Well. She found our notes.'

'Ah, our notes.' He smiled, his eyes travelling to the bureau under the window. I followed his gaze and saw a folded note sitting there.

'Is that tomorrow's?' I asked, excited.

'Yes, but I'm not sure Marin should give it to you. I think he should strike out the lines and start anew.'

'Why? May I see it now?' I was halfway across the room already, my breath half-held, desperate to see what it was Marin shouldn't tell me. It was in my hands in a second, and then Emile was there with his fingers firmly over mine.

307

'Don't,' he said darkly. He was very close. I could feel the heat from his body. His grip was tight.

'Please,' I said.

He slowly let go, and I unfolded the note and read it before he could change his mind.

Moineau, I am falling in love with you.

My senses reeled, throwing me off balance but in a pleasant way, like sand dissolving beneath my feet. 'And is this from you, or from Marin?' I asked lightly.

His own serious gaze did not lighten. 'It must be from Marin, for I ought not fall in love with you.'

The off-balance feeling became instantly unpleasant. 'Why not?'

'It won't end well. You do not know all there is to know about me.'

'Then, tell me. I want to know everything about you.'

'No, you do not. You cannot.' He stepped away from me, then shook his head, the darkness dissolving. 'It is late and I am tired, and not making any sense,' he said.

'Would you like me to go?' I felt silly and afraid.

'No, I . . . I have so missed seeing you. Stay a little longer and we will talk about other things.'

So, I stayed, and we pretended the strange interaction over the note hadn't happened. We sat opposite each other and did not touch, but I could still remember the feel of his hands on mine, and that night as I went to sleep I held the feeling in my mind until it dissolved into blackness. I dreamed of standing by a window, reaching through to grasp Emile's hands on the other side, only to find they were Mr Shawe's hands instead.

CHAPTER 19
Moineau

Three nights in a row Madame Azhkenazy called a séance, and each time I visited Emile after dinner, with my sister urging me more and more strongly. 'Why oughtn't you marry a carpenter?' she said. 'As long as one of us takes Mister Shawe as Father has promised.'

I asked her once, if all of Mr Shawe's money would make up for a lack of love, and she gave me such a look as if my question had been asked in a language she didn't understand.

Why oughtn't you marry a carpenter? Yes, why oughtn't I? My evenings with Emile were pure bliss. We talked, we ate, we lay on the floor one night with Marin between us, listening to light rain on the roof and Emile said, 'Marin is in heaven at this moment,' and I said, 'So am I' at precisely the same time Emile said it. I took this as a sign. I took *everything* as a sign. I had become as superstitious as Harriet. Even the clear weather seemed to conspire to keep Emile and I in our happy bubble, in the plain little house, under the stars.

On the fourth day, in the late morning, I was lying on my bed reading with Basil tucked under my arm, when I heard a great commotion downstairs. I put aside my book and my cat, and descended the stairs to find Harriet howling in the drawing room and Jones trying to get her to take some tea. Harriet had upended the tea tray and was pounding her own chest, shouting, 'He's gone! He's gone!'

'What is it?' I asked, hurrying to Harriet's side.

'Madame Azhkenazy has visited,' Jones said, her mouth pulled down hard at the corners.

'She said there is nothing more to be done,' Harriet sobbed. 'She cannot reach Oswald. He is lost forever to me. Oh, the stubborn fellow! He was always stubborn in life too!'

I held Aunt Harriet against me, surprised by how small and soft she was. She had such a big personality that I'd believed her more robust of body. She shook with sobs. My sister appeared at the door and asked what had happened.

'Aunt Harriet has lost Uncle Oswald,' I said, even though the loss was several months in the past.

My sister asked no questions, and immediately came to comfort Harriet, while I gave a kind nod to Jones, who cleared up the mess swiftly and left the room. We made a little circle: my sister, my aunt and I. We held each other for a very long time, and then Harriet sniffed and gently pushed us away and said, 'If only I could say goodbye to him.' Her face was distorted by an unvoiced sob. 'I didn't get a chance to tell him how much I loved him.'

'Sh,' my sister said, smoothing her hair.

'That was all I wanted. For Madame Azhkenazy to make contact so I could say goodbye.'

'I know,' I said, though I didn't know then how insurmountable the loss of love feels.

My sister met my gaze over the top of Harriet's head. I could tell by her one cocked eyebrow that she had thought of a plan. I nodded to indicate I understood, because it was very simple really. Jones was certain Madame Azhkenazy was taking large sums of money from Harriet. If we offered her a large enough sum, perhaps she would return and pretend to contact Oswald, giving my aunt the chance to say goodbye.

But for now, we stayed with Harriet and eventually she said it was time for her to draw the shades and put on her widow's weeds, and what a fool she'd been. My sister helped her upstairs to dress her in black, and I went below stairs to find Jones.

I found her bent over an open cupboard in the scullery, a crooked little corner behind the kitchen. She was pulling out cleaning brushes and bottles and jars of soap and polish.

'Jones?' I asked.

She stood, gave me a curt nod. 'Miss Breckby. I tidy cupboards when I'm angry.'

'You're angry at Madame Azhkenazy?'

'I knew that Russian witch was up to no good. She made promises she could not keep.'

'Where does she live? My sister and I are going to pay her a visit.'

'She lives over the tea room on the high street in Raven's Head. Hateful woman, leading on poor Mrs Parsons like that. Are you going to get back all the money she's been paid?'

'Actually . . . there may be one last visit from Madame Azhkenazy.' I touched her shoulder gently. 'You must trust my sister and me.'

'Best keep me away from her then, lest I give her a black eye.' Jones made a harrumphing noise. 'I've sent for Doctor Mortensen. He will bring her an anodyne to calm her down, and she can doze on the sofa all afternoon.'

I returned to the drawing room and soon enough Harriet came in, supported by my sister, her bright green gown abandoned for sombre black. We settled her on the couch in time for Dr Mortensen's visit, and soon after she drank the anodyne he gave her, she became settled and sleepy.

My sister and I finally had a chance to talk outside the drawing-room door.

'Raven's Head,' I said. 'We can go tomorrow and find this beastly woman and insist she come and sort this out.'

'Today,' my sister said. 'I don't see why we should wait.'

'We have to arrange a carriage.'

'Mister Shawe will take us.'

'Mister . . . No, we are not going to mention this to Mister Shawe. This is a family matter and we can deal with it ourselves.'

'You are far too independent, sister,' she said. 'Mister Shawe has a carriage sitting there. Besides, I want to see if he'll say yes.'

'Of course he will say yes. It's the gentlemanly thing to do.'

'I want to see if he says yes quickly,' she corrected herself. 'Come, sister. We can be at Raven's Head by one and have this whole mess sorted out.'

I glanced over my shoulder at the closed drawing-room door, remembering Harriet's small trembling body. 'Very well,' I said. 'Though I do not like being beholden to him.'

'He will be family soon, one way or another,' my sister said. Her tone was light but I knew she was deadly serious.

•

Mr Shawe agreed with haste. I was relieved to see that he seemed to have transferred his interest to my sister, and was solicitous and attentive to her, while I stood back as they made plans. Now his attention was solely on her, she relaxed and became her calm, good-natured self, and I liked her a lot better this way than when she was shrill or flirtatious. Within half an hour, we had set off in his fine carriage towards Raven's Head. It was a clear afternoon, with only the slightest breeze, and so he had the canopy back so we could have the sun on our hair. We rolled out of the village, past Emile's lane. I thought of last night's conversation with him, when I had asked him what he thought happiness was. 'A quiet mind and good company,' he had said.

A quiet mind and good company. It was so simple and so powerful, for I knew now this was exactly what I wanted. Not houses and factories and fine carriages, though I didn't blame my sister for wanting those instead.

Mr Shawe asked me teasingly if I had continued to attract stray dogs, and I told him boldly that in fact I had found the dog's owner, Mr Emile Venson, the carpenter who worked at the church.

'A carpenter's dog,' he sniffed. 'Even better.'

'Mister Venson is a very kind gentleman.'

'He may be kind, but if he's a carpenter, he is no gentleman,' Mr Shawe countered quickly.

'Careful, she's quite taken with him,' said my sister, and I wanted to kick her shins for saying it aloud.

'Mister Venson and I are on friendly terms, and no more,' I said.

Mr Shawe eyed me suspiciously. I turned my face away to watch the passing countryside, and my sister distracted him with some other nonsense and it seemed the conversation had moved on. I breathed out in relief. We rattled past wildflowers and deep cool groves, slowly up steep hills, then racing down again. In just over an hour we were slowing down on the high street of Raven's Head. It was a larger village than Millthorne, with an old market square in front of the church, and many new stone buildings.

313

'Jones said there was a tea room,' I told them, as the carriage came to a halt and we made to climb out.

'I see it,' said my sister, as Mr Shawe helped her down, his hands lingering a moment too long on her hips. She smiled at him.

I took his hand to climb down but released it quickly. 'I'm sure you don't need to come, Mister Shawe,' I said. 'It is, after all, sensitive family business.'

'Don't listen to her,' my sister said, already striding off. 'Of course we need you, Ernest. What if she has a terrible Russian husband with knives hidden in his trousers?'

I smiled weakly at Mr Shawe, who gave me a dark look in return. I ignored it and followed my sister. All the little shops looked so inviting with their wares in their windows. We found the entrance beside the tea room and walked up a crooked staircase to Madame Azhkenazy's home. Hanging on the door was a wreath of hawthorn and dangling from the middle of it, what looked to be a bird's skull.

'How dramatic,' Mr Shawe said, recoiling.

I lifted my hand and knocked, and within a few moments the door opened. Madame Azhkenazy, minus her dark head-scarf, blinked back at me. 'What do you want?'

'I need to talk to you about Aunt Harriet.'

'I have nothing to say.'

'Let us in,' demanded Mr Shawe. 'Or there'll be the devil to pay.'

Madame Azhkenazy laughed bitterly, but let us in nonetheless. I found myself standing in a tiny, dark room, with black curtains hanging from the windows, and the greasy smell of tallow candles hanging on the air. There was a small table, but no sofas or easy chairs. She stood in front of us, defiantly, and said, 'My relationship with your aunt is at an end.'

'Has she refused to pay you more money?' my sister asked, in a sharp tone.

'No money in the world is enough to contact the dead if the dead will not be contacted,' Madame Azhkenazy said with an arch of her brows.

Mr Shawe was about to say something but I silenced him with a look and said to her, gently and reasonably, 'We will pay you handsomely to return tomorrow for a last séance, and tell her that Oswald speaks to you.'

'You insult me. I do not perform parlour tricks.'

'Oh, come now,' Shawe boomed. 'Everything you do is nonsense. We know it and you know it, so just do as the lass says. In fact, *I* shall pay you, and I can pay you much more than either of these girls can.'

'Mister Shawe, no,' I said, at precisely the moment my sister said, swooningly, 'Oh, what a perfect gentleman you are!'

Madame Azhkenazy looked from me to my sister, then settled her gaze back on Shawe. 'How much?'

'Twenty pounds,' he said.

'Twenty-five,' she countered instantly.

'Yes, twenty-five,' Shawe said. 'But you must come every night for a week and let her speak with him.'

My stomach swirled with guilt. On the one hand, she had agreed. On the other, we were now deeply indebted to Shawe, and he really had offered her a lot of money – more than triple what I was prepared to give her. Shawe had the money in her hand with showy speed, and the deal was done.

'You must be convincing,' I said to Madame Azhkenazy. 'She is in a mourning gown, but have Uncle Oswald say he prefers her in green.'

'Yes, and that he will try to visit her in her dreams, and she will know him because he will be a young man again.'

We went on, layering the details, giving her specific things to say: things only Oswald would know or mention. Once we had exhausted all the information we had, we finished with a wish that she would tell Harriet that Oswald was sorry to leave her. 'And he will see her one day again, and hold her in his arms,' my sister added, and I pressed her hand, so overcome with emotion and affection.

'I will come tomorrow,' Madame said. 'And now you are here, would you like me to tell your fortunes?'

'What nonsense,' Mr Shawe said, but my sister gave him an appealing look.

'Oh, do go on, Ernest. It's just a bit of fun. Besides,' she turned to Madame Azhkenazy, 'I should like to know my future.'

'I won't hear of it,' he said. 'Come along.'

My sister followed him obediently, but I hung back a little and said softly to Madame Azhkenazy. 'Go on.'

'It looks as though your companions are leaving,' she said, smiling cruelly. Mr Shawe and my sister were already out the door and on the staircase.

I nodded and moved towards the door, but her bony hand shot out and she held me close by her a moment and said in my ear, 'He's lying to you.'

'Who? Shawe?' Then an awful, sick thought. 'Emile?'

'A man. There is a man, and he is lying to you.' Then she released me, and my sister was calling to me from the stairs, so I hurried off.

'That was well done,' my sister was saying to Mr Shawe.

'Poor people always have their price,' he bragged, then gave me a sidelong glance and said, 'Maybe even poor carpenters.'

Before he uttered this, I had disliked Mr Shawe. Now I despised him. I bit my tongue so I didn't tell him so, as I followed them back to the carriage.

·

I couldn't get away to see Emile with Harriet in such a state, so I stayed with her that evening and all the next day, and prayed that Madame Azhkenazy would come soon. My sister and I were solemn and quiet, but always there by her side; and between us all we must have drunk a barrel of tea; Jones declared it was 'just the thing' for troubled times.

When a loud knock at the door sounded through the house, just on dusk, my heart leapt. It would be Madame Azhkenazy, and she would call a séance, and Harriet would be distracted enough that I could leave to see Emile. But it wasn't. The drawing-room door opened, and Toby showed the vicar in just as Jones was lighting the lamps.

'The vicar!' Toby announced, before retreating again.

'Mrs Parsons,' he said, limping in. 'Miss Breckby, Miss Breckby.'

'Good evening, Vicar,' Harriet said. 'Have you come to comfort me, for I'm sure I cannot be comforted.'

'Comfort you? No . . . I . . . has some ill befallen you?'

'My aunt is just now feeling the loss of her husband,' I explained hurriedly.

His face froze as his brain ticked over. 'Oswald?' he said, confused.

'Yes, yes, Oswald, who else?' Harriet cried.

I could not blame him for being confused; he had buried Oswald so long ago. 'Ah, well. I am very sorry. Again,' he said.

'Perhaps come back another day, sir,' my sister said.

'No, no, he has come for some reason,' Harriet said. 'Speak, Vicar. I'm sure I need some distraction.'

'Yes, well. I need your good advice as head of the church renovation committee.'

'Go on.'

'Our man, Venson.' He looked pointedly at me before he continued. 'Emile. He's had an accident while sawing some wood and won't be able to work for some time.'

It was as though the room went white, and everything became muffled. I needed to speak, but couldn't. Bless my sister, who said, 'What kind of accident? Is he badly injured?'

'No, not badly. Just inconveniently. He's cut his palm quite deeply. Obviously, he can't do anything useful until it's healed.'

I relaxed a little, but still longed to get out and see Emile.

'And what advice would you have of me?' Harriet asked.

At that moment, there was another knock on the door.

'Busy in here tonight,' said the vicar. 'What I'd like to know, Mrs Parsons, is whether you'd have me find another carpenter to finish the job, or wait for him.'

'Oh, but you must wait for him,' I said, before I had the good sense to hold the words back. 'It isn't his fault he's injured.'

The vicar gave me the full weight of his cold gaze. 'Miss Breckby, thank you. I had asked your aunt, though, who is the head of the renovation committee.'

Harriet looked at me sideways then turned her attention back to the vicar. 'The man does good work and it might take us just as long to find another,' she said. 'We shall wait for him.'

Tears pricked my eyes and I wanted to throw myself onto Harriet and hug her.

'A wise decision, my lady,' the vicar said, and was about to say something else when the door to the drawing room opened and Toby stood there again, this time with Madame Azhkenazy.

'Madame Azhkenazy!' he announced, then withdrew.

They faced each other across the room, the vicar and the medium. Harriet said, 'Oh!' and the vicar said, 'Harriet, *really*.'

I leapt to my feet. 'Vicar, let me see you out.'

'Come in, Madame,' my sister said to her. 'How lovely that you have returned.'

I took the vicar by the elbow and led him away, closing the drawing-room door behind us.

'What is that witch doing here?' he asked.

'She gives my aunt comfort,' I said.

'God should be all the comfort she needs.'

'Yes, I see that. But if Aunt Harriet is happy, where's the harm?'

'The devil laying claim on her soul might be quite some harm,' he muttered, but he knew he fought a battle he couldn't win. We paused at the front door; it had started raining lightly and I could see he had no umbrella.

'Allow me to walk you back to the vicarage. I have an umbrella we can both fit under.'

'That won't be necessary,' he said, but I could tell he was unsure and so I said it more forcefully, pulling a large umbrella from the stand beside the door.

We moved out into the street and down towards Church Lane. His limp was exaggerated if we walked faster, so I kept the pace slow and talked about anything but Madame Azhkenazy and Emile. Weather, flowers, if he preferred cats to dogs. Finally we were at the vicarage and he thanked me and then said, 'Take care of your aunt.'

'I assure you, I do.'

'And yourself,' he said.

I chafed against this. I knew he meant my feelings for Emile, and it infuriated me that anyone would think I would be taking care of myself better by choosing a rich husband over the man I loved. I didn't answer, and he went inside.

I, of course, went directly to Emile's house.

The street was deserted, dark and mournful and mizzling. I put my foot in a muddy puddle in Emile's lane, and my feet squelched uncomfortably the rest of the way. But none of this could dampen my hope and my desire, because I was going to see Emile again and the time without him had been unbearably long.

Marin barked from the other side of the door as I knocked, and I called out to him to be quiet, that it was only me. Within a few seconds, the door was open and Emile was smiling down on me.

'*Moineau*! What a delight!'

I saw his bandaged left hand and said, 'It's true, then? You are injured?'

He held up his hand. 'I wasn't paying attention and I slipped. Come in out of the rain.'

I went in, and the warm, plain house with its modest candlelight felt like home.

'You are here in good time, actually. I wonder if you'd help me change this bandage. The physician said I should change it every evening, but I don't know how I am meant to with only one hand for the task.'

'Of course,' I said, pleased beyond expression at the idea of playing nurse to him.

He gave me instructions and I boiled some water and mixed it with the water from the jug to make it tepid, then I fetched the clean bandage and the salve, and brought it all on a tray to the living room. I sat beside him and he gave me his hand, palm up, in my lap.

'It hurts like the blazes,' he said.

'Let's see it,' I answered, and carefully unwrapped the bandage. The inner layers were quite bloody and I promised him I'd boil it and hang it up before I went, so that he could use it again. The wound was diagonal across his palm, like two cuts overlapping. It looked deep on the heel of his thumb, but less so elsewhere. I sponged it carefully, then held his hand in mine while I let it dry.

'Thank you,' he said.

He was so close. I could feel his pulse in his wrist. I couldn't meet his eye, I was so overcome with desire. I blew gently on the wound to dry it, and he sighed softly.

'*Moineau*,' he said, his voice thick with feeling.

I put the tray on the floor, picking up the fresh bandage. Carefully, I began to wind it around his palm, then under his thumb and around his wrist to keep it secure. I tied it, but couldn't let him go.

I couldn't let him go.

And he pulled me towards him, even though it must have hurt him to close his hand over mine. He pulled me towards him and opened his arms and I sank between them, my head on his chest. His good hand was in my hair, stroking it gently, while his injured hand rested on my back. 'There,' he said. 'There.'

What perfect bliss. What perfect, perfect bliss. I allowed myself to be folded into his embrace and he did not let go, and nor did I, as the rain deepened overhead and Marin watched us curiously from the rug.

'*Moineau*?' he said.

I turned my face up and he grasped my chin in his hand, then bent his head to kiss my lips. Every nerve in my body lit up with a sweet, hot feeling. *Emile is kissing me*, I thought, and the knowledge of its forbiddance inflamed me even more. I did not know how to kiss, but he did. His lips parted mine and my body went weak. He kissed my top lip, then my bottom lip, then both, then I felt the tip of his tongue in my mouth and I was completely undone. He could have done anything to me then, I was so thoroughly under his spell. I moaned a little, and seemed to hear myself from far away.

Then he pulled back, and saw my stunned expression and laughed at me gently.

'Oh, *Moineau*. I am so sorry. I oughtn't have taken such a liberty with you.'

'Please, take it again,' I said.

'No, no. I was overcome with feeling but now I have my rational head on my shoulders again. Forgive me, my love.'

My love. I lurched forward and pressed my lips against his, and all his talk about liberties and rational heads could stay outside in the rain. Now he had kissed me, I would never let him go. We spoke only with kisses until the rain stopped, and my lips were burning as I made my way home in the damp dark.

•

What a dreamy-eyed fool I was for the next week. Harriet was completely distracted by the return of Madame Azhkenazy; the messages from Oswald were coming so regularly that Harriet moved Madame into the servants' quarters so she did not have to continue to travel between Millthorne and Raven's Head. My sister continued to prevail on Mr Shawe for his carriage to take her sightseeing. I wandered free as a pagan, which meant to Emile's house, Emile's garden, and the long green grass of the stream behind.

We played a game, Emile and I. We called it 'If anything were possible', and under its guise we said everything that we wished for in life.

'If anything were possible,' I said to him one day, as we sat by the stream with the sun in our hair, 'I should like to leave Yorkshire behind and come to live right here in Millthorne.'

'If anything were possible,' he said, 'I would have you here by me, every waking hour, and every night as well.'

And so it went: declarations of impossible plans. At the end of every game he would say, 'But not everything is possible,' and it would make me sad. But then he would kiss me, and my brain would be wiped blank for long enough to forget I was sad, and for hope to grow anew.

We were so happy.

These things don't last.

•

It was a Tuesday. The least interesting day of the week. Madame Azhkenazy was leaving that morning, and Aunt Harriet, once again resplendent in her green gown but slightly more subdued than I had found her when I arrived, had enlisted me to help see her off. My sister had disappeared directly after breakfast to have a picnic with Mr Shawe. She had asked me if I knew any cosy spots and I didn't tell her about the Hawthorn Well, because if I wasn't allowed to picnic in love there, then why should she be?

So, I was helping to organise Madame Azhkenazy's bags by the door, while Harriet effusively kissed her and told her that she was a divine gift and was she sure Oswald had nothing more to say, when my sister returned up the street. The slump of her shoulders and the bend of her head told me she had suffered some blow and I waited curiously by the door for her arrival.

'What's wrong?' I asked, as soon as she was in earshot.

She glanced up, but shook her head. Toby was to take Madame to the carriage, and Harriet was pushing money into her hand for the driver. My sister forced a smile for my aunt and for Madame, and then the Russian witch was on her way. We watched until she and Toby turned the corner and headed towards the coach stop, and then my sister and I enfolded Harriet in a warm, quick hug.

'Will you be all right, now she's gone?' I asked her, as we moved back into the house and along the hallway to the drawing room.

'I expect so. I'll need you girls about me for a day or two, until I find my feet.'

'Of course, Aunt,' my sister said.

I nodded too, but I was desperate to get out and see Emile and so I couldn't respond as forcefully.

'But I have some grim news, I'm afraid,' my sister continued, taking off her bonnet and gloves and laying them on the mantelpiece. 'Mister Shawe is readying himself to leave for London at first light tomorrow. He said he was too busy to picnic today, on account of all the packing and organising he has to do.'

'London isn't far, my dear,' Harriet said. 'Here, come and sit by me.'

My sister slumped onto the couch next to Harriet and said, 'He goes to London early because he has to sail away to India tomorrow, Aunt.'

The relief that flooded me then nearly took my knees from under me. I sat opposite them. 'Has he been called away on business?' I asked.

'Yes. What abominable timing, though! Once again, both of us on the shelf. It will not do, I tell you. Father must make him declare his hand.' She put her hand on her head. 'I believe I am coming down with something, Aunt. My head is thudding.'

'Poor lamb. I'll get Jones to call Doctor Mortensen.'

'No, never mind that. I will rest today and perhaps feel better tomorrow. Blast it all. I want to get on with my life. He is making us wait forever!'

'Don't go writing to Mister Peacock to come down here,' I said, and although I intended it to sound like a joke, it landed darkly and my sister gave me a sharp glance.

'I don't see a third option that Father will actually approve of,' she said imperiously.

324

Harriet looked from one of us to the other and said, 'You girls will always be sisters, no matter whom you marry. Be gentle with each other.'

Neither of us felt like being gentle, but we pretended for Harriet's sake. We repurposed my sister's picnic and we went to the Hawthorn Well and enjoyed the summer day, knowing that they were on the turn now. The oak leaves looked tired. Autumn would be here soon enough.

After lunch, we sat in the drawing room and played cards, and now and again Harriet would tell us some other message that Oswald had sent to her via Madame Azhkenazy, and we would smile and pat her wrist. Although I missed Emile fiercely, I was sensible that today was a good day, a companionable day. My aunt missed Oswald just as much, and my sister missed Mr Shawe. The three of us were well matched in mood.

As Harriet was shuffling the cards once more, there came a knock on the door. Harriet looked at us curiously. 'Are you expecting anyone?'

We shook our heads, and soon enough Toby was there announcing Mr Shawe's arrival.

'Ernest!' my sister said, rising to greet him.

'Forgive me,' he said, removing his hat and holding it across his chest. 'I know I have come at an awkward time but I couldn't leave without . . . Mrs Parsons, would you allow me to take your niece to the formal parlour to speak privately?' As he said this, his eye fell on me.

The others saw it.

'My niece?' Harriet asked, gesturing to my sister.

He fixed me in his gaze. 'Miss Breckby? May I speak with you privately?'

'Whatever you have to say, you can say in front of us, surely,' my sister said, in a jovial tone that was brittle over her fear and anger.

'I do apologise,' he said. 'I will only take her away for a few moments, and then I will be on my way.'

I rose, my knees loose beneath me. He offered me his arm and I took it stiffly, then we crossed the hallway and went into the parlour. The curtains were still open, letting in the last of the afternoon sun. No lamps had yet been lit.

'Miss Breckby,' he said, once the door was closed behind us, 'I expect your sister has told you I sail for India tomorrow?'

'Yes,' I said, and realised that my lungs were tight with held breath. I forced myself to relax, and sat on the sofa with my hands folded on my knees.

'After spending this time with the both of you, I am reluctant to leave without first settling the issue of marriage,' Mr Shawe said, still standing. 'Lord Breckby has given his in-principle blessing for me to marry either of you, and so I am asking you to be my wife.'

Shock drained the blood away from my face. I could feel it grow cold. 'Me? But . . . why not—'

'Your sister is very entertaining company, but as a wife she would exhaust me.' Here he smiled, conspiratorially. 'The headaches. The moment she thinks I am not listening to her . . .'

'I am well acquainted with my sister's follies, Mister Shawe,' I replied sternly. 'You have led her on terribly.'

'I led nobody on. You were always my choice. I need a steady hand in the home, and a wife who is independent enough to withstand my long absences. Your sister is entirely wrong for me and you are entirely right. So, put any guilt out of your head, so that you may say yes.'

'No,' I said.

He blinked in shock. 'Please, Miss Breckby. As I have said, your sister will get used to the idea—'

'I don't say no on account of my sister,' I said. 'I say no on account of the fact that I don't love you and I don't want to marry you.'

His bafflement might have made me feel pity, were I not so desperate to escape the situation. Once the confusion on his face passed, anger took its place. 'Your father will make you,' he said.

'Is that what you want? A wife forced to be with you? How would that make me any different from a prostitute?'

'Miss Breckby! I never thought to hear such things from your sweet lips.' He jammed his hat on firmly. 'This is not the last of this issue, I assure you. I will write to your father before I leave.'

Then he threw open the parlour door and my aunt and sister were both there, and had clearly been listening through the keyhole.

'Good evening,' Mr Shawe said, embarrassed and angry.

'Let me see you to the door, Ernest—' my sister started, but he brushed her off and now she turned to me with furious eyes.

Harriet had scurried after Mr Shawe, and my sister used the time alone with me to unleash her rage. 'How do you dare, you horrible girl?' she said. 'How do you dare to turn him down?'

'I thought you would be glad. Now he might marry you.'

'He won't marry me. I heard his summation of my faults. But to insult me further by turning him down. Do you think yourself so superior to me?'

'What?' I said, astonished. 'No! This has nothing to do with you.'

'It has everything to do with me, as your sister. As a member of your family, all of whom want you to marry him. Father will be monstrously enraged with you, and I will not blame him one whit. If you were not so enamoured of that wretched carpenter—' She was not so furious with me that she was careless. When she heard Harriet returning she immediately stopped.

Harriet grasped my upper arms. 'I have smoothed things over for now. My dear, what have you done? Why have you done it? You know that you were promised to Mister Shawe.'

'I can't bear him.'

'He has a lot of money and is away a great deal. Be sensible, Little Sparrow. You may grow to like him.'

'How can you say this, Aunt? When you loved Uncle Oswald so fiercely and with all your heart? How can you ask me to marry somebody I despise?'

Harriet's brow drew down. 'There is no need to bring Oswald into this.'

'But it's true. You fell in love with him and married with your heart. Why do you want less for me?'

'I will not have this! I will not!' she cried. 'Not on the very day after my dear husband said his last goodbye to me from beyond the grave.'

Then they both started speaking at the same time, admonishing me and insulting me until I had had enough and ran upstairs to my room and slammed the door, startling Basil.

I went to the window and pushed it open, leaned out and gulped the evening air. Everything was ruined and my heart ached. I turned my eyes in the direction of Emile's house. Minutes passed. I heard Harriet go to her bedroom and close her door. My pulse beat hard at my ears.

Quietly, I left my room, closing the door and locking it behind me. Let them think me still here. Let them think me silent and furious and let them say, *Well perhaps she will be more communicative in the morning.*

As I crept down the stairs I heard their voices in the drawing room, but I daren't open the front door and go out past Toby and Jones. I slipped instead into the dining room and closed the door behind me. The smells of roast meat and gravy still filled the room. *I expect you eat meat every night of the week.* Emile had been right. Ever since he asked, I'd paid attention. Lamb and beef and ox and bacon. I was never without everything I needed, except love. And that was what I needed most of all.

I opened the window and pulled myself up on the sill, swung my legs over and jumped out the other side, landing with a thud and catching my skirt in the hedge. I picked myself free and then ran to Emile.

●

This time I didn't knock. I simply opened the door and walked in. I said his name, and that was all that emerged from my lips before I started to sob.

'*Moineau*, what is it? What has happened?'

'My father . . . Mister Shawe . . . I will never . . .' More sobs, and he stopped asking me questions. Instead he held me close and I tried to take comfort in his warm, hard body, but I knew that it couldn't last, I wouldn't be allowed to have him, and happiness would forever be beyond my grasp.

When I had sobbed myself dry, he sat me on the couch and made me tea, and Marin came and put his head on my lap. While Emile was not looking at me, I found I could tell him the truth more easily.

'My sister and I have been promised to husbands,' I said. 'It is the way in families like ours. Mister Shawe came tonight to ask for my hand and I turned him down, but my aunt and my sister are entirely sure that I cannot say no. That my future is not mine to make.'

He set the tea tray down in front of me, and his eyes were sad. 'I see.'

'I love you, Emile. I want to marry you, not him. You are an infinitely better man.'

329

'I knew we could not marry, *Moineau*,' he said simply. 'Not everything is possible, remember?'

I looked up at him and I began to cry again, big sobs that came from all the way in my soul. 'Please, Emile,' I said to him, though I don't know what I was begging for.

He reached for my hands and pulled me to my feet, embraced me hard and planted his mouth on mine. As always, the kisses made my head swim, made my trouble recede momentarily, so I kissed him hungrily, my hands against the small of his back. His hands roamed too, the bandaged one coming to rest on my waist, and the other on my bustle, pushing me against him.

I lost all good sense and so did he. Here, on the edge of the end, we both let passion override our heads. His hand was on my bodice, picking open the buttons, and I let him. I let him walk me to his bedroom, kissing me all the way. I let him lay me down among the covers – they smelled spicy and warm like him – and remove his shirt and press himself down on me. The first jolt of his hand against my bare breast was stronger than my body could stand, and I began to tremble violently.

'Sh, sh, *Moineau*,' he said against my lips, my ears, my neck. 'I will take care of you.'

He helped me out of my clothes, and removed the remainder of his own. I could see him in the candlelight that reflected through the doorway, and he was beautiful and strong and hard. I had thought a moment like this (because of course I had imagined it) might feel awkward or strange, but instead it felt natural and earthy. He lay down beside me and touched me so expertly, and kissed me from my crown to my toes, and that is the night, my child, that you were made.

•

You will never read this, of course. That is why I can tell you such things that a mother should never utter to a child. You are loved by someone else, and they will make sure you never find me; perhaps they will even make sure you never know you grew in another woman's body. I am telling this story to myself, as all the saddest stories are shared.

Afterwards, our bodies entwined, we fell asleep. I remember waking once, and thinking I should go home, but then the bliss of being in his slumbering arms chased away sense, and I slipped under again. When I did wake, he woke too, and it was because somebody was thundering at the door, calling his name. And mine.

'Quick,' he said, throwing my shift and pulling on his trousers. But the door was not locked, and they burst in and found us.

The vicar, Harriet, my sister. I was in nothing but a thin cotton chemise, he naked from the waist up.

'I'm sorry,' said my sister.

•

It was Basil's fault. He had been trapped in my room and he needed to go out, so he had miaowed and clawed at the door until Harriet, at one in the morning, had found the spare key and opened it. I was gone and she didn't know where I was, and she'd got herself into a flap and my sister told her everything. They went to find the vicar, who knew where Emile lived. So we were undone.

I do not know if I believe that my sister was truly sorry. Nonetheless, Emile was dismissed from his work at the church, and I was to be dispatched on the next train home to Yorkshire. My chest was sore from sobbing as my sister and I climbed into the carriage to London, and as we rolled out of the village I took—

The Present

'There,' I say. 'It's unfinished.'

'I think it's very near the end,' Mum says. 'It wasn't much thicker than this. I remember it came in an old collection of books from a library in Yorkshire. The librarian found it tucked into a volume of Cicero. I became quite obsessed with it for a while.'

'What happens?'

Mum sighed. 'I can barely remember what happens.' Then she brightened. 'I spent quite a bit of time and money trying to find the people in the letter. I never did find out the lass's full name, but I tried to find Emile Venson. I got my research assistant on it, made a visit to Millthorne. Nothing. Such a shame. I would like to know what happened to them.'

'Me too.'

'Could you . . . Do you think Andrew Garr may be able to help us find the rest?'

Progress. I smile. 'I can ask him.' *When I see him at dinner.* A little glow warms me as I think about it, but then a twinge of guilt. I still haven't called Geoff.

But then, he hasn't called me either.

CHAPTER 20
Agnes

A gnes was given twenty-four hours to orient herself, once the *Persephone* had sailed from Colombo, before she was due to report to Dr Angel for duty. In some ways, the clipper ship was similar to the steamship she had boarded in London: the names of the rooms and the decks, the hatches and ladders between one place and the next. In some ways, however, it was vastly different. No hum of an engine; instead, the rattle and snap of rope and sail. No faint odour of coal smoke laid over the fresh briny smell of the sea. Even the way the ship moved felt different. Rather than the steady, predictable pace of steam, the *Persephone* rode the wind, cutting through the water almost as if by instinct.

Agnes's situation was vastly different too. Rather than the comfortable second-class cabin she had shared with Tempie Dartforth, she found herself consigned to a tiny windowless cabin in the middle of the ship, which smelled faintly of grease. Her narrow, hard bunk folded down from the dark wood-panelled wall at night, and was stored during the day. There was barely room for the washstand and her trunks. The heat in the cabin was unbearable, and sleeping that first night had been impossible. She'd locked the door and slept completely naked on top of her covers, but even so wherever her skin touched the bed grew almost immediately damp with perspiration.

So, she was tired and hot when she reported to Dr Angel's office below the foredeck for her first day of work as his Nurse Assistant on board the *Persephone*. She had met Dr Angel already, in Colombo, where she had spun him a tale of vast experience working in the infirmary at Perdita Hall. She need not have exaggerated so fully, though, because the doctor had told her that the last Nurse Assistant had fled them on their brief stop in Colombo, that he was quite desperate because he couldn't find an English-speaking girl willing to replace her at short notice, and as long as she could read and follow instructions, that was all he really cared about.

A sign saying SURGEON hung on the door. She knocked once and let herself in.

Dr Angel sat behind a small desk that overflowed with papers and books; some had also scattered on the floor around, as though they had been tossed there by high seas and never retrieved. He had his feet on the desk and his eyes turned to the grimy porthole window, deep in thought. The office also had a wooden examination table built into the wall with a thin mattress upon it, and many cupboards and drawers where, Agnes suspected, the surgical instruments and medicines were stored.

'Good afternoon, sir,' she said.

He roused out of thought. He was a young man, perhaps in his mid-twenties, with a florid complexion and eyes that bulged slightly. His hair was mousy and his beard and sideburns untrimmed. 'Good afternoon, Miss Resolute. Found your way about the ship yet?'

'Only my small portion of it, sir. It has been too hot to do owt but sit in the shade and wish for a breeze.'

'Ah, well. Once you start work you'll find a few more nooks and crannies. There are fifty-one passengers in steerage. Men to the aft, ladies and children to the stern, with the ladder to the upper decks between them. I will take care of the male passengers, but you are responsible for the health of the ladies. If I need you in the aft among the men, you must be accompanied by me.' Here he laughed. 'You wouldn't want to go in there without a chaperone, believe me. And likewise, I am not allowed in the stern without you.'

'Why is that, sir?'

'They are all savages in the 'tween decks,' he said, without any trace of humour. 'It's for our safety: so you don't get molested by the men, and I don't get accused of molesting the women. Don't give me that look. It has happened.' He lifted his feet off his desk and opened the drawer, slipped out a large silver flask and took a quick belt from it.

'And the other passengers, sir?'

'First- and second-class cabins are on this deck towards the prow. There's only twelve of them; most joined us in Colombo so won't have their sea legs yet. You can expect to be vomited on. Not much interesting happens on this run but report anything unusual you see.' Here a great wave picked up the ship and slammed it back down, and everything shook and rattled. Agnes steadied herself on his desk. Another book slid to the floor and she bent to pick it up and hand it to him.

He took it, saying, 'The first two berths in women's steerage have reported creepers. There's carbolic in the cupboard somewhere . . . you'll find it.'

'Yes, sir. What are creepers?'

'Bed bugs. You'll have to wash all the sheets in carbolic, sprinkle it on their beds, and if they complain about the itching, tell them to come to see me for a tonic.'

'Yes, sir. Where will I find the laundry?'

336

He looked amused. 'There is no laundry. There's a water pump, and some soap, and then get one of the lads to drag the sheets behind the ship for a while. They'll tell you how to do it.' He waved her away. 'You've a lot to learn. Go away and learn it.'

Agnes made her way down the ladder to the between deck, where the steerage passengers were located. It was dark down there, with no natural light except what little fell through the open hatch. The berths were separated by walls, but had no doors; and the beds were little more than thin hammocks suspended from bolts on the walls. A pervasive smell of urine and sweat greeted her. She walked around two little boys playing with stones on the ground. Deeper into the dark along the corridor, she heard evidence of at least someone in their berth – the soft sounds of breathing and shifting, someone murmuring to herself – but most were likely out on deck trying to escape the suffocating heat. The residents of the first two cabins, one on her right and one on her left ('Starboard, port,' she muttered to herself) were nowhere in sight, but they had stripped their linen and left it on the floor. Agnes sprinkled the carbolic powder on their hammocks, and scooped up the thin grey linen to take upstairs.

The pump was near the stern of the ship, and she had to work the lever several times before anything shot out. When it did, in warm rhythmic squirts, it was water the colour of weak tea. She sprinkled more powder on the sheets, then scrubbed them against each other under the pump. She was mostly sheltered from the sun here but could feel its bite on the hem of her skirt. She kept an eye out for a passing sailor, and called out when a young fellow – he couldn't have been more than sixteen – went past with a pail. He was dressed in plain brown clothes and wore no hat. His nose was red and peeling from sunburn.

'Excuse me, but Doctor Angel said you could tow these behind the ship for me?'

'Give them to me, Miss. I'll take care of them.'

She handed the sheets over and followed him, and watched as he and two other sailors tied the sheets to a rope and lowered it into the water. They told her they'd return in an hour, and in that time she watched the sheets skim along behind them for a while, then found some shade to wait. Once they were rinsed under the pump, she passed them over to the sailors again, who climbed up into the ship's rigging to hang them. They flapped in the breeze and the sun, and Agnes was completely charmed by this unorthodox laundry method. She stayed outside while they dried, moving about the decks in any shade she could find, and greeting the crew and passengers she encountered. Everyone seemed much happier on this ship than they had been on the steamer; she had to admit she felt quite happy herself.

Once the sheets were dry and returned to their berths, Agnes reported back to Dr Angel's office to see if there was anything else he needed from her. By now, the heat of the afternoon had become unbearably damp, and she only wanted to sit up on deck and feel the cool breeze on her cheeks. She knocked, then when he didn't answer, let herself in, only to find Dr Angel asleep behind his desk. She could hardly breathe in here – how could he bear it in this heat? But then she smelled the strong odour of brandy, and realised he wasn't asleep so much as passed out drunk.

Agnes smiled to herself. At least he wasn't going to be a tyrant. She went back up on deck to find some fresh, cooler air.

•

The first two days of work were spent mostly dealing with passengers who had boarded in Colombo and weren't yet used to the rhythms of the sea. Her shoes and hem were vomited on more than once, and she had to scrub them clean under the pump. Dr Angel had her tidy his desk and organise his cupboards, watching her the whole

338

time with bleary eyes. Agnes couldn't see herself warming to him, and in turn she thought about Julius, who was almost the same age and had the same training. What a calm, gentle and warm soul he was. At night, in her narrow bed in the cabin, she imagined him receiving her letter. Would he be angry? Or would he be proud of her? Would this latest adventure test his patience so far that his love would be diminished? She tried to harden herself to the thought, but could not. His regard for her mattered too much.

On the morning of the third day, when they crossed the equator, Agnes was up on deck with everyone else. The captain rang a bell, and everyone cheered, and somehow they had passed from one side of the world to the other. It seemed odd that she couldn't feel it. Paradoxically, it was cooler today. Clouds covered the sun, the wind was behind them and a fresh salt-laden breeze streamed in her hair. One of the sailors told her to enjoy it while she might, because soon enough they would hit calm weather and the heat would be insufferable. Dr Angel came to find her just as the first- and second-class passengers were moving back to the well-heeled end of the ship, with its shaded open saloon for playing cards. She and the other intermediate and steerage passengers fought for a place out of the sun among ropes and buckets. The smell of human sweat was strong.

'Agnes,' Dr Angel called, beckoning from the hatch.

'Coming, Doctor,' she said, picking her way over ropes and feet.

She climbed down after him into the hot wooden interior of the ship, and stopped at the bottom.

Dr Angel indicated the next hatch. 'Down in steerage. Berth four. There's a little lad of one or two who's quite sick. Not sea-sick. His mother says he's just about vomited himself inside out.'

'What's wrong with him?' she asked.

'I've no idea. Go and see them. Give him some salts, perhaps.' He waved her away. 'I'm not good with children.'

'Aye, sir,' Agnes said, and walked towards the hatch to the 'tween deck. She climbed down and felt the heat and dark swell around her. She counted the berths as she walked past – one, two, three, four – and stopped for a moment, peering in. Once again, she could hear the soft murmuring from deeper down the corridor. She made a note to look in on that person at some stage, and advise her to get up on deck for fresh air.

'Is this little lad poorly?' she asked the harried-looking woman in berth four.

'As you see, ma'am. Is the surgeon coming?'

'I . . . Let me see him.' Agnes moved in to the berth. The little one was on the top bed, pale and listless. 'Doctor Angel said he's been vomiting.'

'Yes, ma'am. He's been poorly since we left Colombo, and I put it down to the motion of the sea. I was ill m'self. But he's not keeping anything down and he's gone very quiet.' She stroked the little boy's sweaty curls. 'He's *never* quiet.'

Agnes took a deep breath. She knew she wasn't qualified to help, but this woman didn't know that and trusted her. She recalled to mind Nurse Maggie from Perdita Hall, and asked herself what she would do.

'What has the child been eating?'

'Nothing. Only milk from a bottle.'

'Let me see the bottle.'

The woman rummaged among the covers and produced it. 'Doctor Angel gave it to me when we were anchored in Colombo,' the woman said. 'He said milk from a bottle would stop him getting rickets at sea.'

'Where do you get the milk from?'

'Doctor gave us a ration of powder.'

Agnes sniffed the bottle. It smelled foul. She stepped out into the little bit of grim light in the corridor and pulled the teat from the bottle. It was flowered with green mould. She didn't remember much from her brief stint under Nurse Maggie's instruction – she had been fifteen and determined to be terrible at sickroom work because the infirmary depressed her – but she did remember that they kept the little ones' bottles much cleaner than this. 'Don't give him any more milk for a few days,' Agnes said. 'This needs to be cleaned. I'll bring it back tomorrow. What food do you have for him?'

'Just our rations, ma'am. Some salt pork and rice and some boiled pudding.'

'Give him a little rice water, but no milk until his stomach settles. And some fresh air up on deck will help.'

'Thank you, ma'am. I'm awful worried about him.'

Agnes knew the woman was looking for reassurance, so she said, 'He will be fine. You'll see.' Almost immediately, she regretted it, because she didn't know that at all. She would have to convince Dr Angel to visit. But then, he was the one who'd given the boy's mother the bottle in the first place, and not advised her to keep it clean. Agnes felt the weight of the responsibility she had taken on. All the other little lies she had told to get by were harmless by comparison.

Agnes climbed the ladder and made her way up to the galley. It was a cramped room with a low roof behind the captain's quarters, near the front of the ship. A long cabinet built into one wall housed the stove and the sink, and a railing stood in front of it, for keeping the cook steady in high seas. The room was horrifically warm, with boiling pots on the go and nowhere for the steam to escape. A slender man stood at the sink, a bag of potatoes at his feet. Agnes cleared her throat and said, 'Excuse me.'

The cook turned, and it wasn't a man at all but a woman of about thirty, dressed in men's clothes. 'What is it?' she said in a

341

thick Scottish accent. She was red-faced and glassy-eyed, and wore an apron smeared with stains over her trousers and shirt.

'I'm Doctor Angel's assistant. I need to clean this bottle. The infant who's been drinking from it is sick.' She took off the teat and held it out as evidence. 'It's full of mould.'

The cook indicated one of the boiling pots with an inclination of her head. 'Go on, then. Put it in there. It's just boiling water for these potatoes.'

Agnes moved closer to the stove, the steam hitting her full in the face. She dropped the teat and the bottle in and stood back. The cook had returned her attention to the sink, and Agnes took a moment to look at her. Her hair was cropped below her ears and slicked back with hair oil.

'I can feel you watching me, you know,' she said.

'I'm sorry.'

'I don't suppose you've met a woman who dresses like me before, have you? Well. There aren't many like me.' She wiped her hands on her apron and offered one to Agnes. 'I'm Jack.'

'Agnes,' Agnes said, taking her hand.

Jack shook it firmly then returned to her task. 'I suppose you'll be wondering why I'm wearing men's clothes.'

'I . . . yes.'

'I wanted to go away to sea. Didn't fancy being a whore or an actress. Too stupid to be a nurse like you.'

'But the captain must know you're a—'

'He's a good man and he doesn't care. Has his own quirks that he hides at sea. I started by scrubbing pots in the scullery and now I run the galley and the dining room.'

'How do the crew treat you? The other men?'

'They were a bunch of bastards at first, but they're used to me now, and I'm used to them.' She reached for a pair of cast-iron tongs and pulled the bottle and the teat out of the boiling water and dropped them in the sink. 'Go on, give them a scrub.'

Agnes picked up a scrubbing brush and scrubbed the mould off the bottle and teat. 'So, if they know you're a girl, why don't you just dress like a girl?'

Jack gave her a swipe on the bustle with a wooden spoon. 'What? And wear this kind of nonsense. No, I like my life just the way it is. Open seas. Freedom. You'll never have that.' She began to drop the potatoes into the boiling water.

'I might.'

'You'll be marrying some sir and having his babies before you know it,' she said over her shoulder. 'Like little anchors, babies are. Enjoy that.'

Irritated, Agnes gathered her things and left the galley. Trapped in a stinking hot kitchen, boiling potatoes was hardly freedom and the open sea. She made her way back to the 'tween deck, to drop off the bottle.

•

That night, sleep was impossible in her tiny hot cabin. She remembered the steamship, and how some of the passengers slept up on deck. She knew the steerage passengers on *Persephone* had been forbidden from being on deck at night, and she wouldn't be welcome among the first- and second-class passengers. Perhaps some of the crew were up there, but the crew were all men. Well, except Jack.

She tossed and turned, unable to get comfortable, feeling as though her lungs were stuffed with hot cotton, then finally gave up and rose, pulling her blanket and pillow down, and heading up on deck.

Plenty of men slept up on the aft deck, and she could see a few bodies in the grey starlight up at the foredeck. She hesitated. Already, a big brutish sailor was propped up on his elbow whistling at her.

'Hey, lassie. Plenty of room here next to Old Dom.'

She walked a little way towards the foredeck, nearly tripping over a pair of legs in the dark.

'Watch where you're going.'

'Jack?'

'Oh, it's you. I wondered if you'd come up here.' Jack lay between two barrels. She inched over and made room for Agnes. 'They won't come near you if you're with me. They know I'll spit in their food. Or worse.'

'Thanks.' Agnes laid down her blanket and pillow next to Jack and squeezed herself into the gap. 'Aren't I going to make you hot?'

'Not up here. We'll be fine. There's a breeze, and look at the sky. The clouds have cleared. It's magic.'

Agnes looked up through the rigging. The sky teemed with stars, like another ocean above them. The breeze ran over her then, rattling the ropes and sails, and Agnes sighed. 'Oh, thank the Lord for that.'

'Aye. I'll never get used to the heat.'

'How long have you worked on this ship?'

'Two years now. Melbourne, Perth, Colombo, Calcutta, then all of those in reverse again. Back and forth across the line, full of cinnamon and tea one way, full of failed gold miners the other. I hope you're not thinking you'll make your fortune in Australia, Agnes.'

'No. Not at all. I'm looking for my mother.'

'Your mother? Did she run away?'

'Aye, but not from me. She never knew me. I was abandoned as a baby, left at a foundling hospital.'

Jack huffed a bitter laugh. 'If she's managed to get rid of you once, she'll find a way to do it again.'

Agnes didn't answer.

Jack shifted onto her side, propped up on her elbow, her cheek resting in her palm. For all her short hair and her men's clothes, she was unmistakably a woman. Her nose was fine and slightly lifted at the end, her dark eyes surrounded by thick lashes. 'Agnes was my mother's name,' she said, in a softer tone. 'It means lamb, you know.'

'I didn't know.' Agnes had trouble thinking of herself as something so soft as a lamb.

'That's what my mam told me. God bless her soul.'

'She's dead?'

'Aye. Six years now. She was a good woman.' Jack smiled mischievously. 'Never abandoned me at a foundling hospital.'

Agnes flared with irritation, but then realised that this was Jack's way of making friends with her: through dark jokes. 'Well, she called you Jack, so she wasn't all that grand, was she?'

This made Jack laugh, and now Agnes felt she understood her better. 'What is your real name?' she asked. 'Because I'm certain it isn't Jack.'

'It is now and that's all that matters,' she said, then was defiantly silent. She turned onto her back and a few moments passed before she asked, 'How are you finding Doctor Angel?'

Agnes sighed and closed her eyes. The breeze had dropped, and the sweat was pooling under her again. 'He's allus drunk, and not pleasantly so either. Drunk and passed out at his desk.'

'He's been that way as long as I've known him. He's a terrible surgeon. The only place he could get work is aboard this ship. He's the reason the last Nurse Assistant left.'

'Really? Why?'

'He wouldn't treat a sick little girl on the run from Perth to Calcutta. He said, "Just give her some salts," and the nurse tried that and it made everything worse. The lass was dead the next morning. We put her little body overboard that night. The mother wailed and shouted at us not to put her in the sea, that the sharks would eat her. Probably dead right too. The sharks always seem to follow the ship when there's somebody aboard who's ailing.'

345

Agnes shuddered.

'The nurse left the ship in Calcutta and refused to come back,' Jack said. 'She's gone to work with the missionaries, I think. I can't bear missionaries. Well, they can't bear me either. We've had a few on this ship over the years. If they see me, they call me a devil. I'm not a devil, Agnes.'

'I can see that.'

'Best place for me is at sea. Out of society.' She turned on her side so Agnes could see her face. 'Anything goes.'

Agnes fell silent for a few moments, and the breeze returned. 'Do you ever miss life on the land?'

'No. Worst years of my life.'

'Because you wanted to dress like a man?'

Jack smiled ruefully. 'Because I loved somebody and it didnae work out.'

Agnes could not imagine Jack being in love. 'Why didn't it work out?'

'Because I'm hard to love, Agnes. What about you? Is there a young sir back in England waiting for you to return?'

Agnes couldn't hide her smile and Jack pounced, making knowing noises. 'Oh, aye. A young sir! What's his name? Go on, tell me everything.'

Agnes told her about Julius, and Jack listened and made a few crude jokes but smiled kindly the whole time.

'I feel that I must be very bad at love,' Agnes said, after she explained about rejecting Julius's offer of engagement. 'I didn't know what to say or what to do.'

'Well, don't ask me, lassie. I've no idea. I wear trousers.' And then she went off into peals of laughter and Agnes joined her. Finally, Jack said, 'Describe him to me, Agnes. In three words.'

'Only three?'

'There's the trick. If you need more than three, there's something wrong with him.'

Agnes considered for a few moments, then said, 'Kind and true.'

'Good. But you need one more.'

'Fine-looking. Very, very fine.'

'Too many words,' Jack said laughing. 'But I'm glad to know you've got some warm blood in you, despite having grown up in the north.' She tapped Agnes on the top of the head. 'Goodnight, Agnes.'

'Goodnight, Jack,' Agnes said, and lay awake watching the sky and thinking of Julius.

•

Agnes saw the little boy with his mother up on deck the next morning, and he was much better. A little pink had returned to his cheeks and Agnes gave him the custard apple she had swiped from Jack's pantry and been benignly threatened over. 'Now the captain won't get his favourite dessert,' she'd said. 'What sick child could be worth that inconvenience?'

Agnes had laughed and taken it anyway, and when she saw the little boy eating the soft innards of the fruit on a spoon, she felt a warm glow. She had helped. This wasn't so hard.

That first week she saw her fair share of coughs and belly aches. She also stood by as Dr Angel, shaking before his first brandy of the day, set a sailor's fractured forearm while the poor young fellow howled like a dog. She tended to bruises and abrasions from hatches that hit heads, and elbows that hit floors when the sea was high. Her time was largely free, though, and she spent a lot of it standing in the threshold to the galley, trading light-hearted barbs with Jack. She had never met somebody with such a gallows humour. Jack made endless jokes about how rotten life was and how everyone died in the end, and laughed herself silly at them. Agnes was fascinated by her, and Jack seemed to have warmed to Agnes, sneaking extra food to her cabin and making sure she got the best cuts of meat in her weekly rations. Jack was nowhere to be seen on Sunday mornings for the shipboard service, presided over by Dr Angel, but then neither were a lot of the sailors or passengers.

•

It was precisely one week since she first reported for work that Dr Angel told her to go and check on the 'pregnant lass in berth fifteen'.

'Is she unwell?' Agnes asked.

'I don't know. She boarded in Calcutta, told me as she was being allocated to a cabin, that she's in the family way, and I said I'd keep an eye on her. Been rather busy, though.' He spread his palms to indicate the mess of papers and books that had reaccumulated on his desk. 'Just realised I haven't seen her since.'

'Certainly, Doctor. I'll let you know.'

He waved her away. 'Fine, fine.'

Agnes made her way down to the 'tween deck again, and as she passed along between the berths, counting them until she reached fifteen, she realised it was where she had heard the murmuring from time to time. It was dark down here, and hot, and the smells seemed to gather. She could see now the faint flicker of candlelight, and peered into the berth curiously. Two hammocks; the top one empty, in the bottom one, a woman holding a book in front of her face, reading softly aloud to herself by candlelight. Agnes could see from the tattered dust jacket it was a children's storybook.

'Excuse me, Miss,' Agnes said.

The woman put down her book. She saw Agnes and sat up in shock, blinking rapidly. 'Is that . . .'

Agnes jolted. 'Gracie?' she cried. 'Gracie Badger!'

CHAPTER 21

In a second, Agnes had Gracie in her arms, the children's book fallen to the floor. Then she sat back and a million questions bubbled on to her tongue at once: 'What are you—where have you—how—'

Gracie laughed softly. 'Of all the people in all the world, Agnes Resolute. You see, we have been shepherded together by God. That's the mark of a true friendship, that is.'

Agnes looked around the dark, stuffy little cabin. 'But Gracie, you oughtn't be under here in the dark. You'll be better off up on deck.'

Gracie shook her head sadly. 'With my eyesight the way it is, I'm afraid of going up and down the ladders, or tripping over something on deck.'

Agnes stood and pulled her to her feet. 'Come on, then. I'll take you up and stay by you. Doctor Angel told me to look in on you, so—'

'Doctor Angel? But why?' Then she took in the white pinafore over Agnes's dress. 'You're the ship's nurse?'

'Nurse Assistant,' Agnes corrected her. 'I may have exaggerated my suitability for the job. But do come upstairs, Gracie. Your clothes are musty and you must be so hot and tired from being buried down here. We can explain ourselves to each other in the cooler air.'

Gracie hugged close to Agnes's side. Agnes noticed she wore a grey serge dress from Perdita Hall, and wondered if she had any other clothes. Agnes helped her up the ladders to the deck.

As soon as the fresh air hit Gracie's face, she burst into laughter. 'It's very bonny up here.'

'Aye,' Agnes said. 'Good for you too. You and . . .' She indicated Gracie's belly. If there was any swell or curve, it was hidden beneath her skirts.

Gracie's face went bright red. 'Sorry. I still feel I should be ashamed of it.'

'Let's find a place to sit and you can tell me everything,' Agnes said.

Gracie was right. The ship's deck was no place for someone who had trouble seeing anything that wasn't directly in front of her good eye. Too many ropes and beams and barrels and pails. Agnes took her down to the bench at the stern of the ship, and sat with her. The sun blazed on them, but the breeze was stiff and cool.

'You go first,' Gracie said.

'No, you. I have been wondering for months where you were. Where is Cole? Is he in the men's quarters?'

Gracie was already shaking her ginger curls, which were frizzy from the humid air. 'Cole has gone ahead to Perth. There's talk of gold. He told me to join him at the end of the year but then I found I was in the family way, and I didn't want to wait that long to go on the ship.' She looked down at her tummy. 'I already feel enormous. And I've been poorly the whole time. Aches and pains . . .' She dropped her voice. 'Bleeding.'

'Heavy?'

'You sound like a nurse. No, light. But most days, and always with pain.'

Agnes's blood lit up with alarm. If Gracie really was sick, she had no idea what to do, and she wondered if Dr Angel would be any more help. But then, Agnes knew nothing about pregnancy, and perhaps Gracie's symptoms were normal. 'I will come to your berth with Doctor Angel tomorrow,' she said, reassuringly. She would have to ask him before he started drinking. 'I'm sure it's nowt that fresh air and dry land won't fix.'

Gracie sighed, her eyes going to the horizon. 'That's the thing. Cole doesn't know I'm coming. I sent him a letter, but I've sent him so many and he doesn't write back. I hope I'm still welcome.'

Agnes kept her opinion of Cole Briar to herself. 'He's your husband. He has to take you in,' she said.

Gracie was already shaking her head. 'We haven't exactly got around to marrying yet. When we got to Liverpool, there wasn't time before the ship left. Then we were in India and we'd already been travelling as man and wife, and it seemed easier to let everyone believe we were married rather than confirm we weren't and endure the shame.' The colour had risen in her cheeks again, and Agnes squeezed her hand.

'Still. He has to take you in. You're having his baby.'

'I do love him. Though there are days I can't quite remember how we came to this, and he seems vague and not real, like a character in a story.' Gracie bit her lip, her expression pensive.

Agnes did not recognise the feeling she expressed; Julius was vivid in her thoughts. She watched her friend for a little while. She thought about Gracie getting off the ship, alone and pregnant, and trying to find Cole in a town so far from home, and she felt almost sick at the thought.

'But tell me your story, Agnes,' Gracie said. 'For I am tired of thinking of my own troubles.'

351

'I would love to,' Agnes said, 'but let's get out of this sunshine before we are both burned alive.'

Agnes took Gracie up to the place she and Jack slept. Here, tucked against the barrels and beneath the sails, Agnes unfolded her whole adventure, much to Gracie's delight.

When she had finished, Gracie said, 'Do you remember when I said that London was a long way to go to find your mother?'

'Yes,' Agnes laughed. 'It did seem so at first, and now it is so far behind me.'

'I do admire you so, Agnes. It's one of the reasons I ran away with Cole.' She blushed again. 'Well, I could never run away by myself. I'd trip over something.'

Agnes put her arm around Gracie and hugged her tight. 'I won't let you trip,' she said. 'Now, come and let's sponge you down. You smell atrocious.'

•

It rained that night, and so Agnes had to sleep in her cabin. She woke early, hot and sticky, and lay for a while thinking about Gracie. Agnes wanted the surgeon to make sure everything was all right with her friend, but wondered how she could get him to do that before he took his first belt of brandy on arrival at the surgery.

Then she had an idea. She rose and gave herself a quick sponge-down at the washstand, then pulled on her dress and pinafore. Dr Angel had given her a key to the surgery, so she let herself in. The weather was grim and the seas high, so it was dim inside and all of his books had slid off the desk again. She could hear bottles rattling against each other in the cupboards. She went behind his desk, opened the bottom drawer and withdrew his flask. Closing the drawer silently behind her, she left the surgery and hid the flask in the centre of a tall coil of ropes just outside the door. Then she went back to her room to make herself breakfast.

When she returned to the surgery two hours later, Dr Angel was pulling out all the contents of his desk and piling them haphazardly on the table, where they were dropping off to the floor as the ship rocked.

'Doctor Angel?' she said.

He looked up. His fair hair was wild. 'Have you seen my silver flask?'

'No, sir. I wonder if you might come with me to see the pregnant lady in berth fifteen?'

'Yes, yes. As soon as I find my . . .' More papers being thrown about. Then he stood and turned to the cupboard. 'You could help,' he said.

She came to stand in front of him. 'Doctor Angel, I need you to come and look at this patient.'

Then the door to the surgery opened and a sailor with blood pouring over his face came in. 'Doc?' he said.

Agnes held tight to the railing beside the examination bed. She had never seen so much blood.

Dr Angel looked up and tried to compose himself. 'What's happened here?' he said, grasping the man's elbow and moving him to the examination bed.

'I slipped and hit my head,' the sailor said, lying down. He was a man of about forty, with a grey beard that was now stained red with blood.

'Agnes, clean him up,' Dr Angel said, once again burrowing in his cupboard. 'Where is the damned thing?'

Agnes filled a bowl from the pump over the tiny sink, and using a cloth began to sponge away the blood. The wound was more than an inch long, over his right eyebrow. Once she had most of the blood off his face, she pressed the cloth gently against the wound in the hope it would stop bleeding.

Suddenly Dr Angel shouted a curse so vulgar that even Agnes was shocked. 'What is it, Doctor?' she asked.

'I can't. Find it.'

'Leave it a minute then, and come look at this fellow's head. It'll need a stitch or two.'

Dr Angel came over and took the cloth away. Agnes felt the blood drain from her face as she saw the depth of the wound. Dr Angel probed it with his finger, and the sailor stiffened with pain under him. 'Yes, this will need stitching. Agnes, have you seen my flask?'

'No, sir.'

He turned away and opened one of the cupboards, filling an enamel bowl with items. 'Keep him still, Agnes. Keep the cloth on that wound.'

Agnes did as she was told, smiling down weakly at the sailor, who was clearly in terrible pain. Dr Angel joined them, shook some carbolic acid onto a new cloth and patted it on the wound. The sailor's entire body tensed up.

'I'm going to stitch it,' Dr Angel said.

The sailor nodded, setting his jaw. Dr Angel set down the bowl, removed the needle from a slip of velvet, but his hands were shaking too hard to thread it. Agnes intervened, threading the curved needle with the hard thread and handing it back to him.

'Hold the wound together, Agnes,' he said, so she took a deep breath and gently pressed an index finger either side of the wound.

With the needle in one hand and scissors in the other, Dr Angel leaned over the sailor. There was sweat on his brow and his hands shook violently.

'Damn it all to hell,' he muttered, forcing his hands to be still.

The ship rolled. The bowl fell off the examination table and rattled onto the bare floorboards. Dr Angel steadied himself, the needle poised. But his hands were shaking so much that the needle entered the skin a full inch from where it should. He cursed again, then withdrew the needle. The sailor was quaking with pain and fear, the boat rolled again, and Dr Angel, without his customary breakfast brandy on board, could not control his palsied hands.

'I'll do it,' Agnes said. She was a good needlewoman, with steady hands. 'If you instruct me, I'll do it.'

The sailor moaned a little, but Dr Angel eagerly handed over the needle and scissors. 'Yes. Yes, good idea, Agnes. You do it.'

'Where do I start?' she asked.

'Across the middle. Bisect the wound, that's it.'

Agnes pushed the needle into the man's skin. It did not give easily. Dr Angel held the wound together and the curve of the needle popped out the other side.

'Now tie it and snip it,' he said, releasing the wound.

Agnes crossed the thread over itself and made a knot, then cut the thread. The wound stayed closed in the middle.

'Good, good. Next one, Agnes. One either side.'

Slowly, while the poor sailor writhed in pain beneath her, Agnes stitched the wound. The ship rolled and Dr Angel shouted cursory instructions from his desk, where he still sought his flask of brandy. Every time she entered a new stitch, she met the sailor's eyes and said, 'Sorry,' gently to him, and he gritted his teeth and told her she was doing a fine job.

Finally, it was done. Agnes helped the sailor to sit and then to stand, and Dr Angel told him he should return to his cabin for two days and then come back so they could see if the wound grew infected. The sailor thanked Agnes and went on his way.

Agnes stood back and watched as Dr Angel ransacked the cupboards, looking for his brandy.

'Doctor Angel? The pregnant lady in berth fifteen?'

'Rather more pressing matters at hand, Agnes,' he said. 'I've lost something quite important.'

'Doctor Angel?'

He stopped. Looked up.

'I know where it is and I will give it to you only *after* you have seen Gracie Badger with me.'

'What do you mean you know where it is?'

'I hid it. You are forever drunk and it's bad for the patients.'

He strode over to her, and Agnes thought he might strike her. His face was red with rage. 'How dare you pass judgement on me? Did you see my hands shake? That was because I needed my brandy. Do you not understand?'

Agnes remained cool. What could he do to her now? They were at sea and he needed her. 'Away with you. I'm not afraid.'

He took a step back, glaring at her.

'Gracie Badger. Berth fifteen.'

He seized his little bag from by the door and strode out of the surgery. 'You may regret this, Miss Resolute.'

Agnes followed him, quite confident that once he had his morning brandy, he would barely remember what had transpired between them. They descended the ladders to the 'tween decks, and Agnes led him along to Gracie's berth.

'Agnes,' Gracie said, putting down her book. 'And Doctor Angel.'

Agnes came to stand next to Gracie's head. 'Doctor Angel is going to make sure you and the baby are all fine,' Agnes said. 'You must tell him all your symptoms, even if you are ashamed to do so.'

Gracie swallowed hard. 'Very well.'

'Raise your nightgown,' Dr Angel said, and she inched it up so that her bloomers were showing.

Dr Angel pushed it all the way up to her breasts, and put his hands over her round tummy.

'How many months along are you?' he asked.

'I'm not sure. Perhaps four?'

'Hm.' He rummaged in his bag, pulled out what looked like a wooden tube with a flare on each end. He put one end against Gracie's belly, and leaned his ear on the other.

'What's wrong?' Gracie asked.

'Sh,' he said sharply. 'Nothing's wrong. But you must be silent.'

Agnes held her breath and waited. Then Dr Angel put away the wooden tube and said. 'You're quite big for four months. I couldn't say for sure, but you might have twins on board.'

'Twins?' Gracie gasped.

'Can't say for sure.'

'When might I know?'

'When you're a little further along you might feel two in there. The best way to know is to birth them, of course. If one comes out with another behind it, well that's definitely twins.' He said this without any trace of humour.

'Gracie says she's been bleeding a little, and there's been pain,' Agnes interjected, afraid that Gracie would be too embarrassed, or too shocked by the latest news, to say it.

Dr Angel pursed his lips. 'To be frank with you, I've never treated a woman with twins before. That could be normal. You look otherwise well. I wouldn't worry about it. If you get griping in your guts, then get Agnes to give you a dose of salts.'

Agnes's heart fell, then. He didn't know, and neither did she. Gracie was stuck on a ship in the middle of the ocean, pregnant possibly with more than one child, and there was nobody aboard who could help her. She stroked Gracie's hair. 'See?' she said. 'Nowt to fret over.'

Gracie smiled up at her.

'Now, Agnes, I believe we have some business to finish?'

'Yes, sir. This way.' She gave Gracie's hand a squeeze and led Dr Angel away.

Once he had his flask back in his hands, Dr Angel's mood lightened. He warned her not to hide it again and she promised she wouldn't. What did it matter if she lied to a drunkard?

•

That day Agnes took Gracie up on deck again, and spent a little time with her. But Dr Angel sought to punish her for hiding his brandy by having her work in the surgery, cleaning out and organising the cupboards. The heat was intolerable. It seemed the ship stood still under the blazing sun, and all the boards soaked up the heat and trapped it in the airless spaces below. Her dress clung to her. She would have gladly worked naked.

She brought Gracie to her cabin to eat, and they sat on Agnes's bed after and talked into the night. Gracie had her knees under her chin, and she looked so young. She was only seventeen years old after all, and the idea that she might have two babies growing inside her was more than Agnes could comprehend. As they talked, she sounded like the Gracie Agnes had always known. 'Do you remember that time Lewis Antigone climbed in through the senior girls' dorm window?' 'How on earth did Bess Albertus get so big, when she ate the same as the rest of us?' 'I believed for a full month that Cook Carmody was trying to poison me because I called her mutton too salty.' 'Charlotte Pelican was not so bad. She was just pious.' They shared memories and laughed and, apart from the gentle rocking of the ship on the swell, Agnes could almost imagine they were back there, at Perdita Hall, when life was simpler.

Still, Agnes would not go back. Not for anything.

Eventually Gracie grew tired. Agnes tried to convince her to sleep up on deck with her and Jack, but Gracie said she preferred to be safely tucked away below. Agnes helped her back to bed and then took her pillow and blanket up the ladder.

Jack moved over for her. 'It's going to be hot, even up here,' she said.

Agnes slid into place. There wasn't a breath of wind. 'This is unbearable,' she said.

'It always hits us after the equator. A bit later than usual this time, but predictable nonetheless. It will pass soon enough. We'll get storms in the horse latitudes. That'll be interesting.'

'Are we moving at all?'

'Probably a little. In a hurry to get to Melbourne, are you?'

Agnes shifted a little away from Jack. Their body heat was mingling and making the discomfort worse. 'I'm in a hurry to get one of the passengers to Perth, actually,' she said. 'A lass in the 'tween decks. Pregnant, possibly with twins, and poorly.'

'Now, don't you go getting attached to your patients. They're hard to bury when you like them too much,' Jack said darkly.

'She's an old friend, actually. I went to school with her.'

'Truly? And she's on this ship?'

Agnes nodded.

'Still, not the greatest coincidence I've heard,' Jack sniffed. 'One of the lads told me that one time he followed a fellow for two streets in Calcutta, to slip a wad of pound notes out of his back pocket. Said they were just poking out there ripe for it. Took the money, the fellow turns around: it's his own brother! Hasn't seen him for five years.'

'Is that true?'

'True as I'm here in front of your eyes. They fought so violently that our man came back aboard with an eye like a split peach. Sibling rivalry goes deep.'

They laughed together and made a few more jokes, and then Agnes said. 'I'm worried about Gracie and her baby, or babies. If you have summat for her—'

'Which berth?'

'Fifteen.'

'I'll make sure she gets some fruit and a nice pudding in her ration sack,' Jack said.

'Thank you.'

'In any case, you oughtna worry. You're a good nurse. You'll take care of her just fine. Bill Collie was singing your praises today, after you stitched him up this morning. Neatest stitches I've ever seen.'

Agnes looked up at the slack sails and prayed for a breeze. She didn't tell Jack she had done a good job because she was a seamstress, not a nurse. 'He was very brave. It must have hurt like the devil.'

'You're good at this, Agnes. You should stay aboard. We'll be moored in Melbourne for two days. After your Mam tells you she didnae ever want you, you should come back. You and I could cross the ocean a few more times together. I'd like that.' She lightly punched Agnes's arm. 'You're better off having a Jack than having a mam that doesnae want you.'

'She might want me,' Agnes said. Gracie had spoken already in aching tones about how much she wanted her baby to be safe and happy. Surely all women wanted their babies, no matter how much time had passed. 'You don't know.'

'Well, *I* want you,' Jack said. 'Even though you are an awful mope sometimes, you're still a good nurse.'

'I'm not a nurse,' Agnes said.

'Nurse Assistant. Whatever your title is.'

'I'm not that either. I lied to get the job.'

Jack stared at her in the starlight. 'Oh, you didnae, Agnes. Tell me you didnae.'

Agnes's pulse thumped guiltily in her throat. 'I did.'

Then Jack burst into peals of laughter. 'Oh you're a bad one. With all that blonde hair like a halo, and yet you're a bad thing.'

Agnes suppressed her laughter. 'But it's terrible, isn't it? What if something serious happens?'

'That's Doctor Angel's problem, not yours.' She waved Agnes's concerns away with a slender hand. 'He's been to a fancy college and he's been aboard this ship for two years. Nothing too bad will happen, don't worry.'

'I wasn't worried until I found Gracie aboard.'

Jack didn't speak for a few seconds, and then she said, 'You worry too much, Agnes Resolute. Your name should have been Agnes Anxious. Anxious Agnes.' She chuckled at her own joke. 'Lasses have been having babies since the start of it all.'

'I suppose you're right,' Agnes conceded. 'That's why you and I are here.'

'Yes! You especially. See, it's so easy that sometimes lasses have them accidentally and abandon them on a doorstep.' Jack settled on her back. 'Though maybe you weren't an accident and she abandoned you because you were a bad baby.'

Agnes laughed. 'How bad could I have been at a few days old?'

'Maybe you cried a lot.'

'I never cry.'

'Maybe she could tell you were born a liar and a worrier. She thought, *Oh I must get rid of this one or it'll drive me mad.*' Jack nodded, feigning seriousness. 'She had no choice.'

'I'll ask her when I meet her.'

'*If* you meet her.'

'*When*,' Agnes replied.

Jack grew tired of her joke. 'Your friend's biggest problem is feeding and clothing the wee ones when they come out. I take it there's no father?'

'There is, but . . .' Agnes didn't finish the sentence. 'You know, if I have to get off with her in Perth and take care of her, then I will.'

'That's noble of you,' Jack said. 'Mighty noble. Mighty foolish, too. That gentleman Julius may not wait for you, then you'll be sorry.'

'He'll wait,' Agnes said, hoping she was right. 'At the very least, he will understand. Gracie's the closest thing I have to a sister. I don't think I have a choice.'

•

The weather remained hot and calm for days. Without any sense of direction or motion, the ship seemed trapped between warm sea and hot sky. The humidity and the lack of progress made everybody on board irritable. Fights broke out between sailors, Dr Angel had taken to shouting at Agnes rather than speaking to her, Jack's dark humour grew black. Only Gracie retained her sweet equanimity, always happy to sit in the shade on deck, watching the horizon with her good eye. Agnes longed for the steamship: the noise and smell were a small price to pay for continuous motion.

On the fourth day they were becalmed, Agnes went to fetch Gracie in the morning to take her up on deck, but Gracie refused.

'Not today, Agnes. I think I'll stay here.'

'You'll die in this heat,' Agnes said.

'I'm feeling poorly,' Gracie replied. 'I just want to lie still.'

Alarm flashed in Agnes's blood. 'What kind of poorly?'

'Pain.' She rubbed the underside of her belly. 'I'm sure it's just something I ate. I've been on the pot five times since the midnight bell. It's passed now, but I think I'll just stay here and try to sleep.'

Agnes stroked her hair away from her forehead. 'This heat must be hell for you.'

'It's all quite hellish, really,' Gracie said.

Agnes picked up Gracie's book of children's stories, and began to wave it like a fan, stirring up the warm, dead air.

'I wish we would move,' Gracie said. 'I feel . . .' She trailed off, but Agnes had heard the urgency and frustration in her voice.

362

'Hush now. Perth isn't so far away.'

'But we are stranded so far out to sea. Oh, don't stop fanning me please, Agnes; that is the smallest comfort.' She sighed. 'I wish Cole had taken me with him to Perth. If he were here I would feel better.'

'I'm here,' Agnes said.

'Yes, and you are a dear. Life is so dark just now, Agnes. I shouldn't have left Perdita Hall. I should have stayed. Even *you* stayed until you turned nineteen, and you'd told me often enough that the place felt like a cage to you! But you are sensible, and you knew to wait until you'd finished your apprenticeship and had all your papers so you could be independent . . . I was a good lacemaker, Agnes. I might have made something of myself.'

'There's no changing the past,' Agnes said gently.

'Do you still have that shawl I made you?'

'I left it back in London.' Agnes thought of Marianna, and felt a pang. Had Julius received the letter? Had he told her where Agnes really was? Agnes hated the idea of Marianna thinking she'd abandoned her. 'But it's in safe hands. And you are in safe hands too, Gracie, for I am here and I will take care of you.'

Gracie started crying. 'Oh, I had the most terrible dream last night.'

Agnes laid the book down and leaned forward to grasp her friend's hands. 'Hush, now. Don't upset th'self.'

'I was back at Perdita Hall, and I was in our old dormitory looking for something, but I couldn't remember what it was. All was hollow and shadowy, and finally I remembered I had forgotten about my babies! I ran downstairs and across to the infirmary as fast as I could, but when I got there, the infirmary had grown a mile long and I had to look under beds and in cupboards. When I finally found them, they were both dead. Just two tiny cold bodies.' She took a big gulp of air between her sobs. 'They looked like dolls.'

Agnes repressed a shudder. 'It was only a dream.'

'I know, but it has left me feeling so low. What will I do with two babies, Agnes? How will I cope? I'm not even sure how to find Cole.' She palmed tears off her face. 'It's a disaster.'

'I will come to Perth with you and help you find him,' Agnes said. 'Or you can leave him behind and come to Melbourne with me. Either way, I will stand by you.'

This shocked Gracie's tears away. 'You would do that for me?'

'It's only what you would do for me and no more,' Agnes said.

'You had nous enough not to get th'self into such a mess in the first place,' Gracie said. 'I can't let you do that. You are nearly at the end of your quest.'

'Genevieve and I have done without each other for nineteen years, another year or so won't matter,' Agnes said.

'But what about Julius? You love him, don't you?'

'He is a good man and he will understand,' Agnes said, and she both knew it was true and hated that it was true. If he were passionate or jealous he would demand she return and she could simply say to Gracie that she must go back to London. 'The important thing is that you are not alone with a baby. Or two.'

Gracie nodded. 'Well, then. I will ask you to come to Perth with me, just for long enough to find Cole. It will not take too long, and then you can continue on your journey.'

Agnes didn't point out that she was almost certain Cole had disappeared on purpose. But if they did find him, then good. She would punch his oily face.

Gracie rolled onto her back and gazed up into the dark, hot air above her. 'I am so tired.'

'The heat makes you so. That and the upset.' Agnes stood. 'I will get you a tonic from Doctor Angel. Once we start moving again, you will feel better. I promise it.'

Gracie smiled up at her. 'Do you not think God put us on the same ship, Agnes? So you could look after me? I might pray all day. I haven't prayed properly since I left Perdita Hall. Maybe that is why my luck has gone so badly.'

'I'll be back in a minute,' Agnes said. 'We can pray together.'

CHAPTER 22

Agnes was asleep on the deck when the weather finally broke. She woke to the sound of rattling ropes and sails, the shouts of sailors. A cool, damp wind ran over her body and she sat up and shook Jack and they watched the sails fill under the stars.

Agnes expected Gracie to feel better now they were moving, so was alarmed to see her looking worse when she went to check in on her after breakfast.

'You're very pale,' Agnes said, putting her hand to Gracie's forehead. 'How do you feel?'

'The pain is worse.'

Agnes smiled down at her. 'At least it's cooler. Do you think you can come up to see Doctor Angel with me?'

'Must I, Agnes? Do you think it is bad?'

'Give over with your fretting. I don't like you being in pain, so you must come to see him.'

Gracie sat up, with difficulty, and Agnes helped her to her feet. She was aware of how much both of them stank of sweat, and made a resolution to get them both baths and clean clothes as soon as possible. With the wind high, laundry would dry quickly.

Dr Angel helped Gracie up onto the examination table, and she clung onto Agnes's hand as he – rather roughly, Agnes thought – examined her. Gracie's expression was muted pain and unbridled shame all in one. Then Dr Angel smoothed down her skirts and turned to Agnes with an expression of regret she recognised. Julius had worn it when he'd spoken to her of having to give up on sick children: regret and helplessness. It chilled her blood. 'These babies can't be saved,' he said.

'What?' Gracie cried.

Dr Angel addressed her. 'You are in labour. The babies are far too little to survive.'

'But we are sailing again? Can we not make it to land? They would be safe on land.'

He was shaking his head long before she finished her volley of questions. 'No matter where you have these babies, it is far too early for them to live. I am very sorry.'

'How soon will they come?' Agnes asked.

'It's impossible to say. My strict advice is for her to stay in bed. Her body will do the rest. There is nothing anyone can do.' He strode to his desk and sat down, then opened the drawer. 'Stay with her when you can, Agnes. Take some extra linen for the blood.'

Agnes embraced Gracie. 'I'm so sorry,' she said.

Gracie cried a little, then said, 'Perhaps it is better this way. I wouldn't have been able to look after them. Perhaps that is the reason God put you on my ship, so I wouldn't be alone when it happened.'

Agnes helped her down. 'You won't be alone,' Agnes said. 'I promise it.'

•

Jack smuggled some books out of the captain's cabin while taking him breakfast, and Agnes read to Gracie in the dim little room. Gracie endured the pain bravely, though every now and then she would cry and say she felt sorry for the poor little mites, that they didn't even get a chance. Jack brought them meals and didn't make a single dark joke in front of Gracie.

Even though Agnes missed the stiff breeze on deck, the cabin was not so stuffy as it had been. She climbed into the spare hammock and slept with Gracie the first night. They fell asleep telling stories about their schooldays, and Agnes was glad to hear Gracie sounding more cheerful.

•

Agnes was woken in the early hours of the morning by the violent rocking of the ship, and the sound of the boards creaking and moaning. She sat up. Even from deep inside the ship where they were, she could hear the wind roar. Objects rolled about on the floor between the berths, and somewhere a child cried in fear.

'Gracie, wake up,' Agnes said, climbing down.

Gracie mumbled, 'What is it?'

'We are in a storm—' Agnes's stomach lurched as the ship seemed to fall and slam into the water. She grasped the edge of her hammock but it didn't stop her from falling over. When she climbed to her feet, Gracie was up. 'We are in a storm, and I do not want to be this far down in the ship.'

'Why? Are we not safer down here away from it all?'

'We will certainly drown quicker if she goes down. Come on. I'm taking you up to the surgeon's office.'

With one arm around Gracie's waist, and the other feeling her way from one berth wall to the next, Agnes got Gracie to the ladder.

'You go up first. I'll catch you if you fall,' Agnes said.

A shudder thundered through the ship and Gracie cried out.

'Go!' Agnes said. 'Don't lose your nerve.'

She followed Gracie slowly up the ladder, noticing that the back of her nightgown was flowered with dark blood. Once up on the next deck, Agnes held Gracie again, one hand on the railing, and took her to the surgery. She unlocked the door on the third try, the violent swaying of the ship continually threatening to send her over again. A sudden sound of running water caught her attention and she turned to see seawater pouring through the crack around the hatch. She looked at the floor around her feet, and realised she was standing in half an inch of sea.

The door opened, and she got Gracie inside and up on the examination table. With the lamp lit, she went to the cupboard and pulled out two long bandages. 'Hold still and lift up your arms,' she said to Gracie, and then she lashed her friend to the examination table, under the table's legs, around her chest and hips. The boat shuddered again, with a violent cracking sound. The wind roared monstrously, and Agnes heard men shouting to each other on deck. She felt her way to the grimy porthole and pressed her face against it. At first it was all black, but then a bright bolt of lightning illuminated everything. For an instant, she saw a flash of a topsy-turvy world, with the ship on a wild angle and the waves seeming to stand higher than it, but then it was gone. She returned to Gracie, busying herself so she wouldn't panic. Her feet slid about in seawater, her balance was pulled from under her again and again. She held on to whatever she could, to get towels and linen for Gracie's bleeding.

'Are we going to die?' Gracie asked in a tiny voice.

'One day,' Agnes said. 'But storms at sea are common, are they not? Imagine th'self telling this story one day. About how Agnes had to tie you to the bed.'

This made Gracie cry. 'I won't have any children to tell it to.'

'You may. Take heart. There may be more babies. Dozens, if you want them.'

'If Cole wants them.' Her mouth turned down in the shaking gas-light. 'If Cole wants me.'

Once again came the horrible sensation of the ship being lifted up and then falling and slamming. Agnes clutched her stomach. 'Hell fire. I may be named after a ship, but I can do without that.'

'I'm named after a ship too,' Gracie said. 'The HMS *Badger*. Do you know what happened to it? They broke it up when I was ten. Captain Forest told me.' She shivered. 'I hope I don't get broken up.'

The cupboards all rattled and more water sloshed into the surgery. Agnes hung tight to the examination bed. A cupboard door opened and jars and bottles tipped out, some of them smashing on the floor. She would be busy tomorrow, cleaning up but also tending to minor injuries. There wouldn't be many that survived the night without a cut or a scrape of some kind, and Dr Angel was probably even now treating fainted ladies up in the saloon. She wondered if Jack was all right, then told herself that Jack had probably survived a dozen such storms and would chide her for worrying.

Then another shudder moved through the ship and this time they tilted so violently that the lamp fell on the ground, shattered and extinguished in the seawater. Gracie let out a little yelp of fear, and Agnes ended up on the floor, her elbow in a mess of broken glass and oil. She cursed and tried to stand, but slipped and fell again. Gracie called out to her. The ship pitched again. Agnes put her hands around the leg of the examination table and held on as hard as she could as a series of violent shudders shook the ship and seawater sloshed around her. Men's voices swirled on the wind above them. Gracie called out again.

'It's fine, Gracie, I'm fine,' she said.

'I'm not!' Gracie cried. 'I'm not.' Then she let out such a cry of pain that Agnes would almost have believed there was a wild animal in the room. She scrambled to her feet as Gracie again howled in pain. She had pulled up her dress and Agnes could see her white thighs in the gloom but little else.

'Is it the babies?' Agnes asked.

In answer, Gracie took a deep breath and howled again. With no light, the sea sloshing at her feet and the ship pitching violently, Agnes closed her eyes for a moment and took a deep breath. It all seemed a nightmare, everything moving slowly and darkly around her. But nature wouldn't wait, and her friend was frightened.

'Gracie?' she said, opening her eyes and taking her friend's hand. 'I'm here. Just let me get another lamp.'

So, as the men shouted above the deck, the two women shared the first and last journey of Gracie's babies. By lamp-light, Agnes whispered calming words to Gracie as two tiny infants, no bigger than Agnes's palm and without a breath or sound, slid out of her body onto the bloody linen between her legs. Much blood and other matter followed, and Agnes stumbled back and forth in the dark for water from the pump to clean up the mess. She folded the tiny bodies in a towel and handed the bundle to Gracie, who clung to it in shock. The wind had started to die down, but the ship still swayed ferociously. Agnes wanted to fetch Dr Angel, but it was too dangerous to do so in such dark and savage conditions, so instead she bundled bloodied sheets and cleaned Gracie, and restored order as best she could. Gracie still bled, so Agnes tied a towel between her legs and smoothed her skirt back down and kissed her forehead.

'I am so sorry, Gracie,' she said.

'It's fine. This is a dream. I will wake up soon.' She nodded. 'Don't worry about me. A dream can't hurt me.'

Then she began to cry, and Agnes's heart was sick with sorrow.

•

The storm passed as dawn glimmered, and Agnes finally went to find Dr Angel. He was with the first-class passengers in the saloon, where they had all gathered to be near the life boats. Everywhere she went, there was mess; food and clothes and other items littered across the decks and hallways, shredded sails hanging from the masts, seawater sloshing about. Some of the crew were already up with mops and buckets. The captain, a large silver-haired man whom Agnes had only seen from afar – she certainly had never been invited into the saloon before – greeted her by name and put a weathered hand on her shoulder, promising her better conditions for sailing today.

Dr Angel had begun to gather the injured passengers and crew in the saloon. Against a wall covered with a mural of Poseidon, turquoise seas and beautiful sailing ships, all of the chairs and tables had been stacked up and chained into place. Behind this, the walking wounded were gathered.

'Agnes, I was just about to come and get you,' Dr Angel said. 'We'll be busy today. Can you start by cleaning up some wounds while I go to fetch my case?'

'I . . . Gracie Badger had her babies this morning. Both were born dead. She's still bleeding.'

'I see.'

'She's in your surgery.'

'I see. I see. Well, I will check her over and give her a dose of ergot then send her back to her berth.'

'She doesn't see very well. You'll have to help her back to her berth.'

He indicated the row of people. 'Agnes, we are *busy*.'

She couldn't bear the thought of Gracie having to find her way back on wet and uneven ground after the horrible shock of losing the babies. At that moment, Jack ducked her head into the saloon.

'You're still alive, then?' she called to Agnes.

'Jack! Can you go with Doctor Angel? Gracie's had her babies and she needs help getting back to her berth.'

'Right you are,' Jack said. 'Come on, Doctor. I hear you're in need of a Scotswoman to keep you in order.'

Agnes watched them go, wishing she could be there for poor Gracie. In front of her were half a dozen wealthy people with cuts and scrapes; they couldn't possibly need her more than Gracie did now.

'Nurse!' a thin, well-dressed woman said sharply.

Agnes turned without smiling, and got to work.

•

Dr Angel put Agnes in charge of all the stitching, and for hours, she worked. Around them was a whirl of motion and sound as the ship was put back to rights. Agnes missed it all: the cleaning up, the hanging of new sails, the untangling of ropes. She heard snatches of tales about the young man nearly washed out to sea, only saved by the captain's iron grasp; about the fear that the mast would split under the power of the storm; and the brave sailors who had hung on to ropes and each other, even as the deck was awash with sea and the wind had torn the sleeves from their shirts. She didn't have time to think about herself, about how she hadn't slept or eaten; she barely had time to think about Gracie, who, Dr Angel had said, was 'sad but fine' on his return. Sometime around midday the young lad who assisted Jack in the scullery came by with a slice of pie for her and the doctor, and they ate in seconds before turning to the next patient. Most of the injuries were cuts and abrasions. One was a fracture and one seemed to be entirely made up in the passenger's head: in his extreme fear he had begun to believe he was dying. No matter how many times Dr Angel told him he was fine, he continued to beg for medicine, until Dr Angel gave him an anodyne and told him to go to bed for twenty-four hours. Finally satisfied, he left. Dr Angel had muttered to Agnes that the 'anodyne' was really just a finger of his brandy, which he kept close by during the whole crowded day.

In the middle of the afternoon, they were finally done. Agnes made her way back to Gracie's berth via newly tidied and mopped walkways. It seemed the ship was almost back to normal already. A good wash through of seawater had freshened the air, and the 'tween deck smelled better than it ever had. She held still a moment, waiting for her eyes to adjust to the dark, and heard singing. Beautiful singing. A woman's voice, a sad and lilting song. Curious, Agnes made her way to Gracie's berth.

Jack sat there, next to Gracie's bed, on an upturned crate.

'Jack?' Agnes said. 'You sing?'

'Aye, so here you are,' she said, climbing to her feet.

Agnes sank down next to Gracie, who smiled up at her weakly.

'Have you been here all day?' Agnes asked Jack.

'Aye,' Jack said. 'I hope the lad fed you like I told him to.'

'He did.'

'Jack's been so kind,' Gracie said.

'She's not too bad,' Agnes joked. 'Can't keep her opinions to herself.'

'Was never abandoned as a baby, though,' Jack said.

Gracie looked slightly horrified, and Agnes assured her they were joking. 'Did she take good care of you, then?' Agnes asked.

'Oh yes. Though I feel very unwell. The singing helped.'

Agnes turned to Jack. 'Thank you.'

'Ah, it was no trouble. Your friend Gracie is as sweet as a sugar lump, and she's had as bad a day as she'll ever have, haven't you, pet?'

Gracie's eyes were closed, her breath rising and falling shallowly.

'Agnes,' Jack said quietly. 'I need to tell you something.' She grasped Agnes's arm and walked her out of the berth and down the corridor.

'What is it?' Agnes asked.

374

'She's probably going to die.'

Agnes's blood cooled. 'Why would you say such a thing?'

'I've seen how much blood she's losing. Doctor Angel's packed her up with cotton but she's bled right through it, and she's still soaking through all the linen I put beneath her.'

'Jack, none of your dark nonsense. She might be fine.'

'I'm going now to get Doctor Angel, but I'm telling you to prepare yourself. There's only so much blood in a woman.' Jack firmly patted her shoulder. 'Sorry, Agnes. Go be with her.'

Agnes hurried back to the berth. Gracie was still sleeping, so Agnes sat on Jack's upturned crate and held the candle as close as she dared to Gracie's face. Her skin was white, clammy. Was Jack right? She put the candle back, wished she had a voice like Jack's with which to sing to her friend, and waited for Dr Angel to come.

•

By the second day, even Gracie knew. Dr Angel, a drunkard though he might be, was kind and careful with her, but his face and voice said everything he hadn't said in words. For Agnes, the horror of the situation dawned on her in increments. She focused on making Gracie comfortable, and the task kept her mind from dwelling on it. But later, as Gracie slept, breathing raggedly, and Jack came back and sang, the knowledge of what was happening blossomed coldly in her body. Gracie was dying. She was here now, but soon would be nowhere. In the world, then out of it. It was too much to comprehend, so she listened to the words of Jack's song, in the candlelit berth, as Gracie grew weaker and weaker.

Let us go, lassie, go to the braes o' Balquhither,
Where the blackberries grow among the bonnie
*   Highland heather.*
I will twine thee a bower by the clear silver fountain,

And I'll cover it o'er with the flowers of the mountain.
I will range through the wilds, and the deep glens so dreary,
And return wi' their spoils, to your bower, oh my dearie.
I sha' never leave your side, though the winter breeze
   be swelling,
And I sha' lay you when you've died, 'neath the flowers
   around our dwelling.

Her voice, pure and melodious in the quiet, creaking hull of
the ship, kept Agnes from falling apart, as she held Gracie's hand
and smoothed her brow and told her God was waiting for her. Jack
was still singing when Gracie drew her last breath, just before the
midnight bell.

•

A clear, fresh day dawned, with a stiff breeze keeping away the
cloying humidity. It was near to eleven when arrangements had
finally been made for Gracie. Agnes had had the ghastly task of
scrubbing out her cabin and bundling up all the bloody linen.
It would have been a terrible task under any circumstances, but
unbearable in these. She was called up on deck by the toll of the
bell. It clanged over and over, every two seconds. Agnes climbed
up the ladder, the metallic odour of blood clinging to her.

   They had wrapped Gracie in canvas, weighted down with
lumps of coal, the canvas then stitched together. Agnes glanced
at the stitching and felt indignant. It had been done so hurriedly,
so carelessly. Surely Gracie deserved Agnes's own fine hand. At
one remove from herself, she could see that her fury over the poor
stitching made no sense, and yet she held on to the thought as
passengers and crew began to gather on the deck, heads uncovered,
to pay their respects for Gracie. Some of the crew climbed up in the
rigging to watch, solemn but curious. They hadn't known Gracie,

though word had got around that she was beloved of Agnes. Jack arrived, a threadbare jacket over her usual shirtsleeves, and a clean pair of trousers on. She said nothing, but came to stand next to Agnes very close, her shoulder just behind Agnes's. Four sailors gathered around Gracie's body and lifted her up. As they did so, she bent a little in the middle, and Agnes caught a glimpse of her shape, and then they straightened her out and she was just a lump in a sack again. Dr Angel read from the Bible and Agnes thought about Gracie's face; about Gracie's blind eye that wandered to the side and how much Gracie had hated it and thought it ugly. But now it was the thing Agnes missed most of all.

Agnes's chest began to burn.

Dr Angel finished his reading, and the bell stopped tolling. The sailors walked to the side of the ship with their bundle and slid Gracie over the side. There was a pause, then a dull, heavy splash. With that splash, the burning in Agnes's chest seemed to break open, like a coal fallen from a fire, and the embers spilled through her blood. She tried to breathe but couldn't, and realised it was because she was crying. She was crying and crying, and it shook her to her foundations.

Jack pulled her into her embrace. 'Hush now, lassie,' she said, as Agnes cried. 'Jack's got you.'

•

Empty sky. Empty sea. No sight of land. *I'll be crushed by how big the world is.* Agnes remembered Marianna's words, said them in her head over and over as she sat on the foredeck watching clouds gather on the horizon.

The ship, still on course, headed for Australia.

CHAPTER 23

J ack was on deck with Agnes as they passed the lighthouse at
   Cape Otway, three weeks to the day after Gracie died. They
crossed the bar, the ship pitching and yawing over the rolling sea,
but then in a few hundred yards the bay was as still as a mill pond,
and Agnes could see the hills and trees of Melbourne. Dozens upon
dozens of ships lay at anchor, a forest of masts and rigging. Jack
predicted they would have to wait overnight for the pilot to come
aboard and guide them to a berth.

'You may as well put those away,' Jack said, pointing to Agnes's
trunks, which were stacked between them. 'We'll not be off this
ship until morning.'

Agnes was itching to be on land. Now that she had endured
Gracie's illness and death, the only happiness she could imagine
was a reunion with her mother. She quieted the voice in her head
that taunted her with the possibility of Genevieve not being in
Melbourne either.

'Perhaps I can have somebody row me over,' Agnes said.

'Row you over? Now you're talking like a mad person. Just stay on board. In the morning, they'll berth us right on the railway pier and in ten minutes you'll be in Melbourne on the train.' Jack cocked her head, considering Agnes. The last of the afternoon caught an auburn sheen in her short hair. 'Aye, you'll need me to take you to town.'

'No, I will be right on my own.'

'Where will you stay?'

'I'll find a hotel.'

'There's your first problem. Any old building of boards with a corner for a stove can call itself a hotel. They're always full of drunks and whores.' Jack clapped her on the shoulder. 'I'll come ashore with you and put you in a temperance hotel. I know one on Lonsdale Street.'

Agnes could see that Jack's protective instinct could not be argued with; and, it would be good to have somebody show her to a safe hotel: she'd had enough adventures with drunks and whores. 'Be right then, Jack. But you must let me pay your fare on the train.'

'Aye.' Then in a softer voice she said, 'Will you come back to us, Agnes?'

'I don't know what is going to happen.' Dr Angel had all but begged her not to leave him. They would be in port for forty-eight hours and he hadn't a hope of finding a replacement for her, unless it was another desperate liar like Agnes. She had told him what she had told Jack: she could not see her future. He should not wait for her.

Jack turned away now, seeing that Agnes was not going to be moved. 'Och well. If you change your mind, be sure to get back before we sail.'

The captain came by then and confirmed what Jack had suspected: they wouldn't berth until the morning.

Agnes hurried along after him, reaching out to grab his sleeve with gloved fingers. 'Captain, wait. Would it be possible for me to get to shore on a row boat?'

He turned and looked at her with his hard, silvery eyes. 'Agnes, I've never seen you so well dressed. Were you going to town? You'll have to wait.' Then he was striding off and Agnes returned to her trunks.

Jack smirked. 'I told you. You laced your corset for nothing.'

One more night, then. One more night between Agnes and her mother.

•

The *Persephone* was finally at the pier by ten the next morning. Jack helped Agnes off the ship with her trunks, and they negotiated their way around ropes and containers and bollards and men shouting and pulling loads, to the waiting train. A conductor helped them into the passenger car and Agnes gave him sixpence for their fares. There was a long wait on the train, which filled up rapidly with sailors and weary-faced ship passengers, as cargo was loaded behind them. Jack chatted away to Agnes, but she was warm and felt shut in. She opened a window on the train to let in sea air, the smell of fish and the cry of seagulls. Still more people crammed into the carriage. Finally, the train began to move. Off the pier, past stores and warehouses, then out into a countryside of watercolour ochres, silvery grass and pale green trees. As the train swung round, she could see the town of Melbourne in the distance, flat and spread out to a dusty horizon.

The journey was mercifully quick, and within fifteen minutes they had pulled in at the Melbourne Terminus on Flinders Street, next to a large market building covered in advertising signs and surrounded by horses and carts. The train disgorged its passengers; Agnes and Jack were the last off. Jack took Agnes's larger trunk, and Agnes the smaller.

'This way,' Jack said.

They fought their way across the busy street and headed away from the river and the railway. The buildings were a mix of wood, some of which looked as though they'd been erected in a hurry, and English-style stone. There weren't many trees and the sun seemed bright, even though it was a mild day. Agnes noticed that Jack attracted attention wherever she went. Although she dressed and walked like a man, there was no hiding the softness of her face. Some folk stared at her with hostility, some laughed, some quickly glanced away. Agnes thought about how Jack had said the best place for her was at sea. *Out of society. Anything goes.*

'Do you mind people staring at you, Jack?' she asked.

'Aye, but I'll only be on land for an hour. I can stand a little staring if it's to help you avoid the worst of this town.' She pointed ahead of them. 'There you go. Hardwicke's Temperance Hotel. I hear the rooms are cheap. You got your three quid from Doctor Angel, I take it?'

'I . . . yes I did. But I have a little money saved.' She thought about the twenty pounds left from the money Julius had given her.

'Och, do you now?' Jack teased. 'I expect this is why you're wearing your fancy clothes today, so everyone will know how well-to-do you are? Well, Miss Moneybags, shall I leave you and your trunk here?' She put the trunk down at the front entrance to the hotel. It was a large stone building with two floors of arched windows, and the words *APARTMENTS. COFFEE PALACE. TEMPERANCE HOTEL* painted across the front awnings.

'Thank you, Jack.' She opened her arms and Jack pulled her close and hugged her hard.

'I shall miss you, Agnes Resolute.'

'And I you.'

'Come back if your mam don't want you.'

Agnes didn't reply. It was a possibility she could not for a moment entertain. She watched Jack go, and saw the many pairs of eyes following her progress. When Jack was out of sight, Agnes picked up her trunks and shouldered open the door to the hotel.

Inside, the walls were panelled wood, trapping the dark. The windows were too grimy to let good light in, and Agnes paused for a moment allowing her eyes to adjust. An elderly, exceedingly short woman with a querulous voice greeted her from the front counter.

'May I help you, madam?'

'Mrs Hardwicke, I take it?' Agnes said, removing her gloves. 'I'd like to rent a room.'

'For how many nights?' Mrs Hardwicke replied. She must have been at least seventy. Her crepey hands shook as she turned the pages of the guest register.

Agnes hesitated. She had a strong urge to say two, so she could be back on the *Persephone* in time to sail back to Colombo with Jack. But she didn't know how long it might take to find Genevieve. Her money would run out eventually, a thought that left her stomach cold as she remembered the nights she slept in the paupers' house in London. But she shook herself. It wouldn't be so bad this time. She could sell her expensive dresses and even Genevieve's jewellery if she had to, and if she needed to find work as a seamstress she at least had samples this time. 'Two nights, for now,' she said, as smoothly as she could. 'Though it may be longer depending on how my business goes.'

As Mrs Hardwicke signed her into a room and handed her keys, she explained to Agnes that there was strictly no drinking, no dancing, nor any kind of music or singing in the rooms or about the premises. The cost of her room included her meals in the dining room. Then she led Agnes, very slowly, along a corridor hung with amateur paintings, and to a room at the very end.

'The bathroom is right across the hall,' Mrs Hardwicke said. 'Mind you don't hog the bath. We have a full house at the moment.'

'Thank you, I shan't. Ma'am, would you be so kind as to tell me where the theatre is?'

Mrs Hardwicke looked puzzled, her little face crinkling up. 'Theatre? Which theatre?'

'I'm . . . I don't really know. But I'm looking for an actress—'

'No actresses in the rooms or on the premises,' she said.

'I understand. Where might I find a theatre in town, if I promise not to bring any actresses back with me?'

'You're not an actress?'

'No, ma'am. I am not.'

'There are a lot of theatres. The Princess, the Queen's, the Pavilion. There are smaller theatres and music halls too, mostly down on Bourke Street.' The woman shook her head. 'I wouldn't recommend going near any of them, dear.'

'Aye, thank you for your concern, ma'am. Where is Bourke Street?'

'Two blocks back towards the river,' the woman said, laying a soft hand on her arm. 'But do be careful.'

Agnes smiled sweetly. 'Thank you.'

She finally let herself into her room. It was narrow with one window that looked out onto an alleyway. She stored her trunks and went straight to the bathroom and drew a bath. Ignoring all warnings, she stayed in it for a long time, as six weeks at sea sloughed from her body. Then she dressed, locked her room, and went in search of her mother.

•

Agnes tried two of the bigger theatres first, presuming Genevieve would be a star of some kind. The young lass in the foyer of the first had never heard of any Genevieve Breckby who could also be Genevieve Valentine or even Genevieve Pepperman. At the second theatre, an older man with thickly oiled hair and a strong Irish accent told her that Pepperman operated further down on Bourke Street, and so she headed in that direction.

Her stomach was rumbling, eager for lunch, as she made her way along Bourke Street, and past the Cobb and Co offices where stagecoaches waited across the road. The presence of playbills told her she was near a theatre, and she stopped in front of a two-storey stone building, with two elaborate lamp posts standing sentinel on either side of the vestibule. She waited for a carriage to rattle past then crossed the street to look closer at the poster: *PEPPERMAN'S THEATRE ON BOURKE presents THE WINTER'S TALE by William Shakespeare.* Her heart ticked hard, her eyes scanning the cast list in smaller writing below. And there it was: *Genevieve La Breck as Queen Hermione.* Agnes began to tremble, her eyes almost unable to focus as she scanned through the playbill for Genevieve's stage name again. This was the only performance she was listed as taking part in, and Agnes returned her gaze to the date. *Please let it be soon. Please don't let it be in the past.*

Tonight. She would meet Genevieve tonight.

•

Agnes let her imagination run away. She was so close now, it didn't matter if she toyed with incautious thoughts. In just a matter of hours, she would see Genevieve in the flesh. She wouldn't be told that Genevieve had once again fled; so, she was free to create whichever story she liked in her head.

She paced her room, sat down on the bed, stood again. Her appetite had abandoned her. Genevieve would welcome her. They would have dinner together after the show. They would talk about all their favourite things. There would be no need to return on the *Persephone*. She would tell Genevieve about Gracie, and Genevieve would give her a maternal embrace to comfort her.

384

They would return to England together. Marianna and Genevieve would be reconciled. Julius and Genevieve would be reconciled. Genevieve would be in attendance at Agnes's wedding. Happiness. Completeness. All of these scenarios and more played out in her mind's eye, affecting her so viscerally that at times she shook.

As dusk came, she pulled on her evening gown from Paris, then took it off again. Too fancy. The striped grey-and-black travel dress, then. No, too dour. The evening gown came out again, and she thought of Julius telling her how beautiful she looked in it and it seemed an age ago. She had difficulty lacing the back, and contorted herself in front of the mirror until it was tightly fastened.

She hadn't eaten since she left the ship, so she descended to the hotel dining room and was greeted with an alarmed expression by the elderly gentleman who brought her meal. Agnes spent a good ten minutes wondering if her dress was too revealing and planning to change it, when she realised he simply had an alarmed-looking face. He took dessert orders with the same raised eyebrows. Agnes dispiritedly pushed the roast pork meal around her plate, eating just enough so that she wouldn't get a light head.

Then she was off, out into the evening air. The traffic had slowed, but couples and small groups strolled along the footpaths. It was chillier than she'd imagined it would be, and she thought about going back for a shawl but her steps would not bend anywhere but towards Pepperman's Theatre, towards the reunion she had so fervently imagined.

A queue had formed outside the theatre. Agnes stood in the general line, where the tickets were only one shilling, even though she was dressed for the six-shilling queue. A number of women glanced sidelong at her gown, and Agnes straightened her back and let them look at her. What did she care which queue she stood in? She had the most intimate connection with one of the actresses, and that made her more important than all of these people.

Inside the theatre she was herded through to the general seating on the floor. The theatre was not as large or as grand as the one she had attended with Julius in Paris, and she was seated between a family who talked incessantly, and an old man who smelled like cabbage. She glanced around at the balconies. All of these people, here to see her mother perform. What would they think if they knew Agnes was among them? She returned her attention to the stage, to the heavy crimson curtains. Her blood seemed to buzz. Gas-lights dimmed. A hush fell over the crowd. The curtains opened. Agnes held her breath.

Two men stood on stage, among a set that looked vaguely Greek: white columns and square patterns. Who were the two men? Where was her mother? Agnes couldn't concentrate on what they were saying. She had never read *The Winter's Tale*. She had never read any Shakespeare except for a few sonnets in school. They talked for a little while, then the set went dark and there was a murmur of movement through the crowd before the lights returned.

Agnes let out a little cry.

There she was, striding in between two actors, in a set very similar but not identical to the last. Agnes wanted to stop time, to soak in the moment. This tall blonde woman with the imperious face was Genevieve, the woman she had crossed oceans to find. Finally, they were breathing the same air. Agnes hung on every word she said; her voice was mellifluous and assured. Agnes could not follow the plot. Not simply because they used a stilted language she could barely understand, but also because her mother's voice was so clear and sharp in her mind, that all else sounded like mumbling. At length, Genevieve exited the stage, and Agnes waited for her to return.

When she remembered it later, she saw the performance in her mind's eye as a series of entrances and exits by Genevieve, with some interchangeable others milling about. At one point, it seemed her character, Queen Hermione, was dead. Agnes fidgeted in her seat, waiting for the play to be over, but then she came back to life from a statue, and this moment seemed to embody everything Agnes felt. A woman – a real woman – coming to life from a series of stories she had heard.

The moment the play finished, Agnes didn't wait for encores. She bumped along her row, striking every second person's knees with her own, and got herself into the vestibule and then out into the street. She had to find the stage door, to get in and introduce herself to Genevieve.

I knew there was someone special in the audience tonight, Genevieve would say. *I felt your eyes on me the whole time.*

Agnes made her way around the side of the building and into an alleyway. A gas lamp hung over a dark little double door, and she approached it and knocked loudly. Nobody answered, so she knocked again. The door creaked open, and a burly man with a huge curly moustache peered out.

'What is it?'

'I need to see Genevieve La Breck.'

He laughed. 'What makes you think she wants to see you?'

'Please. I have come all the way from England to meet her.'

'Well, well. We've had some zanies in our time, but this takes the cake. No, pet. Off you go.'

'But I need to see her. She's . . . we are—'

'Here.' He shoved a program into her hands. 'There's your souvenir. If you want her to sign it for you, make an appointment via Pepperman's office.' He began to close the door.

'Wait! Where is Pepperman's office?'

'In behind,' he said with a nod of his head towards the building behind the theatre. 'They open at ten.'

'Ten in the evening?'

He laughed again. 'You've drunk too much,' he said, and slammed the door.

Agnes thought she would go wild with frustration. To be so close, and to be denied. She would not wait until ten in the morning and visit Pepperman's office, only to be fobbed off again. She would sit right here – she found an old crate in the adjacent doorway – and when Genevieve emerged, she would call out to her.

Agnes sat and waited. It had grown cold but she wouldn't shiver. She was from Yorkshire; a bit of cold wouldn't hurt her. A breeze whipped up. She could smell horse manure and rotting vegetables. A mist of rain passed over. Still she did not move.

Then, men's voices. She leaned forward and peered down the alleyway. Two men approached. She shrank back into the doorway. One of them began thumping on the backstage door.

'Oy, open it up!' he called.

The burly, moustached man opened the door again. 'What is it?'

'Genevieve Pepperman,' the man said. Agnes could see now that he was well dressed, with severely parted hair. His companion, a much younger and less well dressed man, smoked a pipe. The tobacco was sharply aromatic.

The door man shook his head. 'You and everyone else wants to see her tonight. The answer's no. Find her at Pepperman's office in the morning.'

'Pepperman's office,' said the pipe-smoking man, 'is unmanned. They're going to run, and they owe us.'

'Not my problem,' the door man said. 'Go on. Away with you.'

There was a short scuffle as they tried to push the door in, but the door man was stronger than them and slammed and bolted it.

The two men turned to each other, exchanged a few words in low voices, then headed off the way they had come. Agnes then realised she was out there in the cold and dark alone, and felt very vulnerable. But she couldn't wait until tomorrow, not now the men had said Pepperman's office was unmanned. What did that mean?

Then the backstage door opened and the door man was there again, peering out. 'I see you out there,' he said. 'Genevieve's gone. She went a different way. You can't sit in an alley all night, not in this town. Go home to bed.'

'Those men said Pepperman's office was unmanned.'

'Tomorrow's Wednesday. Somebody will be there.'

Agnes hesitated.

'Go on, away with you. I've seen Genevieve to her carriage. She's gone. I wouldn't have let her out the back door with those thugs about.'

Agnes dragged herself to her feet, and could barely bring herself to thank him. He could have left her out here all night, after all. She made her way back the two blocks to the temperance hotel, which was all in darkness. She found the right key, let herself in, then walked the dark corridor to her bedroom.

Agnes cast her gown on the floor in the dark, stepped out of her corset and lay down to wait for the next day to arrive. Sometime, in the early hours of the morning, she drifted off, a vision of Queen Hermione emerging from a statue playing out in her mind.

CHAPTER 24

Agnes made her way to the breakfast room in a hurry the next morning, having overslept after a night of tossing and turning. She was corseted and wearing the striped grey-and-black dress, chosen to impress her mother. Mrs Hardwicke was clearing away cutlery, and glanced up at Agnes with a little frown.

'Breakfast is over. It's nearly ten.'

'I know. I'm sorry and I have . . . so much to fit in today. Would you please . . . ?'

'A message came,' Mrs Hardwicke said, not meeting her eyes. 'This morning. Before you woke.'

'A message?'

'A policeman came down to see you.'

Agnes's heart picked up its rhythm.

'Somebody named Jack has been taken to gaol,' Mrs Hardwicke continued. 'Apparently this person is known to you.'

The floor fell out from beneath Agnes's feet. 'Jack's in gaol!'

'I must say, Miss Resolute, that between the actresses and the prisoners, you don't keep good company.'

'Where is the gaol?' Agnes asked.

The woman sighed. Whatever she thought of the company Agnes kept, she couldn't refuse to help. She gave detailed instructions to Franklin Street.

'Thank you, Mrs Hardwicke. You have been so helpful.' She hurried away.

'Wait. Your breakfast.'

'I'll have to skip it. There's no time.'

'Please, Miss Resolute,' Mrs Hardwicke called after her, 'if you find this Jack and bail him out, don't bring him back here.'

'*Her*,' Agnes said. 'Don't worry; this is the last place she'd want to be.'

Within fifteen minutes, Agnes was approaching the grim front of the Melbourne Gaol. The huge arch above her, hewn out of dark stone, enclosed locked wooden gates. To the right, she saw a small window and approached it, up two narrow stairs.

'Hello?' she called.

A man appeared at the window, and Agnes could see through into a small, enclosed space. 'Madam?' he said. 'Can I help you?'

'I'm here to see a friend.'

'A prisoner?'

'Yes.'

'Wait at the gate.'

Agnes stepped back onto the ground, and a small door opened in the gate. The guard let her through. 'You'll have to report to the office,' he said, leading her across a courtyard of dry, crackling grass. Guards stood at the far end, under another arch. Agnes noticed that some of the stones in the walls were rough and uneven, as though hewn by inexperienced hands.

Within a moment she was delivered into the hands of another warden, this one with a crisper uniform and accent. He had a

391

round, kind face and frizzy blond hair cut very short against his scalp. 'How may I help you, ma'am?' he asked.

'I'm looking for my friend, who was brought in last night.'

'Surname?'

'I don't know,' Agnes said. 'I know her as Jack.'

'Ah, the woman in trousers. She's in the bail yard. Follow me.'

They returned to the courtyard where the guards stood with grim faces. Once under the arch, they were in a long dark corridor that towered above her. She could hear shouting, men's voices, the sound of water and quick footsteps on metal stairs. Her eyes lit on the rope hung from the gallows, and she quickly looked away, head down, watching her feet on the dark stone floor. Then out into the sunlight again, in a different, smaller grassed area surrounded by high brick walls. The area was full of men. And Jack, sitting with her back against a wall, watching the world nervously with a black eye.

She leapt to her feet and ran towards Agnes.

'You have five minutes,' the warden said, and moved to stand by the entrance to the dark corridor.

'You came!' Jack cried. 'Och, I've had the worst night of my life.'

'What happened to you?' Agnes asked. She was aware that some of the men in the bail yard, ill-favoured and raggedly dressed, were staring openly at them. Agnes dropped her voice. 'It's not safe for you in here.'

'Aye, you think I don't know that! I've been begging them to put me in the women's wing but they think it a great game to tell me I'm finally where I belong.' She gestured around. 'Surrounded by wife beaters and street brawlers.'

'I don't understand. How did you end up in here?'

'After I left you, I stopped by the markets to buy me some new clothes. Men's clothes. The gentleman behind the counter took exception and started pushing me about. I took a crack at him.

Don't know how I did it – must have got my fist right in the perfect spot – but I popped him square on the jaw and he fell over, and then there were others piling on, trying to hold me back, one of them trying to tear off my trousers. I was kicking and screaming when the police came.' She leaned in close. 'Agnes, I'm ruined. They say they're keeping me in for two months, because I haven't got the bail. I'll miss the ship; I'll be beaten – or worse. They'll make me bathe in front of the men.'

Agnes's stomach flipped over. She could smell them, the men. Sweat and stale clothes.

'You have to convince them to put me in the women's wing. That nice warden there at the gate, he kept an eye on me last night, but who's to say what's coming? They think it a great trick, all of these men, a woman dressed like this. They've already made jokes about what they'll do to me the minute they can. But look at you, you're well dressed and you've a sweet face. You can persuade them to move me.'

'How much is the bail?' Agnes asked.

Jack narrowed her eyes. 'More than you can afford.'

'How much?'

'Aye, they tell me it's usually ten pounds for disorderly conduct, but because of the way I'm dressed, the bailiff set it at twenty.'

Twenty pounds. All the money she had. Agnes swayed slightly, struck by the horror of the situation. But then she remembered Jack, singing Scottish folk songs to Gracie as she died, and she knew she couldn't leave her in here, not even in the women's wing.

Agnes turned, then beckoned the warden over.

'No, Agnes. I cannae let you do this,' Jack was saying.

'Kindly direct me to the bailiff,' Agnes said to the warden. 'I'm taking Jack with me.'

•

Even though she was desperate to get to Pepperman's office, Agnes insisted on walking with Jack all the way back to the railway station. As they stood on the platform, the noon sun direct but distant above them, Jack finally asked Agnes, 'Do you have any money left after that?'

'Aye, be right,' Agnes lied, knowing Jack was already stricken with guilt. 'Don't worry about me.' But Agnes was worried, so worried. She had to speak to Genevieve today. If, as Jack suggested, she wanted nothing to do with Agnes, she had to get back on the ship before it sailed tonight. If, as Agnes hoped, she welcomed her with a warm embrace and offers of somewhere to stay, *Persephone* could head back to Ceylon without her and it wouldn't matter.

But she had to know today, and today was already half over.

'Go on, away with you,' Jack said. 'You've got a faraway look in your eyes and nothing will happen between now and five minutes when the train comes.'

'If you're sure.'

'Go on. Go find Pepperclogs or whatever his ridiculous name is. Go find your mam. And tell her from Jack, that you grew up as fine as can be without her.'

Agnes leaned in to hug Jack, and she didn't want to let go. Fear made her feet tingle. She wanted to jump on the train and head back to Colombo, see if the steamer company would accept her return ticket, go back to London to Julius and Marianna.

Now, though, she was so close.

She released Jack. 'Goodbye, friend.'

'Aye, find me someday. You're good at finding people.' She laughed.

'Aye, Jack. I will.' Agnes turned and began to walk away. She crossed the street just as she heard the train rattle and whoosh into the station, its trumpet whistling. She glanced over her shoulder, but Jack had disappeared into a cloud of white steam.

Agnes walked past Pepperman's office four times before she found it. The door man had told her it was directly behind the theatre, so she reoriented herself, and tried again. The problem was that she had been expecting something bigger, grander. In fact, the office was not marked from the street. The building she stood in front of was rough, wooden and had a sagging verandah. It was only when she rang the bell, waited a while, then pushed her way inside without being invited, that she found a set of dark stairs to her right with PEPPERMAN painted on a wooden sign in the shape of an arrow, hung on the wall. The stairs creaked under her feet as she ascended and found herself on a landing with bare floorboards, with three closed doors facing her. One was marked as George Pepperman's office, so she opened it and went in.

A young woman with a face like a mouse glanced up at her. 'Who are you?' she demanded.

Agnes took in the office: one large room with doors that opened onto the verandah. The only desk was the ink-splattered one where the young woman sat, sorting papers. No other furniture. Boxes packed up. She thought of what the crooked-looking men had said last night: *They're going to run, and they owe us.*

'I'm looking for Genevieve,' Agnes managed.

'Genevieve will not be in today.'

'Where might I find her?'

The mousy girl smiled a little cruelly. 'That is her own business.'

Agnes felt herself at breaking point. To have come so far only to have Genevieve slip through her fingers again was too much. She thought about begging, but then decided she was better at deception than supplication.

'Can I tell her who was looking for her?' the mousy girl said.

'Agnes Resolute,' Agnes said. 'Goodbye.'

Agnes made her way back down the stairs, and across the road to a coffee house with blue-and-white striped awnings and petunias in window boxes. She took a table near the front window and spent sixpence of her salary from Dr Angel on coffee and a sandwich. That meant, after paying the Hardwickes, she would have seven shillings left. Seven shillings and here she was on the other side of the world. She took a deep breath and pressed her toes down hard in her shoes. A group of rowdy men argued in the opposite corner. Agnes sat and watched the wooden house across the road. Time seemed to crawl. Despair crept close.

Finally, the door to the house opened and the mousy woman stepped out and headed across the road. For a horrible moment, Agnes thought she might come into the coffee house, but she turned in the other direction and hurried off. To lunch, to the bank, who knew? The important thing was that Agnes needed to get into Pepperman's office.

Agnes waited for a horse and cart to pass, then crossed the street and went up the stairs. The door was locked, of course. She fished two pins out of her hair and squared her shoulders; maybe this time.

Time ticked. She fiddled with her pins in the lock, but it wouldn't give and her hands began to tremble. 'Hell fire,' she said under her breath, stilling her hands and going in again.

'Locked yourself out, have you?'

Agnes turned to see a middle-aged gentleman with a shining bald head and a well-oiled moustache looking at her. 'I . . . yes.'

'Here,' he said, pulling a key from his pocket and unlocking the door for her. 'Don't say I'm not a good landlord.'

'Aye, you are the very *best* landlord,' Agnes said, and said a silent prayer for her silk gown and kid gloves, which made her look anything like the sneak she was. 'I will make sure to tell Mister Pepperman.'

He smiled at her, his eyes crinkling kindly, and then let himself into the opposite office.

Agnes slipped into Pepperman's office and closed the door behind her, her heart thudding hard.

Where to start?

She went to the mousy woman's desk. Letters. Letters always had addresses. She pulled off her gloves and rifled through the drawers and found nothing but empty ink bottles and blotting paper. She pulled out a small iron box from beneath the desk and opened it. Letters! But all of them were addressed to here, at the office. No home address.

Wildly, now, she went to the packed-up boxes. Their lids were not yet nailed shut, so she opened them, one after the other. Playbills and accounts and posters and books and maps, an adding machine, pens and ink bottles. Her fingers were raw from prising off box lids. Finally, she found a bunch of letters tied together. She untied them, fanned them out. All the same business address, except one. It felt as though it had a card in it. She flipped it over and saw it was addressed to Mr and Mrs Pepperman on Gertrude Street.

Where was Gertrude Street?

She remembered she had seen a map of the city in one of the other boxes, and now she hunted it down and pulled it out, her eyes reading too far ahead. Found it. A distance of no more than a mile.

Leaving the boxes open and their contents strewn about, Agnes ran.

•

The address was on a quiet street of terraced houses. Agnes opened the gate and it squeaked loudly. She winced. She passed the tiny, overgrown front garden and walked up three steps to the front door. Heart hammering, she rang the bell.

Nobody answered. She rang the bell again and then she knocked and, nearly crippled with frustration now, started calling, 'Hello? Is there anyone here?'

She tried the door. To her surprise, it opened.

Agnes glanced behind her. She was concealed from the street by a hawthorn hedge, and she could hear no footsteps or hoofbeats. The last time she'd found a house open like this, it was the abandoned house in Colombo. She needed to see if this one was empty too. Guiltily, she slipped inside.

'Hello?' she called again. 'Genevieve?' With relief, she noticed there were still signs somebody lived here. She stood in a hallway with rooms branching off either side. She walked in a little further, opened doors and looked in rooms. She couldn't imagine why the door was unlocked – the house was still furnished richly, though she noticed the walls and mantelpieces were bare of pictures and ornaments. She came to a set of stairs and ascended. Two tiny rooms looked out over the street; one of them had a canopy bed covered in embroidered linen, the other had a sitting chair under a window and nothing else.

Agnes moved back downstairs, puzzled. Was this Genevieve's house? Why was it unlocked? Would she be home at any moment, and if so, what would she think of Agnes being inside? Agnes was in the hallway, moving towards the front door, when she heard the gate outside squeak. Somebody was coming back.

Desperate, she glanced around her. A hat and coat cupboard stood to her left, built into the wall of the hallway. She opened it and ducked inside, closing the door just as she heard the front door open, and smelled a sharp, aromatic, familiar scent.

Then came the men's voices, and she knew it was the two fellows she had seen at the backstage door of the theatre the night before.

'So, how much did you have to pay the housekeeper to leave

the door unlocked?' one, she imagined the younger one, asked the other.

'She did it for two shillings. Would have done it for free, I'm certain. No love lost on Genevieve by anyone.'

'Except Pepperman.'

'Idiot.'

Agnes shrank against the back wall of the cupboard, and lowered herself to the floor, coats and sleeves brushing against her. It was very dark, with only the barest crack of light where the door met the jamb. Her heart thudded so hard she had trouble hearing her own thoughts. She expected the men were here to steal things because Pepperman owed them money. Did that mean they would open this cupboard, to go through pockets? Maybe they would go upstairs first and give her a chance to escape.

But then one asked the other, 'When's she coming back?'

'Housekeeper says she's always home between two and three.'

'Won't she get a surprise when she finds us?'

'Won't Pepperman get a surprise when he has to pay us to give her back?'

They sniggered, and then one said, 'Put your pipe out, man. She'll smell us before she sees us.' Then the voices withdrew into the room across the hallway. 'No, no, leave the door open. We want to hear when she's coming.'

So, they weren't here to steal things, they were here to steal Genevieve. Agnes forced stale, musty air into her lungs. She closed her eyes and tried to bring to mind everything she'd seen in her quick tour of the house. The room they were in was diagonally opposite the coat cupboard; depending on where they sat, if she dared open the door, they might see her. She doubted they would let her go, because they would know she would go straight to the police.

She pictured the house again in her mind's eye. The front door was only four yards away, but might as well be on the other side of the world. Even if she got to the door, it was hidden from the street and they could grab her in the garden. She opened her eyes and felt around in the cupboard for a weapon of some kind. Was Genevieve the type to keep a pistol in her coat pocket? Agnes edged to her feet, bumping her head softly and freezing for nearly a whole minute wondering if they'd heard. Nobody came. As quietly as she could, she twisted around and rifled through the pockets, then felt about among the hats on the shelf above her. Nothing. Then she remembered that by the front door was a leather basket with walking canes in it. If she could get to one of those first . . .

It was impossibly risky. She sat again, curled over on herself, closed her eyes and rocked. She didn't know what time it was, but she felt a half-hour slip away. Occasionally the men would talk, but not about Genevieve. About their wives, about their plans, as though kidnapping somebody were nothing significant at all. Agnes felt trapped in a bad dream, and found herself wishing she had got on the ship with Jack that morning. But no. Then these men would abduct Genevieve and who knew what would happen? Could Pepperman even afford to pay to get her back? It certainly looked as though they had already sold their valuables, and his office showed he was going out of business. Would they murder her or leave her somewhere to die?

Agnes may have found herself in the middle of a drama she was ill equipped to deal with, but she was glad. She had a chance to warn Genevieve, to save her.

Filling with determination, she forced her thoughts to become ordered and devised a plan. Out of the cupboard; three steps and she'd have a cane in her hand; out the door, fighting them off if she had to; then run. She didn't know where the police station was, but she could find the gaol and they would know. The criminals would be caught, Genevieve would be safe. And grateful. So very grateful.

Agnes put her hand on the door, ready to push it, when she heard the gate squeak again.

'No,' she breathed in the soft dark.

'She's coming,' one of the men said.

Agnes froze. The front door opened, followed by footsteps in the hallway, then the cupboard opened and Genevieve stood there, shrugging out of her coat. She saw Agnes and her eyes went round. This moment, this long dreamed of moment, when she came face to face with her mother, was not meant to be like this. She had imagined studying Genevieve's face, learning every line of it, before they even spoke.

Instead, Agnes said, 'Run!'

Genevieve didn't need a second warning. She ran.

•

All that happened after was noise and chaos, lit brighter than regular life. As the front door opened and sunlight fell in, the two men, dressed in dark clothes, blurred past after Genevieve. Agnes acted on instinct, propelling herself out of the cupboard despite her cramped leg muscles and leaping towards the walking canes she had seen. Her hand closed over the brass end of one, and she saw that Genevieve was shouting and struggling with the two men on the first stair. Agnes took two steps, the cane raised high, and swung it with all her might down onto the back of one man's head. A cracking noise cut through Genevieve's shouts for help. The man fell to his knees and landed on the top stair awkwardly, then slid down at a sick angle and woozily fought to get on his feet. Genevieve kept shouting and trying to get away, the other man dragging at her sleeve. She got to the gatepost and held onto the iron bars of the fence with all her might, while the fellow tried to pull her away.

'Who are you?' he screamed at Agnes, who approached with her cane raised.

'I'm her daughter!' Agnes shouted and brought the cane down. The man reached up to stop it, caught it in his hands but in doing so let go of Genevieve, who wrenched open the gate and ran into the street shouting for help. Along the street, doors were opening and people were peering out, and a burly fellow with a bushy blond beard was making his way over from the adjacent house.

The man's eyes flicked from Agnes to the bearded man and back. Genevieve had run, was already halfway down the street.

'Wait!' Agnes called, making after her.

The man grabbed her as his fallen companion climbed to his feet. But the bushy-bearded man thundered towards them shouting, 'Let her go!' and he released her. Agnes didn't stop to see what happened. She heard shouts and pounding footsteps, but that drama meant little to her, compared to that of losing Genevieve, who was now a hundred yards away.

'Come back!' Agnes called, running as fast as she could. Her heart pounded and her breath became short. 'Genevieve, wait!'

Genevieve didn't slow, but Agnes was younger and faster, and finally caught up with Genevieve two blocks from the house. 'Where are you going?' Agnes gasped, falling into step beside her. 'The police station?'

'Who are you? Why do you care?'

'I'm Agnes. I'm your daughter.'

Genevieve glanced her up and down quickly, never breaking her stride. 'No, you're not.'

Agnes's heart went cold. 'I am, I can explain. We need to go somewhere quiet.'

'I'm going somewhere quiet now. You can come with me. Hoy!' She put her hand out to a passing horse and cart. When it didn't slow, she reached into her purse and pulled out a five-pound note, waving it frantically. The driver abruptly stopped a few yards ahead of them. Genevieve ran to catch it up, Agnes behind her.

'I'll not be moving my crates,' the driver said.

'I don't care. Here.' She handed him the money then hoisted herself up and held her hand down for Agnes to climb up too. 'Take us to the Albion. North side of Bourke Street.'

'Right you are, ladies,' the driver said, and they were off.

Agnes sat between two fruit crates, Genevieve across from her, cheeks flushed.

'So, you think you are my daughter?' Genevieve said, as the cart rocked along and she caught her breath and very carefully restored the pins to the right place in her fair hair.

Agnes looked behind them to see if the men were following, but the street was silent and calm, as though the drama had never happened. 'I am Agnes Resolute. I grew up in Perdita Hall foundling hospital in Hatby. You know it?'

'Yes, I do. I spent my childhood in Hatby. But that doesn't make me your—'

'I was left there as a baby with a unicorn button, just like the buttons on a jacket you sent to the hospital for charity, ten years later. And Miss Candlewick once said I was like you. Cut of the same cloth . . .' Saying it out loud to Genevieve made her realise how thin it sounded.

Genevieve studied her face for a moment, and Agnes could see her mind ticking over. 'So, that's what happened to the button? That's why I eventually gave the coat away. It was my favourite, and the buttons had been handmade for me by Mrs Connor down at the haberdasher. She'd died, I couldn't replace it, so I couldn't wear it any more. A real shame.'

Agnes fought for words. She had imagined Genevieve welcoming her with a mother's embrace and she had imagined Genevieve rejecting her outright. But never had she imagined that Genevieve would simply sit there talking about Mrs Connor who'd handmade her buttons and what a shame she'd not been able to wear her favourite riding coat.

'In any case,' Genevieve said at last, smoothing her skirt. 'I'm not your mother.'

'I know that it's a surprise, me showing up, but—'

'Really,' Genevieve said more firmly. 'I think I'd know if I'd borne a child. I haven't.'

'But—'

'You seem a nice lass, but I'm not your mother, dear. My sister, Marianna, is.'

•

In the shock, there is a pause. Time seems to slow and Agnes finds herself back inside a memory. The quiet house on Belgrave Place. She sits in companionable silence next to Marianna, working on a corner of embroidery. Marianna gazes out the window at the orange trees. The day is windy and rainy, but inside they are still and warm. Marianna turns to her and says, 'Do you know how rare it is to find somebody to be quiet with?'

'Very rare, I imagine,' Agnes, whose life has never been quiet, replies.

'We are cut of the same cloth, Agnes,' Marianna says.

Agnes smiles. Cut of the same cloth. Yes, they are, she and Marianna, in the warm bubble that is familial love.

•

When Agnes drew breath again, the cart was rattling to a stop a few blocks south, outside the telegraph office. The road was choked with horses and carts, stopped on the side of the road.

'Here will do,' Genevieve said imperiously. She was already climbing down, smoothing her skirt again.

Agnes climbed down after her. 'Where are you going?'

'You can't follow me,' Genevieve answered, but she helped Agnes down and steadied her when the cart took off at a pace.

Genevieve strode to the neighbouring building, a two-storey stone place with a statue of Queen Victoria standing on the gable. She pushed open the door and went in, Agnes scurrying after her. The smell of cigar smoke gathered around her. Inside, a row of men stood at a bar. Behind the bar were tables, largely empty, though one family sat eating a meal. Genevieve went to the back corner and sat down, removing her hat.

'Are you still here?' she asked.

Agnes pulled out a chair and sat opposite her. 'I've come all the way from England. I came to find you and—'

'But I'm not your mother, dear,' Genevieve said slowly. 'You do understand that?'

'Yes, of course. But how did it happen?'

A tall man appeared beside their table and said, 'Mrs Pepperman, your bag.'

Genevieve looked up and smiled at him. 'Fourteen pounds and not an ounce more?'

'All weighed and measured, ma'am.'

'Thank you, James. You have been a good friend to George and me.' She opened her purse and handed him five pounds.

The tall man shuffled off and Genevieve returned her attention to Agnes. 'Fourteen pounds. That's all I'm allowed to take with me.'

'Take with you where?'

'On the stagecoach. That's the Cobb and Co office across from us. I leave in two hours to join George, my husband.' She smiled demurely. 'My *current* husband. We've some rather bad debts, you see. I'm starting a new life, with fourteen pounds of possessions.'

This was the woman Agnes had thought Genevieve would be; but now that she had met her in the flesh, she found herself profoundly unimpressed.

405

'Where are you meeting him?'

'Well, I'm hardly going to tell you, dear. When somebody flees debts they're usually quite secretive about it, so don't take it personally.' She glanced at the clock over the bar. 'You're not going to leave without me telling you about Marianna and Emile, are you?'

'Who's Emile?' But she knew. That was her father's name. *Emile.*

Genevieve launched into her tale, eyes constantly flicking from the clock to the entranceway, fingers drumming on the table. She told Agnes everything, and at the end of it Agnes understood all, and she knew what she must do.

'So, there,' Genevieve said. 'Are you quite satisfied now? You've come a long way for that story. Will you go to find Marianna? I can give you her address.'

'I know where she lives,' Agnes said, grudgingly. She didn't want to share any of the secrets of her adventure with Genevieve. 'I'll be returning directly to London. Do you have any message for me to pass on to your sister?'

'I expect she won't want to hear from me, dear, and I really have nothing to say to her or the little fellow, Julius.' Then Genevieve impulsively put her hand to her hair and withdrew a comb. 'Here. A souvenir of meeting your aunt. Thank you for helping me out with those crooks.'

Agnes didn't point out that if Genevieve owed them money and was running away so she needn't pay it, that technically made her the crook. She took the comb, a marcasite butterfly studded with pearls, and felt very keenly that she was on the wrong side of the ocean.

'When do you sail?' Genevieve asked, her eyes going to the clock again.

'The ship I came here on leaves her berth this evening.'

Genevieve focused on her for a moment. 'You'd best hurry, then, dear. It's nearly five and the last train to Sandridge Pier will be leaving soon.'

'The last . . .' There was a *last train*? The thought had never crossed her mind. She had been fixated on the idea that the ship would leave without her, not the train. 'Which direction is the station?' she gasped, leaping to her feet.

Genevieve pointed. 'That way. Oh, but don't go without giving your Aunt Genevieve a hug.'

Genevieve stood and embraced her. 'What a pleasure to meet you,' she said.

'And you,' Agnes said, but the words felt like dust on her tongue. It had been anything but a pleasure.

•

It wasn't simply a case of heading 'that way'. Agnes had to return to the Temperance Hotel and collect her trunks. Mrs Hardwicke demanded an extra day's fee because she'd not been able to let the room to anyone else, and was so slow at totting up the account that Agnes threw all her remaining money at her, took the trunks and ran.

She made it to the railway station only to see the last train speeding off into the coming curtain of rain. Agnes said every curse she knew, standing on the long platform as the smell of coal smoke and fish markets filled the air.

She dropped her trunks and sat, with her head in her hands. No money to hire a carriage or even bribe the driver of a cart, as Genevieve had. Her ship sailing tonight and no way of—

Agnes lifted her head. The railway line went straight to the pier. She didn't need a train to find the *Persephone*. Jack had said it was only three miles.

She stood and lifted her trunks, then realised the larger one would slow her down. She opened it and pulled out the sapphire blue evening gown, the one she had worn on that beautiful night in Paris with Julius, and stuffed it into her smaller trunk. Then the smaller trunk wouldn't close, so she removed her spare corset and spare shoes and anything else she wouldn't need, and left them on the platform.

Agnes picked up her small trunk, jumped down onto the train line and began to walk, sleeper to sleeper, towards the sea.

●

Rain fell. Drizzle that intensified to a deeper shower then passed, leaving her damp. The clouds parted on a pale sky. One foot after the other, over the river and out of the town, and across bushland as the sun set gold and red on the horizon. The cry of seagulls told her she was drawing near. Agnes kept going, all the way past the stores and warehouses and out onto the pier, her feet damp and aching, her hand raw from clutching her trunk. An hour from where she started, the ships at the pier came into view. She eyed each in turn, looking for the *Persephone*, but couldn't see it. She turned and went back. Still couldn't see it.

'You right, lass?'

Agnes jumped, then saw a man smoking a pipe, sitting on a barrel a few yards away. Fighting down frantic feelings, she asked him where the *Persephone* was.

'*Persephone*? She left the berth half an hour ago,' he said.

'No!' Agnes cried. 'I haven't missed it. I can't have missed it. I need to get back to England. Back to my mother!'

'Calm down, lass, calm down,' he said, and he stood and moved closer to her, pointing out towards the sea. 'She's at anchor in the bay. Won't leave until morning.'

'How can I get out there?'

'My friend Frank has a rowing boat. He'll take you if you've got coin.'

Coin. She had no coin.

'Oy, Frank, come over here, then. Can you take this lass out to *Persephone*?'

Frank came over. He was a tall man with big dirty hands and a dirtier cap. 'Aye, for a shilling.'

'I have no money. I . . .' Then she remembered the comb Genevieve had given her. She pulled it out of her purse. 'Will you take this?'

Frank took the comb and eyed it. 'This is worth more than a shilling,' he said.

'I'd say it's worth more than a pound or even ten,' Agnes said. 'But I don't want it as much as I want to be on that ship.'

Frank smiled at her. 'Right this way.'

•

By the time they had walked up to Frank's shed and launched the rowing boat out into the bay, it was fully dark and Agnes was weary to her core. Frank rowed her out across dark waters, between the masts and rigging that were black against the velvety sky. As they approached *Persephone*, Frank began to call out. 'Ahoy! Ahoy, *Persephone*!'

A lamp appeared at the side of the boat, one of the older sailors looking down at them. 'Why if it isn't Miss Agnes. Jack will be glad to see you.' Then he turned away and called for a rope ladder, and within minutes she was aboard. She had made it.

Jack, having heard the news, came running up from the galley. She smelled of boiled potatoes as she folded Agnes into a hug. 'She didnae want you? Grand! We got you back.'

'It's more complicated than that. I . . . I need to rest. Can we talk after supper?'

'Aye, lass. I'll leave you be. Sorry things haven't worked out as you'd hoped.'

'Don't be sorry,' Agnes said, smiling. 'I'm just . . . I'm a long way from where I ought to be, Jack.'

'But are you heading in the right direction?'

'Aye,' Agnes said, looking up through the masts at the stars. 'For once I am.'

The Present

Living with Mum every day for just over a week, it becomes horrifyingly apparent how much she has already declined. She moves in and out of lucidity; at times she speaks in circles, at others in long, intelligent lines. Sometimes, the worst times, she is not there at all. She looks at my face like somebody might look at a puzzle to be solved: finding the parts with her eyes, concentrating hard, and then . . . then she is with me again and we both pretend the grey moments haven't happened.

Dr Chaudry comes every day. She is young and kind, and Mum clearly adores her; though that doesn't stop her from complaining bitterly later, when the doctor is gone. It is early the following week when I call Dr Chaudry's office and make an appointment to speak to her without Mum around. Her surgery is above a health-supplies store behind Portishead's high street. The morning is cool, and the sea fog has rolled away. I love the smell of the air here. It is fresh and bristling with salt, so different from our inner-city apartment back home, where hot days drive me to open the windows to the smell of exhaust fumes and the takeaway shop on the corner. Seagulls cry in the distance. I take a deep breath.

In Dr Chaudry's waiting room, there are two elderly gentlemen and a young mother with a sleeping baby. The baby looks so tiny, so new. The mother . . . she must be fifteen or sixteen and I am struck again by how everybody seems to be able to procreate but me. This girl can't drive or vote, and yet, here she is, a mother. She rocks the baby absently, her lips pressed against its soft forehead.

I have barely sat down in the tartan-covered chair when Dr Chaudry emerges from one of the white doors and calls me in.

'It's nice to see you again, Tori,' she says, as she closes the surgery door behind us. 'I presume this is about your mum?'

'Yes, it is.'

'Take a seat,' she says, and I do. The patient's seat. I feel nervous, but I'm not sure why.

'Your mum is thriving with you here. You're doing a great job,' she says.

'Thanks. All I'm doing is loving her.'

'Yes, well. Love is underrated in medicine, I think.' She smiles at me.

'It won't fix her, though, will it?' I say. 'I was hoping you could give me some details about her . . . condition and what to expect.'

Dr Chaudry begins to explain, sometimes using medical terms and then translating them for me. I catch the key concepts. 'Middle-stage Alzheimer's.' 'Progressing a little faster than we'd usually see.' 'Not safe out of the clinic, or without ongoing care.' 'One to two years, maybe three, before she will have to be institutionalised in full-time care.' 'Not sure what your plans are.' And so on. Mum is sick; she isn't getting better. If anything, she is worsening. She has about two good years left, and then she'll likely be lost; after that she'll have to be nursed in a hospice until she dies. In those two good years, it's the clinic or home with me.

But I have a job. I have a husband. I have a life, on the other side of the world.

I don't cry, although I very much want to. I hold it in, because I need to be strong for Mum. According to Dr Chaudry, I'm really the only person who can convince her to resign from work so she can access her retirement money; I'm the only person who can convince her she needs to move into the clinic. I suggest the idea of paying somebody to come and check in on her once a day at home, but Dr Chaudry shakes her head.

'I'm sorry. She has a history now of wandering. It's too much of a risk for her to be alone for hours on end.'

I think about the wound on her face, turning pink now as it heals. About how what's happening in her brain will not heal.

'Are there nicer rooms at the clinic?' I ask Dr Chaudry.

'I'll see what I can do. Tori, you can count on me as an ally. Margaret is one of my favourite patients. She's so . . .' She trails off, because neither of us can say it any more. Mum isn't bright and brilliant, or at least she is only in flashes now, flashes that are destined to dim.

•

When I arrive back at Mum's, she's sitting on the sofa staring at the television.

'Hi, Mum,' I call, dropping the rental-car keys on the bench.

She turns, looks at me blankly for a moment, then seems to gather herself and smiles. 'Hello, dear. Where have you been?'

'With Doctor Chaudry, remember? I told you before I left.' I immediately regret pointing this out, because she blinks back at me and her expression is hurt.

I pick up the television remote and hit the off button, then set it down on the coffee table once again and sit next to Mum.

'How are you feeling right now?'

413

She glances around the room. 'Oh, well. Could be better, I suppose. I was watching a show and I couldn't remember anyone's names. That troubled me a little.'

'I had a good chat with Doctor Chaudry.' I stop, wait, let the moment grow heavy.

'What is it?' she asks, in a constricted, frightened voice.

'Mum, you have to retire from work.'

'No I don't. I'm fine. I don't operate heavy machinery. I'm not going to kill anyone.' She shoots out of her seat. 'Has Andrew Garr been telling you stories about me? You know that man hates me. And Doctor Chaudry too. She's younger than you! What does she know about anything?'

I stand and gently pin her arms by her side. 'Mum, Mum,' I say softly, until she stops talking and looks at me. Defiantly. 'Mum, we'll bring all your books and papers to you, wherever you are. You can work at your own pace. Just because you're leaving the college, doesn't mean you can't keep doing your research.' I think for a moment about how many books they might let her have at the clinic. I will have to ask about a bigger room. When her retirement money comes, it might be enough to cover it.

She plops back down on the couch and sighs deeply. I wait a few moments, and then she says, 'All that I am is there at Locksley College.'

I sit next to her and put my arm around her. 'Not to me. To me, it's never mattered where you work or how many books you published.'

She leans her head on my shoulder. 'Oh, my darling girl. I am sorry. I'm not very good at being a mother and I am even worse at getting old and sick.'

I squeeze her close against me, and I suspect she is crying a little but secretly. Then she withdraws and looks at me with big,

414

frightened eyes, and she says, 'What if they don't let me have my books with me in the clinic?'

'Then we'll find a clinic that will,' I say, and I am determined but at the same time worried that there may be no such place.

She nods, then says, 'I feel as though I am about to cross an ocean, and it's grey and grim and lonely.'

I am struck speechless by her words, and then she takes a deep breath and says, 'Will you tell them for me?'

'Tell who?'

'Professor Garr, the college, the retirement fund. Tell them . . . I'll be leaving.'

'Of course. Of course I will.'

'I don't want to see their faces. I don't want to see anyone pitying me, not ever. I am—' Her voice breaks and she finishes in a whisper. 'I am bigger than that.'

'Yes, you are,' I say, kissing her forehead. 'I'll take care of everything.'

•

I have already started the process of organising Mum's retirement before my dinner with Andrew. Everyone at the college is warm and helpful, and so very kind. I get to see my mother through their eyes: they tell me they love her humour and her charm and admire how hard she has worked her whole life, and they want to do whatever they can to ease her transition, including taking care of the paperwork and packing up her office for her. I tell Mum about it, but she is distant and mildly angry every time I bring it up, so I love her instead. I read to her. I remind her of things we did when I was young. We don't talk about the clinic, but Dr Chaudry has all but assured me Mum can have one of the larger rooms on the fourth floor when she returns, with a view of the park instead of the brick wall.

I feel guilty and a little worried leaving Mum alone on Friday night, but she tells me that I should go and enjoy myself – even if it is with that Andrew Garr, whom she doesn't trust – and that she will go to bed early. I program my mobile number into her phone so she can call me easily, and together we fill out a sticky note reminding her of where it is and what to do if she gets confused.

'Don't leave the house,' I say.

'I won't. What makes you think I want to leave? I'm in my nightie now. I'll watch the telly and go to sleep.'

I meet Andrew at the Chancellor's Club, which is inside a lovely old stone building with a clock tower, on the western side of the campus. I make my way through a bar where students have gathered around tables and talk loudly and animatedly, and through to a subtly lit dining room. As the door swings shut behind me, the noise dies off. I can hear quiet music; folk guitar. Andrew sits at a table in the far corner with a menu open in front of him.

He notices me on my way over, stands and takes my hand. He wears a smile that I recognise. A smile that he can't stop. A smile too big for the corners of his mouth. I don't know that Geoff has ever smiled at me like that.

'You look beautiful,' he says, and I find his admiration so intoxicating that I decide I will *not* think about Geoff. That my relationship with Geoff has been out of kilter for a long time, and I should simply let myself enjoy Andrew's company.

We fall into conversation, both eager to get to know each other. I tell him about Mum's decision to retire, and his relief and happiness for her is genuine and beautiful. Food and wine come and go and we are talking and talking, and still talking as the dining room empties and the wait staff start putting up the chairs.

'Come on,' Andrew says, standing and taking my hand. 'I want to show you the gallery.'

His hand is warm, and he moves to withdraw it once I am standing, but I squeeze it instead. He considers me a moment, smiles, then locks his fingers between mine. We exit the building, and skirt the cold quadrangle where a pair of drunk students are engaged in the kind of passionate kissing that only the young seem capable of: as if they are trying to climb into each other's souls.

Andrew drops my hand as he pulls out his wallet and removes a swipe card, then swipes us into the tower. He feels about on the wall inside for a light switch, and in front of me a staircase is illuminated.

'This way,' he says, taking my hand again and leading me up the stairs. On the first landing he switches on another light, and swipes us through wooden doors and into a gallery. It is softly lit, with tall glass cases in two rows. The cases hold all kinds of Victorian objects: tea sets and snuff boxes and hairbrushes and wind-up toys and things I can't identify. The things my mother is obsessed with: the signs of daily life as it was lived, not just men's lives, but women's too, and children's. I move along, gazing at the cabinets.

'I have good news,' Andrew said. 'We have approval now to name the gallery after your mother.'

'Really?' I beam. 'That's wonderful.'

'We want to have a ceremony. Do you think she'd come? She needn't speak.'

I don't know what Mum is capable of, whether the idea would confuse or frighten her. 'Perhaps,' I say. 'Can I tell her about it?'

'I'll write her a letter,' he says. 'It might sink in better if she has it in writing. She always seemed to love it in here. She often came in to sit and think or read.'

'I can imagine.' I have stopped at one of the cabinets. 'What is that?' I'm pointing at a black box, with a pattern of flowers on it and multiple small compartments, one of which is open.

'It's a Chinoiserie box for playing cards,' he says.

417

The word, Chinoiserie, sets a bell ringing in the back of my mind. 'Would you . . . can we open it?'

Andrew looks at me curiously, but his swipe card is still out and the cabinet is open a second later. I reach in and pull out the top drawer of the box.

'Well, well,' Andrew says.

I withdraw the thin sheaf of papers, flick to the end and see that it is complete. 'I need to get this home to Mum,' I say.

'Let me walk you to your car.'

•

Mum is asleep when I arrive home, and I regret leaving Andrew so swiftly. I throw myself on the couch and kick off my shoes. I can smell his aftershave on my hand, and I press my fingers against my nose for a moment, eyes closed. I still glow a little, from the wine and from his company.

Then I gather myself and unfold the letter to read.

CHAPTER 25
Moineau

—one last look behind me at Emile's lane. I felt raw and tired, and vulnerable, as though my happiness had been left somewhere carelessly by strangers.

'Don't worry,' my sister said, squeezing my hand. 'We won't tell Father about . . . you know.'

I was mute as we turned towards home.

•

There is not much to narrate for the rest of the summer, nor much of the autumn. On my return to Hatby, I took to my room and didn't leave it for a long time. My sister explained to Father and Mother that I had foolishly fallen in love, that I had refused Mr Shawe, but that she believed I would see sense. She told me all this, and she also told me that neither she nor Harriet had let on that I was 'ruined' (Harriet's word). I certainly felt ruined, but in a different sense completely.

I suppose you think me hopeless. Why did I not write to him? Or run away to be with him? Or use my plucky spirit and cunning rhetoric to convince my father to let me marry with my heart? There were many reasons, some to do with my breeding and some to do with my fear of my father's opinion and my mother's nerves, and some to do with the knowledge that I had already interfered with Emile's life and livelihood. Now that I was back in cool, grey Yorkshire, I saw the affair in a cool, grey light. He had said all along we couldn't be together, that we ought not fall in love. I had ignored him and made friends with his dog and left him notes and pushed myself on him again and again.

I did not stop loving him. I have not stopped loving him.

My agreement to marry Mr Shawe was never articulated directly by me. Somehow, it became true simply because everyone around me believed it to be true and I did not correct them. At some point, my father must have written to him and told him, because I received a long letter from Mr Shawe in late October, describing the weather in Calcutta and a boat ride he took along the river, and obliquely referring to how pleased he was that I was 'recovered from my guilt about my sister sufficiently to accept his offer'. I tore up the letter and cast it out my window, watching the pieces fly away on the autumn breeze.

I felt otherwise well, though I longed for some grand illness to befall me so that I could stay in my room and never have to be coaxed out for walks and shopping trips. My mother was happy to have me sit inside and practise my needlework while she told me the village business, though she told me once or twice I was growing too plump and needed a brisk walk in the park. It was the first of November when I realised, in fact, that something about my body was not quite right. I was eating hardly anything, and yet I was rounding out, especially in my breasts. I had heard enough women's gossip in my life to send me to my calendar, and I was shocked to realise that I had not had my flower in three months.

I stood by the calendar, which hung on the wall above the piano in our music room, and I counted the days over and over. Perhaps I had just forgotten. I always bled lightly; perhaps it had passed with me barely noticing, so flattened was I by losing Emile. But I knew this was not true. Cold shock held me immobile there in the music room for nearly ten minutes, until one of the servants came in to beat the rugs, and I found my way upstairs to my bed. I lay face down, eyes closed, unable to make the truth fit within my reckoning. A rough wind shook the branches outside. Winter would be here soon, and then spring, and there would be a baby. Emile's baby. It was inescapable.

I lay for many hours in that posture, too shocked to cry or to plan, but as the afternoon grew cold I sat up and I knew what I must do. I must tell Emile. Because this changed everything: if we were to bring a child into the world, then Father would rather we married than that I should bear a child out of wedlock. I felt flushed with excitement. I sat down to write him a letter, but then I changed my mind and decided I would go to him.

I knew that Harriet would be highly suspicious if I turned up in Millthorne to visit her, and so I enlisted the only ally I thought I had: my sister.

That night, I knocked on her door before bed and she opened it in her nightgown.

'It's good you came,' she said. 'I could use your help.' She handed me her hairbrush and we sat together on her bed in the candlelit room and I brushed the snarls out of her hair. We sat in silence for a few minutes, but eventually she said, 'Did you want to tell me something?'

'I . . . yes,' I said, brushing and brushing. Her hair was golden by the light of the candle that sat on the gleaming oak dresser.

'Go on, then.'

'This must be a secret.'

'You know I can keep your secrets.'

I took a deep breath, dropping my hands into my lap. She turned. 'Go on.'

'I'm carrying Emile's child.'

Her mouth formed an O of surprise, and she froze like that for a long time.

'I need your help,' I said.

'I will do anything I can,' she replied, grasping my hand. 'Oh, my poor darling.'

'I want to go to him and tell him, and see if he offers to marry me.'

'But . . .' she started, then stopped. 'What are you thinking?'

'That Father would rather have me married to a carpenter than give birth unmarried. That Mr Shawe won't want me anyway: it's not as though a pregnancy is easy to hide. My body will change forever.'

She nodded slowly. 'You may be right. But Harriet won't let you near him.'

'I won't tell Harriet I'm coming. You and I will travel to London; we'll tell Father we are looking in the shops, buying items for my trousseau. I will take a train and carriage directly to Emile's house, and back on the same day. But I need you to come with me to London. For support, but also because Father barely trusts me any more.' There was another reason. Since my return home, I had become increasingly uncomfortable leaving the house. I couldn't explain it even to myself, but I felt vulnerable when outside, and was always glad to slip back inside and close the door behind me.

My sister took the brush from me and put it aside, then she took me in her arms. 'You must be brave now, pet,' she said. 'No matter what Emile says, or Father, or Ernest, or anyone, the baby is coming.'

I was terrified, but at the same time I could see that my plan would work. I had seen in my sister's expression that she thought it would too.

•

It took us several days to organise our journey. My sister wisely told me to wait until the day Mother's friend Elice was returned from a trip to France, because otherwise Mother would almost certainly demand to come with us. Father sent us in his carriage to York, and the train ride was terribly slow due to some problem on the track near Doncaster. We finally made it to our hotel on Grosvenor Square at three in the afternoon. It was too late to travel further, so we looked in the shops and ate some supper in a tiny restaurant where a man played the piano with such little finesse that a small child at the next table to us began to cry. Or at least, that is the story my sister and I told ourselves for our amusement. We were both in high spirits: me because I might not be marrying Mr Shawe, and my sister for the same reason. Perhaps she did love him after all, and not just the idea of living in so many different houses.

That night, when we were reading in our beds, which lay next to each other in a bed chamber with the most unfortunately gloomy wallpaper, she rose and slipped into bed beside me, just as she used to do when we were small. I said nothing and nor did she. She curled around me and put her hand over my tummy and said, 'I shall be an aunt.'

'Yes. A good aunt.'

'Like Harriet.'

'Better than Harriet.'

'I wonder if it will be a girl or a boy. If it's a girl, will you name her after me?'

'No. I think a carpenter's daughter needs an unassuming name. Like, Rose.'

'Rose. That's pretty.' She sighed. 'It was easier when we were little, wasn't it?'

I didn't answer. The truth was, it was easier before I had fallen in love. Up until then, I hadn't a care in the world.

•

I was on the first train to Dorchester and then in a carriage to Millthorne by ten-thirty. The passing landscape was unfamiliar, now that November was here. The riot of colour and leaf was gone. The oaks were all bare, and the chestnuts on their way. The road was muddy, overflowing with leaf fall, and the hedges were the colour of copper. I asked the driver to drop me off just outside the village, so that I would not be seen by peering eyes: especially Harriet's or the vicar's. I walked the last little way, finding a balance between sticking to the side of the road and avoiding slipping in mud.

When I finally reached the top of Emile's lane, I saw a carriage parked on the road directly outside his house. It was a plain carriage, a little worse for the wear, and I experienced a horrible moment in which I thought that Emile had left Millthorne, and new residents had taken his house. But then I heard his voice, among others, and shrank back behind a hedge.

An elderly man and woman appeared, and Emile with them. I watched and tried to listen, though their words were not distinct. Emile hugged each of them in turn and helped them into the carriage, and waved them off as the carriage began to draw towards me. Emile watched it go, and because I was not particularly well concealed, he caught a glimpse of me.

Then the carriage passed between us, and I could see the man and the woman and wondered if they were the parents of his dead wife, whom he said lived in the next village. When the carriage was gone, Emile was still standing at the front of his house and I made my way down the lane.

I did not know what to make of his expression. I had been expecting joy, surprise, maybe curiosity. But I did not expect fear, and for the first time since I had formed this plan, I regretted it.

I arrived and stood before him. Marin galloped out and leapt up at me. I patted his head and pushed him gently away, and he ran excited circles around me and Emile as we faced each other.

'Hello,' I said at last.

'I did not expect to see you,' he replied.

'I did not expect ever to return,' I said. 'I need to speak with you. May we go inside?'

He half-turned, looking back towards the house anxiously, which immediately made me suspicious.

'What is it?' I asked.

Then the weather conspired to intensify the situation. Rain began to spit down.

'May we go inside?' I said again, and my heart was thumping.

Marin had already run off towards the house. Emile glanced at the sky, then turned and led the way.

I became aware immediately that there was someone in the house. A fire glowed in the hearth, and by it in a wooden chair with a high back, sat a woman. Her eyes were closed, and she had a large round scar on the right side of her brow. She sat very still, and I could see that her limbs were withered and wasted, as though she hadn't used them in a very long time.

'Hello,' I said, to be polite.

She didn't answer. I turned to Emile, who looked at me sadly.
'I am sorry,' he said.

'Emile? Who is this? Who were those people leaving?'

'The people in the carriage were my wife's parents. They leave for a week in Spain. A much-earned holiday.' He gestured towards the woman in the chair. 'And this . . . this is my wife.'

Although it was very quiet – the rain on the roof, the crackle of the fire – I remember this moment as though it were deafeningly loud, as though the world were cracking and shifting around me.

'But you said . . .'

'She is not sensible of our voices. If she can see us or hear us, she cannot understand it. We are blurred objects that move around her for no reason she can comprehend. The accident took it all away from her. She cannot feed or dress herself, she sits and sometimes her eyes are opened and sometimes closed. She is not the woman I married.'

'But she is still alive. You are still married.' I said it again, under my breath, to myself. '*Still married.*'

'Her parents took her in so that I could continue to work. They expect nothing from me except kindness and, from time to time, money. *Moineau*, my marriage has ended in all but name. I swear to you that Eleanor is gone. This shell you see here does not know me. She does not need my love, only my kindness and care.'

It didn't matter what he said. The fact was he was married, and even if my fond imagination could see my Father allowing me to marry a carpenter to save the family embarrassment, it could not picture my family being comfortable with bigamy, or with Emile divorcing his catatonic wife and leaving her in the care of her parents so he could be with me.

'Oh God,' I said, tears falling. 'I wish I hadn't come.'

'If you had written to me—'

'What? You would have continued to conceal this from me?'

'No. I might have . . . Why are you here, *Moineau*?'

I shook my head. 'It doesn't matter. None of it matters now.' My condition, my prospects, all of it struck me with full, awful force.

He moved to put his arms around me, but I jumped back as though burned. 'No. How could you embrace me in front of . . .' I gestured towards Eleanor, who had opened her eyes and was staring into space with unfocused eyes. Had she once loved him as I now did? I wanted to cry for her as well. But most of all I wanted to cry for you, the little life that grew inside me, because certainly now the happy story I had told you about your mama and papa raising you happily together, would never come to pass.

Never.

'I am sorry I came,' I said, hurrying to the door.

'Wait. You can't go out in the rain. Do you have a carriage home?' He reached out his hand for me.

'Don't touch me. I will find my own way back. Leave me be.' I ran out into the rain, and up the lane to the road. Then I began to walk. I was not sensible of where I was or where I was going, but on the route I began to feel terrified. Shudders of cold fear ran across me, and all the bare trees and thorny hedges and iron gates looked as though they were hostile towards me. I cannot explain it better than that. It seemed the whole, grey, wet world had decided it despised me, and I began to run, crying, stumbling through mud, my heart being torn by terror. At length, a carriage came by and a kindly gentleman leaned out and asked if I was in some trouble. I was drenched, crying, panicked, and could barely answer him. He quickly bundled me into the carriage, where his wife managed to get out of me where I was headed, and they took me to the next village.

There I sat, in a tea room, still dripping but finally calm now I was indoors and sipping hot tea. The kindly couple had gone on their way, and I had booked a ticket on a coach to Dorchester that left in one hour. The rain ran down the windows of the tea room, and my pain became muted and less frightful. I closed my eyes and told you I was sorry, because I had no idea what would happen to you now.

•

By the time I arrived at the hotel in London, the sky was growing dark and I was shivering with cold, fear and shock. My sister put me in a hot bath and sat on a chair beside me as I cried and told her what had happened. She stroked my hair and spoke to me soothingly. When I had cried myself dry and the bathwater had turned tepid, she said to me, 'I promise you, my dear sister, that I will take care of you. I will speak to Father and Mother on your behalf, I will make all enquiries about what we should do for your little one, and I will even stand by you while you bring the child into the world. I will not leave your side. You must leave everything to me.'

In my addled state, with my very soul bruised, the idea of giving over my trouble to my sister to sort out was more appealing than I can give words to.

'Thank you,' I said, resting my face on her forearm. 'Thank you.'

•

The frosts came to Hatby, and it became more and more difficult to rise in the morning. When I was asleep, warm and insensible, nothing could trouble me. Only when my eyes opened did the world come rushing at me.

The morning my parents called me to speak with them, I had been up for half an hour, sitting by the window and gazing out at the silvered grass. The door opened and one of our new servants – my mother did not keep servants for long; they always disappointed her – gave a little curtsey and said Lord and Lady Breckby needed to speak to me in the library.

I knew, of course, that this meant my sister had finally told them. She had been waiting for the right moment, she'd said. I didn't know what this 'right moment' was, but I had given over the burden to her and so I trusted her with it.

The maid helped me pull on my house dress, but I did not bother with my hair. It still hung in the long plait I wore to bed.

The library is in the west wing of the manor, and so it required me to descend the wide stone staircase and go past the breakfast room, where I could smell bacon and coffee, and across the empty ballroom. I knocked on the door and my father's voice said, 'Enter,' and then I was standing in front of his armchair, while he looked me up and down with his hard, grey gaze. Mother sat on the sofa under the window, a handkerchief pressed against her face, refusing to look at me.

'Sit,' he said, and so I sat in the other armchair. The bookshelves rose almost to the ceiling, but were largely empty of books. Mother liked to read novels, and Father had a good collection of the kind of books a gentleman of his breeding should have, but mostly the library shelves were filled with busts and figurines that required dusting every other day. It smelled like wax and lemons.

Father glared at me a moment longer, and I grew tense, digging my fingernails into my palms. When had he become so silvery-grey? I remembered him as fair and strong. But this morning, with this burden on his mind, he looked old and tired.

429

'Your condition is known to us,' he said at last. 'I cannot let you marry Ernest Shawe. I will write to him this morning and tell him he must marry your sister. That you are . . .' He paused. 'I will think of something. The fewer people who know of this disgrace the better.'

'Will I have to marry Mister Peacock?'

'Peacock married last month. Tired of waiting, I expect. I think it fair to say that your marriage prospects are practically ruined.' Then he leaned forward and pointed an accusatory finger at me. 'I had not expected this from you.'

I didn't know what to say, so I said nothing.

Mother leapt to her feet and paced towards me, stood quivering with rage in front of me for a moment and then slapped me once, hard on the face. 'How *could* you?' she said. 'You need not think we will allow you to keep the child. I have instructed your sister to make enquiries and arrangements. The Breckby family will not raise a bastard.'

At that moment, my child, I felt you move for the first time. I'd had some little sensations before – like bubbles breaking against the wall of my stomach – but this was a clear, soft thud against my insides.

The Breckby family will not raise a bastard.

'Please,' I said. 'Please let me keep it. I will not marry. I will raise it away from home if it will make things easier for you. But do let me keep it.'

'No!' Father roared. 'Have my daughter running about, unwed, with a child? It doesn't matter where in the world you are, you will bring shame on our family. If you insist upon it, know that I will cut you off. You will not be part of this family, nor will you have any of the benefits of it. No house, no money. What will you do, alone with a tiny child? How could that be good for either of you? The only right thing to do is to give the bastard away.'

I quailed before his infamous temper. My fate was sealed, and so was yours.

·

The winter wore on, and it was too cold to be out; and then my belly grew and grew and my family were keen for me to stay inside and away from company, and I became more and more afraid of the outside world. I feared a return of the ghastly fear that had gripped me leaving Emile's. Somehow I became a creature of the indoors, and I have been that way ever since. Such a fear takes hold of me outside. I dreamed of you sometimes, outside the safety of my womb, and you were in a cold, dark world that gave no consideration for your care or comfort. These dreams and my fears became intertwined over the ensuing months, and I often crept into my sister's room where she held me and told me stories of the beautiful family who had agreed to adopt you.

She told me Father had paid them off handsomely for taking you but also for their silence, that they were a noble family but had fallen on hard times. That the wife had tried in vain for years to have a baby of her own, and that they would love you so much and give you everything you needed. Sometimes I cried when she told me these stories, and I would beg to know their names but she said Father had forbidden it, that I must have the child and give the child up and never think of it again.

'It's for your own good, sister,' she said to me, over and over again. 'And for the good of the child.'

No child wants to know the pain they caused their mother in childbirth, so I will not tell you about those dreadful fourteen hours, save to say that the pain was over soon enough and I held you for a little while after you were born. The attending physician had said it was a terrible idea and that a pillow should be held between me and you so I would never see you, but my sister was there – as she had promised – and she convinced him that it would do no harm for me to cuddle the little one. The midwife cleaned you up and gave you some sugar water from a dropper, then handed you to me. 'Here is the little girl,' she said.

Ah. This is a pain that never leaves.

What a precious thing you were. Like a bud on a flower, soft and full of promise and beautiful, so beautiful. There, I am crying again. It has been more than a year. Perhaps I will never stop crying. I did love you. I did. I still do. I will never stop.

Then my sister was there, and her face was grim and patient. 'Come along, sister,' she said. 'You must hand her over now.'

I looked at your dear face and I kissed your forehead, and I whispered in your ear, 'One day I will find you,' although I knew it wasn't true. My sister took you from my arms and left, while the midwife sat me up to bind my breasts. I heard you crying all the way down the stairs.

•

So, my child whom I could not keep, here is the end of my account. You will never see this, so perhaps I shall tuck it in one of the books in the library that nobody ever reads. I leave today for London, where my father has bought me a house. My sister is now Mrs Shawe, and Father knows I will never marry and so he must get me out of the manor another way. I fear the journey, but once I am there I need not fear anything except long, empty years.

God bless you, child. Wherever you are.

Marianna

The Present

*O*ne day I will find you.

All I can do is cry. It isn't just that the story is sad, it's that I am sad. I am sad and I have been holding it down for a long time. I am sad that I lost my babies and I am sad that I likely won't ever have one. I am sad that my mother is sick and her future is so uncertain. I am sad that Moineau couldn't be with Emile. But I am especially sad that she had to give up her baby and she never recovered from it. Everyone knows that children need their parents, but is it not also true that parents need their children?

That Mum needs me?

I think of what she said, the day I had persuaded her to finally retire and accept her fate. *I feel as though I am about to cross an ocean, and it's grey and grim and lonely.*

I will not let her be lonely. I will be with her as she crosses that ocean. I know this with such force that I begin to tremble.

I reach for my handbag to pull out my phone. It is time to call Geoff, and tell him I'm not coming home.

CHAPTER 26
Agnes

A s Agnes stepped onto the platform at Dorchester Station, she heard a young woman say to her husband, 'I feel as though I've been travelling forever.'

The rest of their conversation was lost under the hiss of steam letting off, but she didn't need to hear it to know that, whatever the woman thought, she had not been travelling as long as Agnes. She had left England in the summer, and now the trees were all bare and the sky was chilly and grey.

Agnes made her way out of the station and into town, dressed in her second-last gown. All the others had been sold along the way. She had not mourned the two she sold in Colombo to stay in a room for four nights waiting for the steamship, nor the extra two plus Genevieve's jewellery she sold to pay the ticketing fine for changing her date of departure by several months. Jack had been indignant on her behalf, wanting to give the steamship's captain a 'fist in the chops' for what she saw as extortion. Both of them had

434

complained bitterly about the unfairness of it, ranting and cursing rather than saying the sad goodbye that neither of them was able to say. It didn't really matter; they were only dresses.

It had been harder for her, though, to sell the striped black-and-grey dress, which she had worn until it was threadbare on the steamer to London. She really loved that dress: people called her Ma'am instead of Miss when she wore it. But she had sold it for a night in a guesthouse and a train fare to Dorchester. Yes, she might have gone straight to Julius and Marianna, but she'd had a long time to devise her plan, and if either of them had an opinion on it, all might come undone.

Now here she was in Dorchester, preparing to sell the dress she loved most of all: the sapphire blue evening gown. She'd hoped to return to London still in possession of it, but it wasn't to be. The village of Millthorne was not in walking distance. She needed a carriage there and back.

Agnes began to walk, carefully sidestepping puddles. Her shoes were nearly worn through after having been soaked so many times and worn so relentlessly for months. After a good half-mile, she found the high street, with the pretty church spire at its end, and slowed down, looking in the windows. Sometimes she chose a dress shop, or a general store, but this time she chose a haberdasher. They could pull the gown apart: the ribbons and lace and buttons would sell individually, and the satin and velvet could be repurposed. She gulped hard, trying not to think about her beautiful gown anatomised in such a way.

A bell over the door rang, and a sharp-faced woman of middling years looked up from behind the counter. 'Can I help you, Miss?'

Miss. It was the blue cotton dress that had her called Miss. 'I'd like to sell a gown.'

'We don't buy gowns.'

'I don't want much for it. Just enough for two carriage rides and another train fare . . .' She trailed off, struck dumb by how close she was, now, to home.

'We never buy gowns.'

'Let me show it to you.'

Of course she bought it. Why would she not? It was exquisite and Agnes sold it for less than a tenth of what it was worth. Then the haberdasher directed her to the coaching inn, and Agnes found herself a coach leaving for Millthorne at four. She sat outside the coaching inn, cold and hungry, and waited.

Genevieve had told her everything in the pub that day; told it to her as though it were a story about somebody else completely, somebody who didn't matter.

Of course, to Genevieve, nobody really mattered. It had taken ten minutes in her company for Agnes to know that.

Marianna had been in love with a young carpenter by the name of Emile, with a French surname, who lived in the village of Millthorne. She had been sent home in disgrace when it was discovered her lover was already married. 'But the wife was simple, or sick, or something. I can't quite remember,' she'd said. Then Marianna had realised she was pregnant, and Genevieve had been charged with finding the child a good home, and some family friends of family friends had agreed to take the child, but only if it was a boy.

'I thought we had a good chance of getting a boy,' Genevieve had said. 'One-in-two! But alas, it was you.'

Rather than distress Marianna, who had already become withdrawn and afraid to go outside, Genevieve's parents had ordered her to take 'the little mite' to the foundling hospital, which they knew was a good institution that raised fine young people who went on to make good in the world. They told Marianna the other family had taken the baby, so that she didn't sink all the way into despair; giving up her child had made her take to her bed weeping incessantly already. Unfortunately, their father had revealed the fact to her several years later on a visit to London, and that was when Marianna had lost her temper and thrown Genevieve out. Agnes was astonished to learn that Marianna had a temper to lose, and that it had been the true reason Genevieve left England.

'So, you see, if I lost a button that morning I left you at Perdita, or sent a coat missing a button years later, or if Miss Candlesnuff said something about you being as headstrong as me, those facts were simply coincidences you've read a wishful story into,' Genevieve told her. 'You've got some pluck, I'll admit that. But you've gone well beyond your station. I suppose now you wish you'd been born a boy. You would have been quite wealthy.'

Agnes had never wished, and never would wish, that she'd been born a boy.

The coachman came to find her, lifted her impossibly light trunk onto the back of the coach, and handed her inside. He looked at the sky. 'There'll be rain,' he said.

'There always is,' she answered.

•

The journey was slow and muddy, and the rain beat mournfully on the windows of the coach. Village by village they made their way through Dorset, dropping off people along the way, until they rattled into Millthorne. Agnes was the last on board. How far she had travelled since that first coach that left Hatby.

'When is the return carriage?' she asked as the driver untied her trunk.

'First thing, Miss.'

'Would you be so kind as to take my trunk inside the coaching inn and tell them I'll be staying the night. I'll come back to Dorchester with you in the morning.'

'Very good, Miss. What name will I tell them?'

'Agnes Resolute.'

He smiled broadly. 'Is that so? What a fine name. And are you, Miss?'

'Am I what?'

'Resolute?'

'Oh, aye,' she said.

She had seen a little church on the approach to town and headed back in that direction. In a small village like this, the vicar would know everybody. The rain had held off since they'd arrived, but the sky had grown dark and night would soon be full upon her. She hurried her steps, walked up the grass slope to the church and pushed open the doors.

'Hello?' she called, and her voice echoed about. Nobody here; she would have to try the vicarage. But it was a bonny little church, not too chilly, and with beautiful hand-carved pews and candles burning in sconces. She moved inside and ran her fingers along the wood, then sat down and clasped her hands together. She rested her forehead on her knuckles and said thank you for being safely back in England, and was just getting on to asking for help finding Emile when a voice said, 'Miss?'

She looked up and saw an elderly vicar with fluffy white hair. 'Good evening, Vicar. Can you help me?'

He smiled. 'I will do what I can, Miss, and you can pray to God for the rest.'

'I'm looking for a man named Emile. I believe he's a carpenter and he may have a French surname. He's an . . . old friend of my family and I have come a long way to find him.'

The vicar nodded and held out his hand to help her up. 'Emile carved the pew you were sitting on,' he said. 'He's lived in Millthorne for twenty years or more, though he keeps to himself.' Here a small frown passed over his face, but was soon gone. 'I can give you directions.'

'Thank you, Vicar.'

Soon she was on her way again. It was dark and the rain was back, but nothing could stop her now. She walked back along the main street of the village, then turned where the vicar had told her to. She would have known the house by its carved gateposts, even if the vicar hadn't told her specifically which one it was.

She opened the gate, strode up to the front door and knocked loudly.

She heard the sound of somebody moving inside, then footsteps. The scurrying of dog feet. The door opened and a puppy jumped out and began madly scrabbling at her hem. A man held a lamp, looking at her. He was in his late forties, with grey hair around his temples and a vest stretched a little across an expanding middle. His brow looked troubled, but his eyes were kind. Agnes smiled. *Her father.*

'Yes?' he asked.

A spirit of joy took hold of her, despite the cold and the dark and the damp, and she said, 'Hello, Papa.'

His expression froze on his face, as his eyes took her in. 'It can't be,' he said.

'May I come in?'

•

Agnes sat in front of his fire. The pup had settled down enough to sit in her lap, bathing her hands with his tongue. Emile stood at the mantel, unable to relax enough to sit down.

'The moment I saw you,' he said. 'You look so much like her. I didn't know she'd had a child.'

'She did, although her sister left me on the porch of the local foundling hospital.'

'How did you . . .'

'It's a long story.'

Finally, he sat down on the chair opposite. 'I have all the time in the world to hear it.'

So, she told him. As she unfolded her tale, she saw in his eyes wonder and pride and she felt, for the first time in her life, a sense of belonging so strong and so deep that nothing would ever shift it from under her again. Here he was, her father, and he was *proud* of her. She embellished the story a little to make him laugh or gasp, and finally they were back, here in the room, on this rainy night in Millthorne.

'And you, Papa?' she said. 'What of you?'

'I've done less in the twenty years since I met Marianna than you've done in the time since you left the foundling hospital,' he said with awe. 'But I will tell you my wife, Eleanor, died fourteen years ago, and I have not remarried. You have no wicked stepmother to concern yourself with.'

'I'm well supplied with a wicked aunt, I'd say,' Agnes replied. 'Have you never thought to seek out Marianna in those fourteen years?'

He was already shaking his head. 'Her family would have forbidden it. She was set to marry another man.'

'She didn't. She never married.'

He cleared his throat then said, very softly, 'How is she?'

'Lonely, still beautiful in her way. Afraid.'

'Afraid?'

'She doesn't leave the house.'

'That can't be right. Nobody could ever keep her indoors.'

'She's changed.' Agnes paused a beat and then said, 'You should come to London and see her.'

Emile turned his eyes to the fireplace and watched the flames; he didn't reply.

'I know she would welcome it,' Agnes added.

'You don't know that. As you say, she's changed.'

They fell into a long silence, and Agnes felt her weariness keenly. She needed to come to rest; she had been too long in motion. 'May I write to you?' Agnes said. 'May I keep in touch?'

'But of course. You are always welcome here too. My home is yours. I'm sorry, I do not know what to say or do. I never expected . . .'

Agnes stood. 'I never expected either. Let me write down our address so you may correspond with me, or come to visit. You needn't announce it. In fact, it may be better if you don't.'

He rose and led her to a side table, where she found pen, ink and paper, and scribbled down the address. She handed him the slip of paper, but instead of taking it from her fingers he enclosed her in a hug. She allowed herself to be engulfed by him, and felt his body shake slightly. He was crying. Agnes smiled against his shoulder. But she didn't cry. She hardly ever did.

•

At three o'clock the next afternoon, Agnes finally made it back to Belgrave Place. It surprised her how nervous she was. She had mailed a letter from Colombo, but had no idea if it had made it ahead of her. Did they know she was on her way back? Was Julius angry with her? Worse, had he fallen out of love with her?

She wasn't sure if she should knock on the door or simply open it, so she did a little of both, opening it with a knock and calling out, 'Hello there?'

Daisy was the first to see her, and lost control instantly of her mouth, calling, 'Marianna, Julius, you must come. *You must come!*'

Footsteps. Running footsteps. Julius appeared from around the side of the stairwell. With a shout of happiness he picked her up and spun her around. 'My love! You are returned!'

441

'Put me down,' she laughed. 'I'm far too tall to be swung around like a child.'

He put her down. 'You're as naughty as a child, disappearing for so long. But Agnes, Marianna knows that—' He stopped, because at that moment Marianna stepped out of the hall to the drawing room, her face a mask of wonder and joy. Julius took a step back and Agnes turned to face her.

'Agnes,' Marianna managed. 'You have come back to me. My baby, my lost child, you . . .' She dissolved into speechless tears.

'Aye, be right,' Agnes said gently. She stepped forward and put her arms around her mother, and Marianna was warm and soft and loving, just as mothers always are.

●

It was night-time before Julius and Agnes had a moment alone. Marianna had gone to bed, exhausted from crying, by six o'clock; but Annie, Daisy and Pamela all wanted to hear about Agnes's adventures and so she drank hot cocoa with them in the kitchen and told them everything. Julius listened on, his shirt sleeves rolled up so he could almost pass as somebody who belonged below-stairs. They were particularly interested in stories about Jack, who engendered Annie's speechless admiration for running away to sea in trousers. But eventually Julius hinted that Agnes was tired from all her travelling and the staff should release her to bathe and turn to bed. He followed her up the stairs, caught her hand and said, 'Just one moment with you, my dear, in the drawing room?'

Agnes allowed herself to be led. Pamela had turned the lights down hours ago, and the fire had burned down to smouldering embers. It was dark and cold when Julius shut the door behind them. The curtains remained open and Agnes could see the half-moon through the bare branches of trees.

Julius did not wait to light a lamp. He turned Agnes towards him and took both her hands in his left hand. With his right, he reached out to touch her cheek. 'Agnes?'

'Aye, Julius. I will marry you. If you'll still have me after I've been roaming all over the world.'

'I will. Of course I will. I love you more for your wisdom and experience, for your strength of character.'

'But promise me, Julius, that the adventures aren't all over? That we'll travel? We will go to visit Jack?'

He smiled, and she caught her breath at the truth and kindness in his face. 'I promise you, Agnes, the adventures are not over yet.' Then he pulled her against him and pressed his lips over hers. She heard her pulse rushing past her ears and it put her in mind of angel wings.

•

Two weeks after the day she returned, life had assumed a regular shape. Now Agnes was a noblewoman's daughter and soon to be a doctor's wife, she could command people to wait on her, but she hated to be idle and she did not think herself above anyone. Julius had a new position with the government, visiting schools to perform health checks on students, and sometimes she accompanied him to help him with his notes and talk kindly to the children. He was much happier being around well children than ones who were poorly. Sometimes she stayed home with Marianna, and she still read to her but no longer at three in the morning. That was now Daisy's job, as she was learning to read and Marianna was happy to hear her stammer her way through children's books just as long as she had company. Marianna didn't wake as much in the night anyway. Having Agnes back seemed to have mended whatever it was that had frayed the edges of her soul.

Agnes had been out in the morning buying lace and silk. She was determined to make her own wedding gown, and Marianna's mother-of-the-bride gown too. She returned to Belgrave Place with her purchases wrapped in brown paper, tucked under her arm. She let herself in and was accosted at the door almost immediately by Julius.

He put a finger over his lips.

'What is it?' she asked. 'Why are you home?'

'I was on my way out when a visitor came,' he whispered.

'Who?'

'Come and see.' He relieved her of her packages, laying them on the hall table as he led her towards the drawing room. He opened the door and she saw through the window that there was somebody in the garden.

Agnes's heart stood still.

Seated on the bench was Emile. In front of him, on the cold ground on her knees, was Marianna, her head in his lap. A beam of weak sun was in her fair hair, and his hand cradled her crown.

'Agnes Resolute, I do believe you are crying,' Julius teased.

'I'm not,' she sniffed, palming tears off her face. 'I hardly ever do.'

The Present

The email pings into my inbox as I worry at the corner of my pinkie fingernail. I am waiting for an email from Geoff, about the house settlement. It hasn't been pleasant. None of this has been pleasant, but there are small joys. And big ones, like Andrew.

But this email isn't from Geoff. It's another I hadn't hoped to wait for. A reply to something I shot off out of curiosity. When I see it, I almost laugh with delight. I print it and call out to Mum.

'Mum? Where are you?'

'Out here.'

I slide open the doors to the little sunroom. The weather has turned bitter – I'd forgotten about the English cold in my sun-drenched Australian existence – and Mum likes to sit here in the sunroom because it feels like the last warm place in the house. Don't misunderstand: there is no sun. There is unyielding grey sky. But there is an electric heater, and the glass keeps the warmth trapped inside.

She has been reading. The book bristles with sticky notes. This is how she remembers characters and their histories. I tread carefully, not wanting to upset or frustrate her with my news, but hoping she is in a lucid-enough spell to comprehend what I'm about to tell her.

'Mum, do you remember that letter we both read? Moineau and Emile?'

She nods, but I see she doesn't remember because she blinks rapidly.

'It was in the back of the book by—'

'Cicero!' she says, a small note of triumph in her voice. 'Yes, yes, I remember. The poor lass who lost her baby. The lover with the injured wife.'

'Yes. Well, I have just received the most exciting email. You tried to find him, remember? Emile Venson?'

'Nobody could find him for me,' she says.

'Well, I had a hunch, and Andrew got his research assistant to follow it up for me.'

A muscle tightens in her jaw. Mum is still unimpressed that I am seeing Andrew, but I am confident he will win her over eventually.

'Venson,' I say. 'It's an unusual name.'

'It is.'

'And he was French. It didn't sound like a French surname to me, but what if Moineau simply spelled it as she heard it? Venson . . .'

Mum thinks for a second, then says, 'Vincent. The French would pronounce it Venson.'

'Exactly. I sent the research assistant off to see if he could locate Emile Vincent, carpenter of Millthorne, Dorset.' I wave the email. 'And he did.'

Mum sat up, electrified. 'Tell me again. Andrew found Emile Venson?'

'His research assistant found Emile Vincent, yes.' I was getting used to repeating things, making sure they embedded themselves. I crouched on the floor next to her so she could see the sheet of paper as I read off it: *Hi Tori, I found your Emile Vincent. I have no date of birth but he appears in the marriage records in 1875 when he wed Marianna Breckby of Belgrave Place, London. He appears again in the records on the date of his death, in 1896. The* Dorchester Daily *writes that he is survived by Marianna, their daughter, Agnes, their son-in-law, Julius Halligan, and their granddaughter, Grace.*

Mum clutches her hands together over her heart. 'They found each other!' she exclaims. 'They married!'

'They had a child!' I added. 'Agnes.'

'I wonder if it's *the* child,' Mum says. 'The one she wrote the letter to?'

'Well now, it could be. We would have to do some research on the dates.' I think this unlikely, but Mum is so delighted by the possibility, and I try as much as possible to let her enjoy any moments of brightness and happiness that come. Crossing the grey ocean is not so bad if there are stars along the way.

Mum reads the email over and over again, and for a little while she is back with me. I hang on to it. The weather will change. Everything does. Calm seas don't last forever. Clouds will cover the sun.

We set our course together, my mother and I.

Acknowledgements

In the composition of this novel, I have never been more aware of the people and communities I rely on to get books written.

Thanks to everyone who helped with my research: Oliver Chadwick, Anna Madill, Karen Pymble and the staff at the National Maritime Museum archive, and Alan and Trevor at the Old Melbourne Gaol.

Thanks to Stacey Clair, Karen Ward and Vanessa Radnidge, who helped trim sails and set course.

Thanks to my writing support group: Meg Vann, Charlotte Nash, Liz McKewin, Bek Turner, Fiona McMillan and Nicole Cody.

Thanks to my neighbours: Adele Bird, Lynne Marsh and Margaret Wolfe, none of whom are in any way doo-lally.

Thanks to my soul sisters: Kate Forsyth and Mary-Rose MacColl.

Thanks to my World Domination team: Lisa Fletcher and Beth Driscoll. Sorry about any deadlines I missed because I was writing a novel.

Thanks to my understanding children: Luka and Astrid. Your permanently distracted mother adores you.

Thanks to my husband because he's lovely in more ways than is possible to enumerate.

Thanks to my author management: Selwa, Brian and Linda. I love you with all my heart.

And to my mum. Everything that's good about me comes from you.